THE WOODEN CROWN

Book One
of
The Blackwater Chronicles

PAUL HEWER

BookReality
Helping Writers Become Independent Authors

For Mum
You will be missed

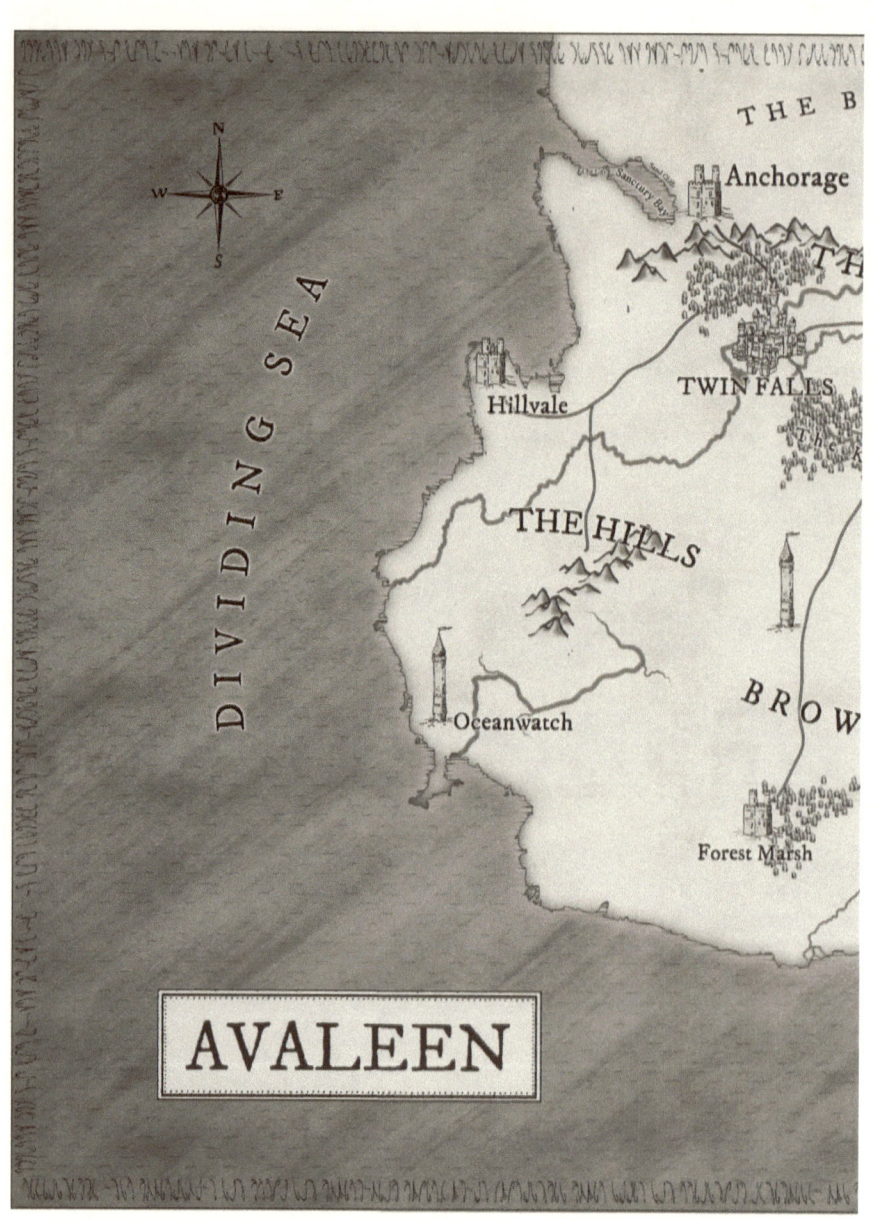

THE B

Anchorage

Sanctuary Bay

TH

Hillvale

TWIN FALLS

THE HILLS

BROW

Oceanwatch

Forest Marsh

DIVIDING SEA

AVALEEN

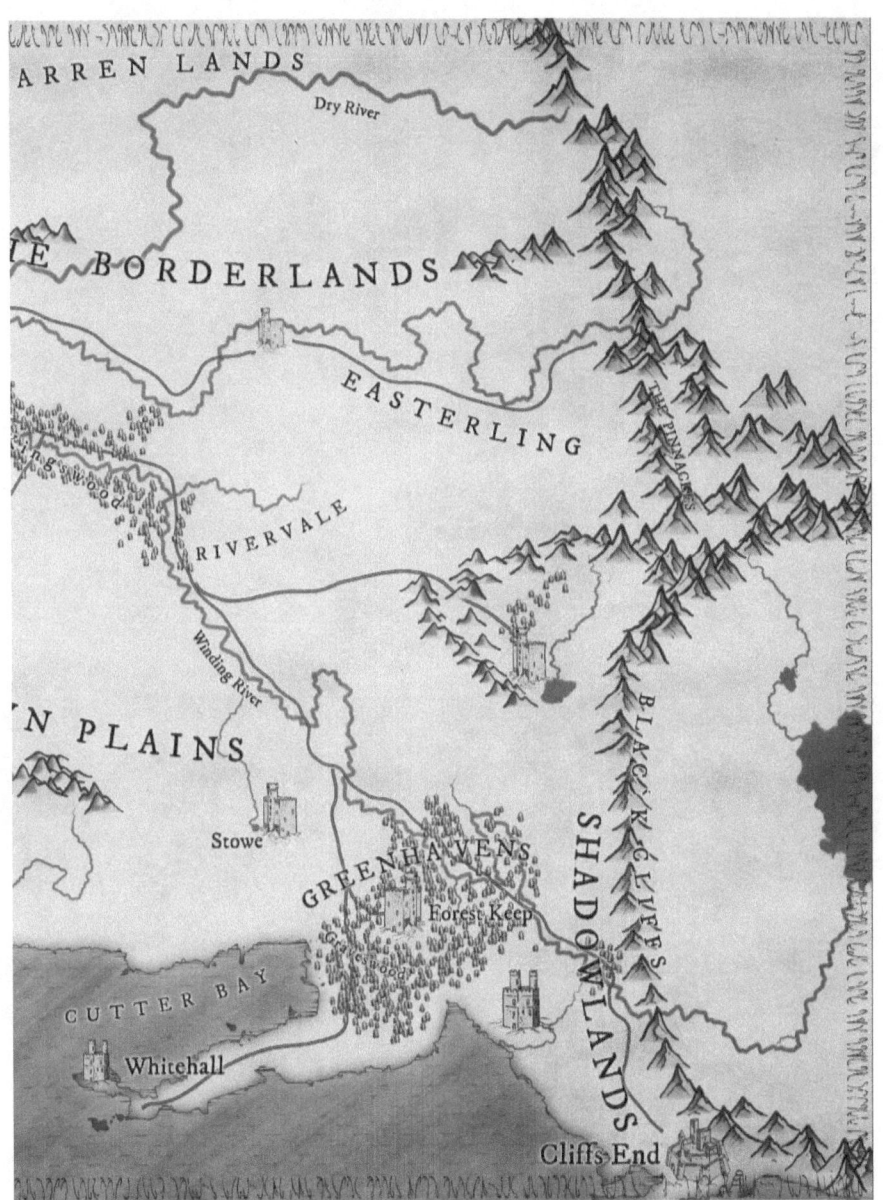

The Great Houses of Avaleen

Blackwater
(The Royal House)

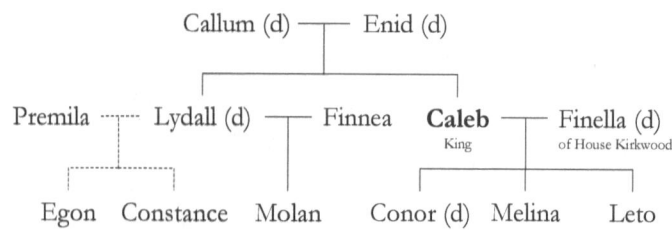

Callum (d) —— Enid (d)

Premila ···· Lydall (d) —— Finnea   **Caleb** —— Finella (d)
                                  King   of House Kirkwood

Egon   Constance   Molan   Conor (d)   Melina   Leto

Fergus Trotter   Peyton Holmguard   Jacob Rivers
Noble Guard   Knight Commander of the Noble Guard   Companion of Leto

Kirkwood

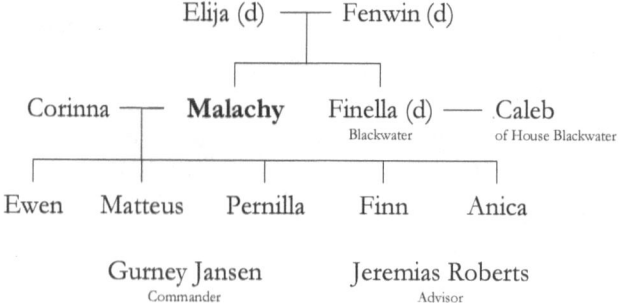

Elija (d) —— Fenwin (d)

Corinna —— **Malachy**   Finella (d) —— Caleb
                                Blackwater   of House Blackwater

Ewen   Matteus   Pernilla   Finn   Anica

Gurney Jansen   Jeremias Roberts
Commander   Advisor

Redstone

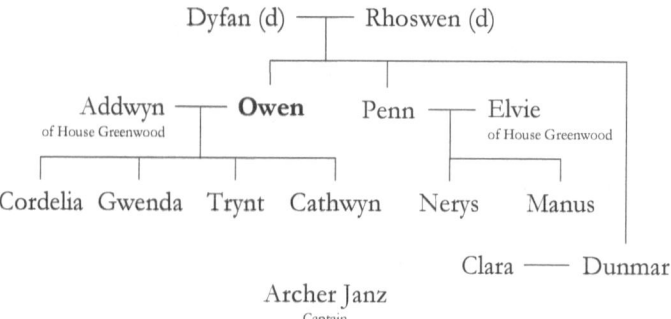

Dyfan (d) —— Rhoswen (d)

Addwyn —— **Owen**   Penn —— Elvie
of House Greenwood   of House Greenwood

Cordelia   Gwenda   Trynt   Cathwyn   Nerys   Manus

                                          Clara —— Dunmar

Archer Janz
Captain

THE GREAT HOUSES OF AVALEEN

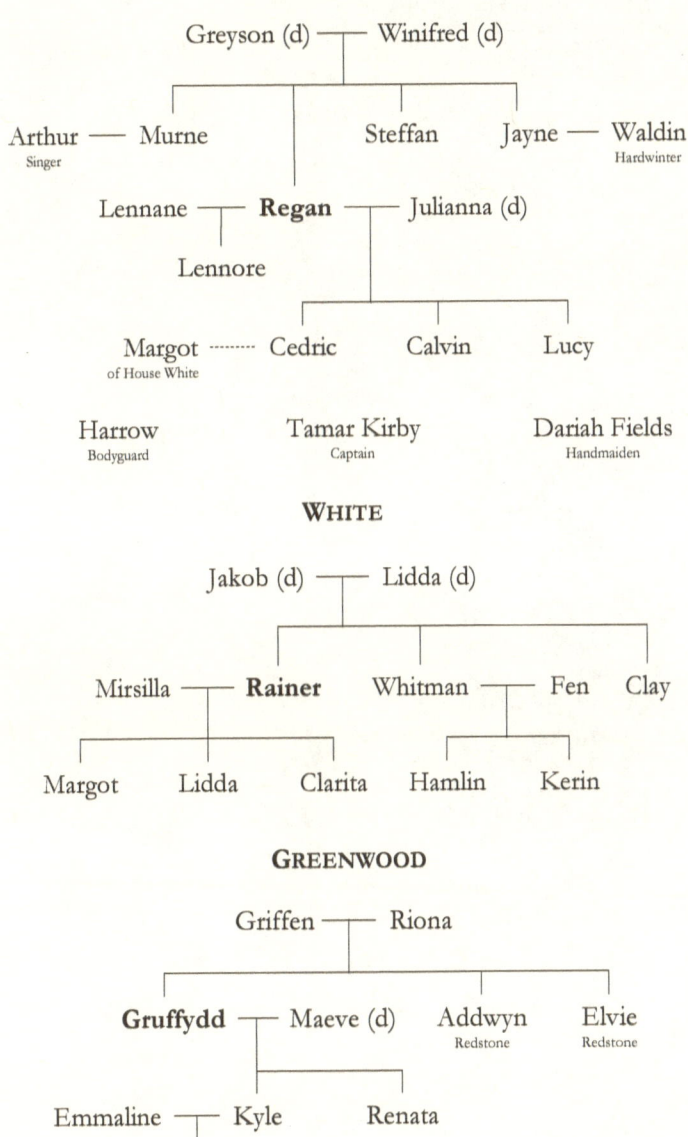

GREYTHORPE

Greyson (d) —— Winifred (d)

Arthur —— Murne   Steffan   Jayne —— Waldin
Singer   Hardwinter

Lennane —— **Regan** —— Julianna (d)

Lennore

Margot ········ Cedric   Calvin   Lucy
of House White

Harrow   Tamar Kirby   Dariah Fields
Bodyguard   Captain   Handmaiden

WHITE

Jakob (d) —— Lidda (d)

Mirsilla —— **Rainer**   Whitman —— Fen   Clay

Margot   Lidda   Clarita   Hamlin   Kerin

GREENWOOD

Griffen —— Riona

Gruffydd —— Maeve (d)   Addwyn   Elvie
                                    Redstone   Redstone

Emmaline —— Kyle   Renata

Griffen

He knew death was near.

He felt his life slipping away as he fell to his knees in an expanding pool of his own blood.

Go!

He reached up towards the gallery, arm heavy as iron, as pain shot through his chest.

He searched, but an ever-darkening mist clouded his vision.

They must not find you!

He tried to rise, but they kicked him back to the ground.

He propped himself up, but every breath felt like a knife in his chest.

Shadowy figures moved about, their muted voices taunting him.

Run!

'Get away!' he shouted, blood spraying from his mouth and nose.

He still felt pain, but from where he could no longer discern.

He coughed and slumped onto his back as they shoved him again, his shallow breathing now a series of short, wet gasps.

Get away…my boy!

He closed his eyes and surrendered to the darkness.

1

LETO

Leto leapt from the wall to an abutting battlement and dropped to the rampart below, barely making a sound. He glanced over the edge at the rocky ground below. It was a long way down.

'Damn you,' Jacob said in a loud whisper. 'Slow down!'

Leto grinned as his friend stretched his arms out for balance, took a few quick steps and jumped, landing next to him with a thud.

'Quiet!' Leto said, keeping his voice low. 'Are you trying to get us caught?'

'No, because if we're caught up here again, it'll be my head, not yours.'

Jacob was several years older than Leto, a couple of inches taller and, despite a more heavyset body, almost as quick and nimble.

Ten summers ago, Leto couldn't tighten the girth on his saddle. The pony had puffed himself up, making the task difficult for a boy of seven. He continued to struggle until a tall, scruffy, dark-haired boy offered to help. Leto accepted in a heartbeat. The boy pulled the girth tight and kneed the pony in the side. The pony snorted in surprise and relaxed its chest. The lad pulled the girth tighter, waited a few moments, kneed the pony again, tightened the buckle and tied it off.

'These ponies can be stubborn. A couple of good whacks usually gets them in line.'

'Thank you,' Leto said, embarrassed at his weakness.

From there, their friendship grew, and now they were inseparable. Being a prince made it difficult for Leto to make real friends. He'd lost his older brother, Conor, over ten years ago, so he clung to Jacob's friendship. It didn't concern Leto that he worked in the stables and Jacob didn't care Leto was royalty. He treated Leto like a person, not someone special, and that's all that mattered.

However, more than a few complaints had come from members of the household about their behaviour, causing friction with his father, the King. Ultimately, the King had made Jacob an offer he couldn't refuse: to be Leto's squire and bodyguard or get packed off to Anchorage and muck out the harbour stables. From then on, Jacob always prioritised Leto, and took his new position very seriously, often to Leto's annoyance. He watched out for Leto, regularly preventing him from making foolish decisions. However, through no fault of his own, he was not always successful.

Leto loved him like a brother, but right now, Jacob would not be pleased with him. He wasn't afraid of heights or of Leto injuring himself. They were both fit and agile and could make even the most difficult climbs. The cause of Jacob's anxiety was Leto's father.

'He wouldn't punish you too badly,' Leto said with a wry smile.

Jacob rolled his eyes and shook his head in disapproval.

'Don't worry,' Leto assured him. 'He'll only put you in the stocks for a day or so.'

Leto started towards the nearest tower.

'You wouldn't let him do that to me, would you?' Jacob asked, following along.

'I'd protest. You have my word.'

Jacob sighed as they approached the bastion. 'I don't doubt your sincerity, but he'll do what he pleases.'

'If it makes you feel any better, it would hurt me as much as it'd hurt you.'

'I doubt it.'

They stopped near the tower opening.

Leto glanced at Jacob. 'Are you scared of my father?'

'Of course! He's the king!'

His father's rank, and therefore Leto's position in society, was something of which he was acutely aware. He loved his father more than anything; he gave Leto all kinds of advice and life lessons to prepare him for when it was his time to rule, but Leto just wasn't interested.

'You do realise we could both avoid punishment if you behaved,' Jacob added.

'Are you saying I'm irresponsible?'

'Extremely.'

'You realise you've just insulted a prince of the realm.'

'A real prince wouldn't be scrambling over castle roofs in the middle of the night against the express instructions of his King.'

Leto chuckled, even though his friend spoke the truth. His father had forbidden them from climbing onto the roofs of Riverview. It was too dangerous, apparently, but court life was boring. He just wanted to have some fun.

'Did I tell you I'll make you a knight when I'm King?' Leto asked.

'I thought you didn't want to be King?'

'True enough.'

'So where does that leave me?'

'An excellent point, Sir Jacob.'

'You are unbelievable,' his friend said, shaking his head in mock frustration.

Leto leaned through the battlement, peered over the edge, and smiled. The guards were standing just where they should be.

'Oh, I forgot to tell you,' he said, turning to Jacob. 'My betrothed arrives today, or tomorrow, I forget which. Anyway, I plan to produce a son or daughter as soon as possible, and they can rule the kingdom and leave me out of it.'

They continued past the tower.

'I hope she's pretty,' Leto added.

'Are you stupid?' Jacob said. 'They don't betroth princes to ugly girls.'

'I suppose you're right, and maybe I should begin acting more like a prince,' Leto said. 'I don't want my future wife to think I'm a childish brat.'

'No one would want that.'

Leto grinned.

Jacob's eyes narrowed. 'Assuming you mean it, of course.'

'I do. I really do,' Leto said and stopped, and glanced over the wall again. 'I'll start tomorrow.'

He scrambled over the battlement, lowered himself to the apex of the adjoining roof, and began making his way across, taking care with each step.

'Damn it!' Jacob said, rushing to follow.

They moved along the roof, climbed down to a walkway and burst into a run towards the other side of the castle.

'Where are we going now?' Jacob asked, climbing after Leto onto a roof below.

'You'll see.'

Leto moved across the roof to the second storey of the timber building in front of them. He inched across the edge of the roofline, stepped to the adjacent balcony and climbed up to the next roof.

Jacob pulled himself up from the balcony. 'Isn't this the ser –'

Leto silenced Jacob with a finger to his lips and pointed at some broken wooden shingles a few yards from where they stood. Leto crept over, lay face down and beckoned to Jacob. With the utmost care, he pushed aside one of the shingles and peered inside.

The small room below contained an old wooden bed, a lighted candle and a chair with a dress draped over the back. Leto was thinking it much too fine a garment for a mere servant, when a murmur from the bed caught his attention. The blanket was pushed aside, revealing the face and arm of a gorgeous fair-haired girl. She rolled over towards the middle of the bed, dragging the blanket and exposing her naked body. The candlelight flickered off her porcelain buttocks.

Leto grinned and glanced at Jacob, who stared transfixed through the other broken shingle.

The girl whispered something that Leto couldn't make out as she moved across and sat astride her lover, her body obscuring him from view. Whoever hid under the blankets was a lucky man, Leto thought, mesmerised by the beauty straddling him. She glanced at the table where the single candle burned low.

'We don't have much time left,' she said, her voice soft and melodic.

She bent down and kissed her lover.

'Of course, one more time, my lady.'

What? Did he hear correctly?

The young woman shuffled backwards, pushing the blanket down the bed, revealing the girl's lover. Leto's eyes widened. The lover was another woman, but not just any woman. It was Lady Lennane Greythorpe, wife of the Governor.

A stunned Leto watched as she knelt between the older woman's legs and buried her face between her thighs. Leto was captivated as Lady Greythorpe moaned at the girl's ministrations. Her whimpers of pleasure increased in volume, and her breathing became more rapid.

Leto shuffled around to find a more comfortable position without success, his arousal beginning to cause discomfort. He ignored it and continued to watch one of the highest-ranking women in the aristocracy being serviced by one of the servants.

'Yes!' Lady Greythorpe's hips began to move around.

Leto heard a crack, like that of breaking timber, but he ignored it and continued to stare.

'Don't stop,' she breathed, clutching the girl's head as her hips bucked.

Another crack, louder this time, as the roof under Leto began to cave in.

'Help!' he cried, forgetting all thoughts of being silent.

He scrambled to get up as the roof began to give way. The women screamed as Leto fell into the room, preceded by a pile of timber debris and dust that hit the floor near the bed. At the last moment, Jacob grabbed Leto's right hand and halted his descent. He dangled in the space for a few moments, swinging back and forth, then got his bearings and glanced down at the women now covered with the blanket. A flash of recognition crossed Lady Greythorpe's face.

Jacob strained hard, and Leto could feel his hand slipping out of his friend's grasp; he reached up with his free hand. After a few attempts, he managed to find a hold, and with Jacob's help, he pulled himself back up onto the roof.

Leto lay on the roof breathing deeply.

'Let's go!' Jacob said and helped Leto to his feet.

They descended to the balcony, crossed the roof of the adjoining building, scaled the wall and ran off into the darkness.

2

DARIAH

She waited.

Her mistress paced around the bedchamber, oblivious to everything else. Dariah had become accustomed to being ignored. As a servant, she came when ordered, was diligent with her assigned tasks, and didn't look for any appreciation, but this time she needed a response.

'My lady?' she prompted.

Lady Lennane Greythorpe stopped her pacing and glared at Dariah. 'What?'

'Do I have your leave to visit the Abbey? I promise I won't be long.'

'Whatever for?'

'After last night, I just need to think about …' she lowered her eyes, '… about what happened.'

Dariah's mistress eyed her for a few more moments, her gaze severe.

'What we do is not wrong,' she eventually said with a touch of annoyance.

Before she had come into Lady Greythorpe's employ, the closest Dariah had come to any form of sex was with the son of a drunken merchant. While working in her uncle's tavern, he tried to kiss her, groping her breast and pushing his other hand under her skirt. Uncle Leon and her cousin, Edmund, had come to her rescue and gave the young man a sound beating and threw him out onto the muddy street, threatening him with castration if he ever showed his face again.

As arrogant and self-righteous as the rest of the nobility, for some reason, Lady Greythorpe had taken quite an interest in Dariah. At first, she had reservations, but her mistress encouraged her, and the things she did to her, she had never experienced anything like it and made her feel wonderful.

'Most men don't think of a woman's pleasure,' she had said to Dariah one night as they lay entwined in her bed. 'They just want to stick their cock inside you, usually before you're ready, then thrust away, and before you know it, it's over.'

Dariah wouldn't know, but it certainly wasn't like that with her mistress.

'That's not what I meant at all, my lady,' Dariah said. 'I enjoy our … err … intimate encounters immensely. I only hope the prince finds it in himself to keep our secret.'

Lady Greythorpe approached her.

'The prince won't be telling anyone.'

'How can you be so sure?'

'He's been in trouble many times for being in places he shouldn't. He won't say anything.'

This made Dariah feel a little better about last night's incident, but she still needed to get to the Abbey.

'I'm going to see my husband soon,' Lady Greythorpe informed Dariah. 'You can toddle off to pray then.'

Before Lady Greythorpe's interest in her had grown, there were more opportunities for Dariah to get away from the castle, but recently it had become much more difficult. She had even resorted to slipping out after everyone had fallen asleep. At least this time, she didn't have to sneak out.

'Thank you, my lady. You are most gracious.'

'Yes, yes,' she said and waved her hand dismissively. 'Now I must pick a dress. Something not too revealing.'

Lady Greythorpe had been trying to regain her husband's favour since before Dariah had arrived, without success, and more often than not, took her frustrations out on the servants. Not even Dariah was immune to her tantrums, and there was never an apology afterwards; not that she ever expected one.

Her mistress turned and contemplated her image in the nearby the wall-hung crystal mirror. The undergarments and corset she wore did little to hide her curves.

'He should take me seriously,' she said, turning side to side, hands on hips.

'One of the blue ones, my lady, with long sleeves and a high neck,' Dariah said. 'No ruffles.'

'Excellent idea. The sky blue, I think.' Her mistress began to play with her hair, continuing to study herself in the mirror. 'Up or down?'

'Definitely up.'

'Yes, up. You have a good eye. We'll make a lady of you yet.'

Dariah didn't know what to make of that last comment. She came from a frugal farming family, and her father always looked down on those who thought themselves better, calling themselves lords and ladies. Did her mistress want Dariah to become a lady and be more like her? She pushed aside the thought and rushed to the next room where Lady Greythorpe stored her favourite clothes. Scores of gowns, in assorted styles and colours, filled the room. Dariah knew the exact location of the suggested dress, so it took her only moments to return to the bedchamber with it in her arms.

'This one, my lady?' Dariah said, holding it up for her mistress to view.

'Perfect,' Lady Greythorpe replied, briefly glancing at the dress before looking back at the mirror.

Dariah carefully laid the dress on the bed, relieved her mistress hadn't changed her mind and scolded her for bringing the wrong one. It wouldn't have been the first time.

'Actually,' Lady Greythorpe said, 'call in that young girl, Gretchen? She can help me dress. You can go and pray but be back by midday. I may need you afterwards.'

Dariah welcomed her mistress's capitulation.

'Yes, my lady,' Dariah said and hurried out of the bedchamber.

She found Gretchen in the nearby common room. The petite but plain girl of fifteen years sat next to Hilma, engrossed in being instructed in the proper repair of her lady's dresses by the old woman. Dariah ordered her to attend Lady Greythorpe at once and gave her strict instructions on dressing their mistress.

'Take Hilma with you,' Dariah added.

The old woman had been part of the Governor's household longer than Dariah had been alive. She couldn't move very fast but listened well, had a good memory, and could help Gretchen if required. Dariah shooed them out and hurried out of the castle, stopping off at her room to retrieve her shawl.

She made her way through the east gate into the city. The air still carried a chill despite being mid-morning. Dariah clutched her woollen shawl around herself as she navigated the crush of people and carts that occupied the streets and laneways. At least the rains had not yet set in. Most of the streets were unpaved and would turn to mud in winter, making travelling through the city on foot a very unpleasant experience.

Dariah slowed as she approached the Abbey. The large stone edifice dwarfed everything in this corner of the city. She regarded the bell tower. Despite being only a hundred feet high, she still found the sight impressive. When first built, the Abbey had been surrounded by grass plains and the nearby river, but the city had grown over the years until it encompassed the Abbey and the adjacent monastery.

Dariah entered through the arched timber doors. Her nose twitched at the scent of incense. The rich, such as nobles and those in the royal household, bathed at least once a week. Not so for most folk, hence the requirement for incense, even in a large airy building like the Abbey. It burned day and night to mask the smell of the unwashed who flocked to the Abbey for prayer, to listen to the Abbot's sermons, or just for some quiet reflection.

On this visit, Dariah wasn't interested in any of these. She approached a nearby monk, who smiled as she caught his attention.

'Good morning, Father,' she greeted him in a whisper.

'And a good morning to you as well,' he whispered back.

Unlike the monk she'd spoken to on her earlier visit, he wore a cheerful smile.

'Would you be so kind as to tell Abbot Alwen that Winnie is here to see him?' she asked, returning his smile.

'The Abbot, you say?'

His smile didn't disappear, but he hesitated.

'He is expecting me,' she said.

'If that's the case, wait here, and I'll see if I can find him for you. He's a busy man, so he may not be able to come straight away.'

'Thank you, Father … ?' she said, prompting him for his name.

He gave her a quizzical look before his smile grew even wider.

'Oh! How rude of me. I am Bryan,' he said, leaning closer to her, 'and I'm not a monk, yet. I'm still a novice.'

She smiled at his admission.

'Now stay here, and I'll notify the Abbot of your arrival,' the novice continued.

He turned and disappeared into the cloisters.

Dariah gazed up at the three large, stained-glass windows above the stone altar at the far end of the Abbey. She loved the vibrant colours, and the way the glass pieces had been formed into a collage of images bounded by lead strips, each window representing a different time in Avaleen's history. Coloured glass windows were rare and expensive, and she had only seen them in the Abbey and Riverview Castle.

She banished the smile as two monks exited the cloisters and headed towards her. Bryan looked grim as he trailed another monk she didn't know. His head lacked a single strand of hair, and he stood about half a foot shorter than Dariah. He also sported a rather large, crooked nose. They stopped in front of her, Bryan behind the short monk.

'You aren't the Abbot,' she said.

'No, I am not,' he said, his voice abrupt. 'What business do you have with Abbot Alwen?'

'That's between me and the Abbot.'

'He's a very important man and cannot see every little girl wanting to chat.'

'Excuse me?'

She knew her presence had been requested. Yesterday, just after dawn, she had wandered through the crowded market and stopped at the stall of a silk merchant. Whilst examining a scarf she thought her mistress might like, Dariah heard the words she had begun to dread, this time from what sounded like an older man.

'Your patron wishes to see you tomorrow.'

She froze momentarily and then whirled around in an attempt to identify the messenger, but the crowded market made it impossible.

No! She had not imagined it. High sun wasn't long coming, and she wouldn't have this obnoxious little monk delay her any longer.

'May I have your name?'

'Why would you need my name?' the short monk said. 'I am a simple Monk of the Brotherhood.'

'Fine then, monk!' Dariah said, her voice raised above a whisper. 'If you don't tell the Abbot I am here, I will leave. Later, when I am asked why I didn't attend when ordered, I will say I was turned away by a rude little –'

The sound of a throat being cleared interrupted her. Dariah and both monks automatically turned towards the noise.

A white-haired old man with a short, white beard appeared and closed the door behind him. Abbot Alwen glanced at Dariah and gave her a polite smile before glaring at the little monk.

'Prior Fren, what's going on?' he said, his voice soft but full of authority. 'This is a place for quiet reflection; you are not haggling in the market.'

'My apologies, Brother Alwen,' said the prior. 'But this girl insists that she was expected, but –'

'That's because she is,' the Abbot said, interrupting him. 'Not everyone in this city is out to deceive.'

'Yes, Brother Alwen,' Prior Fren said, bowing his head several times.

'And call me Father or Abbot!' the old monk's tone was brusque, but still a whisper. 'Both are titles I deserve, don't you think?'

The prior lowered his eyes, accepting his admonishment.

'Yes, Father. I humbly apologise and ask for your forgiveness.'

Dariah thought about saying something but kept her mouth shut. Abbot Alwen glared at the prior for a few more moments.

'Of course, you're forgiven,' the Abbot said, his soft smile returning. 'We don't hold grudges here in the Brotherhood, but we do learn lessons. I will deal with this young lady. You're dismissed.'

The prior and the novice nodded, but she could see the annoyance on the prior's face as the two monks moved away in silence.

The Abbot held open the door to the cloisters and beckoned to her. 'Winnie, please come with me.'

'Thank you, Father,' Dariah said, relieved the altercation had ended.

She found it strange being addressed by a different name. She didn't especially like it either, but that's the name she had been told to use for this arrangement.

'I apologise for Prior Fren's behaviour,' he said as he shuffled by her. 'He's new to the capitol and isn't used to how we do things here.'

'That's perfectly fine, Father,' she said as she entered. 'I'm sure he was doing what he thought best.'

He followed her inside and closed the door. Whilst much smaller than the Abbey's main hall, the cloisters had the same high gabled roof, with an abundance of comfortable seating and more valuable decorations. She stopped to admire the huge tapestries that hung along one of the walls. After a few moments, her attention shifted to the coloured glass window that dominated the end wall. In the same style as the windows in the main hall, it had a more intricate design, and Dariah thought it stunning.

'Beautiful, isn't it?' Abbot Alwen said.

Dariah turned to him with a smile.

'It is.'

'But we should get started. We can't have you being late. Your mistress can be quite … err … emotional, and we've spent a great deal of time and resources getting you where you are.'

He opened a door on the other side of the room, and Dariah hurried through. The Abbot gestured towards a chair, and she sat. He picked up a jug and goblet from the table.

'Would you care for some wine?'

It would calm her nerves, but Dariah politely declined.

'I don't want to explain why I smell of wine when I was supposed to be praying.'

'Clever girl. We don't want to risk your position just yet.'

As the Abbot poured some wine for himself, Dariah recalled he had mentioned *we* on her earlier visit and again just now. At first, she had thought the Abbot was her patron, but she now suspected otherwise. Abbot Alwen was quite an important and influential figure in Avaleen, so whomever he reported to must be even more powerful. This made her more nervous.

'I'm glad I please you, Father.'

'It's not a case of pleasing me, though I am happy with your progress.'

She nodded, and he sat on the chair closest to her.

He took a sip of his wine and leaned back.

'As you have informed us previously,' the Abbot continued, 'The Governor has been ignoring Lady Greythorpe. Is this still the case?'

'Yes, and she continues trying to return to his good graces, but without success.'

'Hmmm,' the Abbot sounded troubled by this news. 'Well, we can only work with what we have, can't we?'

Dariah nodded, not entirely sure of the Abbot's meaning. She had only been brought into this intrigue after she entered the Governor's household. However, within a week of beginning her new job, a Sister of Avaleen, a female acolyte had approached her. She said a senior member of the Brotherhood was looking for young people to aid them with their work. Dariah already had a job, but she followed the old lady to the Abbey and, to her amazement, met with the Abbot himself. He promised there wouldn't be any danger and that she should go about her everyday work. She only needed to pay attention to everything she saw and heard. Despite her awe at being approached by a person as important as the Abbot, she thought about refusing, not wanting to jeopardise her new job. However, when told that her family would also benefit, she changed her mind and agreed. What could go wrong, she thought afterwards? It sounded exciting, and she only worked in the kitchens, so she couldn't see the harm in it.

Soon after, everything changed when the Steward of the Governor's Household strode into the kitchens.

'The damn woman has dismissed another handmaiden! That's five so far this summer!'

He glanced around and pointed at Dariah. 'You'll do. She likes the pretty ones. Have a bath and report to Lady Greythorpe at once.'

It was clear to her now that they wanted information on the Governor, not her mistress, so if Lady Greythorpe continued to be unsuccessful in her overtures to her husband, Dariah's services to the Abbot may no longer be required. Her family sold their produce at the city markets, and she knew they depended on the business being directed their way.

'My mistress is seeing Lord Greythorpe today and seemed quite confident when I left.'

'Let's hope your confidence in your mistress is not misplaced.' The Abbot stood and moved towards the door. 'You may go now, Winnie.'

'Is that all?'

He had only asked her one question.

'Unless you have anything else to add?'

'No, Father.'

'Then that's it. That wasn't so hard, was it?'

He opened the door.

'Err … no.'

'Well then, we'll be in contact again soon.'

'Thank you, Father. I'll try and bring better news next time,' Dariah said, glad to be leaving, but she still harboured concerns about being cast aside for her lack of information.

'Don't force it, my dear. Whatever happens, happens.'

His smile reassured her. Dariah made her way back through the cloisters and out to the main hall of the Abbey. The novice was near the main doors, and she smiled, nodding at him as she exited the building. He nodded and grinned back.

The sun had not yet reached its zenith, but she hurried back to the castle as fast as the crowded streets would allow. The Watchers had become familiar with Dariah's comings and goings, so she wasn't delayed as she passed back into the castle grounds.

Dariah entered Lady Greythorpe's empty quarters. Given how long it would have taken her mistress to dress and the unusually short visit to the Abbey, she had a little time on her hands, so she poured herself some water and tidied up the bedchamber.

Dariah decided to arrange food and refreshments for her mistress's return. With the kitchen as her destination, she opened the main door and jumped, giving an involuntary yelp, surprised by a man who was about to knock on the door.

'Oh my! I'm sorry. I wasn't expecting anyone.'

'I apologise for startling you, ma'am,' he said.

'Lady Greythorpe is not in right now,' she said, still trying to catch her breath, 'and I don't know when she's expected back. May I ask who has called? I will let her know as soon as she returns.'

'I am Sir Walter Guy, and I'm not here for Lady Greythorpe; I'm looking for Dariah Fields,' he said. 'Would that be you, by any chance?'

At the mention of her name, she looked up into the face of a Noble Guard!

'Y-yes. I'm Dariah,' she said, now noticing the shining white and gold armour and black cape of the King's Protectors.

'Excellent. I am to tell you that your presence is required at the Hall of Law mid-afternoon on the morrow.'

Her heart sank. Had she been discovered passing on information to the Abbot? She had tried to be careful.

'Don't be late, but be prepared to wait awhile,' the knight continued. 'Sometimes the rule of law can drag on so.'

'What does the Master of Law want with me?' she uttered, barely able to get the words out.

'Oh no. Lord Ramin hasn't called for you,' Sir Walter chuckled. 'You've been summoned by the king.'

Her heart skipped a beat as terror struck, and she fainted dead away.

3

REGAN

He threw the parchment onto the desk.

Damn! The letter didn't explicitly say it, but he knew another shipment had been lost. House Redstone had been a thorn in Lord Regan Greythorpe's side for many years. A history of animosity and distrust had long existed between their houses, particularly now that their patriarch, Lord Owen Redstone was a staunch ally of the royal family; it complicated matters no end. On a personal level, Regan just didn't like the man; however, you always knew where you stood with him.

Being Governor, head of the Ruling Council, and chief advisor to the king, Regan should have been the second most powerful man in the realm. However, unlike Owen Redstone, King Caleb kept his feelings in check. Regan found him difficult to read and, as a result, much more of an enigma. Therefore, he had to utilise his power more subtly to not attract undue attention. Some said the King could read minds. An absurd theory, of course, otherwise Regan would have lost his head long ago.

This morning's foul mood wasn't all Owen Redstone's fault, however. Several of Regan's allies had not considered it important enough to reply to his recent missive calling for their support.

Regan began reading another letter, this one from Carson Hightower,

17

pledging his allegiance and giving thanks for a recent loan. He'd never see a copper repaid, but at least the man had replied promptly. Regan needed options in case he had to move an army down the coast instead of via the main road down the centre of Avaleen. If the others would deign to reply, he could solidify his plans sooner rather than later, but Regan had received barely any responses, and it irked him.

A knock at the door interrupted his pondering. He sighed and looked up from his papers.

'Come.'

The door opened, and his wife Lennane entered the room, closely followed by their daughter. As usual, Lennane had dressed immaculately, her hair put up in the current fashion. If she had tried to dress modestly, she failed despite the long sleeves and high neckline. The combination of her generous breast size and small frame produced a spectacular sight, no matter what she wore. Her angelic face and curvy body would distract most people, but he'd long been aware of her masterful skills of manipulation. Lennane rarely did anything without a reason.

Dressed in a similar style to his wife, their daughter Lennore, stood just inside the door, not following her mother to the desk. His only child with Lennane had her mother's striking looks, and from the limited time he had spent with her, he suspected a quiet intelligence; now he ignored them both and returned his attention to the letter.

'Good morning, husband,' Lennane chirped, then glanced at Lennore, widening her eyes briefly.

'Good morning, Father,' his daughter said, her voice barely audible.

'We missed you at the morning meal,' he said to Lennane without looking up.

Regan usually enjoyed the peace and quiet her absence provided, but still considered it important enough to mention that he had noticed. His daughter always attended, but wisely, she stayed quiet unless spoken to.

'I know,' Lennane said. 'I was up late dealing with a servant issue and was extremely tired.'

Regan put down the letter and looked up at his wife. There had been an incident in the servants' quarters last night, part of the morning report from the guard-captain on duty. He claimed they had it all in hand, so Regan hadn't given it further thought. However, his wife's concern now for the servants intrigued him. She barely acknowledged a servant unless one had caused her a personal affront or had not completed a task to her satisfaction.

'It must have been serious for you to bother yourself with it. Is there anything I can do to help?'

Lennane dismissed his offer with a flick of her hand.

'Nothing in which you need to get involved,' she said. 'Your time is too precious to waste on domestic problems.'

He couldn't agree more.

'If you say so,' he said, picking up Hightower's letter for a second time and returning to its contents.

'What's bothering you, my dear?' she asked after a few moments of silence.

His wife had a surprising gift for politics and subterfuge. She also knew his moods.

'Since you ask,' Regan put the letter down again, 'I am yet to receive responses from some of our southern allies.'

The northernmost border lay a hundred miles north of Twin Falls, with Cliffs End six hundred miles away at the southern-most tip of the Black Cliffs. If you needed to find someone or go somewhere, more often than not you headed south.

'You know they're loyal. You don't need a piece of paper to say it,' Lennane said, smiling. 'Don't let it bother you. They need us, or more to the point, need our ships to chase off the pirates near their ports.'

Not that Regan would acknowledge it, but her thoughts had merit, and he noted she had referred to *our ships,* and *they need us.*

'Thank you for your advice.'

'You know I'm right. You worry too much.'

Maybe, but he liked things done correctly, and it annoyed him when others did not cooperate.

Lennane wandered around the room, taking in his small collection of books. She momentarily paused in front of the small iron dragon statue on the mantel given to him by his first wife. She even touched his desk and rubbed her fingers together as if inspecting it for dust.

'Is that all?' he said.

'Whatever do you mean?'

'You interrupted me just to apologise for missing the morning meal?'

Lennane pouted. 'Can't a wife just want to see her husband? I hardly see you anymore.'

Regan sighed. He couldn't deny her beauty. Being nearly thirty years her senior, he used to be proud to show her off at court. At thirty-four, she still turned heads, but couldn't fool him anymore.

'Lennane?'

'I'm bored,' she finally said, giving him a mournful look. 'Life in this place is so dull. All the ladies want to discuss is the latest fashion, who's betrothed to whom and how lucky we all are to be living in Riverview!'

Regan suppressed a smile.

Early in their marriage, when they shared a bed, they would talk for hours on many subjects, but after a while, she forgot her place. She became more forthright with her opinions and would complain when he ignored them. He had moved out of their shared apartment into the Governor's tower, where he now spent most of his time, either in his private quarters or working in his solar.

'It's horribly tiresome.'

'I thought you enjoyed all of the court rumours and scandals?'

'Even I can stomach only so much.'

'And what would you like me to do about it? I can't very well outlaw gossiping.'

He glimpsed her annoyance at his flippant remark, but the doleful look soon returned.

'I want to help you like I used to. You know I'm smarter than your advisors,' she pleaded. 'Let me back in.'

Lennane did have an aptitude for politics. He suspected that was how she'd arranged her introduction to Regan in the first place, many years ago, but her compulsion for power caused him some concern.

'If you can't find me something useful to do, you may as well send me back to Hillvale. At least there, I'll be at home surrounded by family.'

'I don't think Calvin would appreciate his stepmother second-guessing his every decision.'

'I only want what's best for the family.'

She may be a power-hungry schemer, but maybe it could be time to let her back into the fold to some extent. She had never actually broken his trust, and occasionally her counsel had been enlightening.

'Very well,' Regan said. 'Organise an evening meal in your private quarters tomorrow night, and we will talk … '

… and see if she's learned her lesson.

'Keep it simple,' Regan added. 'Nothing too elaborate.'

Lennane danced around the desk.

'You won't regret it.'

Let's hope not, he thought as she leaned over, pushed her bosom into his shoulder, and kissed him on the cheek. He stole a glance at her chest. Maybe tomorrow night he'd see more of it.

'Now, if you don't mind, I have some work to finish.'

She skipped and glided towards the door.

'Goodbye, my love.'

Regan forced a smile. 'Goodbye.'

Lennore opened the door for her mother and followed her out without a word. Regan breathed a sigh of relief as the guard closed the door and left him in peace.

He retrieved the carafe from the sideboard and poured himself half a goblet of wine. He sat, took a sip of his wine and picked up the letter he had been reading before he had been interrupted.

He finished reading it and reached for another, but raised voices, the sound of metal hitting a stone floor, and a loud thump against the door interrupted him. What now? Regan rose from the desk and strode towards the door. He could make out voices as he approached.

'You broke his nose!'

'I'll break more than his fucking nose if he gets in my way again!'

Regan yanked the door open. Two of his guards lay on the floor; one crumpled in the corner and the other groaning, holding his bloody face.

The man standing over him had a sword, resting the point of it on the guard's chest. He gripped a long dagger in his other hand, and pointed it at the third guard. The standing guard had drawn his weapon, but his arm trembled.

'What's going on here?' Regan bellowed.

'I'm sorry, my lord,' said the guard. 'We wouldn't let him in, so he killed Jarvis and hit the Sergeant.'

The man with the dagger had not moved. 'He's not dead, but you will be if you don't drop your weapon.'

'Who are you?' Regan demanded.

'Lord Steffan sent me,' the man said, without taking his eyes off the guard.

He gave no name, no apology, and no 'my lord' honorific, but a slight smile appeared on Regan's stony face.

'Come in,' Regan said and headed back toward his desk.

The man sneered at the guard and entered the room, closing the door behind him before sheathing his sword. Regan towered over the man, a full head taller, but as he had just witnessed, you wouldn't want to face him in combat.

'Harrow, I believe?' Regan said.

The man nodded once.

Regan had sent word to his brother Steffan at Kings Hill with his requirements a few weeks earlier, and he had sent this man, a grizzled twenty-year veteran soldier of the Greythorpe family. Harrow had a reputation for being a first-class swordsman and a completely ruthless killer. He also sported a perpetual sneer, and the scar that stretched from his brow down across his nose and right cheek added to his notoriety.

'My brother told you what to expect?'

He nodded again.

'Do you have any questions?'

Harrow shook his head.

'Where is Lord Steffan?' Regan asked.

'He'll be following shortly.'

'What does that mean? Next week, after the next full moon, what?'

'He didn't say.'

Damn him! Regan needed people in the city who could be relied upon for support, and he felt he could only trust certain members of his family. As for his own safety, Harrow looked dangerous enough, discouraging most who would dare challenge him.

'You're now in charge of my personal guard,' Regan said. 'Recruit anyone you wish, but loyalty is paramount.'

'I don't need anyone else.'

'Don't be stupid,' Regan said. 'You might be tough, but you still need to sleep and eat. But first, clean up that mess you made outside my door.'

Harrow didn't even bat an eye at the rebuke, simply turning and leaving the room. The man had come highly recommended. With any luck, he wouldn't be too difficult to manage.

Regan sat, picked up the next parchment and resumed his reading.

4

LETO

Leto fidgeted.

He'd stood in the hall next to Jacob for hours, watching his father dispense justice. For those who disagreed with a decision made by Sir Ramin, the Master of Law, the King's court gave them a forum for their grievance.

The King relaxed on the small throne in the centre of a raised circular dais. A pitcher and goblet sat on a small table to his left. Sir Ramin stood to his right, leaning on a long wooden staff. The staff, nearly seven feet long, didn't have a formal title, although most called it the Staff of Law. Nowadays, the old Master of Law mainly used it to hold himself upright.

It had been two nights since Leto had seen Lady Greythorpe in a midnight tryst with her handmaiden, and since he and Jacob had returned to the safety of Leto's apartment, still puffing from their exertions of fleeing the servants' quarters.

'Are you alright?' Jacob had said.

Leto hadn't even thought about whether he'd been hurt, having been too intent on making their escape. He performed some different stretches with his legs and arms. On raising his right arm, the one which Jacob had caught him by, he winced.

'Sit down and take off your shirt,' Jacob instructed.

Leto removed his jacket and shirt, tossed them on the bed, and sat on a nearby chair. Jacob examined his shoulder.

'No bruising, at least not yet,' Jacob said, pressing his fingers into Leto's back and shoulder in several places.

'Oww!' Leto jumped up from the chair. 'Yes. It hurts.'

'No archery for at least a week,' Jacob said, chuckling. 'You'll have to use your left hand for sword practice. Master Alexei will be pleased. He always thought you were favouring your right side, anyway.'

Leto had been trained by the finest sword master in Avaleen, Alexei Mets, since he was a child, and had become one of the best exponents of the sword in the realm. The opinion of his sword teacher was the least of his worries.

'She saw me, you know,' he said.

'You fell through the roof of her bedchamber,' Jacob said, grinning. 'It would've been hard not to see you.'

'No, I mean she recognised me.'

'Are you sure?'

'She looked straight at me!'

'Do you think she saw me, too?'

'I doubt it, but if she saw me, you'd be guilty by association.'

'Well, that's great.'

After a few moments, Leto turned away from the window to face Jacob. 'We could be in serious trouble this time. It could get political.'

'You think so?'

'Maybe,' Leto said. 'We better get some sleep. I have a feeling we're going to have a big day tomorrow.'

Jacob started towards the door.

'Thank you,' Leto said.

His friend stopped and faced him. 'For what?'

'For saving me, again. I could have broken my neck if you hadn't grabbed me.'

'An apology and a thank you in one day. I'm honoured.'

Jacob acknowledged Leto's thanks with a nod of his head.

'Just doing my job keeping the prince of the realm safe from harm, even if it was self-inflicted and due to his own stupidity.'

Leto's frown turned into a smile.

'Just close the door on your way out.'

Grinning, Jacob pulled the door and left, leaving Leto to close the shutters and wonder how much trouble he could possibly be in.

He had expected a summons yesterday morning, either from his father or the Commander of the Capitol Guard, so he had woken and bathed before dawn. He had also dragged Jacob out of bed, but no summons came. Perhaps Lady Greythorpe hadn't recognised him, or she didn't want to bring attention to herself this way.

Well, today he may find out. Just as he and Jacob were finishing their lesson with Master Alexi, a member of the Noble Guard instructed Leto and Jacob to attend the King's Court at once.

He couldn't figure out how his father had found out about their midnight hijinks. This could be about something else entirely, but he doubted it. Lady Greythorpe would be unlikely to make a complaint, and except for the handmaiden, she had been the only one who saw him. But here he waited, as he had for most of the afternoon. And his stomach rumbled at not having had anything to eat since the morning meal.

Leto's reverie ended as Sir Ramin struck the staff on the stone floor, signalling the end of business for the day. The final petitioners bowed to the King, turned and hurried out. The King stood and conferred with Sir Ramin in hushed tones. After the conversation finished, Sir Ramin harried his clerks to gather their parchments and inks.

The Master of Law hobbled towards the door, leading the clerks out of the hall. Once they had left, the King faced Leto and Jacob. Despite being unable to read his father's mood, he started towards the dais but stopped when his father turned away and spoke to Sir Mabon Rhys, the Captain of the Noble Guard.

'Bring them in, Captain,' the King ordered, sat back on the throne and took a sip from the goblet.

Captain Rhys signalled to the guard nearest the main doors. Leto glanced across to Jacob, who looked as weary as Leto felt. His heart sank as Lady Lennane Greythorpe entered the hall. She strode towards the dais with her handmaiden who struggled to keep up. Lennane and the girl stopped a few yards short of the dais and curtsied.

'Your Grace,' Lennane said.

'Lady Greythorpe,' the King said. 'My apologies for keeping you waiting. I was unaware you would be accompanying your servant.'

'No apology necessary, Your Grace,' Lennane said, tilting her head slightly in acknowledgement. 'She became quite nervous when she was summoned into your presence, so I thought it best to be here to support her.'

'That's very noble of you,' the King said, and moved forward a little and gazed at the handmaiden, who still stared at the bottom step of the dais. 'What's your name, young lady?'

'Dariah, Your Grace,' she said, her head still bowed.

'Look at the King when he addresses you,' Lennane hissed.

'Yes, ma'am,' Dariah said, glancing at Lennane. She looked up at the King. 'S ... sorry, Your Grace.'

Poor girl, Leto thought.

'Don't fret,' the King said. 'Just a few quick questions and this will all be over.'

Dariah continued to tremble. 'Yes, Your Grace.'

'I understand there was an incident a couple of nights ago in your quarters?' the King asked, his eyes flicking towards Leto before returning to the handmaiden. 'Someone fell through the roof?'

'Yes, Your Grace.'

'Were you hurt?'

'No, Your Grace,' Dariah replied. 'And Lady Greythorpe kindly found me a place to stay until the damage is repaired.'

'That's very kind of her,' the King said. 'Now, let's get down to business.'

Dariah nodded and bit her lip.

'Did you see who it was that fell through your roof?'

'No, Your Grace.'

'Would you recognise this person if you saw him again?'

28

'I didn't see his face.'

She lied! The girl lied to the King. Lady Greythorpe must have put her up to it. She must be more afraid of her than his father.

'What were you doing when this incident occurred?'

'I was sleeping, Your Grace,' Dariah said. 'But I woke when he fell through. I think I screamed as well.'

'I'm sure you did,' the King said.

Leto could see his father's disappointment.

'One last question,' the King continued. 'Were you alone?'

'What?' Lennane blurted out.

Lennane stiffened as she realised her error. Dariah glanced at Lennane with horror as the King glared at her mistress.

'I am so sorry, Your Grace,' Lennane said and bowed. 'Please forgive my outburst. It will not happen again.'

'I certainly hope not,' the King said and returned his gaze to the handmaiden. 'Now, was there anyone else in the bed with you?'

'N … -no, Your Grace,' she said.

The King raised his arm and gestured at the guard captain.

'Captain Rhys reported that a candle was still burning when his men arrived.'

Leto realised he had been holding his breath, waiting for the King's justice to fall on the poor girl.

'I find it difficult to sleep without candlelight,' Dariah said. 'I've been that way since I was a child.'

The King glared at the two women for a few moments, then sighed. 'Fine. You may go. Lady Greythorpe, always a pleasure.'

'Your Grace,' Lennane murmured.

Both women curtsied, turned and marched towards the door. Lennane's eyes flicked to Leto as they passed, and then exited the hall, eyes forward,.

The King beckoned to Leto and Jacob with a quick movement of his hand. As they approached the dais, Leto tried to read his father's mood again. He looked more irritated than anything else. They stopped a few steps from the throne and looked up at the King.

'What do you have to say for yourself?' the King said, glowering at Leto.

'I don't know what you mean, Father.'

The King jumped to his feet, and both Leto and Jacob stepped back in surprise.

'You will address me as Your Grace, or sire! Am I not your king?'

'Yes. Sorry, Your Grace,' Leto said.

'That's better. Now stop feeding me that rubbish. I know it was you and your sidekick here,' his father said, Jacob now receiving the royal glare.

'The guards saw you run away,' the King added.

With the route they had taken, even with a near-full moon they would not have been seen until they had returned to the royal apartments. But he couldn't use that as an argument. It would be as good as admitting their guilt.

'They must be mistaken. We were on the roof near the southern parapet overlooking the falls, Your Grace.' Leto said.

Better to admit a minor transgression to deflect attention from the much larger one, he hoped.

'Really? How long were you, if my memory serves me correctly, in a place I have forbidden you to go on several occasions already?'

'We were back in our quarters before the night guard change. I'm sure the guard captain can confirm that.'

Leto hoped that the guards weren't too exact in the timing of their reports.

The King looked across to Captain Rhys, who nodded in confirmation. He directed his gaze at a nervous Jacob, who stood eyes to the front like a soldier at attention.

'Did I or did I not task you with keeping the prince safe?'

'Yes, Your Grace,' Jacob said.

'So why were you up on the damned roof?'

Jacob opened his mouth to reply, but the King interrupted him.

'I don't forbid these things for my own amusement.'

Jacob glanced at Leto and back at the King.

'I did remind the prince that you had forbidden it, Your Grace.' Jacob eventually said. 'But I thought it best I be there … to protect him just in case something went wrong.'

'Well, he doesn't listen to me, his King,' his father said, his mood softening, 'so, I don't see why he would heed your warnings.'

'He's quite headstrong, Your Grace,' Jacob said.

'Yes, he gets that from his mother,' said the King. 'You may go.'

Both Leto and Jacob turned to leave.

'Not you.'

Leto stopped.

'Good luck,' Jacob whispered.

'Thanks,' Leto muttered and turned back.

The King looked over to Captain Rhys.

'That'll be all, captain. Clear the hall. I want a private word with my son.'

'Certainly, Your Grace.' Captain Rhys said.

The guards behind the dais marched passed him and headed towards the doors. Captain Rhys followed and closed the doors from the outside. With them now alone, Leto looked up at his father.

'What I don't quite understand,' the King said, 'is why Lady Greythorpe waited all that time outside with her servant without as much as a complaint. She's never been one to take an insult, accidental or otherwise, even from me.'

'I wouldn't know, Your Grace,' said Leto.

'You can drop the pretence now. There's no one else here. I know you did it. I'm not a fool.'

Leto smiled.

'I received another letter from your sister today,' the King continued. 'She's doing well. Says you should write to her more.'

'She never stops writing letters,' Leto said, glad the subject had been changed. 'I can't keep up. I think she has too much time on her hands.'

'Be a good brother and write to her.'

'Yes, father. I'll try.'

The King took a drink from the goblet on the table beside him.

'I was a lot like you when I was your age, but at least I had respect for my King, your grandfather.'

Leto couldn't count how many times he had heard this.

'I do respect you.'

'Then what was that farce we just went through?'

'She has a secret,' Leto said. 'Well, I didn't know about it, anyway.'

'Does she now?'

'She didn't attend to assist her servant. She was here to ensure the servant told the correct story.'

'The girl lied?'

'Yes. But don't punish her for it.'

'She lied to her King!'

His father wasn't pleased even though Leto was sure he'd suspected it all along. He sensed that his father wouldn't punish the girl but wanted to see Leto's reaction … to test him. Everything was a test, a learning experience, all to prepare him to assume the throne he didn't want.

'No good would come from it,' Leto said. 'It'd just give the Greythorpe family another reason to despise ours. '

'But why the big charade?'

'The handmaiden wasn't alone.'

'Is that so?' the King raised his brows. 'Who was with her that is so important that Lennane Greythorpe would want to protect them by deceiving me so openly?'

'I didn't say she was protecting anyone else.'

The King gave Leto a puzzled look and a few moments later, burst into laughter.

'Now it all makes perfect sense.'

Still chuckling, the King stood.

'What are you going to do?'

'Nothing, my boy, nothing. I thought you'd know by now; information is often more valuable than gold.'

'Why would she try so hard to hush that up.'

'Yes, it is a little odd,' his father conceded. 'Lennane Greythorpe is quite the social climber and certainly not above manipulating anyone to feed her ambitions, including me.'

The King came down the steps to Leto.

'Maybe she doesn't want people to know she's consorting with the help. Who cares? If she doesn't want this little tryst of hers known, it's valuable to us.'

'I don't know how you can stand it,' Leto said. 'Secrets, gossip, intrigue and heavens knows what else. I hate it.'

'So do I,' his father said. 'But it's one of the many things you must work through when you're king. If you pay attention now and listen to what I tell you, it'll make it much easier when it's your time.'

Leto gulped.

'I don't want to be king,' he blurted out and glanced up at his father, unsure how he would react to this revelation.

His father stood before Leto and placed his hand on his shoulder.

'When I was your age, I didn't want to be King either, and I told my father as much. He wasn't thrilled about it, but here I am.'

This surprised Leto.

'But you're a good king. The people love you.'

'I don't know about that, but I'll tell you something my father said to me.' His father paused momentarily. 'One who covets the crown will ultimately fail in their duty to the people – or something to that effect. Like you, I didn't pay attention to everything my father said, but you understand what I mean?'

'I suppose you're right,' said Leto as his father put his arm around his shoulders and directed him towards the closed doors.

'You care about people and the truth, despite the farce we just went through,' the King said. 'Which is more than do most people around here. You'll make a fine King one day. Better than me, I have no doubt.'

Leto kept silent as they approached the doors.

'So, tell me,' his father continued, 'is there anything else you can remember about Lady Greythorpe that I should know before we put this sordid affair behind us?'

A cheeky grin appeared on Leto's face as they stopped at the doors.

'Nothing, Your Grace,' he said. 'Nothing at all.'

The King gave Leto a bemused look.

'Open!'

At the King's command, the large oak doors creaked as they began to inch open. The day hadn't turned out as badly as Leto had expected. It could have been far worse. The doors opened wide enough for them to pass through, and a smiling Leto walked out with his father's arm still around his shoulders.

5

OWEN

Owen Redstone, Knight Eldar of Avaleen, Lord of the Shadowlands, long-time advisor and friend to the King, and one of the most powerful men in the realm, had been reduced to escort duty. However, he couldn't keep the smile from his face and joy from his heart as he escorted Addwyn, his wife of seventeen years, and his fifteen-year-old twin daughters, Cordelia and Gwenda, to the capitol. His family had already been travelling for nearly three weeks from Cliffs End, the place the Redstone family had called home for generations.

Owen hadn't seen his family since before summer, which had already begun to make way for what felt would be another cold winter. His brother, Penn, was the only member of his family he saw with any regularity, and he, along with Owen, sat on the Ruling Council.

Owen and his retinue had left Twin Falls just after daybreak and had arrived in Southern Brook by mid-morning to accompany his family on the last leg of their journey. He savoured any time away from the capitol.

He had bought a house on the western edge of town, overlooking the river. It wasn't luxurious, but the taverns had much to be desired, and it afforded him and his family privacy.

His daughters had taken the opportunity to bathe and dispense with their riding clothes for something more formal, which meant they could no longer ride and would have to complete their journey to the capitol in a horse-drawn covered wagon. Cordelia had a renewed obsession with her appearance – she would be meeting her future husband for the first time since their betrothal the previous year. Owen still remembered the day he told Addwyn that the King had agreed to the union between his son, Leto, and one of their daughters.

'But which one?' his wife had said.

If Cordelia hadn't been a twin, it would have been a simple decision. When he had informed them of the decision, excitement, apprehension, and disappointment ensued. Gwenda congratulated her sister, who would now one day be queen, but Owen could see her distress at not being the one betrothed. To no one's surprise, Cordelia's first reaction had been unadulterated excitement, but soon after, she turned to her father.

'What about Gwennie?'

Owen threw up his hands, apologised that the King only had one son left to marry off, and retreated from the room, leaving Addwyn and Cordelia to console Gwenda.

Dappled light shone through the forest canopy as they rode through the Kingswood at a walk, Owen on his black stallion and Addwyn beside him on her favourite grey mare.

A dozen soldiers protected the family, including the four Owen had brought with him from the capitol.

'I still don't understand why they changed their clothing,' Owen said. 'They aren't scheduled to meet the prince or the King until the day after tomorrow.'

All Redstone children learned how to ride horses as soon as they could walk. After all, their house emblem consisted of a prancing horse, so Owen felt they should ride.

Addwyn chuckled. 'They want to make a good impression. A future queen must always look her best for her people.'

'Her people? She has people now?'

Addwyn smiled as Owen looked her up and down.

'I noticed you didn't change.'

'I'm not trying to impress anyone.'

'What about me?'

'I impressed you ages ago, my dear.'

Owen laughed. 'That you did.'

He glanced back over his shoulder at the twins.

'She's going to be impossible to live with, isn't she?'

'I'm the one who has to put up with them, not you,' Addwyn said. 'They feed off each other. If one is being difficult, invariably the other is as well.'

'And you've done such a wonderful job so far, and I appreciate it.'

'Really?'

Owen leaned closer to Addwyn with a grin on his face.

'I'll show you how much tonight, my beautiful wife.'

'I know you will, husband,' she said with mock seriousness. 'I didn't come all this way to be ignored.'

They burst into laughter.

The twins had quietened down since leaving Southern Brook, but once they exited the forest and the capitol became visible in the distance, the chatter and wonderment started all over again.

Twin Falls could be seen for miles, with Riverview Castle soaring above everything around it. The dark-stone castle had been built between the two main rivers in Avaleen, the Dry River to the southwest and the Winding River to the southeast. They flowed very near to each other but did not meet. Riverview imposed itself on the city around it, but the magnificent waterfalls that gave the capitol its name dwarfed the castle.

Queens Falls was considered one of the most beautiful places in Avaleen. It consisted of over a dozen smaller waterfalls, each flowing into one another. Members of the aristocracy often swam in the pristine pools. Fed by the Winding River, which flowed from the mountains to the east, it snaked its way southeast of the capitol to the Shadowlands.

It did not flow into the sea like the other rivers in Avaleen but disappeared into the Dragon's Throat, a dark crack in the face of the towering Black Cliffs bordering the southeastern edge of Avaleen. No one knew where it went from there, and those who had been washed over the falls into the Dragon's Throat had never been seen again.

Kings Falls bordered the west of the capitol. They started higher up the hill than Queens Falls and were about five times as wide; the water fell straight into King Lake five hundred feet below, with a roar that could be heard for miles around. The water flowed from the Dry River out of the desert beyond the Borderlands in the north. From King Lake, it flowed southwest to the coast, emptying into the Dividing Sea south of Oceanwatch.

By now, the shadows had lengthened significantly.

'Captain!' Owen said.

A soldier at the front eased his horse to the right and stopped. When Owen had caught up, he urged his mount to a walk beside him.

'My lord?' the captain said.

Captain Archer Janz had been with Owen since being recruited at fifteen and had risen to the position of his personal guard. He hated the idea of constantly being shadowed, but Archer's discretion made it easier to handle. In the last few years, Owen had spent more time in Archer's company than anyone else's, even that of his wife. Owen trusted him with his life.

'Speed things up a bit. I want to get back before dark.'

'Yes, sir.'

Archer stopped his horse again, and Owen knew the twins would be warned. They would not be pleased as it could be an uncomfortable journey in the wagon, but that's the price they would pay for not riding like everyone else.

'On my command!' Archer called out. 'Slow canter. We want to make the capitol before sundown.'

He trotted past Owen, took his place up front and raised his hand.

'Forward!' Archer kicked his horse to a canter, and everyone behind urged their mounts forward to match his speed.

The sun had just touched the horizon, and the air had begun to cool as they rode through the South Gate, the first of the gates on their way to Riverview. The twins had last visited the capitol nearly ten years ago as young children. In the excitement of seeing it again, Cordelia had forgotten her position as future queen, and encouraged by Gwenda,

38

started with shrieks of excitement, pointing out people and sights, giggling enthusiastically.

He and his wife looked back at their daughters.

'They're still little girls at heart,' Addwyn said.

'I sometimes wish they'd never grow up.'

Archer called a halt at the main castle gate, a large timber and iron structure set into the even higher stone wall that enclosed the outer part of the castle grounds. Archer spoke to the Watcher on duty, so it would only be a short wait before the gates opened.

Once in Riverview, they would be surrounded by scheming nobles and swallowed up by the politics and greed of the royal court. Part of Owen wanted to turn tail and make for Cliffs End as quickly as possible, but he had responsibilities to his family and the King.

'Everything will be fine,' Addwyn said.

Owen managed a smile. She could always read his thoughts. 'I'm sure it will, my dear. I'm sure it will.'

'Forward!' Archer called, and the procession moved through the main gate into Riverview.

6

DARIAH

The click of her heels against the stone floor echoed through the corridor as Dariah hurried back to her mistress's quarters. The previous two days had been a blur, and exhaustion had almost claimed her.

When Sir Walter Guy had told Dariah of the King's summons, a thousand thoughts ran through her mind, and she found she could hardly function.

The next thing Dariah remembered, she lay on her mistress's bed, Sir Walter and Lady Greythorpe looking down on her.

'What happened?' she murmured.

'You fainted,' the Noble Guard had said, concerned. 'It took me quite by surprise.'

'Sir Walter picked you up and put you on my bed,' said Lady Greythorpe, clearly not amused, and turned away. 'Gretchen! Water!'

The room began to spin when Dariah attempted to sit. Putting her hand to her head, she felt the rough cloth of a bandage.

'The Maester left this for you,' Sir Walter said, holding a cup. 'Drink it and rest here for the remainder of the day, if your mistress will permit, of course.'

'For the moment,' her mistress said. 'Now drink.'

She took the proffered cup and sniffed the contents. She screwed up her nose at the pungent smell. She looked up at her mistress and across to Sir Walter.

'Drink!' Lady Greythorpe ordered.

Dariah tentatively put the cup to her lips, took a sip, and nearly retched. It tasted worse than it smelled.

'The Maester said you must drink it all,' said Sir Walter.

Dariah forced herself to drink the bitter liquid. She heaved and almost vomited but managed to keep it down.

'Good girl,' Sir Walter said and held out his hand.

Dariah gave him the empty cup, and the Noble Guard handed her another.

She hesitated, glancing at him with raised eyebrows.

'It's water,' he said with a smile.

Dariah took the cup and drank. The cool water soothed her throat and cleansed her mouth of the tart medicine.

'I should go back to my room,' Dariah said.

She tried to get out of bed, but Lady Greythorpe touched her shoulder.

'Stay!' she said. 'I don't want Sir Walter having to pick you up from the floor again.'

'Yes, my lady,' Dariah said, looking at the Noble Guard. 'Thank you, Sir Walter. You have been most kind.'

He gave her a broad grin.

'Think nothing of it. I'm just glad to see you weren't badly hurt.'

He faced Lady Greythorpe. 'If there is nothing else, I will take my leave.'

'Sir Walter, you also have my thanks,' she said.

'The pleasure was all mine, my lady,'

He performed a short bow, turned and left the room.

Dariah yawned as the door closed behind him. Her eyelids felt heavy; she lay back on the bed.

'I'm sorry, my lady,' Dariah said and yawned again. 'I'm so embarrassed.'

'Rest,' she said. 'When you wake, we will talk.'

Dariah slept dreamlessly through the whole afternoon and into the night. She woke to the flickering light of the fire in the hearth. She sat up, the dizziness returned, and she remembered. A movement beside her caught her attention. It was only her mistress sleeping.

Dariah slipped out of bed. Unsteady on her feet, she managed to make her way to the privy, using furniture and the walls to steady herself. She returned without incident, stripped off and crawled back into bed. She snuggled up against the warm body of her mistress and put her arm around her. Lady Greythorpe moved slightly in her sleep and took her hand, clutching it to her breast.

Dariah smiled and closed her eyes.

The following day also became another she could not forget and would rather not repeat. Lady Greythorpe had wanted her to lie to the King. People had been thrown into the dungeons for much less, but she promised her mistress she would do as instructed. Lady Greythorpe must have sensed Dariah's agitation because she decided to go with her to see the King. This settled her nerves, and she was glad of the company.

Unfortunately, her mistress kept coaching her on the story she was to tell, which only made her more anxious. She began to shake and found it hard to draw breath; waiting outside the great hall for so long made it even worse. Lady Greythorpe had arranged for a secluded area nearby where they could wait away from prying eyes. Still, Dariah had worked herself into such a state that she could barely walk through the doors when the summons finally came.

The actual meeting with the King wasn't as bad as the waiting. His grace had been gracious and polite, reminding her of Sir Walter with his considerate manner. She stammered and made mistakes, but not as big as Lady Greythorpe's outburst when the King asked Dariah whether she had been alone in her bed. Dariah almost fainted then and there.

Also, she felt sincere relief when she came up with the reason for the candle, and the King seemed to accept her explanation. She remembered that her little brother couldn't sleep unless there was a candle burning. Thinking of Dirk still brought a tear to her eye.

And tonight, Lady Greythorpe's evening meal with her husband had kept Dariah busy. She had worked extra hard to ensure everything would be perfect. Lady Greythorpe even had a mantra for the evening, simple but elegant. She had arranged with the Governor's kitchen to cook some of Lord Regan's favourite dishes. Dariah convinced Winston to supply one of the best wines from the Governor's collection without first getting permission from Lord Regan.

Dariah rushed into her mistress's apartment. She surveyed the living room and smiled, satisfied everything was where it should be. A smaller table had been brought in for this occasion to give it a more intimate feel. The fire in the hearth burned nicely, and Gretchen had just lit the last of the candles.

'His Lordship is on his way. Tell the kitchen to ready the first course,' Dariah said.

'Yes, ma'am,' Gretchen said and hurried out.

Dariah entered the bedchamber. Lady Greythorpe stared at herself in the mirror.

'Lord Regan is on his way, my lady,' Dariah said.

'Late, as expected,' Lady Greythorpe said and faced Dariah. 'How do I look?'

She seemed oddly nervous. Usually calm and confident, sometimes to the point of arrogance, she now acted like a young girl at her betrothal.

'Stunning, my lady.'

'You think so?'

She wore a deep red dress with a simple but elegant design that accentuated her womanly curves. She looked positively beautiful.

They both left the bedchamber, and Dariah waited by the main door. Her mistress went to the sideboard and filled two goblets, one smaller than the other, and Dariah recalled her explicit instructions about the wine.

'It's too good to be watered down, and I want my husband to relax tonight.'

Dariah assumed that she meant for His Lordship to get a little drunk.

She heard footsteps and opened the door. Lord Regan Greythorpe approached, and Dariah bowed her head and curtsied.

'My lord. Lady Greythorpe has been expecting you.'

Lord Regan barely paused in the doorway.

'I'm sure she has.'

'Good evening, my love,' her mistress said, approaching him and kissing his cheek.

Thankfully, he leaned over so she could reach him. This small act suggested a promising start to the evening. Lady Greythorpe guided her husband to the table, and he sat at the offered place. They had ensured he could see the door from his seat, as he preferred.

'The first course will be here directly, my lady,' Dariah said.

Her mistress brought over the goblets of wine.

'Go to the kitchen and wait for it,' she instructed, 'and no one else is to enter this room except you, understand?'

'Yes, ma'am.'

Dariah left and made her way to the kitchen. The head cook, Garrick Manse, had just put the final touches to the first course. He drove his kitchen hands hard, his booming voice a constant echo throughout the kitchen, but he always had a smile for her.

'It's almost ready,' he said when she entered the kitchen. 'The serving girls will bring it up momentarily.'

'Lady Greythorpe wants privacy tonight, so I'm the only one to attend them.'

'Well, aren't you the lucky one,' Garrick laughed. 'But there's too much here for you to deliver yourself, and I'll not have you serving cold food to the Governor.'

Garrick's skills in the kitchen were only exceeded by Hendo, the Royal chef.

'But my lady was very specific,' Dariah protested.

Garrick raised his hand to stop her objection. 'Don't worry. The girls will bring the food and wait in the common room. You can take it from there. The first course will be brought up shortly, so you can personally serve the Lord and Lady.'

He was poking fun at her situation, but Dariah didn't mind having to serve her mistress and the Governor. She may even overhear something that may be valuable to her patron.

Weariness dogged her, so she didn't hurry back, and by the time she arrived at the common room, Gretchen and the serving girls were on her heels.

'Follow me,' Dariah instructed and led the girls to the door of Lady Greythorpe's apartment. 'Wait here.'

She grabbed the platter from the nearest girl and went in.

Smiling and chatting, her mistress either didn't notice or chose to ignore that the Governor's attention seemed elsewhere. Not a promising start. Dariah hurried out and returned with the second platter. Lord Regan took a drink of his wine, all the while eyeing Dariah as she placed the platter on the table.

'Would you like me to serve, my lady?'

'No, I will be serving my husband tonight.'

Dariah bowed her head, turned and left.

When she brought up the second course, a similar scenario greeted her. Her mistress had been doing all the talking while the Governor stared into his wine goblet, his plate of food hardly touched.

She set out the new platters and hurried out of the room. She returned to the kitchen with Gretchen and waited for the next course to be prepared.

The future didn't look very bright. She could do nothing to help her mistress and would again have nothing helpful to report to her patron. To make matters worse, Lady Greythorpe would be moodier than usual afterwards and make Dariah's life hell.

With the next course finally ready, she and the serving girls took the two platters of meats to the common room. Dariah dreaded that the situation had deteriorated even further between Lady Greythorpe and her husband. Still, she took one of the platters and entered the apartment.

'-and I had to order him not to escort me. Otherwise, he'd be standing over there watching you right now.'

Lord Regan pointed towards the door as Dariah put the food on the table. 'And he'd be wondering whether or not you were going to kill me.'

'That's absurd,' her mistress laughed. 'Why did your brother send him, anyway? And where is Steffan? I thought he was supposed to be here by now.'

Dariah retrieved the other platter.

'-he's quite scary looking,' her mistress said.

'He's supposed to be scary,' the Governor said. 'What's the point of having a bodyguard who doesn't look threatening?'

Dariah left the room and returned to the kitchen, silently thanking the gods. Lord Regan wasn't overly happy, but at least he now participated in the conversation.

After the prescribed amount of time, she grabbed the single platter of sweet rolls and returned to Lady Greythorpe's apartment.

' – will you be able to control him?' her mistress said as Dariah entered the room. 'He looks harmless, but if he's anything like his father –'

As Dariah approached the table, Lord Regan glared at his wife, and she stopped talking and poured more wine for her husband and herself.

Later in the evening, after Dariah had cleared the plates away, she collected another jug of wine, which the Governor himself had requested. The special vintage came from the Governor's private store, so she had needed to find Winston, who had the only key. He wasn't pleased with the interruption to his evening, but he did as asked.

Wine in hand, she entered the living room and heard laughter. Dariah had never seen Lord Regan smile, so to hear him laugh surprised her. They both watched her as she moved towards the sideboard.

'Bring it here, girl,' he said. 'I'm tired of my lady wife getting up and down serving me like a common wench.'

Dariah changed direction and headed towards the table.

'Is this the one I asked for?' he said as he grabbed the jug and filled his cup. 'The Masterran?'

'It's the one Mr Morgan gave me, my lord.'

He sniffed the cup and took a sip. 'Probably isn't, knowing Winston. He's a cagey one. Doesn't want to waste good wine on people who have already drunk too much. But it will suffice.'

Lord Regan ogled her, his gaze moving up and down her body.

'She's a pretty little thing. How come she's serving you and not me?'

Lady Greythorpe's smile never wavered.

'You aren't going to take away my best servant, my dear?' she said, her lips pouting slightly.

She leaned close and whispered into her husband's ear. Lord Regan eyed her again and smiled. Dariah felt uncomfortable under his continued gaze.

'Would you like to serve me?' he said, his voice slurring slightly.

'I would be honoured, my lord,' she said, unsure of the service he had in mind.

'Yes, I'm sure you would.'

He took another drink of his wine and turned away.

'You're dismissed for the rest of the night,' her mistress said and returned her attention to her husband.

'Thank you, my lady. Have a good evening,' Dariah added, and gave the Governor a short bow. 'My lord.'

With mixed feelings, she made her way to the door. She assumed her mistress would bed Lord Regan tonight. At least Dariah would get a decent night's sleep, which she badly needed after the past couple of days.

In the common room, she found Gretchen had been replaced by Amelie, the young girl who would perform night duties for Lady Greythorpe. Dariah instructed her to clean up the living room once their mistress had retired for the evening and to wake Dariah should any problems arise. Even though she disliked being awakened at all hours, being the most senior member of Lady Greythorpe's staff meant she needed to bear the responsibility.

She went back to the room her mistress had assigned to her. Dariah fully expected to be back in her old servants' quarters in a few days, but until then, she would enjoy the soft bed and warm blankets.

Her head seemed to have just hit the pillow, and she could feel herself being shaken awake.

'Dariah, get up,' a voice said.

She opened her eyes. 'What's wrong?' she murmured.

'Mistress is calling for you.' The voice belonged to Amelie.

Dariah became alert. She sprang out of bed and began to dress.

'What time is it?'

'It's just before dawn,' Amelie said.

Dariah chose a simple shift. She'd dress properly later. There wasn't time for anything else.

'Is she alright?'

She slipped on her shoes, went to the water bowl, and splashed some water on her face. It had the dual effect of washing her face and waking her up.

'She seemed fine to me,' Amelie said.

'What did she say?'

Lady Greythorpe could be fickle at times, so any clues to her mood would help in dealing with her on this occasion.

'Only to fetch you and to arrange her morning meal in the main dining room.'

'Then go to the kitchen,' Dariah instructed. 'Though don't rush them.'

It would take her a while to dress Lady Greythorpe. As the maid left, Dariah gave her own hair a quick comb and hurried out the door.

Dariah entered Lady Greythorpe's bedchamber to find her standing naked at the window, the shutters wide open.

'My lady!' she said. 'You'll catch a chill.'

She grabbed her mistress's nightgown, carelessly thrown over the back of a nearby chair, and made her way around the bed, noting that more than one person had slept in it. She came up behind Lady Greythorpe as her mistress let go of the shutters. Dariah expertly threaded her arms through the sleeves and up and over her shoulders.

'I like the cool breeze on my skin,' her mistress said. 'It makes me feel alive.'

Dariah wrapped the gown around the front of her, and moved closer as her mistress grabbed her hands and held them to her chest.

'It went well, my lady?'

'Better than expected, much better.'

'I'm so happy for you,' Dariah said, slightly squeezing her hands.

Relieved some progress had been made, Dariah just needed to find out what type of progress.

'I need you to do something for me.'

'Anything, my lady,' Dariah said.

'I need you to find me a new body servant,' her mistress said. 'I don't want a stranger. Promote one of the existing ones. Maybe that Gretchen girl.'

Dariah pulled her hands away and stepped back. She didn't understand. Had she just been dismissed? What had she done to become the latest victim of Lady Greythorpe's fickle behaviour?

'A … a new body servant?' she didn't understand. 'Have I not performed to your expectations?'

Dariah knew her mistress could be ruthless but making her find her own replacement seemed the height of cruelty.

'What have I done to offend you so?'

Would she be sent back to the kitchens or thrown out of the Governor's household entirely? Her thoughts shifted to her family. They would also suffer if she had outlived her usefulness to Abbott Alwen and her patron.

Lady Greythorpe turned around, her untied gown falling open.

'Stop fretting,' her mistress said with a smile and stepped forward to wipe away the tears trickling down Dariah's face.

How can I not? thought Dariah. This is all I have, and you have ripped it away from me.

'Don't cry,' her mistress said. 'Ladies-in-waiting have to be strong for their mistress.'

Dariah stared at her in confusion, tears still flowing as her anguish turned to bewilderment. Lady-in-waiting? She had to be playing a cruel joke. Only daughters of noble families were ever appointed to such a position. She was just a farmer's daughter.

'Really?' she asked, hopeful.

Lady Greythorpe nodded, stepping forward and kissing her with exquisite tenderness.

Eventually, she stepped back and slipped out of her gown, letting it fall to the floor.

Breathless, Dariah smiled through her tears. 'I … I am honoured.'

Her mistress held her cheeks between her hands and pulled Dariah towards her, kissing her again. Lennane eventually stepped back and allowed Dariah to remove her shift and undergarments, letting them fall to the floor. Goosebumps rose on her naked skin as the morning breeze blew through the open window. Lennane began planting light kisses on her neck and moved down to tease one of her small but upright nipples with her tongue while she gently squeezed the other between her fingers. Dariah gasped at the unexpected sensation and leaned against the bedpost for support.

After what seemed like an eternity, she stopped and grabbed Dariah's hand, leading her around to the side of the bed. Her mistress pushed her curves up against her own, giving her another soft lingering kiss on the lips.

'You deserve it,' Lennane said as she placed a cool hand between Dariah's breasts and pushed her back onto the bed.

7

REGAN

Regan arrived early for the council meeting, so he waited near the hearth, partially to keep warm but mostly to be away from the others. His head ached, and he continued to chide himself.

Lennane had filled his goblet, he couldn't remember how many times. He enjoyed quality wine, but by the fourth, he'd felt a slight tingling in his nose, and he should have stopped there. Her handmaiden had cleared the third course away, leaving them alone again, and he had begun to think this may have been a bad idea.

'Where's your new bodyguard?' Lennane had asked.

Finally, a real question, instead of the inane prattle about the current rumours circulating the castle. Regan despised court gossip.

He pointed towards the door. 'If I hadn't ordered him not to escort me tonight, he'd be standing right over there watching you right now, and he'd be wondering whether or not you were going to kill me.'

'That's absurd,' Lennane said with a faint titter. 'Why did your brother send him, anyway? And where is Steffan? I thought he was supposed to be here by now.'

'He was.'

Regan wasn't concerned yet, but if his brother didn't arrive soon, a search party would need to be organised.

'Well, Harrow; is that his name? He's quite scary looking.'

'He's supposed to be scary. What's the point of having a bodyguard that isn't threatening?'

Regan took another drink of his wine as the serving girl placed the other platter on the table.

'I'll need him,' he added when she had left the room.

'Why?' Lennane said, taking a sip from her goblet. 'You have the whole Capitol Guard at your disposal.'

Before he could stop himself, he told her. The words had barely left his mouth and he stiffened, unable to believe what he'd just said. He hadn't gone into detail, but he'd said enough. He glanced at his wife, who had frozen, holding her goblet inches from the tabletop, staring at him with her mouth agape.

Only his brother and the Commander of the Capitol Guard knew the full extent of Regan's grand plan – until now.

He stared at his goblet of wine. Pushing it aside in disgust, he glared at Lennane. 'Do you know how much trust I've placed in you?'

Even with the veiled threat behind his gaze, her look of surprise evaporated, and she visibly relaxed.

'I do,' she said and leaned towards him. 'I want to help.'

He had hoped she'd acknowledge his perceived trust and promise to keep it to herself. She'd be chafing at the bit to be involved in a dangerous scheme amongst the highest echelons of power in Avaleen.

He had spent the rest of the evening fending off her probing questions.

'Why now?' and 'How will you be able to control him?'

Some he answered, some he did not, but at least it wasn't the idle gossip she had started the evening with. At one point, he cut Lennane short with a glare when the servant came in, and she had continued to talk.

After the girl left, his wife reached forward and placed her hand on his. 'You can trust me.'

He wasn't convinced, but realised he had no choice.

'I sincerely hope so.'

Later, he ignored the sweet rolls before him and ordered more wine. When the servant girl eventually returned with it, he took the jug from her and filled his cup.

'Is this the one I asked for?' he said as he grabbed the jug and filled his goblet. 'The Masterran?'

'It's the one Mr Morgan gave me, my lord,' she said.

'It probably isn't, knowing Winston,' Regan said as he sniffed the cup and took a sip. 'He's a cagey one. Doesn't want to waste good wine on people who have already drunk too much. But – it'll suffice.'

He found himself watching the handmaiden again, inspecting her. Regan knew his wife took other women to her bed and assumed this one to be the latest. He looked her up and down.

'She's a pretty little thing. How come she's serving you and not me?'

Lennane had protested, albeit mockingly, and leaned closer, whispering into his ear. 'But if you need her for any reason, I'm sure we can come to some arrangement.'

He inspected the handmaiden again and smiled.

'Would you like to serve me?'

'I would be honoured, my lord,' the young woman said.

He felt a stirring in his loins.

'Yes, I'm sure you would.'

He downed his wine and turned back to Lennane, his gaze lingering on her ample breasts. Lennane dismissed the handmaiden for the night, and after the girl left, she had sat astride him and kissed him hard, grasping at his groin, which responded as she'd hoped.

'Come, husband,' she said, grabbing his hand.

He had let her lead him to her bedchamber without any objections, knowing that bedding his wife wouldn't be the usual chore.

Regan rubbed his temple. He'd have to make the best of this rare error of judgement and hoped his wife would be true to her word.

Despite being in no mood for aggravation today, he glanced across at the large oak table with frustration. Someone of the stature of Lord Owen Redstone should take these meetings more seriously and be on time.

Regan had fought, schemed, and utilised his family's substantial influence and wealth to reach his current lofty position. However, he suspected the King had handed Owen Redstone his position on the council so as to keep Regan on a short leash.

Owen's brother, Penn Redstone, had been on the Ruling Council for several years. He wasn't an ally and had tried to block many of Regan's proposals, but at least he seemed to respect the position and the responsibility that went along with it. On the other hand, Owen acted as though he didn't want to be here, only turning up and participating at the King's insistence. It infuriated Regan no end.

It didn't matter. The leash would soon be broken, and House Greythorpe would have all the power and influence they deserved. His father would have been proud.

Regan noted that most members of the council had arrived. They included ruling guild heads, wealthy landowners, the High Chamberlain, Arturo Exley, and Sir Baltair Drum, Commander of the Capitol Guard and reassured himself he'd have majority support.

The Commander sat across the corner from where Regan would sit and could be relied on to support Regan. Not because they liked or respected each other but because they both hated the Blackwaters, and he had discovered Baltair had a penchant for the younger male form, a revelation Regan used to his fullest advantage.

Opposite the Commander sat the two apprentices, a couple of youngsters who attended the council meetings in order to learn how the realm functioned, the scheme being another of the King's grand ideas. All the noble families whose children had not yet come of age tried to have them selected for the honour. Appointments only lasted a year, but they put the recipients in good stead for any future prospects.

Fortunately, Regan chose the apprentices. This year, they were Fenwick Anderson, the son of a knight recently killed in the line of duty, and Waldin Hardwinter, Regan's nephew by his sister, Jayne.

The apprentices could not vote, but Regan still had four definite votes in any decision. He only had to convince at least one of the other three who didn't directly support Owen Redstone. The King could overrule any council decisions, but that rarely happened.

Regan glanced again at the still unoccupied chair at the other end of the table. The Lord of the Shadowlands had better get here soon. Across the corner of the table from the empty chair sat the monk, Abbot Alwen. Regan thought the man to be a complete waste of space, but the King wanted someone on the council to give some spiritual guidance; being friendly with Lord Owen, the Abbot couldn't be relied upon for support.

As he turned back towards the hearth, the large oak doors at the other end of the room creaked open. Lord Redstone wandered in, a skin of wine in one hand and a goblet in the other. He ambled towards the other councillors in no apparent hurry, pausing to refill his goblet.

'I'm here!' Owen boomed, as he stopped just short of the table. 'Where do I sit?'

Regan detested Owen Redstone, but as a senior council member and, more importantly, a staunch ally and friend of the King, Regan had to treat him with respect, even though it pained him to do so.

'You're late,' Regan fumed.

Owen bowed a little too low towards Regan.

'Apologies, my lord. It will not happen again.'

If anyone noticed Owen's mocking tone, no one said anything.

'That's what you said last time.'

'And I meant it last time, only I have been distracted recently with the arrival of my beautiful family.'

Ah, yes, the betrothal. Something else that would bring the Redstones and Blackwaters even closer, but it wouldn't make any difference in the end.

Alwen gestured to the vacant chair near him. 'Lord Owen.'

The others took their seats as Owen ambled to the chair near the monk, and sat.

'Thank you, Father,' Owen said.

'Let's get started, shall we?' Regan took his seat. 'We have important business to discuss.'

8

LETO

He had hardly eaten anything all day. Apprehensive about meeting his future wife, Leto's anxiety had only increased when he caught sight of her. The last time he'd met Cordelia Redstone she'd been a scrawny girl of ten. She had changed a lot in the past six years, and Leto couldn't hide his delight. Mature and well-spoken, she had grown into a stunning young woman.

Leto's mother had died ten years before, and his father had not yet taken another wife, so the King almost gleefully handed over the responsibility for organising the royal wedding to Addwyn, Leto's future mother-by-law. Even though she had no choice, she accepted the task gracefully. Ever the diplomat, Addwyn invited Leto's Aunt Finnea, the widow of his uncle, Lydall Blackwater, to help with the organising, but her cool acceptance exposed a distinct lack of enthusiasm.

The King's private dining room, usually for entertaining members of his Ruling Council and people of importance such as foreign dignitaries and merchants, could easily accommodate thirty people. But for the betrothal celebration, only twelve sat around the table with the King at its head, and except for Jacob, all were family or family to be. Leto glanced at his betrothed, who sat beside him. They had been exchanging pleasantries throughout the meal, Leto regaling her with stories of the capitol, which she seemed to enjoy.

Once the remnants of the main meal were cleared away, the servants brought out platters of small cakes and sweets. Gwenda and Jacob immediately reached for a sweet, neither shy about being the first to eat.

Cordelia didn't take a sweet, and Leto wondered if she was waiting for him to offer her one, or had she already eaten her fill? Leto wanted to get her alone, away from the prying eyes and ears of their families. He sensed a naivety about her but found it quite endearing and didn't have the faintest clue why.

His thoughts were interrupted by the raucous laughter of his father and Lord Owen, his future father-by-law.

' ... where do I sit, I said.' Owen laughed again. 'Of course, I knew where, but it was worth seeing the look on his face.'

'You shouldn't tease Lord Regan like that,' Addwyn said. 'You know he doesn't forget a slight.'

'She's right,' said the King. 'Don't poke the wolf, my friend.'

'Yes, yes,' Owen admitted. 'But it was still hilarious to see.'

Penn Redstone smiled. 'I thought the bastard was going to blow his top.'

When the laughter settled, his father stood, drink in hand. Silence descended on the room.

'I would like to thank you all for attending this evening to celebrate the future joining of our families through Leto and Cordelia. Whilst this is a joyous occasion, I have two regrets: one is that my darling Finella is not here to see our son betrothed to such a beautiful young woman.'

The King lowered his chin and sighed. A moment later he looked up and cleared his throat.

'She would have been so proud.'

Leto hadn't seen his father this emotional for a long time and felt his own throat constrict.

The King glanced around the table. 'The other is that Melina could not be here, though I console myself knowing she'll return well before the wedding next summer.'

His eyes momentarily settled on Leto. They moved to Cordelia, and a modicum of joy returned to his face. He raised his goblet to Addwyn.

'She is a credit to you.'

She acknowledged with a smile and nod. Everyone else nodded their assent, especially the twins, who beamed.

The King settled back into his chair. 'Addwyn, I know I've kept Owen busy with the business of the realm here in the capitol, and for that, I apologise.'

'You are forgiven, Your Grace,' she said.

'The children probably turned out better than they would if I was at home all the time,' Owen said.

'I don't doubt it,' the King replied.

Addwyn turned to Leto. 'Your Highness, perhaps you and Cordelia would like to take a walk out on the terrace?'

'Excellent idea,' said the King. 'Off you go.'

Leto nearly tripped over himself in his hurry to move behind Cordelia's chair, pulling it out for her.

'Thank you, Your Highness,' she said as she rose.

He offered her his arm. 'Call me Leto, please.'

She smiled and slipped her arm in his. 'Of course, Leto.'

Her touch sent a slight shiver down his spine as they strolled towards the doors. Gwenda started to rise.

'Where do you think you're going?' demanded Addwyn.

'I'm her lady-in-waiting,' she replied. 'Shouldn't I be going with her … in case she needs something?'

'You will do no such thing, young lady,' Addwyn said. 'Sit.'

Gwenda pouted and sat. 'Yes, ma'am.'

'Let them be alone for a while,' Addwyn added, her tone softening.

Leto and Cordelia exited the dining room and walked out onto the terrace. They headed towards the balcony overlooking Kings Falls and stopped at the stone balustrade, the full moon casting enough light to see for miles.

'It's beautiful,' said Cordelia.

'It is,' he agreed. 'Though I probably don't appreciate it as much as I should.'

'You do see it every day,' she pointed out.

'Most days,' he said and turned towards her. 'Would you like to see this every day?'

'Of course.'

'Do you really want to marry me and live here in Riverview, hundreds of leagues away from your family?'

Cordelia now turned to face him, her hand slipping off his arm to her side, her brow knitted in confusion.

'Of course. We are betrothed.'

'But you don't know me.'

'You don't know me either.'

'Doesn't it bother you?'

'I don't understand. Don't you want to marry me?'

Leto could hear the agitation in her voice.

'What's wrong with me? Aren't I pretty enough?'

'No, there's nothing wrong. I think you're beautiful.'

'Then why ask such stupid questions?'

'I don't think you understand my —'

'Are you saying I'm stupid?'

'No, no, certainly not.'

'Then what are you saying?'

Leto racked his brain to work out what he had done to annoy her.

'Please explain it to me, Your Highness,' Cordelia persisted.

Leto hadn't expected this fragile young girl to be so combative and forthright.

'Well?' she said.

His plan was going awry, and he had no idea why. His father would not be pleased if he ruined this. The Redstones were their closest allies and Lord Owen, his father's closest friend. He couldn't think of anything to say, so out of desperation, Leto reached for her hand. It looked so small as he held it.

'What are you doing?'

He placed his other hand over hers, enclosing it. She didn't try to pull it away.

'Just forget everything I said, and let me start again, please.'

The scowl slowly disappeared from her face, and she nodded.

'Firstly, you're wonderful and would make a most exquisite Queen.'

Cordelia smiled.

'And I certainly don't think you're stupid. Far from it,' Leto said. 'You seem to know your mind and are not afraid of expressing it.'

'I get that from my mother.'

'From those two things alone, I can see we will get along famously. Just promise me one thing.'

She looked at him dubiously. 'And what is that?'

'Jacob tells me that twins like to play tricks on people, and if I'm honest, I can't tell you and your sister apart yet. Is this true?'

'Well, Your Highness, Gwenda and I are awfully close, as you can imagine. So, I'm not sure whether I can abide by that promise,' Cordelia said with a grin. 'Besides, wouldn't two of me be better than one?'

'I think one of you would be quite enough.'

'Are you sure? Gwennie will be most disappointed.'

Surprised at how Cordelia's teasing stirred his emotions, Leto felt more confident in his plan.

'Let me put it another way. Would you like me to do this to Gwenda?'

Leto leaned forward and gave Cordelia a gentle kiss on the lips. For a moment, she did nothing, before responding in kind. After a time he pulled away and found his hands on her hips and hers on his shoulders. She opened her eyes and smiled.

'I think I will keep you all myself, my prince.'

'I'm glad,' Leto said and felt her shiver. 'You're cold. We should go back inside.'

'I wish we didn't have to.'

'We have all winter to get to know each other.'

'I look forward to it.'

'As do I.'

They turned away from the balustrade and headed back inside.

'Of course, we'll have to find Gwenda a nice man. It's the least we can do,' said Cordelia.

She took his proffered arm, and they returned to the dining room. Jacob had moved around next to Gwenda and their conversation seemed very animated. Leto leaned towards Cordelia.

'She may not need our help.'

9

CONSTANCE

Her heart pounded as he kissed her again.

A hand slid down her back and rested on her buttocks. Their lips parted, and he began kissing her neck. Constance felt his warm breath as he nuzzled her. His hand started rubbing and grasping at her. She thought about protesting, but he kissed her again. She knew they shouldn't be doing this, but she put her hand on his neck and pulled him to her, kissing him harder. He moved his hand across, reached further down and began pressing between her legs. She broke off the kiss and buried her face in his chest. Even through her dress, she could feel the pressure of his fingers.

No … no, she shouldn't be doing this. She let go of his neck and tried unsuccessfully to push him away.

'No,' she whispered. 'We shouldn't.'

He ignored her and kissed her again. She kissed him back as he kept massaging her. She felt a tingle up her spine. It felt so good, but she broke off the kiss and pushed him again.

'Hamlin, please!'

He let her go, and she stepped back, head down, averting her gaze.

'I'm sorry,' he said, his breathing still heavy. 'I thought you wanted to.'

'I do,' she said, looking up at him. 'But … we can't. I don't want you to get into trouble.'

She did want to lie with him. Unlike other men, the tall, handsome young man of eighteen years treated Constance with respect, despite her lowly position in the world.

'I don't care about them,' he said. 'I care about you.'

Gentle and kind, Hamlin would make the perfect husband for anyone, but not her. Commoners rarely married into nobility and such a union was usually frowned upon. However, a noble marrying someone like Constance would be quite out of the question. She had been labelled a bastard at an early age, and, Hamlin being the nephew of Sir Rainer White, Lord of Whitehall and head of one of the more powerful houses in Avaleen, a marriage between them would be so far-fetched it would never be contemplated.

Constance had royal blood in her veins, but people still labelled her a bastard. Her father, the brother of the King, had taken her mother as his lover. They had two children, Egon and Constance. Not surprisingly, she and her brother weren't welcomed by many in the aristocracy, constantly taunted or simply ignored, especially as children. However, some members of the Royal household ignored their heritage.

Given the circumstances of her birth, she felt blessed, but Constance knew the encounters with Hamlin had to stop before they went too far.

'I care about you too, but we cannot do this again,' she said.

It would not go well for either of them if his family found out.

'But ... but I love you,' he told her.

'You aren't allowed to love me,' she said and rushed out before the crying started.

Whitehall Castle sat perched on a cliff near Lonely Point at the western tip of the peninsula known as Sisters End. A chill breath of breeze brought Constance back to the present and she shivered. Winter had begun early, but the shutters had not been closed and unfortunately, she had neglected to dress for the cooler weather.

Often, the Maester would take them out on a day trip to a nearby farm, the forest, or even the tiny stretch of white sand down at the cove, depending on the lesson he wished to teach. She loved the outdoor classes, but on the colder days, she preferred to be inside with the shutters closed and a fire in the hearth. The Maester would not brook any interruption to his class to allow her to leave and fetch a shawl, so Constance rubbed her arms and turned her attention from Hamlin and the weather back to Maester Arkham, who meandered around the room with his arms clasped behind his back spouting his current lesson. She tried her best but found numbers difficult, unlike letters, at which she excelled, often writing long messages to her brother.

However, history proved to be her favourite subject, especially when the Maester told tales of the lands across the Dividing Sea, the great capitols of Masterra and Aru, the vast plains of Nubar in the west and the ice city of Tunia in the far south. He'd even described a place where they had carved a whole city from inside a mountain. He could talk for hours without pause, and she would listen with rapt attention.

She glanced at the girl beside her. Princess Melina Blackwater, the fifteen-year-old daughter of the King and second in line to the throne, adored Constance. Fortunately, her mother, Queen Finella, had been accepting of Constance and her brother, so she and Melina had been constant companions since childhood. Now she attended the princess as handmaiden, but loved her like a sister.

Melina excelled in all her classes, becoming one of the Maester's shining lights, only outshone academically by Willem, an acolyte of the Followers of the One God, a sect of monks from the Eastern Woods. He even dressed like a monk, in a simple dull tunic tied at the waist with a string of leather, and on his feet bare leather sandals. He and Melina often read together in the library.

Constance joined them many times, and despite Willem's shyness, they had struck up a friendship. He had confided in her that he wanted to become a Maester and teach the new acolytes in his Order.

The class was small, with only four others in attendance. They included Margot White, the daughter of the Lord of Sisters End, who often drove

Maester Arkam to distraction with her stupidity and high opinion of herself. Gayleen Marchesi was the daughter of Ferris Carver, himself a lauded knight and son of a minor lord. She glanced at Nerys Redstone, the daughter of Sir Penn Redstone, the only other person Constance could call a friend.

Later that evening, Constance sat in the apartment she shared with Melina, repairing one of the princess's dresses. The princess sat opposite, writing another letter to her father.

'Are you going to write to Leto?'

Melina stopped writing and looked up. 'I may do, but he's such a horror. He only writes back once for every five I send.'

'Tell your father. He'll make sure he writes,' Constance said and continued to repair the dress, careful not to tighten the loose stitches too much.

'I've tried, but it doesn't seem to help.'

Melina wrote to them constantly. Not even her father could keep up with her, and he probably had royal scribes who could do it for him.

After a while, Constance could no longer hear the scratch of quill on parchment and looked up from her sewing. Melina held the quill loosely in her hand and seemed to be daydreaming, gazing right past Constance at the stone wall behind her.

She had a fair idea what the princess was pondering, or more to the point, about whom. Melina and Constance shared everything, including their lessons, dreams, and fears. The most recent topic of conversation had been men and marriage, and they had several lively discussions about them. Melina had already passed the usual age of betrothal, but her father had not yet broached the subject. Melina had confided in her that the thought of marrying someone she did not at least like filled her with dread. Despite Constance's reassurances, the princess continued to fret.

'I'd rather not wed at all,' she had told Constance.

'Don't be like that, Mellie,' Constance had said, using her nickname, something she only did when they were alone together. 'I'm sure you'll marry a good and brave lord. And handsome, too.'

'I doubt it. He'll be old and ugly, and I'll vomit when he touches me!'

'Don't be so dramatic.'

'I don't think I'll wed a knight or a lord.'

'Who then? There aren't any princes or kings in Avaleen other than your brother and father, and you can't marry them, regardless of what they used to do back in the dark ages.'

Melina sighed. 'I guess a knight it'll have to be.'

'I'm sure you'll have your choice of handsome suitors.'

As one of the most beautiful and eligible women in the realm, there would be many a knight and lord calling on the King for a betrothal.

'Who are you thinking about now?'

'Err … what?' Melina asked, and her guilty look turned into a coy smile as she put down her quill. 'What about Jacob?'

'You can't marry Jacob,' Constance blurted out.

Her heart skipped a beat as she realised how she had spoken and hoped the princess had not noticed.

'He's just a stable boy,' she added, in case Melina wasn't jesting.

'You're probably right, Connie.'

Melina had only mentioned Jacob occasionally, mainly when reading her letters from Leto, who often wrote about him. Constance had more chance of marrying Jacob than Melina did, and she found the thought pleasing.

'But he's not a stable boy anymore,' Melina said. 'He's a squire, and Leto said Father will make him a knight one day. And he's one of the best swordsmen in the realm.'

'If you say so.'

Constance thought Jacob would be a good match for herself; the stable boy and the bastard.

'If you want my opinion, I think he would be better suited to someone who is not royalty,' Constance said, her eyes on the dress she had been repairing. 'Like me, for instance.'

'You have as much royal blood as me.'

'I might have the blood, but I don't have the name.'

'If my father can make me marry someone else, then Jacob is all yours,' Melina said. 'I'll even ask my father to order him to marry you.'

Constance loved Melina like a sister and hoped to be her lady-in-waiting once she came of age. However, it occurred to her that if Melina married some lord, she would have to live with her new husband at his estates, and Constance wouldn't be able to marry Jacob anyway, as she'd be with Melina. But if the princess wed Jacob Rivers ... she didn't know what she'd do.

Don't be silly, Constance told herself. It's just a young girl's wild imagination. Her loyalty to the princess surpassed everything else. She'd never willingly leave her.

'I know you, Melina Blackwater. You're as stubborn as an ox and will convince your father to allow you to wed whomever you please.'

Constance knew that the King had a soft spot for his only daughter, but he wouldn't hesitate to use her for an alliance if he deemed it necessary.

Melina laughed.

'Don't worry yourself, Connie. I'll make sure we find you a good husband,' Melina said, picking up her quill. 'We should go riding tomorrow, maybe down to the shore before it gets too cold. We should invite Nerys as well.'

'I'll get Sir Fergus to saddle the horses after the morning meal.'

Constance tied off the thread, put the dress away in the chest, and reminded herself to put out warm clothes for the princess tomorrow.

10

LETO

Leto hadn't been able to think of anything but his time spent with Cordelia on the terrace. The thought of her radiant smile had been distracting him ever since. He'd been questioning himself with nearly everything he'd done in the past two days: What would Cordelia think? Would she approve? When we spoke last, did I say anything infantile?

The morning after the betrothal dinner, Jacob couldn't remove the grin from his face. Leto assumed he had thoughts of Gwenda.

'I didn't get a chance to ask you last night,' Jacob said. 'What do you think of your betrothed?'

'I can't stop thinking about her.'

It felt odd, a foreign feeling he hadn't experienced before.

'Sounds like you're in love, my friend.'

'Don't be absurd! I only met her a couple of days ago.'

'Tell me this then, do you remember the size of her tits?'

'What kind of question is that?'

'I'm not asking you to tell me how big they are, just whether you noticed.'

Leto opened his mouth to rebuke Jacob again but stopped, closed his mouth, and thought for a few moments.

'I have no idea.'

Jacob chuckled. 'See, you're in love.'

'How do you figure that?'

'The first thing you usually notice about a girl is her tits. Unless she's facing away from you, then it's her arse, and you always tell me about it.'

'I do not!'

'You do, and you know it.'

'Rubbish!'

'I can't remember the last time you were so besotted with a girl,' Jacob said, wiping up some gravy with a hunk of bread. 'What colour are her eyes?'

'Green,' Leto said straight away, surprised at himself.

'See what I mean. Up until last night, girls were all curves and smiles to you. You're smitten, no doubt about it. Did you kiss her?'

'A gentleman never tells.'

Jacob laughed aloud.

'By the gods, you did! She has bewitched you.'

'You seemed taken with Gwenda.'

'Don't try to change the subject, but yes, she's quite striking. But you know that already since they're identical.'

'If you wed Gwenda, we'd really be brothers,' Leto said, enjoying the thought of Jacob being his brother.

'Don't go marrying me off just yet. Besides, I *did* notice the size of her tits,' Jacob said and raised his hand. 'But don't worry, I'm not going to tell. They're probably the same in every way, so I won't spoil the surprise for you.'

'You're such a good friend,' Leto said, not hiding the sarcasm.

'And don't you forget it,' Jacob said as he shoved the gravy-laden bread into his mouth.

Thoughts of Cordelia had also distracted Leto during sword practice. With his right shoulder still recovering, he trained with his left arm. This should have been fine since he usually practised with both hands. However, with his concentration absent, Master Alexei brutally punished him, penetrating his defences on more than one occasion with painful blows. Jacob found it all quite amusing, but the sword master had not.

'Bah!' Master Alexi called off the session early. 'I hope she's worth those bruises, young prince.'

She certainly could be, Leto thought.

He'd briefly met Cordelia again and they had made plans to go riding. He looked forward to the outing, but the fact that Jacob, Gwenda, her mother and a small contingent of Noble Guard would be escorting them, tempered his excitement.

His upcoming nuptials had given Leto a new sense of responsibility, which led him to the old viewing gallery in the throne room, to see his father in action.

He and Jacob sat in the back row, leaning against the stone wall. The old gallery had no windows, just a small door from the royal residence. They hadn't lit any torches, so they couldn't be seen, concealed in the shadows where the lighting from the hall couldn't penetrate. Leto wasn't even sure if his father had noticed him come in.

Just twenty yards away, the throne stood on a large, raised stone dais making it easy for Leto to hear his father's conversations.

Now he peered over the balcony. The day's work had barely started. He could see the Noble Guards behind the throne, one on either side, and Leto knew two more guards covered each side wall and two more at the door.

He hoped that by watching his father, he would learn more about the way the realm worked, especially the art of diplomacy, an essential skill required by a monarch, according to his father.

The King listened to one of the Ruling Council apprentices, the only other person in the hall. He was delivering the council meeting update. Leto couldn't remember the boy's name.

The door to the throne room opened with a loud creak, followed by the thump of many boots hitting the stone floor. His father looked up and stood. The Noble Guards stiffened, placing a hand on the pommel of their swords.

The doors creaked closed as Regan Greythorpe strode into view with Sir Baltair Drum, Commander of the Capitol Guard, close behind. Leto also recognised Greythorpe's new personal bodyguard, Harrow, followed by at least eight fully armed members of the Capitol Guard.

'Lord Regan, explain yourself,' his father demanded. 'Why do you bring armed guards into my throne room?'

All Capitol Guards wore swords, as did most nobles, their guards and anyone else who deemed themselves in need of one. Still, Leto knew it was the crossbows they carried that had caused his father's outrage. The Noble Guards behind the throne gripped their swords, ready for combat, but didn't unsheathe them. Only the Noble Guard were allowed to carry ranged weapons in the throne room.

'Your Grace,' said Regan. 'I apologise for this unexpected intrusion, but we received word of an immediate threat to your person and concluded that it would be prudent to act.'

His father glanced across at the Commander. 'Is this true?'

'Yes, Your Grace.'

Sir Baltair didn't sound as confident as usual, though Leto put it down to the gravity of the situation. Death threats against the King were serious.

'Very astute of you, but why not just post extra guards outside?'

'Not if the threat was from within,' said Regan.

'Don't be absurd,' the King said, directing his glare at Sir Baltair. 'Commander, remove your guards at once and have them wait outside, then we'll discuss this threat.'

Lord Regan glanced at Sir Baltair and nodded.

'Of course, Your Grace,' said the Commander.

The Capitol Guards turned to leave, but without warning, the whistle of flying crossbow bolts filled the air. The two Noble Guards behind the throne went down, one with a bolt through the heart, the other through the neck. Elsewhere in the throne room, shouts rang out, and a howl of pain pierced the air, but it ceased moments after it had started.

'M … my lord?' the apprentice stammered. 'What's ha-'

The apprentice expelled a muffled scream and dropped his scroll as Harrow came up behind him, clamped one hand over his mouth and ran him through, a sword protruding from the centre of the boy's chest.

Leto started towards the balcony, but Jacob held his arm in a vice-like grip.

'No!' Jacob whispered close into his ear. 'Don't do or say anything, no matter what happens.'

Harrow yanked his sword out and the boy crumpled to the ground.

Leto fought to get free, but Jacob wouldn't let go. The Capitol Guards took up positions around the throne, their crossbows ready.

'Why, Regan?' his father said, showing no anger. 'I trusted you.'

'Don't blame yourself, Your Grace. This discord started long before you and I were even born. I'm just the fortunate generation that gets to finish it.'

'That was all over with decades ago,' the King said. 'I thought you were better than that.'

The Governor stepped up onto the dais. 'I am better than that. Much to my father's dismay, I even considered calling it all off.'

'So, what happened?'

'I'll tell you,' Regan's voice hardened as he stepped closer to the King. 'You and your family took something from me, and I realised my father was right after all.'

The King's brow furrowed. 'Regan, what did we take? If it's within my power, I'll gladly return it.'

Lord Regan took another step forward, now barely a foot separating him from the King.

'Really?' he glowered at the King. 'Are you a god?'

'Of course not.'

The glint of a blade caught Leto's eye.

'Then you cannot return what you have taken.'

A long dagger had appeared in Regan's hand, which he swiftly plunged deep into the King's side. His father grimaced but did not cry out. Regan leaned forward and whispered something into the King's ear.

Leto went to move forward again, but Jacob held him back. Regan's voice became louder as he withdrew the dagger and stuck it back into the King's body.

'You stole her from me!' Regan yelled as he stabbed Leto's father repeatedly in an increasingly frenzied attack, piercing his stomach, side, chest, and arm.

'You stole her from me and then killed her!' Regan continued to rage.

The King started to fall, but Regan held him up and continued to thrust the blood-covered dagger into his body.

'It was meant for you, not her!'

'My lord!' Sir Baltair's voice eventually rose above the screaming.

Regan ceased his attack, stepped back and let the King fall to his knees.

Leto watched on, helpless, as his father clasped at his wounds with both hands. Blood ran through his fingers and spilled onto the stone floor, pooling around his knees. He raised a bloodied arm towards the gallery and tried to stand, but Lord Regan, covered in the King's blood and still grasping the murder weapon, shoved him to the ground with his foot.

Leto whimpered as his father propped himself on his elbow and looked toward the gallery. Blood sprayed from his mouth and nose as he shouted something incoherent. Harrow stepped up beside his master and kicked the King's arm out from under him, forcing him onto his back. The gold crown tumbled from his head, bounced and rolled across the stone floor, hit the throne, and lay upside down.

'Check the guards. Make sure they're dead,' Lord Regan said, his voice raspy through his laboured breathing.

Harrow moved off towards the body of the nearest Noble Guard.

Leto could just hear his father's short, moist gasps for breath.

'We have to get out of here,' Jacob whispered.

Leto ignored him, gripped by the horrific scene below.

'Now get this cleaned up and alert the Brothers,' Lord Regan commanded. 'Make sure they treat his body with due respect. He was the King, after all.'

'Yes, my lord,' Sir Baltair said.

'I'll be calling a meeting of the Ruling Council for high sun. We need to keep this quiet until then.' Lord Regan said. 'And find the boy!'

Leto's eyes widened at the Governor's last order.

'We have to go now!' Jacob said, an urgency in his pleading whisper.

Finally, Leto moved. He and Jacob dropped down and crawled through the rear exit of the gallery. They stood and looked at each other in horror.

'They killed him. I should have done something!' Leto said and shoved Jacob. 'Why did you stop me?'

'There was nothing you could've done except get yourself killed. Do you think your father would have wanted that?'

Leto leaned against the wall, fighting back tears. 'He's dead.'

Jacob went up to Leto and placed his hands on his shoulders.

'You're King now, and you must act like one.'

'But I don't want to be!'

'You don't have a choice. Do you want that bastard, Greythorpe, to win?'

'No,' Leto whispered.

'Good. So, let's get out of here.'

'Alright.'

Jacob let go of Leto and stepped back. 'We have to get out of the capitol.'

Leto wiped the tears from his eyes. 'How are we going to do that?'

'I have no idea yet,' Jacob admitted, pacing back and forth.

'They'll be guarding the gates.'

'I have an idea,' Jacob said and stopped. 'They're looking for you but won't necessarily be looking for me.'

'So? I'm the one that needs to get out of here.'

'Do you remember when we climbed down the west wall near the falls and couldn't get back up? We had to walk around the outer wall to the main gate in the middle of the night?'

Leto nodded. 'Father wasn't happy about that at all.'

'You should be able to do it again without anyone seeing, even in the daylight. I can get our horses and meet you outside of the capitol.'

A thousand thoughts ran through Leto's mind. 'Where do we go?'

'I don't know.'

'We should go to … to Anchorage. My uncle will hide us.'

'North? You'll have to cross the river.'

'I know.'

'Are you crazy? We tried that two summers ago and almost got washed over the falls.'

'I'm much stronger now,' Leto said, despite not liking the plan. 'What other choice do I have?'

Jacob stared at Leto for a moment. 'Fine. We'll meet a few miles past the North Fork along the western road. There's a scattering of boulders near the forest; we'll meet there.'

'That's Greythorpe territory!'

'Exactly. Even if they suspect you've gone north, they wouldn't think to search there. Once I bring the horses, we can cut through the forest to the North Road.'

'Are you sure this will work?'

Jacob shrugged. 'You have a better idea?'

Leto shook his head.

'Then let's get you to the wall. The longer you stay, the more chance you'll be caught.'

They made their way to the west side of the castle. The King's death and the search for Leto would not yet be common knowledge, so none of the Noble Guards they met paid them any heed. He thought about warning them, but his father already lay dead, and nothing could change that. Leto and Jacob entered the small turret at the end of the walkway.

Leto leaned out of the small arched window and glanced down towards the rocks below. It seemed much higher than he remembered, and the various protrusions that poked out of the wall seemed smaller than when they had last used them.

Leto turned to Jacob. 'I can't leave.'

'Why not?'

'I … I've got to get word to Cordelia.'

'No!'

'I can't leave without saying goodbye.'

'If you don't leave now, it could be a permanent goodbye.'

'But –'

Jacob cut him short and pointed to the turret window. 'You're going out that window right now. I'll go and see her, I promise.'

Leto didn't want to leave, but deep down, he knew he had to. 'Just tell her I'm thinking of her.'

'I will. Now go.'

'Go to Lord Owen,' Leto said. 'He'll know what to do.'

Jacob nodded.

Leto removed his sword belt and handed it to his friend.

'Hold this for me. It'll just get in the way on the climb down, and the less weight I have when I cross the river, the better.'

Jacob began to protest.

'Don't worry,' Leto said. 'I still have my daggers.'

'Just stay out of trouble,' Jacob said as he took the sword.

'Well,' Leto said, his tone sombre. 'This is it then.'

'It'll all work out. You'll be back at Twin Falls before you know it,' Jacob said.

Leto embraced his boyhood friend. 'Thank you. You've always looked out for me.'

'Just don't fall off the wall or drown in the river, and I'll continue doing so.'

Leto broke the embrace 'See you soon, my friend.'

He climbed onto the ledge, glanced down, and with great care lowered himself to the first foothold. It held his weight, so he began his descent, escaping from the only home he had ever known.

11

OWEN

Owen had nearly settled into his new solar, part of the quarters in Riverview Castle assigned to him by the King. He'd only recently moved into these larger apartments, as more members of Owen's family would be arriving in the capitol as the wedding day approached.

He ignored the knock at the door and continued to rummage through one of his many unpacked chests. Out of it, he picked a small wooden carving; he smiled. A gift from his twin daughters at eight summers old. He remembered so clearly them presenting it to him. They had been so proud of it. Even after all these years, he still wasn't quite sure what it meant to signify, but it had two heads. He thought they resembled heads coming out of a simple block of wood. A head for each of them, he surmised. How time passes. Now, one of his daughters would soon be married, her betrothal signalling significant changes for the Redstone family.

Another knock sounded, this time louder, more urgent.

'Come!'

A very solemn Captain Archer Janz entered the room.

'We have a grave problem, my lord,' he said.

That Archer didn't wait to first be addressed by Owen immediately put him on edge. He took another step inside, turned towards the door and beckoned.

Jacob Rivers entered, projecting a gloomier expression than his Captain's.

What in hell was going on?

'Jacob,' Owen acknowledged him.

'My lord.'

Both Archer and Jacob kept silent.

'Well?' Owen said to Archer. 'What's going on?'

Archer took another step forward.

'The King is … dead,' his voice broke; he practically whispered the words.

Owen stepped back as if he'd been struck.

'It was Greythorpe,' Archer continued. 'Jacob and the prince witnessed it all in the throne room.'

Owen shifted his stony gaze to Jacob. The young man just nodded.

'I wanted proof of such a fanciful story before I came to you,' Archer continued. 'So, Jacob took me to the old viewing gallery in the throne room. The place was empty. The King's body wasn't there, but I saw the bodies of his guards, and there was still blood on the floor near the throne.'

Owen stiffened. He had never expected to hear news like this and steeled himself against the oncoming shock and grief. His closest friend … his King … had been murdered, but he couldn't grieve just yet. Owen had to think. What should he do? He needed to protect his family, and he also had to protect Avaleen from Regan Greythorpe and his conspirators.

'Find Penn,' Owen finally said to Archer. 'I don't care what he's doing; just get him here, now!'

Archer nodded, turned and departed, leaving the door open.

Owen had to act quickly, or they could all be in great danger. He didn't know Regan's ambitions, but until they became fully understood, he would plan for the worst. Jacob hadn't moved since he'd entered the room.

'Sit,' Owen said, gesturing towards a chair near the desk. 'We'll wait until the others return, and then I want you to tell us exactly what you saw and heard. Can you do that?'

Jacob nodded and sat.

'Where is the prince now?'

'He's safe,' Jacob said. 'He's out of the capitol. I'm to meet up with him. We're planning to go to Anchorage.'

'Good. We'll talk more about that later.'

Owen still held the carving but hadn't noticed how hard he had been gripping it. He placed it on the table and went to the doorway, ignoring the red welt that the carving had made in his palm.

'Addwyn,' he called out. 'Some wine, please, and make it quick.'

He glanced back at Jacob, who had started to fidget. Owen looked back into the living room. His daughters stood near the hearth, aware something was amiss but knowing better than to ask.

'Wine?' Addwyn said. 'It's still early.'

'Just bring it, woman!'

Owen rarely raised his voice to his wife and regretted it at once. Addwyn stopped in the middle of the living room and glared at him.

'Bring some wine, please,' he added, his manner more conciliatory.

Without a word, she picked up the nearby tray and approached him. Even with this grave situation brewing, he still loved watching his wife. She practically glided across the room. He stepped back, making way for her as she moved past him and placed the tray on the sideboard.

The tray held only three goblets. 'We'll need more. Penn will be here shortly. I want you to stay as well.'

Addwyn gave him a questioning look. Owen always welcomed her advice and unique perspective on things. Occasionally, he invited her to attend meetings with the men. She could read Owen's emotions, so maybe instead of questioning him again, she glanced at Jacob and left the room. She returned with extra goblets and placed them on the tray with the others. Owen closed the door.

She glanced back at Jacob again.

'Owen, what's going on?'

Owen picked up the pitcher and filled one of the goblets.

'We'll wait for Penn,' he said, handing Jacob a goblet. 'Drink this, but not all at once.'

Jacob took the wine.

Owen returned to the sideboard and started pouring another cup.

'Has something happened to Leto?'

Owen put down the pitcher and turned to Addwyn. 'I said we wait,' he said. 'Please sit down and have some wine.'

He handed her the goblet he had just filled.

'I don't want wine,' she said.

'You will.'

Addwyn's mouth opened as if to snap off a retort, but the door swung open, revealing Penn and Archer. They entered the room. Archer closed the door as an irritated Penn glanced around, his gaze paused on Jacob before settling on Addwyn.

'Addwyn,' Penn acknowledged her with a slight nod and turned to Owen. 'I was busy writing a letter to Nerys, and then Archer came in and was most insistent that I go with him. I'm sure he would have dragged me here had I declined. So, brother, would you care to tell me what's so urgent?'

'Yes, we're all here now,' Addwyn added.

Owen glanced at Addwyn and Penn. 'What we discuss here must never leave this room, understood?'

They all nodded. Owen started to speak, but the words didn't come out, as if saying it would make it more real, but he had no choice. He could not think of a good way to pass on the devastating news, so he kept it simple.

'Caleb is dead,' Owen said.

Addwyn gasped, covering her mouth with her hand, and sank into the nearby chair.

Penn kept his composure, but Owen could see his brother was as stunned as he had been. 'How? When?'

'Murdered barely an hour ago.'

Owen dropped into his chair opposite Jacob.

No one spoke, but their faces reflected disbelief. Owen watched Penn closely. Politically savvy and well deserving of his place on the Ruling Council, he could see his brother's mind working.

'Greythorpe?' Penn broke the silence.

Owen confirmed his brother's suspicion with a nod.

'And we know this, how?' Penn continued.

'Jacob and the prince witnessed it all,' Owen said.

'Where is Leto?' Addwyn said.

'He's safe for the moment,' Owen said, turning to Jacob. 'Right, son, we need you to tell us exactly what happened.'

'Yes, my lord.' Jacob stared at his wine momentarily. 'I … I'm sorry. I haven't had time to think about it all … until now.'

When he looked up at Owen, tears began to form.

'The King is dead,' he stammered.

The young man said it as if what he'd already witnessed had become all too real again. Addwyn got up and moved behind Jacob, placing a reassuring hand on his shoulder.

'It's alright,' she said. 'Take your time.'

Jacob wiped his eyes with the heel of his hand and took another drink from his goblet. Taking a deep breath, he recounted his story from the moment Regan and Sir Baltair Drum first entered the throne room, to the assassination of the King, and Regan's order to find the prince.

'Once Leto had climbed safely to the ground, we waved goodbye, and I hurried straight here.'

This whole scenario concerned Owen. If Regan had the Commander of the Capitol Guard in his pocket, then accusing him – let alone proving him guilty – would be extremely difficult. Regan had played it well.

He looked around the room. The faces betrayed confusion, anger and frustration.

'Well?' he said. 'Now is not the time to keep your opinions to yourselves.'

'I know what I'd like to do,' Archer uttered.

Owen knew exactly what his Captain meant. 'I know, but that's not an option at the moment. He'll be well protected.'

'We have to be very careful,' Penn warned.

'What about the prince?' Addwyn said. 'How can we be sure he's safe?'

'He's already out of the city,' Jacob said.

'And what of the princess?' Addwyn said. 'Isn't she still at Sisters End?'

'She should be safe for the moment, but I'll work on getting her out of there,' Owen said, looking up at Penn. 'I'll get Nerys out as well.'

'Will Lord Rainer let them go?' said Addwyn.

Rainer White was probably Regan's closest ally, so his wife's concern had merit, particularly if the situation escalated.

'I'll march on Whitehall myself if he tries to use my daughter as a hostage,' Penn said.

Owen stood. 'You'll do no such thing. We can't be seen doing anything out of the ordinary; otherwise, Regan will suspect that we know what he's done, and we'll have to trust Jacob to get the prince to safety.'

Everyone's gaze fell on the young man.

'He's my best friend,' said Jacob, uncomfortable at being the centre of attention. 'I'd die before I let any harm come to him.'

'Captain, arrange supplies and horses for Jacob and make sure he gets out of the city,' said Owen.

Archer nodded.

'Then return and organise an escort for Lady Addwyn and the girls,' Owen said.

'Where are we going?' said Addwyn, confused.

'Home,' Owen said, 'and I will brook no discussion on the matter. It's going to become dangerous around here, and I want my family far away from it all.'

'We'll begin packing straight away,' she said.

'No wagons. Pack only what you can carry on the horses. I don't want them overloaded. I know the girls won't like it, but you'll be travelling fast. It will be a hard ride.'

'Don't worry about them. No doubt there will be complaining, but they're tougher than you think. They're Redstones, after all,' Addwyn said. 'I'll go and break the news. We'll talk later.'

She opened the door and left. Owen watched her leave, thankful she hadn't put up a fight. He didn't need to be butting heads with his wife right now.

'I thought she was surely going to argue with you,' Penn said.

'She understands,' Owen replied and turned to Jacob. 'You and Captain Janz go now. Exit via the south gate. It will take longer to make your way around the capitol, but if Regan discovers how you left the city, at least he'll assume you've gone south.'

'Yes, sir,' Jacob said. 'If I may have a word with Cordelia before I go? Leto wanted me to give her a message.'

Owen nodded his assent. 'Say nothing of the King's death. Just say the prince had to leave the capitol urgently.'

Jacob nodded.

'I would've preferred the prince head to the Shadowlands, but it's too late now. I'll send a bird to Lord Kirkwood with a message to expect you both. Just make sure you get him there in one piece.'

'I won't let you down, my lord,' said Jacob.

'I know you won't, lad,' said Owen. 'Good luck.'

Jacob gave him a hesitant nod and followed Archer out.

'I can't believe the bastard did the deed himself,' Penn burst out as the door closed. 'He's either insane or has gained much more power than we thought.'

'We're in deep shit,' Owen said.

'You got that right.'

'Penn, I want all my family to leave, and that includes you, too.'

'What? I can't leave, especially now. I should be here.'

Owen had expected the protest.

'Caleb is dead, and this has gone way beyond normal politics,' he said and stepped closer to his brother. 'I need you to go back home, brother. If anything happens to me, I'll need you to look after Addwyn and the children. We can't risk both of us.'

Penn started to protest again.

'Don't fight me on this,' Owen pleaded.

'Are you sure?'

87

'I'm not sure about anything at the moment.'

Penn nodded his understanding.

'Thank you,' Owen said.

If anything happened to him, he knew Penn would look after his family. Their youngest brother, Dunmar, already took care of Redstone interests in the Shadowlands in his absence, but Penn was more experienced in politics and war.

'As soon as you return, gather our allies in the south and east, shore up our defences and ramp up the recruiting.'

'Will there be war?' Penn's voice took on an even more sobering tone.

'I hope not,' Owen said, 'but we must be prepared. No doubt Regan has been bolstering his allies. He has a head start on us, which we need to close as best we can.'

'Consider it done.'

Owen and Penn embraced. Someone knocked on the door.

'Come,' Owen said and stepped back from Penn.

One of his soldiers, Sergeant Garrat, came in.

'Yes, sergeant?' Owen said.

'A message from the Governor, milord.'

Owen and Penn glanced at each other.

'An emergency Ruling Council meeting has been convened for high sun,' the sergeant said.

'Did he say why?' Owen said.

'No, milord. Just that your presence was required.'

Owen doubted that Regan either wanted or needed his presence, but not to invite him while he remained in the capitol would be unusual. Regan would like to keep up the charade that normality reigned, except that the King was dead.

'Has the messenger been to see my brother yet?' Owen asked.

'I believe Sir Penn's quarters were his next stop.'

'Sergeant, if anyone asks about his whereabouts, you do not know. Understand?'

Sergeant Garrat's eyes shifted to Penn before returning to Owen. 'He was never here, and I'll tell the others the same.'

'Good man,' Owen said. 'Notify the Governor that I will attend the council meeting as requested.'

'As you wish, milord.'

Sergeant Garrat gave a short bow and left.

'I'll get Nerys out of there, I promise,' Owen said to Penn. 'Now prepare to leave. I must bid my family farewell.'

'Good luck, brother,' Penn said. 'You're going to need it.'

Owen could see grim times ahead, and he would need all the luck he could muster.

12

REGAN

He ripped off the blood-soaked clothes and threw them in a bucket.

'Burn them,' he ordered the Commander of the Capitol Guard, and gulped down a goblet of wine.

He had done it, but lost all semblance of control in doing so. He hadn't even been in love with her. Marrying Finella was a means to an end, but a means that the Blackwaters had ripped away. But why had he lost control? It could have been the killing frenzy that soldiers sometimes experienced at the height of battle. Yes, that must be it. What else could it be? Whatever the reason, he couldn't turn back now. It was done. He turned his thoughts to his next task – informing the Ruling Council.

He quaffed another goblet of wine and checked himself over, taking care to clean all traces of his crime from his body. Technically, he had committed a crime, but since no one of sufficient rank knew what he had done, it didn't matter. He was the law, and he intended for it to stay that way for a long time. He dressed in clean clothes and went to his solar, where he began to organise the meeting of the Ruling Council.

As he headed to his solar, something began to nag at him. Sir Baltair was loyal, but his recent behaviour had given cause for concern. Of the eight Capitol Guards who had gone with them into the throne room, three had been killed. One by a member of the Noble Guard and two others by their fellow conspirators using weapons from the dead Noble Guards. That had been part of the plan, to which the Commander had initially objected.

Baltair had stared at Regan in disbelief when given his orders. 'My own men?'

'The Noble Guard are highly skilled,' Regan reminded him. 'That's why they're guarding the King and not watching the city gates or chasing after petty thieves. It would be more believable if they managed to kill at least a couple of them, would it not?'

Baltair had grudgingly agreed.

'I'm sure there are a few troublemakers you could do without,' Regan added. 'Just ensure the others know how to shoot straight and will obey your commands without question.'

Sir Baltair returned soon after and stood waiting for Regan. Now I'm going to test his loyalty again, he thought as he put the finishing touches to one of the notes.

'I have concerns,' Regan said.

'Concerns, my lord?' Sir Baltair said. 'Everything has gone to plan, hasn't it?'

'And I'd like to keep it that way.'

Regan put down the quill and stared at Sir Baltair.

'After the council meeting is over, I want the rest of the guards who were with us in the throne room, taken care of,' Regan said and glared at the Commander.

The Commander looked puzzled.

'You want to give them money? Women? As a kind of reward?'

Regan took a deep breath and shook his head. Was the man an idiot? It seemed he needed it spelled out for him.

'No, I want you to kill them,' Regan said, hoping that was clear enough.

The Commander's eyes widened. 'They're some of my best men,' he protested.

'It only takes one of your best men to get drunk and start telling stories,' Regan countered. 'We can't have any loose ends.'

'No!' Sir Baltair said, outraged. 'No, I will not!'

'Then you better ensure they remain silent,' Regan warned.

'They will be silent, I guarantee it.'

Regan sat at his desk and glowered at the Commander, furious his orders had been refused. Maybe he had pushed him too far this time. Perhaps he should have Baltair killed as well. Harrow would do it in a heartbeat.

No, not just yet. Unrest would be bound to occur once news of the King's death spread; then the Capitol Guard would have its hands full and need leadership.

He looked at Sir Baltair. Who knew he had a backbone?

'You surprise me, Commander,' Regan said. 'Your loyalty to your men is commendable.'

'They are good men. I trust them with my life.'

'You will be,' Regan said, more annoyed now than angry. 'Now go to the council chamber. I need someone I trust to listen as the councillors arrive.'

'Yes, my lord,' Baltair said and left with his head held high.

Alone again, Regan leaned back and rubbed his temple, feeling another headache coming on. He grabbed the pitcher of wine and poured himself a cupful. Bringing the cup to his lips, he noticed a slight tremor in his hand that caused the cup to shake. Most likely an after-effect of the killing, he thought. He had, after all, performed one of the most dangerous and reviled acts : ... regicide. Regan gulped down the cup of wine in one go and poured another. He began writing notes for each council member, summoning them to a specially convened council meeting.

He didn't like killing, but the Blackwaters had been leading Avaleen down a path of subservience for the past hundred years. They had signed various treaties and pacts with those heathens across the Dividing Sea, and King Caleb had continued the tradition. Avaleen needed to be strong and independent, and Regan would do his damnedest to make it so.

Sometimes, he thought of simply killing his enemies and taking the throne himself. It would be a much simpler plan, but flexing his power so overtly could put many of his allies off. This left diplomacy, and his plan to smooth over the disruption of the King's murder should work well. He could rule Avaleen without claiming the crown. There'd be minimal chance of a significant uprising, and he could conduct his business without being the centre of attention. Something he'd be unable to do if he became King.

He lifted the cup to his lips again, but paused, his eyes glancing down at the deep red liquid. The colour of blood. He put it back down on the desk, finished off the letters and arranged for their delivery.

Led by Harrow and with half a dozen guards several steps behind, Regan strode through the corridors of Riverview to the council meeting. He could have sufficed with Harrow and maybe two other guards, but Lennane had suggested a few more may be prudent.

'How will the death of the King affect the people?' she'd said. 'You could be attacked by an angry mob.'

He hadn't planned on mixing with the people, but she had a valid point, and it irked him that Steffan still wasn't at his side making these suggestions. His brother would've left Kings Hill with an entire caravan and an escort, which meant his journey would take a lot longer, though Regan would have expected him by now. Regan and his brother had developed the plan that began to unfold today. Steffan would be disappointed he had gone ahead without him, but they couldn't have waited any longer.

Confident that the meeting would go as planned, Regan still needed his wits about him. The Blackwaters may no longer be a problem, but Owen Redstone could still cause him trouble.

A guard opened the council chamber doors, and Harrow led Regan into the room without pausing. The doors closed behind them, leaving the rest of his escort standing guard in the corridor. Everyone in the room turned as Regan took his usual place at the head of the table. Harrow stood a few yards behind, watching. Regan glanced across to Sir Baltair Drum, who shook his head slightly. Good, no speculation yet.

Regan had arrived early as usual, so seeing Owen Redstone already seated at the other end of the table surprised him. He surveyed the table and noted that one of the several empty chairs belonged to Penn Redstone. Strange, Regan thought, he never missed a meeting.

'Lord Owen,' Regan said. 'If I may enquire, where is your brother? This is an especially critical meeting, and his presence is expected.'

'Lord Penn received word last night that his wife had taken ill, so he left to return home this morning before we knew about this meeting,' Owen said. 'If he'd known, I'm sure he would have stayed a little longer.'

'I know I speak for everyone here when I say we hope his wife's illness is not too serious and wish her a speedy recovery.'

Murmurs of agreement came from the others.

'Thank you for your concern,' Owen said without humour. 'I'll pass on your wishes when next I see him.'

Alwen leaned over and patted Owen on the arm. 'I will pray for her.'

'Thank you, Father,' Owen said, holding up a parchment. 'Lord Regan, before we start this meeting, here is a signed proxy from Sir Penn giving me his permission to vote on his behalf on any items that may come up, since he will most certainly be gone for an extended period.'

Another surprise, but he wasn't expecting support from either of the Redstones anyway, so it wouldn't make a scrap of difference.

'Thank you for your thoroughness, Lord Owen. Now, if there isn't anything else, can we begin?'

Owen nodded his assent. Some of the others nodded and voiced their agreement as well.

'Unfortunately, gentlemen,' Regan said. 'We are here today because a great tragedy has struck Avaleen.'

Some of the men leaned forward in anticipation.

'There's no easy way for me to say this,' Regan continued. 'The King is dead.'

Complete silence fell on the hall, but only briefly, and then they all started talking at once – asking questions, voicing alarm – though only one kept his thoughts to himself. Owen Redstone sat in silence, his face a mask of stone, and he glared at Regan.

Could he know? Surely not.

'Quiet!' Regan bellowed, raising his hand. 'I said be quiet!'

The throng of voices quietened down.

'What do you mean the King is dead?' Owen barked before Regan could continue. 'I saw him just after the morning meal.'

'The death of your King is not easy to talk about, so please be patient with me,' said Regan and paused for a moment. 'Sir Baltair came to me with information that implied an imminent attempt on the King's life. We immediately went to the throne room with a contingent of Capitol Guards. We entered to find the King already dead, surrounded by several Noble Guards.'

Regan waited to let his words sink in.

'What happened when you confronted the perpetrators of this unspeakable crime?' asked Owen, his voice as hard as stone.

'The Noble Guards attacked us, but Sir Baltair's men managed to kill them.'

'All of them?'

'Yes, all of them,' Baltair said. 'Those bastards killed three of my men. I wasn't leaving any of them alive.'

'How did you plan on locating the mastermind of this plot?' Owen said.

'Where is the person who passed on this information?' Abbot Alwen was quick to follow Owen's question.

'He's probably dead as well,' Owen mocked.

The notion of an informant had been overlooked. Regan began to speak, but Baltair interrupted.

'No, he's not dead,' the Commander said.

Regan glared at him with veiled exasperation. You imbecile! His mind raced, wondering how they would produce this so-called informant. Damn him to hell!

'I'm afraid he escaped,' Baltair continued.

Regan breathed a sigh of relief. At least if everyone believed the non-existent informant had escaped, they would only have to arrange a search, which of course would prove futile.

'How convenient,' Owen spat. 'Do you know who it was?'

Baltair kept an uneasy silence.

'You didn't get their name?' Owen prompted.

'I assure you I am not pleased with the situation,' said Baltair.

Owen stood, placed his hands on the table and scowled at the Commander.

'Our King is dead, and you are not pleased?' he boomed. 'I am outraged, as you should be! From what has been said so far, this was an absolute fuck-up from the start. Why did you waste precious time by going to the Governor first? Why didn't you act on it yourself? You're the Commander of the fucking Capitol Guard!'

Owen slammed his fist on the table to make his point. A few of the others voiced their disgust as well.

'Lord Owen is right,' said Alwen. 'We deserve a proper explanation, Commander.'

The interrogation of the Commander had begun to get out of hand.

'Enough!' Regan said and stood before anyone else could add to the barrage. 'Now is not the time for recriminations. The head of this conspiracy is still out there somewhere, but the longer we squabble here, the less chance we have of catching him.'

Those that stood began to sit back in their seats, including Owen.

'Our King is gone. My friend is gone, and nothing can bring him back,' Owen said, again setting his gaze on Regan. 'I agree that the person ultimately responsible for this act is still alive. This was obviously a direct attack on the royal family, so we need to move to protect who's left, namely Prince Leto and Princess Melina.'

'Where is the prince?' the Abbot asked no one in particular.

'We're already searching for him,' Baltair said. 'All the gates have been alerted, and I've ordered extra patrols of the city. He should be found shortly.'

'Excuse me if I doubt your confidence,' Owen said.

Regan needed to play this right.

'Commander, arrange for search parties outside the city for a half-day ride out. He may not yet know about his father's death, so when you find him, just bring him back to Riverview in the name of the King. I will accept the responsibility of being the bearer of this sad news.'

'Poor child,' Alwen said. 'First, his brother, then his mother and now this. He'll need our support even more when he's King.'

'As far as I'm concerned, he is already our King,' Owen said. 'I will provide some of my men to assist in the search for the prince.'

Regan didn't want Owen's men anywhere near Leto, but he couldn't justify the refusal of such an offer.

'That would be most appreciated,' Regan said. 'But to increase the chances of finding the prince, could your men please liaise with the Commander so the search parties can be better deployed.'

He would have Baltair send Owen's men somewhere where he knew the prince was not.

'Certainly,' Owen said. 'And what about the princess?'

'I'll arrange to dispatch a message by bird to Sisters End immediately for Lord Rainer to increase the guard around the princess,' Regan said. 'I will also send a rider. I realise it is not as quick as a raven but is more reliable, and the princess's safety should be our main concern.'

Finally, Regan heard agreement from the others around the table.

'We should also increase the guard around Finnea,' Owen said.

Commander Baltair nodded his agreement.

'Father Alwen, please begin preparations for the King's funeral. We'll decide on the exact day later.'

'Yes, Lord Regan,' Alwen answered. 'I would be honoured.'

'Until we know who is behind this heinous crime, I would advise you all to review your security arrangements,' Regan said.

'Do you seriously think that council members could be in danger?' asked Owen.

'I don't know what to think,' Regan said. 'But precautions should be taken just in case. For those living outside the main castle walls, I would also recommend arranging protection for your homes in the capitol. The bells will be sounding soon, and criers will be dispatched. There may be some unrest. Thank you all for coming at such short notice. This meeting is ended.'

Regan stood without waiting for acknowledgement from anyone. Harrow had already started towards the exit. Regan followed a few steps behind. Owen's dark gaze followed him. You might be popular and respected now you loudmouthed fool, but your time is coming, he thought.

13

OWEN

After Lord Regan had left, Owen rushed from the council chambers. As usual, Captain Janz waited outside.

'Find Sir Peyton and bring him to my solar,' said Owen, keeping his voice low.

The Knight-Commander would still be in the dark about what had happened this morning, so he had to find him fast.

'Impress upon him the importance of the meeting.'

Back in his quarters, Owen waited for Archer to return. He tried not to think about the King. It only made him angry, and he needed a clear mind and calm head if he and his allies were to survive. He thought about his wife and daughters. They should be well and truly out of Twin Falls by now, and on their way to Southern Brook.

As expected, the farewell to his daughters ended in tears. The twins had purposely not been told the whole story, their mother deciding it would be better to keep them in the dark until they had ridden clear of the city, but they knew something was very wrong.

'Is Leto really gone?' Cordelia had asked, her eyes moist.

'Yes, but he's safe.'

'Are we still to be married?'

Owen could not foresee a quick end to this situation, but he wouldn't lie to his children. 'If I have anything to say about it, you will be the next Queen of Avaleen.'

She seemed to accept his words, straightened up, and dried her eyes at the mention of being Queen.

'We'll do as you bid, Father,' she said. 'Won't we, Gwennie?'

Owen smiled at his beautiful daughters. 'Good girls. Uncle Penn will escort you back home, so do what he says.'

'You aren't coming with us?' a teary Gwenda said.

'I'll follow as soon as I can. I promise.' Owen hoped he could keep that promise.

Addwyn had not asked any more questions. She knew the danger. Times like these reminded Owen how much he relied on his wife. If she'd broken down and wept at their forced separation, the confident facade he'd been projecting would have crumbled at once. As they embraced, Owen became acutely aware he may never see his wife again, so he held her tight for a long moment.

He thought briefly about abandoning the capitol and fleeing with them, but as a Knight of Avaleen, he had a duty to the King, his friend of over forty years; he released his wife and bade her goodbye.

'Be safe, my love,' she said, kissing him lightly.

Only Owen, Archer, half a dozen household staff, and twenty sworn soldiers remained. With any luck, they'd all get out of this alive. He had realised too late that only a few Blackwater and Redstone allies currently resided in the capitol, and most had minimal protection or influence. He had learned that Greythorpe allies had been arriving in Twin Falls regularly since the last full moon, and even though they hadn't brought large protective details into the city, Owen had no doubt they had larger detachments camped nearby. With the Capitol Guard firmly under his control, Regan had at least a couple of thousand men to follow his every order. He had played this well.

The door finally opened, and in strode Archer, out of breath, and without the Knight-Commander.

'Come quickly, my lord,' Archer said. 'It's Sir Peyton.'

Owen jumped up from his chair, grabbed his sword and strapped it on as he followed Archer out the door. What kind of trouble could the Knight-Commander possibly be in? Greythorpe hadn't tried to have him killed as well?

Archer led him at a run out of the guest wing and down across the central courtyard. Owen tried to keep up but slowed to a brisk walk, feeling every bit of his fifty-four summers.

They approached the long flight of steps that led up to the throne room. As Owen neared the top, he heard raised voices and looked past Archer.

A body lay motionless, surrounded by half a dozen Noble Guards, all with their swords unsheathed and ready for battle. Another faced away from the rest, sword raised, protecting the backs of his Noble Guard brothers. He recognised Owen and Archer hurrying up the steps and lowered his weapon. About half a dozen members of the Capitol Guard stood between the Noble Guard and the throne room doors, all with their swords at the ready. A couple even had crossbows.

Between the two groups stood Armen Penna, a Captain of the Capitol Guard, and Sir Peyton Holmguard, Knight-Commander of the Noble Guard. Sir Peyton had not yet drawn a weapon but did have one hand on the pommel of his sword.

Aside from his thinning grey hair, he exuded everything a Knight-Commander should be. He stood six feet six, with a muscular body to match, and despite his fifty-one years, continued to be one of the most dangerous men in Avaleen. Owen certainly wouldn't want to be in Captain Penna's boots if this confrontation couldn't be stopped.

Owen could now see the body properly; a Noble Guard, whose blood seeped onto the stone steps from a crossbow bolt lodged in his chest. Damn it! The Noble Guard, known for their skill in battle and forbearance, would have their patience tested by being denied access to the throne room. If anyone else but Sir Peyton had led this group, the confrontation would have been over long ago, and it would not have gone well for Captain Penna and his men.

'No, Captain!' the Knight-Commander's anger threatened to boil over. 'You will stand down and remove yourself and your men from here, or there'll be more trouble than you could handle.'

'As I have said, Commander, I cannot do that. I have my orders,' a very tense Captain Penna said.

The young captain had his sword drawn but still held it at his side and impressed Owen with his composure. However, he still had to diffuse the situation quickly to avoid further bloodshed.

'I don't care about your –'

Owen interrupted Sir Peyton by inserting himself between the two groups of soldiers.

'Everyone, lower your weapons!' he shouted.

No one moved. Archer moved up a few feet behind Owen, putting himself in the middle of the fight as well.

'I said lower your weapons!' Owen repeated and faced the Knight-Commander. 'Peyton, tell your men to stand down.'

'They killed Mabon!' Sir Peyton said.

'He drew his sword,' Captain Penna said. 'I warned him not to, but he did it anyway.'

'But your men didn't have to kill him,' Sir Peyton glanced at the captain, gripping the pommel of his sword even tighter. 'And with a crossbow, a coward's weapon!'

Owen faced Captain Penna. 'Well?'

The captain lowered his gaze. 'That … was a mistake.'

Owen stepped close to the Knight-Commander.

'Peyton,' he said. 'Tell your men to stand down.'

'My lord,' Sir Peyton said. 'You know I hold you in the highest regard, but I cannot back down now. They are keeping me from my King.'

'Things have become … complicated.'

'Complicated?'

'Not here.' Owen glanced past the Knight-Commander to the body of the dead knight. 'This is a futile gesture. No one else needs to die.'

Sir Peyton glared at Owen, not moving.

'Please, Peyton,' Owen implored. 'Trust me on this.'

A few moments passed, and the Knight-Commander removed his hand from his sword.

Owen turned to face the Capitol Guards. 'Lower your weapons.'

Sir Peyton offered his empty hands to Captain Penna.

'We'll leave,' the Knight-Commander said. 'But not with weapons drawn at our backs.'

'Captain?' Owen prompted, knowing Sir Peyton took umbrage at the crossbows, not the swords.

Captain Penna eventually nodded his assent and sheathed his sword.

'Men, do as Lord Owen asks,' he ordered. 'Sheath your swords and unload your crossbows.'

'But Captain –' one of the soldiers began to object.

'That's an order!' Captain Penna yelled.

The Capitol Guards did as ordered. Sir Peyton turned and nodded to his men, and they did the same. Owen welcomed the sound of swords being sheathed.

'Captain Hanson, arrange for Mabon to be taken to the Brothers. I'll write a letter to his family when I return.' Sir Peyton instructed. 'All duties are cancelled, and everyone else is confined to the barracks until you hear from me.'

'Yes, Commander,' Captain Hansen seemed unsure but accepted the order.

With the utmost care, several of the Noble Guards lifted the body of Sir Mabon Rhys and began carrying him down the stairs. The others made up an honour guard of sorts, marching out in front.

'Captain Janz, escort Sir Peyton to my solar,' Owen said. 'I will be along directly.'

'This better be worth it,' the Knight-Commander said, and with a scowl, followed Archer down the steps.

Owen turned back towards the Capitol Guards.

'Thank you for interceding, Lord Owen,' a relieved Captain Penna said.

'A word of advice if you wish to hear it,' Owen said, tersely.

'Any advice from you would be welcome, my lord.'

The captain seemed sincere.

'Two things. Discipline the idiot who fired that crossbow, and personally apologise to the Knight-Commander.'

'I will,' the captain nodded.

'But not today,' Owen warned.

'Certainly,' Captain Penna said. 'Thank you again.'

Owen turned and started down the steps, wondering how many more incidents there would be before things got really out of hand.

He returned to his quarters, went straight to the sideboard, and quickly poured a cup of wine. He might need it for this conversation with Sir Peyton. He approached the door to his solar, took a deep breath and entered. Both Archer and the Knight-Commander stood, waiting.

'Peyton,' Owen stepped forward and grasped the Knight-Commander's forearm. 'I apologise for asking you to back down, but it would have been futile.'

Like Owen, the Knight-Commander remained one of the few old-guard knights left in Avaleen. He carried himself like a true knight of old, unlike some of today's so-called knights, given the title because of whose blood they had in their veins, rather than because of their deeds.

Even though Owen held the rank of Knight Eldar himself, automatically extending the title to his offspring, he'd tried to convince the King to remove the status altogether, ensuring anyone who sought a knighthood would have to earn it. The King had disagreed and would have nothing of it, a rare occasion when Owen and the King's opinions differed.

He missed his friend.

'What the gods is going on? Baltair's thugs guard the throne room and won't let me or my men inside. I don't understand.'

Regan had done an excellent job of keeping the incident quiet. It wasn't a small thing to keep the death of a King a secret, even for a short time.

'Please sit,' Owen gestured to the chair near his desk.

'I'd rather stand.'

He needed the Knight-Commander on his side, so to avoid disrespecting him, Owen remained standing.

'The King is dead,' Owen said straight out.

In four words, Owen had delivered the worst possible news for a man whose sole reason for living was to keep the King safe from harm. Sir Peyton Holmguard had spent the past thirty years protecting the Blackwater monarchs, Caleb, Callum, Conor and even King Cronin – back when he first entered the Noble Guard at twenty-one years of age, the youngest Noble Guard ever. Now, he projected calm, but Owen could see the Knight-Commander's face tighten.

'Explain,' he said after a few moments, his voice raspy but steady.

Owen related Jacob's story and what had happened at the council meeting.

'Does he think he can get away with it?'

Owen could hear the anger in the Knight-Commander's voice.

'He has, for the moment.'

It pained Owen to make that admission.

'I am the Knight-Commander of the Noble Guard. You tell me the King has been murdered and we can do nothing? I cannot believe that!'

'We need to be smart about this, Peyton. Greythorpe thinks his secret is safe. For the moment, we must keep him believing that.'

'If what you say is true, he's going crucify us. How can anyone believe a member of the Noble Guard would want to kill the King? It's absurd!'

'It has happened before,' Archer reminded him.

The Knight-Commander turned on the captain. 'Are you saying it's believable?'

'No,' Owen stepped in. 'He's not saying that, but there is a precedent.'

'That was over a hundred years ago,' the Knight-Commander argued.

'Treachery has a long memory,' Owen intoned, 'and I wouldn't put it past Regan and his cronies to use that to besmirch the good name of the Noble Guard.'

'So, what do we do?' Sir Peyton asked.

'We have to play his game,' Owen said. 'But I need to know I have your support and that of the Noble Guard, should anything happen.'

'Of course, you have it, but you know how my men will react when some of their own have been falsely accused of murdering their King.'

'Yes, I know, but my advice to you is not to tell them the truth.'

'Lie to them?'

Owen understood this request would not sit well with the Knight-Commander.

'It'll make their reaction to this tragedy more believable. If we manage to unravel Regan's story, then the truth can be told. If we can't, then it won't matter.'

'How long will we have to keep up this pretence?' asked Sir Peyton.

'For as long as it takes.'

If Owen couldn't get the Knight-Commander fully onside, he may as well quit the capitol now.

'I don't like it, not at all,' Sir Peyton seemed to have resigned himself to the situation. 'I'll play this sick game, but only because you asked me to.'

'I wish I didn't have to ask,' Owen said.

Owen finished his goblet of wine and dropped into his chair. With any luck, we'll come out of it with our lives, he thought.

14

LETO

It had taken him much longer to get to the rendezvous point than he expected, so he was surprised that Jacob had not yet arrived.

The climb down the castle wall had been straightforward. The first few moves from the turret window had Leto's stomach in knots, but once he got into a rhythm, his confidence returned; still, he felt profound relief when his feet touched the ground.

The river crossing proved to be another matter entirely. Leto would have preferred to attempt the crossing further upstream where the water wasn't as fast flowing, but being too near the North Gate, he feared being seen.

He stood at the river's edge. At about fifty yards across, the distance didn't concern him. Still, it flowed very fast, and only another mile further down, it plunged over the falls into King Lake. If it had been the end of winter, the river would have been flowing twice as fast, and he would have been washed over the falls before he could swim halfway.

Leto looked around one last time. He couldn't see anyone, so he took a couple of tentative steps into the river. The water flowed around his boots and his feet immediately began to cool. He took a few more steps into the river until the water flowed around his hips. He shivered, wondering how water that flowed out of the desert could be so damned cold.

He glanced downriver towards the falls, the point of no return. Leto took a few deep breaths and stepped forward to begin the swim proper, but his ankle turned on a concealed rock. His body twisted with it, and he flopped into the water, facing the wrong way.

The current asserted itself, and Leto began an uncontrolled trip towards the falls. Panicking, he tried to kick himself upright but couldn't reach the bottom. He eventually steadied and realised he had already been swept over a hundred yards downstream from where he'd entered the river. The thought of swimming back to the eastern shore entered his mind, but the rocks that now lined the river's edge decided for him. He turned and swam for his life.

Arm over arm he swam, making slow progress, swearing it wasn't this difficult last time. A few moments later, it dawned on him; when he and Jacob had swum across two summers ago, they went naked, not fully clothed.

Leto renewed his efforts and increased the speed of his strokes as the current swept him towards certain death. Closer and closer he got to the opposite bank. Leto could feel himself slowing, his arms becoming heavy, but the increasing roar of the falls spurred him on. Barely able to lift his arms out of the water, his feet finally touched the riverbed on the north side. He scrambled to the shore over rocks and collapsed in exhaustion on a patch of grass.

After a while, Leto managed to stand, and tried to get his bearings, shocked to discover Kings Falls less than a hundred yards away. Ignoring the magnificent view and how close he had come to death, he turned and headed towards the grassy plain to the north. His exertions in the river had taken their toll, and he made slow progress, but the walk from the river to the North Fork went without incident.

He spent most of his time thinking on the events of the morning. Part of him still seethed at Jacob for making him hide and not allowing him to help his father, but deep down, he knew his friend had done the right thing. Leto and Jacob knew how to handle themselves, but they would've been no match for the detachment of Capitol Guards.

The shadows lengthened as Leto trudged along the West Road, skirting the south side of the Great Forest. He glanced continually at the trees, noting places where he could hide if he came upon someone on the road. The Great Forest stretched for over fifty miles to the west of the North Road, twenty miles to the east, and nearly all the way north to Anchorage.

The boulders he'd been looking for finally came into view, but he couldn't see any evidence of Jacob. He shivered as the wind picked up, sending chills through his damp clothes. He left the road and searched the rocky outcrop for a place to shelter.

He found a hollow between two large boulders, sat on the grass and leaned against the nearest rock. He removed his boots and turned them upside down, half expecting a torrent of water to pour out. It didn't, but he put them aside in the hope they'd dry just that little bit quicker. He pulled his knees up to his chest, wrapped his arms around them and settled in to wait. His injured shoulder began to throb with the cold, but at least the rocks shielded him from the wind.

His thoughts wandered.

Wanted or not, people would assume he'd succeed his father as King. He knew his father's executioners had to be brought to justice. He also knew he had to stay alive, or there'd be no one to succeed his father, except … by the gods, Melina! In all the drama, he had completely forgotten about his little sister. He felt ashamed. He'd asked Jacob to get a message to Cordelia, someone he had only known a few days and didn't ask after his sister. Leto hoped that being far from the capitol would shield her from this madness. Maybe he could get one of his uncle's ships and sail around the coast to rescue her. Yes, that's what he'd do. His uncle wouldn't dare refuse him.

The sound of approaching horses echoed through the rocks. He hurriedly put on his boots, picked his way through the rocks, and looked to the south, ready to admonish Jacob for taking so long … nothing.

'What do we have here?'

Leto spun around to see three men on horseback only thirty yards away and closing fast. He glanced back at the forest; too late to flee now. How could he have been so stupid? An elderly man led the riders. Balding, and with a short grey beard, he sat high in the saddle and wore quality armour and chainmail; a knight. The second rider also wore armour and chainmail, giving the impression of a soldier. The trailing rider looked barely fourteen summers old, probably the knight's squire, and wore only a basic leather jerkin. All had swords at their hips.

The riders stopped about five yards from him.

'Looks like a drowned rat to me, milord,' said the soldier.

Leto realised he probably appeared less than perfect with his torn clothing, now covered in dirt and dust from the walk, despite having taken a dip in the river only hours earlier.

'Who are you?' the knight demanded.

Leto kept silent.

'Answer him, boy!' said the soldier.

'Yes … yes. I'm sorry, milord,' Leto said in his best low-born country accent. 'I was grazing my father's goats, and a deer spooked them, and they ran off. I've been looking for them all afternoon. You seen them? If Father finds out, he'll whip me 'til I bleed.'

'There are no farms around here,' said the knight.

Leto automatically reached for his sword but quickly realised it wasn't there. He reached for the dagger in his belt.

'Don't even think about it, you little imp,' the soldier lifted a crossbow, aiming it at Leto.

He removed his hand from the dagger as the soldier guided his horse behind Leto to block off his retreat. The squire moved his mount up next to the knight. He had two choices: continue to play the lowly farm boy, grovel and hope they'd spare him and move on, or try to bluster his way out of it. Leto turned so he could see all the riders, glancing from one to the other.

'I'm sorry, milords,' grovelling imp it had to be. 'I'm just scared, is all. I have nothing of value save this dagger. You can have it if you want, just don't kill me. I'm the only son my family have since my brother died last winter.'

He hunched over a little, his eyes on the ground. He occasionally glanced up, hopefully in a deferential manner. Leto wasn't used to being subservient except to his father.

'What do you take us for, you little shit? Murderers and thieves?' the soldier growled, not lowering the crossbow.

'No, milord,'

Just because they weren't thieves, it didn't mean he wasn't in danger.

'I'm not a lord,' the soldier said. 'Lord Steffan is the lord here, and you aren't going anywhere until he gives his leave.'

'Yes, sir,' Leto answered.

Steffan? He knew of only one knight with that name. He glanced back up at the older man who had leaned forward in his saddle and scrutinised him more closely.

'You look familiar to me, boy,' the old man said. 'Look at me.'

'I dunno what you mean, milord,' Leto said, turning away. 'I'm just a-'

'Look at him, you little whelp!' the soldier said, not lowering the crossbow.

Taking his time, Leto turned fully towards the knight and stood straight. He took the opportunity to have a proper look at the rider. He could see the resemblance, and the symbol on his armour – a black raven on a grey background – confirmed his suspicions. Leto looked directly at him and recognition sparked in the old knight's eyes.

'You shouldn't be out here alone, Your Highness,' he said. 'It's dangerous.'

'What?' the soldier exclaimed.

Lord Steffan ignored him.

'This wasn't my plan,' Leto had to stall for time and find out how much he knew. 'But I had to leave the capitol in a hurry.'

'I'll escort you back to Riverview,' Lord Steffan said. 'You'll be safe with me.'

He sounded sincere, but Leto wouldn't return with him.

113

'Thank you for the kind offer, my lord, but given the circumstances, I'll have to decline.'

'It wasn't an offer,' Lord Steffan said.

'I'm not going anywhere with you,' Leto said.

He realised he may have to fight his way out of this but couldn't do anything with a crossbow aimed at him.

Lord Steffan sighed. 'Fine, have it your way. Captain, bind him. We'll return to the caravan and toss him in the cart with the supplies. So much for getting to the capitol before dark.'

The soldier put away his weapon.

'With ple —' his voice cut short by a crossbow bolt in his neck.

After a few short gasps, he slid out of the saddle and hit the dirt with a thud. The horse whinnied and took a few steps sideways away from the twitching body of its former rider. Lord Steffan drew his sword as Jacob appeared from behind a nearby boulder with a crossbow raised and pointed directly at the mounted knight.

'Better late than never, I suppose,' Leto said.

'Apologies, Your Highness. Now, if you could grab those weapons,' Jacob said, gesturing towards the dead soldier without taking his eyes from the riders.

Leto retrieved the sword from the now still body, moved around to the other side of the squire's horse, and raised the sword.

Lord Steffan gave Jacob a menacing glare and turned his gaze to Leto.

'You know we can't let you leave,' Leto said. 'Please get off your horses.'

The squire looked to Lord Steffan. The old knight hadn't moved a muscle.

'Get off your horses!' Jacob said. 'Both of you.'

'I will do no such thing,' he replied. 'Do you know who I am?'

'I don't care. Dismount, now!'

A few more moments passed in silence.

Lord Steffan turned to his squire and nodded. 'Eddard, do as they say.'

With an anxious look, the squire dismounted and moved a few steps away from his horse towards Leto, who still pointed his sword at the squire.

'Now it's your turn, old man,' Jacob said.

Without warning, the squire unsheathed his sword and attacked Leto.

'Go, my lord!' the boy yelled, knocking Leto's sword aside and trying to behead him with a quick slash.

The many years of training instantly came to the fore, and Leto stepped back, the sword passing an inch from his face. He batted aside the squire's blade with his own and took a few more steps back to regain his balance.

'Hah!' Lord Steffan shouted and dug his heels into his horse's flanks, which instantly bounded forward.

Jacob fired the crossbow without thinking as he jumped back to avoid the oncoming horse which galloped past him, heading towards the capitol.

'Shit!' Jacob reloaded his crossbow.

The squire thrust at Leto again, who barely avoided the attack.

'Shoot him!' Leto shouted.

'I did!' he yelled back.

The squire stepped up his attack, slashing wildly, but Leto brushed them aside and cut the boy's shoulder with his counterattack.

'Shoot him again!' Leto cried as he continued to be forced backward by the fierce but sloppy onslaught of the squire.

The boy stumbled and lowered his sword arm to balance himself. Leto took advantage of the opening and thrust his sword into the centre of the squire's torso. The boy dropped his weapon, and his face went pale. Leto withdrew the blade, and the boy crumpled to the ground with a whimper. He wore no armour, so Leto knew the blow to be fatal.

'I could have sworn I hit him,' Jacob bemoaned, reloading the crossbow as Leto rushed to his side.

Jacob aimed the crossbow at the fleeing rider, but before he could let loose another bolt, Lord Steffan slumped in his saddle, slid to the side and fell from the running horse. He hit the ground and skidded to a halt in the grass at the edge of the road.

'It looks like you got him after all.'

Lord Steffan's broadsword lay a few yards away in the middle of the road. Leto picked it up as they started towards the fallen knight. The horse had bolted out of sight by the time they reached the body.

'Cover me,' Leto said.

Jacob nodded and raised the crossbow again as Leto crept towards the knight's face-down body. He prodded Lord Steffan with the broadsword. No reaction. Leto examined the body and removed a dagger and a short sword, which had managed to stay attached to his belt during the fall. Leto put down the weapons and rolled the body over with his foot. Dirt covered Lord Steffan's scratched face and his eyes were closed. A small amount of blood had seeped through the hole in the armour made by the crossbow bolt. It had gone straight through his heart, it seemed. Blood oozed from the base of the chest piece.

'Lucky shot,' Jacob shrugged.

'Not for him.'

'He deserved it.'

'I know.'

But it doesn't mean I have to like it, Leto thought.

'We'll have to hide the bodies. Amongst the rocks should be good enough.'

'Leave them out for the crows,' Jacob spat.

'We can't. His caravan will be passing soon. The longer it is before their bodies are found, the better for us.'

'A caravan? Who the hell was he?'

'Lord Steffan Greythorpe.'

'Shit!' Jacob exclaimed. 'This day just gets better and better.'

Leto couldn't disagree.

They managed to catch the horses of the bodyguard and the squire but couldn't find Lord Steffan's horse anywhere nearby. Leto hoped it had run off into the forest or out on the plains, far from the road.

They dragged the bodies of Lord Steffan and his bodyguard from the road over to the rocky outcrop where Leto had rested earlier. They went to move the squire but found him still alive. His hands clutched his stomach, and blood appeared on his lips. The boy didn't have long, Leto thought.

'Should we put him out of his misery?' Jacob said.

'No,' Leto said and knelt beside him. 'Fetch our horses. Leave him to me.'

'We can't wait too long. You said yourself the caravan could be along any time.'

'Just get the horses!'

'Alright!'

Jacob left Leto alone with the squire. He looked at the boy, about to die on a lonely road, holding in his own guts. Damn it! Why did he have to draw his sword? His young face conveyed fear.

'Eddard, is it?' Leto said.

The boy took a few quick, raspy breaths.

'Yes, sir,' he said through bloody, gritted teeth.

He could see the boy suffering. Jacob could be right; he should be put out of his misery, but Leto couldn't bring himself to kill an unarmed boy. He didn't look long for this world anyway.

'How old are you, Eddard?'

Leto guessed it didn't matter what he asked, anything to divert the boy's attention away from the pain and shock of his impending death.

'Th ... thirteen, sir.'

Eddard squeezed his eyes shut and moaned as a wave of pain racked his small body. His breathing became shallower and wetter. It reminded Leto of his father not half a day ago as he lay dying at the foot of his throne; he could barely watch.

He'd seen men die before, but not like this. He felt the squire's blood-covered hand touch his own. His eyes opened, and he looked directly at Leto. Tears ran freely down his terrified little face, mingling with the blood that trickled from his mouth.

'A ... a ... am I going ... to die?'

Leto nodded.

'Did ... did my lord escape?'

'He did,' Leto lied, knowing the boy wouldn't know otherwise.

'Then I did my job, didn't I?'

The boy grimaced again, and blood now leaked freely from the corners of his mouth.

'You certainly did.' Leto put his hand on the boy's forehead. 'You protected your liege lord. You have a knight's heart.'

The boy managed a weak smile. Leto's throat became restricted as the life faded from the squire's eyes. He knelt beside the boy until Jacob came up with their horses.

Leto wasn't a big man, but he picked up the squire in his arms with little effort. He carried him over to the rocks where they had put the other two bodies and wrapped the boy's body in a saddle blanket.

Jacob and Leto mounted their horses, turned north and headed into the Great Forest.

They weaved their way through the trees in silence. He had killed someone. He didn't feel exhilarated, or excited, or proud. He didn't know what to feel. Leto thought he'd feel different somehow. The young squire had been brave, sacrificing himself for his lord. He did his duty, but it cost him his short life. Leto had always imagined his first kill would be a knight in a battle, not a boy with no armour and little training.

Before long, it became too dark to ride through the forest safely, the moonlight unable to penetrate the dense canopy of the giant oaks. They made camp next to one of the larger trees. They were now a good distance from the road, so Jacob collected wood for a small campfire while Leto hobbled and fed the horses.

Once the fire had caught, Leto placed a few simple bedrolls near the flames and stripped off his damp clothes. He hung them on a low branch to dry and wrapped himself in a blanket Jacob had brought. He sat next to the fire, and Jacob took out some food from his bag: cold beef, cheese, and bread.

Leto asked after Cordelia, relieved that the whole Redstone family, except for Owen, had already left the capitol. He thanked the gods that Owen would arrange protection for Melina.

'I'm sorry I took so long,' Jacob said between mouthfuls. 'It couldn't be helped. As Lord Owen suggested, I left by the south gate but then had to ride for five miles before heading east. The Watchers at the south gate stopped me, and I said I was taking the horse to Southern Brook for Lord Owen, so I had to keep riding until the gate was out of sight before turning east.'

'That's a pretty poor story,' Leto said.

'It was the best I could do at such short notice. Thankfully, the Watchers aren't that smart.'

Leto took a bite of the cheese.

'I headed east for about three or four miles, then started north,' Jacob continued. 'But I had to go further east to avoid the search parties that had started looking for you. I eventually made it to the Old Bridge. They really need to fix that. The horses nearly fell through. After resting the horses for a spell, I galloped most of the way here and hoped I wouldn't run into any patrols. When I approached, I saw the riders, and luckily, their attention was on you. I hid the horses in the forest and came up on foot. The rest, you know.'

When he had warmed up, Leto pulled the spare clothes out of the saddlebags. Jacob gazed into the campfire as he dressed. Leto pulled on his boots and sat on his bedroll.

'Was that your first as well?' Leto said.

Jacob looked up, confused.

'The first time you've … killed someone?'

Jacob's gaze returned to the fire.

'Yeah, but I'm not sorry I did it, or that knight either,' he said after a few moments. 'And I'd do it again.'

'At least you killed a knight,' Leto said. 'Killing a boy – not very kingly?'

'It was either you or him.'

He'd seen dead bodies, men killed in minor scuffles and a few executions, but like him, Jacob had never been personally involved in the killing. Now Jacob had killed to protect him, and although it wasn't his fault, Leto still felt responsible.

'I'm sorry,' Leto felt awful for Jacob.

'You've nothing to be sorry about,' Jacob said. 'If those bastards hadn't killed your father, none of this would have happened. By my reckoning, they deserved it.'

Leto could see Jacob was hurting, but nothing could be done about it.

'We should get some sleep.'

Jacob tossed a small branch onto the fire, which crackled and sent sparks into the cool night air.

Leto lay down, pulled the blanket over himself, and stared into the fire awhile. He closed his eyes, and memories of the other tragedies in his life asserted themselves; like being told his brother Conor had been lost at sea, and when he watched his mother die of suspected food poisoning. And this morning he'd witnessed his father's murder, fled his home and killed a boy. Today would be another day that would be forever etched into his memory.

15

CEDRIC

Curse the gods and my fucking father!

The previous day Cedric had taken a dozen soldiers a full day's ride east of Twin Falls, questioning farmers and villagers, looking for that upstart prince.

The little coward is probably still hiding somewhere in the castle, Cedric thought.

As the eldest son and heir, Cedric expected to inherit the Greythorpe's vast estates, but his father still had him running these shitty errands. Deliver this, fetch that, look for this. He should be the one at Highland Keep, sitting in the great hall of his family's ancestral home, making other people do his bidding, instead of his upstart little brother, Calvin.

Cedric remembered when his father first brought him to the capitol to serve as an apprentice on the Ruling Council. He had been so excited and proud, boasting to anyone who would listen. He didn't have much to brag about now.

His uncle's caravan had arrived the previous evening. Since Steffan had his own residence in the capitol, no one had missed him until late into the night when his steward enquired about his lord's whereabouts. Cedric became the target of his father's lousy mood, brought on more by losing sleep than by concern for his missing brother, he thought.

'Ride all the way to Kings Hill, I don't care,' his father had said. 'Just find him!'

Cedric and his men were now searching north of the capitol, past the Fork, and had been since dawn. The shadows had started to fade, and Cedric, eager to return to the capitol, felt the frustration building. But it had been made painfully clear, not to return without Lord Steffan.

He removed his helmet and ran his hand through his long red hair. The helmet itched like hell, but it kept his head warm. He'd also worn extra clothing under his armour to keep out the cold. A rider cantered up behind them.

'My lord,' Captain Tamar Kirby said. 'We've found him.'

About damn time!

'Lead the way, Captain.'

Cedric and his two bodyguards urged their horses to a canter and followed the captain towards a rocky outcrop about twenty yards from the road.

The bodies lay neatly next to each other. Oddly, the small one had been wrapped in a blanket. Captain Wever had a bloody hole on either side of his neck, his face fixed in a contorted look of surprise, and his uncle had no apparent injuries aside from abrasions on his face, which he probably received when he fell. It almost looked as if he had simply fallen over after a hard night's drinking. However, the single hole in his breast plate gave away his fate. It had gone straight through the emblem engraved in his armour, a small hole where the raven's head should be and a little blood covering the rest of the bird.

'Bandits?' Captain Kirby suggested.

Cedric knew full well it wasn't. He liked Tamar Kirby. The man always gave Cedric the chance to show his quality, and unlike many others, he treated him with the respect he deserved.

'I doubt it,' Cedric said. 'No bandits I've heard of lay their victims out that neatly. I'm assuming they weren't killed here?'

'No, my lord,' Tamar said. 'Wes says they were dragged here from the road.'

Wes Brinker, a long-time servant of the Greythorpe family and one of the best trackers in Avaleen, had gained the respect of his father over the years, something very few had done. If Wes couldn't find his uncle, no one could. Cedric hoped this would have meant less chance of him copping any blame if they had failed.

'Well?' Cedric said as the old tracker crouched over the bodies.

'Lord Steffan and the captain were both killed with a crossbow. A quality weapon to be able to pierce this armour. They were dragged here, but the boy was carried. Odd thing though, their weapons are gone but they still have their money pouches.'

'How many killers were there?'

'At a guess, no more than two or three.'

Stupid old man. He should have stayed with his caravan.

'Captain, arrange for the bodies to be wrapped. We'll take my uncle's body back to the capitol,' Cedric said. 'Did Captain Wever and the boy have any family?'

'The captain had a wife and daughter in Kings Hill, my lord,' Kirby said, 'and the boy was an orphan, from memory.'

His uncle liked giving those born into misery a chance at a better life. It hadn't turned out so well for this boy, he thought, glancing at the small bundle.

'Have a couple of the men take the captain's body directly to Kings Hill from here. It should only take a couple of days to get there. He shouldn't smell too badly by then.'

'I'm sure his family would appreciate it,' said the captain.

'I hope so,' Cedric said. 'We'll take the boy's body back to the capitol with us.'

'If it pleases milord, I'd like to stay until the morning and look around a little more,' Wes said. 'I'll be able to see more in the daylight.'

The old tracker could stay out here, if he so wanted.

'Sure, but if you don't find anything, be back by sunset tomorrow. I'll leave you half a dozen men. Use them to send a message to me if you find something useful. To me, understood?'

'Yes, milord,' Wes said.

Whether it was good news or no news, Cedric wanted to know first. Wes owed his loyalty to Cedric's father, but he hoped the tracker would follow his orders. The last thing he needed was for his father to find out details of Steffan's death before he did.

'Now, hurry. I want to be back at Riverview sometime tonight.'

His father would not appreciate waiting until tomorrow for bad news.

The moon peered between the clouds, lighting their way enough that they made good time back to the capitol. They took the bodies of Lord Steffan and his squire to the Brothers, who would preserve them until decisions were made. They had to bang on the monastery door several times before Prior Fren opened it. The prior did not greet them, but called some other monks out to collect the bodies once Captain Kirby explained.

'What do you want me to do with him?' Prior Fren asked as the monks carried the boy's wrapped body into the monastery.

'I don't give a shit,' Cedric said.

'Why didn't you bury him where you found him?'

'Don't question me, monk,' Cedric said. 'Just make sure Lord Steffan's body is preserved properly. Screw it up, and you'll answer to my father.'

'The Sisters will take all due care, milord,' Prior Fren said. 'If that's all, I'll bid you a goodnight.'

He stepped back through the door and closed it before Cedric could say anything further.

'Rude prick,' Cedric said.

Captain Kirby pulled himself up in his saddle. 'Maybe you should have a word with the Abbot?'

Cedric mounted his horse, and they headed for the castle gate.

'That old fart? Not worth my time.'

Leaving their mounts at the stables, Cedric and Captain Kirby made their way to the Governor's tower. As expected, an increased number of Capitol Guards had been given duty within the castle. His father had ordered it after King Caleb's death, murdered by his own Noble Guard. Cedric wouldn't be shedding tears over the King's death, but it still shocked him. If the King could be killed, so could his father, and Cedric didn't want that, even if he had treated him badly.

They entered the foyer of the tower to be confronted by Harrow. Cedric had come across Harrow back home in The Hills, as a boy. He had been known as a vicious killer back then, and Cedric assumed that hadn't changed, and remained on his guard when dealing with the man. Harrow raised a hand to stop them from passing.

'Just you,' Harrow said and glanced at Captain Kirby. 'Not him.'

Cedric wasn't happy at being told what to do. 'I'll bring who I want.'

'Governor's orders,' said Harrow, his voice unwavering in the face of Cedric's demand.

Cedric glared at the grizzled soldier, who stared right back at him. 'Go back to the barracks, Captain,' he directed Kirby.

'Are you sure, milord?' Tamar said. 'I could wait.'

'Yes, let him stay,' Harrow said. 'We could reminisce about the old days.'

'No. I'll be fine.'

Captain Kirby nodded and strode from the foyer. Cedric turned back to Harrow. He'd had more than enough of the man's insolence and placed his hand on the pommel of his sword.

'From now on, you will address me correctly. Do you understand?'

Harrow's eyes flicked to Cedric's sword hand, and he gave a crooked, humourless smile. 'As it pleases you, my lord.'

'Now, take me to my father.'

Harrow turned and swaggered towards the stairs. Cedric followed him up the curved staircase to his father's solar on the first floor. Harrow knocked and opened the door. In all the time his father had been the Governor, Cedric had not once been invited to his father's private quarters up on the third floor, and it seemed tonight would be no different.

Cedric followed Harrow into the room. His father sat behind his desk, quill in hand. If he wasn't writing, he was reading. Cedric stepped around Harrow and stood before the desk. He turned to his father's bodyguard, who had closed the door and taken up position nearby.

'You may leave,' Cedric said in a clipped tone.

Harrow seemed to ignore him but glanced at his father.

'Do you think he needs protection from me?' Cedric said.

'I don't know, milord,' he sneered. 'Does he?'

'You obnoxious prick. Get out!'

Harrow glanced at his master, who nodded. The soldier performed a short bow, opened the door and left the room.

Cedric shook his head as the door closed.

'Father, why do you have him around? He's dangerous and has no respect for anyone.'

His father put down the quill and leaned back in his chair.

'He is very dangerous, and everyone knows it. So, people think twice before even contemplating something against me. His manners could do with a little work, but my brother thought he would suit the current political climate, and I tend to agree.'

Cedric became nervous at the mention of Lord Steffan. One never relished giving powerful men unwelcome news, especially if that man was his father.

'Yes, well, we found Uncle Steffan. He's dead.'

His father's expression didn't change. He probably already knew, despite Cedric having made a hasty return to the capitol.

'We found him about ten miles east of Jane's Folly, along with his squire and bodyguard. I wanted to stay out and search for the killers but thought it best to return with Uncle Steffan's body at once and give him to the monks for the funeral preparations.'

It wasn't an entirely false statement, and his father wouldn't know any better, he hoped.

'I ordered Wes to wait until morning and see if he could track the killers.'

'Good,' his father finally said. 'Keep me apprised of any developments.'

His father's reaction confused Cedric. He usually found fault with anything Cedric did and never hesitated to point it out. Maybe he was grieving, or he just didn't care. Cedric had to admit he wasn't that fond of his own siblings, either. However, if someone had murdered any of them, he would go to the ends of the earth to exact revenge.

'We'll find the bastards who murdered him, Father.'

'I certainly hope so,' his father said. 'We can't have lords of Avaleen being killed out of hand so close to the capitol, can we?'

'Err … no sir,' he didn't know what else to say. 'I'll leave you to your work. Goodnight.'

He turned to leave.

'No, stay,' his father said.

Cedric stopped and turned back, his brow furrowed. He couldn't think of anything he'd done wrong, and his father's expression gave nothing away.

'Do you know why your uncle was coming to the capitol?' he said.

Cedric had no idea, though now under his father's gaze, he felt he should have taken more interest.

'Err … because you summoned him?'

'Of course, I summoned him, you idiot, but why?'

'I don't know.'

'Then let me explain,' his father said as if addressing a child. 'The King is dead, the prince is still missing, and the people are agitated. If we don't have stable rule, there will be unrest, increased unlawful behaviour or even open rebellion. We don't want that, do we?'

'No, sir.'

'I need someone I can trust implicitly to do things that need to be done to keep the peace in Avaleen, but now Steffan is dead.'

Cedric thought about this for a few moments.

'Let me take his place, father.' He said and stepped closer to the desk. 'You can trust me.'

His father leaned back in his chair and looked at Cedric. 'I know you're trustworthy, but I don't know whether you have the intelligence or the skills I require.'

It pleased Cedric to hear his father trusted him, but it also stung to have his intelligence questioned. He had easily done everything that had been asked of him. He wasn't a seasoned knight and hadn't been in any battles, but he knew how to fight. He was particularly fond of the bow, a weapon at which he excelled.

His father wanted a Greythorpe to stand by his side and be his right hand. He could possibly use that to his advantage but trying to change his father's mind about anything usually ended in failure and admonishment.

'You could ask Arthur Singer or Waldin Hardwinter.'

Both men were married to his father's sisters, Arthur to Murne and Waldin to Jayne. Unfortunately, his father thought Arthur Singer an idiot, and Waldin Hardwinter had one foot in the grave.

'But they aren't blood,' Cedric added, denouncing his own suggestion.

He purposely didn't suggest Godwin or Saul Greythorpe because he knew his father didn't get along with his half-brothers.

'I would get Rainer White here if I could, but it would take too long,' his father said.

Damn it! Cedric had forgotten about Rainer White, his future father-by-law. Even though he wasn't a blood relative, the Lord of Whitehall would be a loyal collaborator, given that Cedric had become betrothed to his daughter the previous summer. His father's need must be great if he couldn't wait for Rainer.

'Father, let me help you. I know I'm not the most experienced person, but I am your eldest son ... your heir. I'd die before I betrayed you.'

'Let's hope it doesn't come to that,' his father said, picking up his quill. 'We'll talk tomorrow. You may go.'

Cedric fought to keep a smile from his face.

'Yes, sir. Thank you.'

He turned and headed for the door. Now, he'd be doing more meaningful work and finally get the respect he deserved.

16

LETO

There wasn't a cloud in the sky. Or, at least, he couldn't see any through the small break in the forest canopy. He breathed a little easier as he lay in the dirt and leaves near a fallen tree. Leto and Jacob had just managed to avoid yet another group of horsemen. This time, he counted twenty-one, a single rider leading them and the rest in two columns behind. They flew no flags, and they were too far away to see any house emblems.

It had been nearly a week since he'd fled Riverview. It usually took around three or four days to reach Anchorage on horseback at a leisurely pace, longer if travelling with carts and even longer if it rained, but they had been cautious. They avoided encounters with soldiers and large groups of travellers. When they did encounter someone, they just moved on at a walk, as if they weren't in a rush. People always remember someone in a hurry.

He glanced at Jacob, crouched behind the same fallen tree, peering through the dead branches towards the nearby road. They hadn't spoken much in the past few days. There wasn't much to say. Leto rolled over, got to his knees, and raised his head above the tree trunk. He hoped that their horses, hidden deeper in the forest, weren't spooked and alerted passers-by to their presence.

'We'll never get to Anchorage at this rate,' Leto said as he surveyed the road.

'Ummm … Callum, that's the least of our problems,' Jacob said.

Leto stiffened at the mention of the name. They'd agreed on false names to use if anyone captured them or if they needed to interact with anyone. If that type of situation arose, Jacob wanted to be known as Mort, and Leto was Callum. He glanced at Jacob who was staring into the forest. Leto followed his gaze.

Scattered amongst the trees, ten yards away, stood about a dozen men with crossbows or longbows, all aimed at Leto and Jacob; and he hadn't heard a thing. Some wore armour or mail, though none matched, and some showed signs of rust. The majority wore hardened leather over their tattered tunics. Leto sighed. They managed to get all this way, only to run into bandits.

'What do you want?' Leto said with a confidence he didn't feel. 'Our horses are back in the forest. Take what you want and leave us be.'

They should be able to make it to Anchorage on foot from here. Some of the bandits laughed.

'What's so funny?' Jacob said.

One of the men stepped forward. 'I already have your horses and supplies, for which I am most grateful.'

He wasn't especially tall or imposing, and he only wore leather armour, but his clothes seemed of better quality than the others. He must be their leader. The bandit stopped short of Leto and squatted to look directly into his eyes. He carried a longbow and recognised Lord Steffan's broadsword hanging from his hip. The bandit leader caught Leto looking at the sword and smiled.

'Yes, it was yours, but it's now mine like everything else.'

'It wasn't mine to give,' Leto said.

'But it was mine to take,' he said, laughing at his own joke. 'Now drop your weapons.'

'Just kill us and take them from us,' Jacob challenged.

'We aren't murderers,' the bandit leader said, offended. 'No, you're more valuable to me alive, for the moment. Now drop your weapons.'

Neither Jacob nor Leto moved.

'I'm not going to kill you, but I will hurt you if I have to,' the bandit leader said, turning his head slightly towards his men. 'Deric, if they don't drop their weapons, put an arrow in the big one's leg.'

'Aye,' said Deric, the bandit nearest to Jacob.

A head shorter than Jacob, his tunic stretched across a muscled chest and his unshaven face presented a solid square jaw. He raised the loaded crossbow and took aim.

'Deric's an excellent shot,' the leader said, 'so if your friend moves or does anything stupid, he may get his balls pinned to the tree.'

Leto glanced at Jacob, who wore a look of angry resignation. They had to stay alive at all costs. Hopefully, a chance to escape would present itself. Leto spread his arms wide and stood.

There were too many.

'Now!'

Leto untied his sword belt and let it drop to the ground.

'Scar, get his weapons,' Deric kept his crossbow trained on Jacob.

Another bandit sheathed his sword and approached Jacob, who had now raised his arms as Leto had. The bandit had been given an appropriate name. The scrawny bald man boasted several scars on his face and neck, but they paled in comparison to the colossal wound that extended from below his chin up past his mouth and around to where his ear used to be. The bandit leader stepped forward and removed Leto's sword from his belt.

'Who are you?' Leto said.

'That's not important,' he smiled as he took Leto's daggers and sword and handed them to another bandit, 'but you can call me Cross. Maybe you've heard of me?'

'No, should I have?' Leto said with more sarcasm than he probably should have.

'You have balls, my young friend,' Cross bent down and shoved his fingers inside Leto's boots.

Scar pulled a small dagger from Jacob's left boot and held it up. The bandit leader nodded and turned to his men.

'Scar, Jacks, Gomer, with me. Deric, escort these two back to the camp,' he turned back to Leto. 'He'll treat you well if you behave.'

A tall, muscular man with long, dark, scraggly hair; Scar; and a scruffy young boy began to move towards Cross.

'This shouldn't take long. We'll be back before sundown.'

'Are you sure you want to take the kid?' Deric said, lowering his weapon.

'He needs to be blooded some time, and this is a straightforward thing,' Cross said. 'Are you ready, Gomer?'

The kid smiled. 'Yes, sir!'

Cross laughed. 'See, he calls me sir. He shows more respect than any of you lot.'

Deric gave a deprecating bow. 'As you wish, sir.'

They bound Leto and Jacob's hands behind their backs as Cross and his small band disappeared into the forest. Deric came forward, his smile fading.

'Do not fuck with me,' he said, glancing at Jacob. 'If either of you steps out of line, I'll personally beat the shit out of the other one. Cross usually likes to give his hostages back unmarked, but it's no difference to me. If you're alive, we'll get a ransom.'

'You don't even know who we are,' a defiant Leto said.

'Once we get back to camp, we'll ask you nicely,' Deric said. 'And the longer it takes for you to tell us, the bloodier you will get.'

Would his uncle pay a ransom for him? Trying to keep his identity and location secret would be impossible if he was ransomed.

'Hobble and bag them,' Deric said.

One of the bandits tied Leto's ankles with rope, and Deric put a sack over his head. He assumed they did the same with Jacob. They couldn't escape now.

Several hours later, the bandits ripped off their head coverings. Their camp wasn't much to look at, just a small clearing with a couple of makeshift tents and a central campfire.

One of the bigger outlaws shoved them to the ground near a large tree, away from the campfire. Relieved when they loosened his hands from behind his back, Leto winced when they roughly trussed them again, this time above his head. He gritted his teeth as his shoulder began throbbing with pain.

About halfway through the trek, Leto's ankle binding had snagged on a rock, and he tripped. He twisted his body to avoid landing on his face, but pain shot through his injured shoulder as he hit the dirt. His captors didn't care. They kept pushing, shoving and cursing him and Jacob, causing them to stumble. Jacob returned their curses once, but Leto then heard his grunts and pain as they kicked him repeatedly. Jacob didn't answer back again and stayed silent for the remainder of the trip.

Jacob, his arms also tied above his head, stared at his own feet. His right eye bulged, the skin a dark purple, and he had a split lip with dried blood down his chin and neck.

'Are you alright?'

Jacob lifted his head.

'Yeah,' he said after a few moments. 'Just great.'

'We've managed to get ourselves into a bit of a bind, haven't we?'

Jacob chuckled and grimaced in pain.

'We don't do things by halves,' he managed to say and gave a weak smile.

'Don't worry. We'll get out of here.'

He could see only four bandits. Deric sat at the campfire, sharpening his sword, his back to the prisoners. A fat man with at least two chins had just waddled into camp with buckets of water on a wooden pole across his shoulders. He may have been overweight, but he lifted the buckets over his head and lowered them to the ground without spilling a drop. The other two had pulled guard duty at opposite ends of the camp.

'Hey!' Leto shouted. 'We need a drink.'

Two Chins glanced over in their direction but turned away. Deric continued to work on his sword.

Leto needed something for his parched throat. He'd settle for anything, some water, wine, or even ale, though he doubted these outlaws would give them ale, and they probably didn't even have wine.

'We just want some water.'

Deric stopped working on his weapon and sighed. He stood, sheathed his sword, and turned toward them. 'You want water?'

Deric picked up one of the buckets that Two Chins had just brought into camp and carried the bucket to them.

'Here's your water.'

Deric stopped ten feet away and threw the entire contents of the bucket all over Leto and Jacob. Leto gasped in surprise at the freezing water. The bastard!

'Now shut the fuck up,' Deric warned.

Leto glared at Deric as he strode back towards the campfire.

'I just filled that,' said Two Chins.

Deric threw the bucket to him, which he juggled briefly before catching it. 'Fill it again.'

The fat man didn't argue. He turned and waddled back into the forest, bucket in hand. Deric unsheathed his sword, sat back down, and continued to sharpen the blade.

'I'm sorry,' Leto whispered, but Jacob didn't respond.

Leto couldn't see how they would survive this situation. If they revealed their real names, they could be ransomed back to Greythorpe. If they didn't, they could be killed. Neither prospect offered any solace.

The other outlaws returned around dusk. The stocky one, Leto had heard him called Grub, balanced a small wild pig over his shoulder, already gutted. Spit, the slightly built bandit with the long stringy hair, held a couple of rabbits. The other two had only their bows.

'It's about time,' Deric said as he picked up a small branch from a wood pile near the tent. 'Is that all you got?'

'Next time you go hunting, you lazy prick,' Grub said.

Deric didn't seem like a man to be trifled with, so Grub's retort surprised Leto.

'Fine, you can stay behind next time and watch the camp,' said Deric.

Grub laughed as Two Chins took the pig from him. 'No thanks. I'd rather be hunting. Where's Cross?'

'No idea,' said Deric.

'He said he'd be back by sundown,' Spit pointed out, still holding the rabbits.

'Do I look like his mother?' Deric said. 'He's probably enjoying some comely wench and lost track of time.'

Grub didn't look happy. 'Maybe. But he won't be back until tomorrow if he's not here soon. Difficult to find your way through this forest at night.'

'More food for us then,' Deric said, turning to Spit. 'Skin those rabbits and get cooking. I'm starving and can't wait for the pig to be done.'

'Of course, you've had such a tough time sitting on your arse,' said Grub.

Deric threw the branch on the fire. 'Don't push your luck.'

Grub laughed again.

Darkness enveloped the forest as Spit expertly skinned the rabbits, skewered them with a stick and put them over the campfire next to the already roasting pig. Leto licked his lips as the aroma of roasted rabbit tickled his nose. Hunger ate at him, heightened by the delicious smell of the charred meat.

Most of the bandits crowded around the campfire, ready for their share, but Two Chins approached with a couple of rabbit pieces. Leto licked his lips again, not taking his eyes off the pieces of meat. A sliver of meat would be better than nothing. The fat bandit didn't even make eye contact, which wasn't surprising, but he walked right past and gave the meat to the lookout.

'Please, can you feed us?' Leto said.

Two Chins ignored him as he licked the juices from his fingers and headed towards the campfire.

Leto desperately wanted that small leg of meat. Part of him couldn't believe how fretful he became over missing out on such a tiny morsel of food, but hunger overrode his common sense.

'Listen to me, you fat bastard,' Leto shouted. 'We want some food!'

The conversation around the campfire ceased, and all eyes turned on him except Deric. He'd stopped talking like the others but sat still, lowering his head as if sighing. Two Chins halted mid-step, turning to sneer at Leto.

'What'd you say, little man?'

'We just want something to eat,' implored Leto.

'The only thing you're going to eat is my fist,' Two Chins said.

The fat man moved far quicker than he should have been able to, and before Leto knew it, he stood right before him. Leto lifted his knees to his chest, turned his head away and braced himself.

'Hold!' Deric's voice boomed.

Leto opened his eyes a crack. Two Chins still towered over him, snorting heavily, his fist ready to strike.

Deric approached and patted Two Chins on the shoulder. 'Go back to the fire. I'll take care of these two.'

'He called me a fat bastard.'

'Don't worry,' Deric said. 'He'll get what's coming to him. Now go and make sure that pig's cooking right.'

Scowling, Two Chins returned to the campfire. Deric crouched down next to Leto and made a show of removing his dagger from his belt and casually pointing it at him. The flickering flames of the campfire reflected off the long, thin blade, giving it an ominous glow.

'I want you to listen very carefully,' Deric said, flicking the blade back and forth in front of Leto's face with his right hand.

Leto's eyes followed the knife, dreading what the bandit had in mind.

'I'm going to ask some questions, and if I don't like the answers … '

Leto's head snapped back as Deric's left fist smacked into his face. Unbelievable pain racked his skull. His jaw stung from being struck, and the back of his head hurt from slamming into the tree trunk. This shouldn't be happening.

'Do you understand?' Deric said.

Leto turned his head back to face the bandit and glared at him.

'I asked you a question,' he continued. 'Do you understand?'

He'd only been hit once, but Leto wasn't sure how many of those he could take. His face still tingled with pain, so he just nodded.

'Good. What's your name?'

'Callum,' said Leto.

Deric sighed. 'I'm a fair man, so I'll rephrase my question so you can better understand. What's your real name?'

Leto looked up at Deric for a few moments before he answered. 'Callum.'

Deric's fist moved like lightning and punched Leto in exactly the same spot as before, his head striking the tree trunk once again. Leto grunted and closed his eyes tightly as the pain washed over him. He heaved and nearly vomited. Blood began to trickle down his face, and he tasted it in his mouth. He tried to spit but only dribbled down his chin onto his tunic. Leto suppressed a whimper, not wanting to give this bastard the satisfaction of hearing him cry out.

'Leave him alone!' Jacob said, his words dull through the ringing in his ears.

'Your turn will come soon enough,' Deric said, pointing the dagger in his general direction.

Leto opened his eyes. He could already feel his right eye beginning to swell. It felt like someone was sticking his head with needles. Again, he turned back to face Deric.

'Your horses, weapons, and supplies are all quality stuff, so I know you're rich,' Deric continued. 'So, I'll ask you again, what's your real name?'

'Maybe we stole them,' Leto quipped.

'You aren't smart enough to steal anything,' Deric laughed. 'Now answer my fucking question, boy.'

Deric waited expectantly as Leto glared at him for a few moments before turning his head away. This bandit wouldn't believe him even if he told the truth.

'Ignore me, will you?' Deric said.

Leto glimpsed a flicker of movement out of the corner of his eye.

'No ... '

... and then, blackness.

17

REGAN

Across his desk stood his second wife, and his eldest son from his first wife. Neither of them would have been his first or second choice, but given the limited timeframe, he couldn't wait for anyone more suitable. His insufferable brother had gotten himself killed, and extracting blood from a stone would be easier than convincing Rainer White to leave Sisters End.

Cedric hadn't proved himself yet, but Regan couldn't question his loyalty, and he would do as ordered. Lennane made some of his so-called advisors seem like idiots, having provided him with elegant solutions to some of his recent problems. However, Regan suspected her intentions weren't entirely selfless. He also questioned whether he had her complete loyalty. He would need to keep an eye on her.

Furthermore, his wife and son did not get along.

'What the fuck is she doing here?' Cedric had blurted out when he entered Regan's solar and seen Lennane.

'Watch your tongue,' Regan told him.

Regan never used profanities. He didn't see the point of it. It showed either laziness or a lack of intelligence.

'She's here because that's what I want, which should be enough reason for you.'

'Yes, sir,' Cedric said.

Lennane had expressed a similar attitude towards his son, though in not so crass a fashion.

'He's not very bright,' she'd commented before Cedric arrived.

True enough, Regan thought, but he is my son, nonetheless.

'Three of the soldiers who went out with Wes have returned, but nothing yet,' Cedric began his report on the search for the murderer of Steffan. 'However, he has managed to track Uncle Steffan's killers halfway to the Borderlands.'

Lennane stopped pacing. 'Could it have been the prince who killed Steffan? The Watchers saw Jacob leaving the city on the afternoon of the King's death. They could be travelling together.'

'They reported him heading towards Southern Brook,' Cedric countered, 'on an errand for Lord Owen or something, so I doubt it was them.

'Since when does the prince's squire do errands for Owen Redstone?' she sneered.

'Even if he wasn't, he was heading south,' Cedric repeated.

Lennane couldn't conceal her exasperation, and Regan understood. Politics and subterfuge weren't his son's forte.

'Let's wait and see what Wes turns up, shall we,' Regan said, ending the conversation before it descended into a screaming match. 'To the matter at hand, I'll effectively control the realm once I make this move.'

'Don't you already?' Cedric said. 'You have the Ruling Council, the Capitol Guard, and you're the Governor. What more do you need?'

To the average person, Cedric's observations might seem valid.

'You are correct,' Regan said.

Cedric smiled at his father's confirmation.

'Controlling the council is good,' Regan continued. 'However, the Governor cannot make changes to the council.'

'Only the King can do that,' his wife said.

'You're going to be King?' Cedric interrupted her, surprised.

'No,' Regan raised his hand, rejecting his son's conclusion.

'Why not?'

'Too much scrutiny and not enough privacy. The King can change the council, but so can the Steward of the Realm.'

Cedric gave him a quizzical look.

'The Steward of the Realm is like a regent but not of royal blood,' Lennane said. 'They can either rule if the King or Queen is not of age, or as now, when there is no King or heir. If the prince is not found soon, we'll have to get his sister back to the capitol.'

'That'll be your job,' his father said.

'Me? Why can't Rainer bring her instead?' Cedric said. 'Just order him to do it.'

'I could order him, threaten him, cajole him, but that's difficult to do using a brief message delivered by a bird or rider. I'd have to go down there.'

Regan waited as Cedric processed what he'd just said.

'But then you'd be there and be able to bring her back yourself,' Cedric said. 'So, you wouldn't need to threaten him.'

'I have far too much to do here,' Regan said. 'And threatening one of your most valuable allies is not a good idea. It'll cost us some time, but we'll cope.'

'But winter is closing in,' Cedric said. 'And it'll take nearly half a moon to get there and probably longer coming back with the princess.'

'Those are your instructions, and you will carry them out,' Regan said.

'Yes, sir,' Cedric said, clearly unhappy despite his acceptance.

'At least you'll get to see your betrothed,' Lennane said with a smile, 'and your new father-by-law.'

'Ensure you make a good impression on both of them,' Regan said. 'This alliance is important. Remember, one day, Whitehall will be yours.'

Cedric's mood seemed to lighten at the prospect. 'I'll do as you ask, Father.'

Regan turned to Lennane. 'Get Winston to arrange some food.'

'Certainly, dear,' Lennane said without fuss and left.

Winston would no doubt bear the brunt of her annoyance at being ordered around like a servant, a thought Regan found mildly amusing.

Despite his misgivings about his wife and son, he had committed himself to this path. And because Cedric and Lennane hated each other, he needn't worry that they would conspire against him.

Just after high sun, Regan set out for the council chamber. As usual, a constantly alert Harrow preceded him by several yards. The number of guards increased the closer he got to the chamber. At least the Commander could do some parts of his job properly.

Regan wasn't looking forward to this gathering. While confident the vote would go in his favour, it could not be guaranteed. Whenever Regan had to go against Owen Redstone, it gave him a headache. He suspected this would be no different. It could be worse, given the gravity of the decision.

The guards opened the doors, and Harrow led Regan into the council chamber.

'Stoke the fire. It's cold in here,' Regan said to Harrow, who promptly headed to the pile of cut wood.

Regan noted that Owen Redstone had arrived on time again, sitting in his usual place at the far end of the table. He wasn't sure whether he should be concerned by Owen's newly found punctuality. Whatever his motivation, Regan wouldn't have to worry for much longer.

The meeting began, and the council dealt with several minor issues without any significant disagreements. Baltair Drum, Commander of the Capitol Guard, provided an update on the search for the prince, which impressed nobody. Even Regan thought the lack of progress unsatisfactory.

'He can't have just disappeared into thin air,' said Owen.

'We will find him,' the Commander promised.

'When?' Owen said. 'He could be dead, but you wouldn't know until the next full moon because you're incompetent.'

'That is uncalled for,' Baltair blustered.

'Lord Owen is right,' interjected the High Chamberlain. 'His observations are correct.'

'My men are doing their best,' Baltair said, agitated. 'I repeat, we will find him.'

'Do you have any leads at all?' Arturo asked.

'We only know that his squire headed south the afternoon of the King's death. He told the Watchers he was on an errand for Owen Redstone.'

Baltair looked down the table at Owen. 'What do you have to say about that?'

Regan groaned to himself. The idiot. Accusing a senior member of the Ruling Council was not part of the plan, and of all people, he picked Owen Redstone. He needed to put a stop to this now.

'I think the Commander meant —'

'No, please let me respond,' Owen said, interrupting Regan.

His voice remained calm, but Regan could see the displeasure on his face.

'Firstly, you will address me as Lord Owen or my lord. Do you understand, Commander?' He didn't wait for an answer. 'Secondly, what you have just intimated is so absurd it borders on ridiculous. Why would the prince's bodyguard do anything for me?'

'Yes, why would he?' Clay White said.

To have even Clay White, whose family was Regan's closest ally, question the Commander proved the depth of Baltair's stupidity. Everyone waited for the Commander to answer. Owen leaned forward, placed his elbows on the table, clasped his hands near his chin, and glared at Sir Baltair. Regan also turned to the Commander, interested in what he had to say, but Owen broke the silence.

'Let us assume for a moment that it was true, and I did use Jacob — that's the boy's name. Did you know that, Commander? Let's assume Jacob was on an errand for me. You never know; it could happen,' Owen said, leaning back and spreading his hands, the sarcasm thick as treacle. 'You've known for five days that the prince's squire and closest friend, one who seems never to be separated from His Highness, was seen leaving the capitol by himself after the murder of our King – on an errand supposedly for me.'

Regan could see where this diatribe was going but dared not interrupt. It served Baltair right. You don't implicate someone in a crime without any real or forged evidence, especially not someone like Lord Owen.

'And neither he nor the prince has been seen since,' Owen continued. 'Also, in the five days since, I have not once been questioned by you or any of your men. What does that tell me?'

Sir Baltair opened his mouth to reply, but Owen held up his hand.

'I'll tell you what it means,' his voice a little louder. 'It means that either my knowing of the prince's whereabouts is such a preposterous idea that there was no need to question me, or, and I think is the real reason, that you are inept and should be removed from this investigation immediately, in favour of someone who knows what the fuck they're doing!'

Owen shouted the last few words.

Silence again descended on the hall as all eyes turned to Sir Baltair, whose face was ashen. Maybe Owen's opinion of the Commander wasn't too far from the truth, but the fact remained that Regan needed him at the moment.

'You are correct, Lord Owen,' Regan said, breaking the silence. 'No one here really thinks you are complicit in the prince's disappearance. Emotions are running high, and sometimes people say things they may regret. Isn't that right, Commander?'

Regan had just given the Commander an opening to redeem himself, if only slightly. He'd better not waste the opportunity.

'Yes … yes,' Baltair finally managed to say. 'I apologise if I have caused you any offence, Lord Owen.'

Owen leaned back into his chair, seemingly having accepted the Commander's relatively poor apology.

'But it's been almost a week,' Abbot Alwen said. 'I fear for the prince's safety.'

'Anything could have happened to him,' Bertram Taverner said. 'And I hate to be the one to ask, but what if the prince is dead? Who'll rule then?'

Grumblings of support followed the question from the Master of the Merchant Guild. Regan glanced at Sir Baltair, hoping the Commander had recovered his wits enough to remember the point of this particular meeting.

'Princess Melina?' Alwen said. 'She's next in line and the most logical choice.'

'She's not old enough,' said Arturo Exley. 'And even if she took the throne, she would require guidance until she was of age.'

'Then we'll need to elect a Steward,' Baltair said.

'Isn't this a little premature?' Arturo said. 'The prince's fate is yet to be ascertained.'

'It doesn't matter,' Baltair said. 'If we elect a steward and the prince turns up, the position is revoked automatically when the coronation occurs.'

The Commander had finally gathered his wits.

'Who should it be?' Clay asked. 'One of us, or someone else?'

'The only senior family member left is Finnea, but I wouldn't trust her to wash the vault floor,' the High Chamberlain said.

They all glanced around the table at each other, wondering who would be the first to give their opinion.

'I nominate Lord Regan,' Clay White said.

He glanced at Owen. The Lord of the Shadowlands would either be his only real rival or one of the loudest objectors, but he just sat there, his mood unreadable.

'If no one has any objections or alternatives, I say we vote on it now. Those in favour,' Baltair said, raising his hand.

Regan knew the motion would pass, but that it passed unanimously surprised him. Even Owen had raised his hand, albeit slower than most others. Surely, he knew the possible repercussions.

'Do you accept the position of Steward of the Realm, my lord?' Sir Baltair said.

Regan took a few moments, still distracted by Owen's actions.

'Yes, I accept,' he said. 'I am humbled by the council's show of confidence in me, and I hope I prove worthy.'

Regan did not do humility well, but he tried to sound as humble as possible.

'Congratulations, my lord,' Baltair said and stood.

Everyone else followed suit and applauded, some more enthusiastically than others. Regan likened it to selecting a King, so why shouldn't they celebrate him?

'Thank you,' Regan said and gestured for them to sit. 'But there is at least one more thing before we adjourn.'

He waited until they had all sat before continuing.

'Abbot Alwen, are the arrangements for the King's funeral complete?'

'Yes, Lord Regan,' Alwen said. 'If you have no objections, it will start the day after tomorrow at high sun.'

'Excellent,' Regan said.

He didn't care about the funeral. He'd rather miss it altogether, but being the Governor and now the Steward of the Realm, he would be expected to attend.

'The council thanks you and Lord Exley for their efforts,' Regan said.

The Abbot and the High Chamberlain bowed their heads in acknowledgement.

Regan adjourned the meeting and returned to the Governor's quarters. His plans had progressed as expected, but since leaving the council chamber, he had a nagging feeling that something wasn't quite right. Regan barely noticed Lennane and Cedric when he entered his solar and sat at his desk. They rushed to him as he poured himself a wine and took a long drink.

'Well?' his wife prompted after a period of silence.

'Well, what?'

He wished they'd go away and leave him in peace. He needed to think.

'What happened?' she asked him, concerned.

'Did it work as you thought it would?' Cedric said.

'Everything went as planned,' he said. 'I'm the Steward of the Realm, or at least I will be once Sir Ramin draws up the documents.'

Lennane's concerned expression turned to a smile.

'Congratulations, my love.'

She came around the desk and kissed him on the cheek. She stepped back and the smile disappeared.

'What's wrong?' she said.

Regan didn't realise his concern had been so apparent.

'What do you mean, what's wrong?' Cedric said. 'Father is the Steward. Isn't that what we wanted?'

After all these years, it didn't surprise Regan that Lennane could read his moods so easily, but it still irked him. They both waited for him to explain.

'The vote,' he finally said. 'It was unanimous.'

Lennane laughed. 'Unanimous? Didn't Owen turn up?'

'He was there,' Regan said.

'He's probably given up and knows there's no point in resisting,' she said.

'Possibly.'

Maybe the death of the King and his impotence on the council had broken him. However, Owen didn't even look at Regan after he had adjourned the meeting, which bothered Regan more than he cared to admit. He remembered the end of the previous session as he had left the chamber and felt Owen's glare on the back of his neck, as he often did. This time, the Lord of the Shadowlands just filled his goblet and spoke quietly with the monk, barely acknowledging his existence.

'You worry too much,' Lennane said. 'He's beaten, and he knows it.'

Regan did tend to overanalyse things at times. He liked to cover every possible contingency, and it was because of this attitude that he could now call himself Steward of the Realm.

It would be simpler if the prince did turn up dead. The young princess would be infinitely easier to manipulate, though he couldn't even guess what she would do once she came of age. The girl had intelligence, by all accounts, and if she was anything like her mother, she'd be headstrong as well; a dangerous combination. But they had a few years yet to mould her.

'You're both dismissed,' Regan said.

He needed some quiet time and having them hovering around when they weren't needed, irritated him.

'Lennane, get Harrow to bring some more wine; Cedric, return at dusk.'

'Yes, Father,' he said, glancing at Lennane.

Regan started to sort some letters on his desk but stopped. His wife and son had not moved.

'I said you were dismissed. That means you leave my presence.'

'We have something to tell you,' Lennane said.

We?

Regan indicated his attention.

'Cedric and I,' she continued, 'we know we haven't seen eye to eye on many things over the years, and if I'm to be honest, we don't like each other.'

An understatement if ever he had heard one, Regan thought. Cedric would have put a dagger through her heart years ago if he had given permission, and Lennane would gladly return the favour.

'And we realise that it wouldn't be helpful to you or the family,' Cedric said. 'So, we've decided to put our differences aside and work together to help you.'

Regan looked from Lennane to Cedric, who nodded his agreement.

'Well, this is a pleasant surprise.'

Regan wouldn't rely on this truce for any length of time, but he'd enjoy the peace while he could.

'Now get out.'

This time, they both headed towards the door. Cedric even opened it for Lennane and allowed her through first.

It couldn't possibly last.

18

CONSTANCE

The silence seemed never-ending. Even the servants had stopped moving. The princess stood unmoving, napkin still in hand. Given what they had just learned, this wasn't a surprise, but Constance's concern for Melina overrode her own feelings about the tragic news they had just received. Sir Fergus Trotter, the princess's personal bodyguard, in his usual position several yards behind, moved closer to the princess.

Lord Rainer had invited Princess Melina to dine with them that night. Dinner with the Whites rarely excited anyone, but it had been going as well as expected. Officially, the princess was invited to dine with Lord Rainer whenever she wished. She usually preferred to take her meals in her quarters with Constance and Sir Fergus, but felt obliged to dine with Lord Rainer and his family on occasion, and put up with the overly polite conversation and forced laughter. With expectations satisfied, everyone could consider their duty done.

But not tonight.

The evening had been almost over, and the children had been sent away. Even Margot had been shuffled out the door, much to her chagrin, which had brought a smile to Constance's face. That left Lord Rainer, his wife Mirsilla, his brother Whitman and his wife, Fen, as well as Hamlin and several Whitehall guards. Constance wasn't allowed to dine at the table. She always stood to the side, ready to serve the princess.

'Your Highness,' Rainer had said, addressing her correctly as always. 'I have some sad news from the capitol.'

Melina looked up from the sweet berry cake she had not yet touched. 'What would that be, Lord Rainer?'

It couldn't be that bad, could it? The Lord of Whitehall's expression was more smug than worried, as was Whitman's.

'The King is dead,' he said with what seemed like restrained joy.

Melina bit her lip as the realisation of what he'd said washed over her. She lowered her head and stared at the table.

'When?' her voice almost broke as she put her hand to her mouth.

Constance wanted to go over and hug Melina, but she dared not move.

'Six days ago,' Rainer said.

'Six days?' Sir Fergus didn't hide his surprise.

Being more than five hundred miles from the capitol, Sisters End lived in isolation, with some enjoying it more than others. Travelling to Whitehall from the capitol could take weeks, but information this important should have reached Sisters End before now.

'Yes!' Lord Rainer didn't like being questioned by those below his station, even Noble Guards. 'Six days.'

Hamlin hesitated and glanced at his father before turning to the princess.

'I wanted to tell you earlier, Your –'

'Silence, boy!' barked Whitman White.

'They should have been told,' Hamlin said, defiant.

'I said be silent!' his father admonished him again.

A frustrated Hamlin turned back in his seat, slouching, his head bowed. Melina seemed surprised at Hamlin's further revelation, glancing at him before setting her gaze on Lord Rainer.

'How long have you known?' she said, a slight edge to her voice.

Lord Rainer glanced at his nephew in disgust and addressed the princess again.

'Your Highness, does it really matter?'

Melina jumped to her feet, shoving the chair back across the stone floor, causing a loud, piercing scrape that caused Constance to wince.

And there she stood, napkin in hand, glaring at her host, her face a mask of grief and anger.

'How long?' she questioned him again.

'Four days,' his smug disposition remained unchanged.

'You ... knew for that long and didn't tell me?' her voice louder with each passing word.

Rainer White said nothing, but his contemptuous look concerned Constance.

'What is wrong with you?' the princess railed at him.

Surprise flashed across his otherwise sullen demeanour.

'Well?' Melina demanded.

'Your Highness,' Rainer said. 'It was not my intention to cause you any extra grief. I only wanted to have all the facts before informing you of such a tragic event.'

'Tell me all of it,' Melina said, trembling.

'Maybe that should be for another time,' Rainer said. 'I don't want to burden you further.'

Constance doubted anything could cause her more grief than the death of her only living parent.

'I am not some delicate little flower who cannot hear something they don't want to hear, without running off to their father.'

Rainer's face hardened at the not-so-veiled aspersion on his daughter.

'Fine,' he said. 'I was going to break it to you gently, but since you aren't a delicate little flower, I will oblige you.'

The princess had insulted Margot, but one does not speak rudely to royalty, especially when the King had entrusted to him the safety and wellbeing of his only daughter.

'Be careful with your tone, my lord,' Sir Fergus stepped closer to the princess, who continued to tremble.

Rainer glared at the Noble Guard.

'We don't take kindly to threats here at Whitehall, Sir Fergus,' Whitman White barked. 'I suggest you watch your tone.'

'It was not a threat, my lord,' Sir Fergus said, stepping even closer to the princess. 'Merely some friendly advice.'

'Keep your advice to yourself! And you should remember where you are.'

'Is that a threat?' the Noble Guard asked.

'Just some friendly advice,' Whitman sneered.

It didn't sound very friendly to Constance. Sir Fergus now stood at the princess's shoulder.

'I am well aware of where I am, Lord Whitman. But may I remind my lords that Her Highness's brother is now the King, so it would be in your best interest to –'

'Do not presume to know what is in our best interests,' Rainer White cut off the Noble Guard. 'Now let me tell you and Her Royal Highness what you both are so eager to hear.'

Sir Fergus bristled at the censure, and Constance thought everyone's interests should align with that of the royal family. However, the tone with which Lord Rainer spoke to Sir Fergus and the princess worried her more than what he said.

'The King is dead. Assassinated in the throne room by members of the Noble Guard.'

'You lie!' Sir Fergus accused.

The Whitehall guards tensed at the insult to their liege lord. A couple even stepped towards Sir Fergus, hands on swords. Sir Fergus glanced back, also resting his hand on the pommel of his sword.

Rainer smirked at the reaction of the Noble Guard.

He spread his hands in mock innocence. 'I'm only passing on the information I have been given. I find it difficult to believe it myself.'

'Please advise your men to step back, my lord,' Sir Fergus said. 'I apologise for the slight. Your news took me by surprise.'

Rainer signalled to the guards, who returned to their original positions. They seemed reluctant to do so, which Constance thought strange as Sir Fergus could have killed them both before they had drawn another breath.

'Your apology is accepted this time,' Rainer said. 'Now, as I was saying, The King was killed by members of the Noble Guard.'

Sir Fergus just stood there, silent.

'The assassins were all killed by members of the Capitol Guard. However, it seems the mastermind of this heinous crime is still at large. Lord Regan was elected Steward of the Realm until such time as a new monarch is crowned.'

'The King's son is of age,' Sir Fergus said. 'There shouldn't be any need for a Steward.'

'That would normally be correct,' Rainer agreed, turning his attention back to the princess, 'but Your Highness, Prince Leto is missing.'

'Princes of Avaleen don't just go missing,' Sir Fergus said. 'Was he kidnapped?'

'That was one of the things I was waiting to hear about. Now you know everything I know.'

'Missing?' the princess whispered, her voice barely audible.

Constance took a step towards her.

'Leto … my brother … ' the princess's voice trailed off.

She started to sway, but Sir Fergus caught her before she fell and helped her back into the chair.

'Your Highness!' Constance hurried over to her, ignoring protocol.

Hamlin jumped up and rushed to the princess, getting there just after Constance, with barely a murmur emanating from the others.

'Fetch Maester Vern,' Hamlin ordered a nearby guard.

The guard looked to Lord Rainer, who nodded his assent, and hurried from the room.

'You should take Her Highness back to her quarters,' said Hamlin, who now stood beside her.

Constance barely noticed him.

'Are you alright?' Constance whispered to Melina.

Melina looked up at her, tears trickling down her face.

'They're both gone,' she said, her voice hoarse.

'I know, it's been a terrible day for her. I'm sure she'll feel better after a rest,' said Rainer White, without a trace of concern.

Both Sir Fergus and Hamlin gave Rainer a disdainful look before the Noble Guard bent down and effortlessly lifted the princess out of her chair. Constance blubbered at seeing her like this; small as a child in the Noble Guard's arms.

'She'll be fine, Lady Constance,' Sir Fergus said. 'She's just had a shock. We all have.'

Constance flinched as Hamlin unexpectedly put his hand on her shoulder.

'Sir Fergus is right. Our Maester is one of the best healers in Avaleen.'

Without another word, Sir Fergus turned and made for the door. One of the Whitehall guards had already opened it, so he just walked out with Constance in tow.

'I'll bring Maester Vern when he arrives,' Hamlin said as Constance hurried after Sir Fergus.

The Noble Guard didn't rush, but with his long stride, Constance still had difficulty keeping up without breaking into a run. They eventually arrived at the princess's apartment and proceeded directly to her sleeping chambers. Sir Fergus laid her gently on the bed, and Constance watched over her as the old knight tended the fire.

'Will she be alright?'

'I'm sure of it,' he said.

'I'll stay with her.'

She placed a chair next to the bed.

Sir Fergus stoked the fire and left the room to wait for the Maester. Constance sat and gazed at the princess.

'Connie,' Melina whispered.

Constance slipped off the chair and knelt close to the bed. 'I'm here.'

The princess opened her eyes and glanced from side to side. 'Please tell me it's not true.'

'I'm sorry, Mellie,' she said, almost crying.

Melina turned on her side, brought her knees up towards her chest, and began to weep. Constance went to fetch a blanket from the chest when Melina let out a sorrowful howl. Constance hurried back to the bed and hugged the crying princess, touching her forehead with her own.

'It'll be alright, Mellie.'

She gently stroked Melina's cheek in an attempt to calm her.

'Everything will be alright,' even though she couldn't know the truth of it.

Constance lifted her head at a knock on the door. The door opened and Sir Fergus stepped in.

'The healer is here, my lady,' Sir Fergus said.

A thin man, his hair hanging in long grey wisps, and dressed in a patchy, faded blue robe, entered the bedchamber. He carried a small leather satchel, which he clasped to his side. This is the Maester? Constance and the princess had not needed a healer since they had been at Sisters End, so she'd never met the man. He looked more like a dirty old drunk than Whitehall's best healer.

As he approached her side of the bed, she could see various stains and marks on his robe, and a musty odour hit her as he passed. She didn't want this unclean man touching her mistress. She wanted to tell him to leave, but that would be seen as a discourtesy to Lord Rainer, so she stood back and allowed him to approach the princess. He squatted down near the bed and performed a cursory examination of Melina, who remained curled up, knees to her chest. He reached into his satchel and brought out a small bag tied with a string, which he untied.

'Water!' the healer's croaky voice startled Constance as he held out his hand.

She fetched a cup of water and handed it to him. He took it, sprinkled some of the bag's contents into the cup, and stirred them with a grubby finger. He sniffed the cup as he wiped his finger on his robe and whispered something to the princess. Constance assumed he had encouraged her to drink the concoction. Melina didn't respond to the Maester's urgings. He moved the cup towards her, but she pushed his hand away. He continued to whisper to her and tried again to make her drink, pushing the cup at her face.

'No!' Melina screamed and lashed out with her arm, knocking the cup from the healer's hand onto the floor. 'Get out!'

Maester Vern almost fell backwards as he tried unsuccessfully to avoid the splash from the flying cup.

'Leave me alone!' the princess groaned.

Constance moved past the healer to Melina's side again and knelt, her face close to the princess's.

'Your Highness,' she whispered. 'Please drink what the Maester gives you. It'll help you sleep.'

'Leave me,' she said.

Constance didn't like being sent away, but she had no choice. 'I will come and check on you soon.'

Melina curled up even more and said nothing, so Constance turned to the healer.

'Her Highness desires to be alone.'

'Fine,' he said and shoved the small bag he'd used before into her hands.

She took it, careful not to touch his grimy skin.

'One pinch a day should do it. She's small, so no more than two,' he said and hurried out of the room.

She glanced at Melina and hesitated, then followed the healer out, surprised to see that he had already reached the main door as she exited the bedchamber, only glimpsing his heels as he disappeared into the corridor. She went to the hearth where Sir Fergus stood.

'That man is so rude. I'm surprised –' she stopped as Hamlin stepped into view from behind Sir Fergus.

She'd forgotten Hamlin had been the one who summoned Maester Vern. Also, she wanted to keep their liaison secret, so she had to treat him like any other member of the White family.

'I'm sorry, my lord,' she stammered. 'But he –'

'No need to apologise,' he said. 'Maester Vern does not have the best bedside manner. My uncle constantly tells him to bathe, but he does know what he's doing.'

'You are too kind.'

'How is Her Highness?' he asked, his concern seemingly genuine.

'She refused the potion the Maester tried to give her to sleep, but she is resting.'

'Sir Fergus, Constance,' said Hamlin. 'Let me apologise for my uncle's behaviour. It was not very honourable. I should have told you earlier. I am sorry if this has caused extra hurt.'

'If you don't mind me asking Master Hamlin,' Sir Fergus said. 'Why the delay? I cannot think of any logical reason, nefarious or otherwise.

Hamlin shrugged, 'My uncle doesn't tell me much, I'm afraid, and after today, I'll be lucky if my father doesn't disown me.'

'You're a fine man, my lord,' Constance said, 'and have done nothing to disgrace your family.'

'If anything, it's the other way around,' Sir Fergus said. 'You are an honourable man.'

The Noble Guard were regarded as the epitome of honour in Avaleen and Sir Fergus did not dish out compliments lightly, so approval of any kind from him was considered high praise, indeed.

'Thank you,' Hamlin said. 'Now I must return before my father thinks further ill of me. Sir Fergus, if there is anything I can do, please let me know. Lady Constance.'

Hamlin bowed in her direction and went to open the door, then turned back.

'I will return tomorrow, if you allow me, for an update on Her Highness?'

'Certainly, my lord,' Constance said before realising Hamlin had probably addressed the Noble Guard.

'Umm … with your permission, of course, Sir Fergus,' she added.

Hamlin smiled when Sir Fergus nodded his agreement. After Hamlin had left, the old bodyguard gave Constance a knowing look.

'That was all a bit odd,' he said.

She didn't know what to say or where to look.

'What was?'

He couldn't possibly know about her and Hamlin.

'Young Hamlin offering to help us, knowing the trouble he would probably bring down upon himself. His family don't seem the forgiving type.'

'Maybe that's his way of being polite,' she said. 'He's more decent than the rest of them.'

'You're probably right, but we should now be cautious about whom we trust. Until today, I simply dismissed Lord Rainer as an ungracious host.'

'I don't understand.'

Sir Fergus beckoned her closer.

'From this moment forward, we should treat everyone here as an enemy,' he said, his face grim, 'including young Master Hamlin.'

This confused Constance. Hamlin loved her, or at least he had until she'd spurned him. Even so, she couldn't imagine him doing anything to hurt them. However, if Sir Fergus proved correct, they could be in quite a lot of trouble.

For the first time since they had arrived at Whitehall, Constance felt frightened.

19

LETO

Leto's head swam in a haze of misery and pain. He opened his eyes but could only see dull light. His mouth felt as if he hadn't had anything to drink in a week, and his jaw throbbed when he tried to swallow. He grunted as he moved, pain shooting through his arms and back, and the memory of his predicament came sharply back into focus.

His eyes adjusted to the darkness and he realised a sack had been pulled over his head again. His nose wrinkled at the stench of something rotten that was in the sack before. He tried to move again, but more pain flashed up and down his body. He heard some shouting but couldn't make out any words. He tried to flex his fingers but could hardly feel his hands.

'Leto!' a hushed voice said.

The last thing he remembered seeing was Deric's fist.

'Leto!' the voice repeated. 'Are you awake?'

The voice belonged to Jacob, but he wasn't supposed to use his real name.

'Callum,' Leto croaked, his mouth parched. 'It's Callum.'

'It doesn't matter anymore.'

Of course, it did, he thought as some moisture finally began forming in his mouth, making speaking a little easier.

'It matters.'

'I told them,' Jacob said. 'I told them everything. I'm sorry.'

So, the bandits now knew their identities. It didn't worry Leto anymore.

'I'm sorry,' Jacob sobbed. 'They were going to kill you.'

What's done is done, his father used to say. If you can't change it, just deal with it.

'It's alright,' Leto said.

'I'm so sorry,' Jacob whimpered.

Someone ripped the covering from his head. Light flooded his vision, and he clenched his eyes shut. He kept them shut while he took a lungful of fresh air.

'It seems we have a problem, Your Highness,' the now familiar voice enunciating the honorific.

Leto began to open his eyes but still couldn't quite see properly. Had he been unconscious all night? And he couldn't tell if it was morning or afternoon. He blinked a few times, and his vision began to clear.

'What are we going to do with you and your friend?' Deric continued, crouched in the same position as when he'd questioned Leto the night before.

The memory made him wince. He had the dagger in his hand again.

'Some of my brothers think that you're too dangerous to ransom. They say we should just kill you and leave your corpses for the wolves. The others think letting you go is too dangerous, so they also want to kill you.' Deric turned and gestured at Two Chins, who stood only a few yards away, scowling at Leto. 'And my rather large friend here wants to beat the shit out of you first and then kill you.'

'Slowly,' sneered Two Chins.

'Just get it over with,' Leto said.

He no longer cared and refused to play their game anymore. His father never begged in his last moments, so why should he? Tears welled in his eyes.

'Do it!' he yelled at Deric. 'Kill me, you cowardly shit!'

Deric stared at Leto for a moment and raised his dagger. 'Okay, have it your way.'

160

'No!' screamed Jacob. 'Leave him alone!'

'You'll be next, squire boy,' Deric pointed his dagger at Jacob.

He returned his attention to Leto. 'Did you know he cried like a baby before he gave you up?'

'Just kill me and be done with it,' Leto said, wanting all the hurt to disappear. 'Do it, damn you!'

Deric put the dagger to Leto's neck, the metal cool on his skin.

'No!' Jacob pleaded.

Leto wondered how it would feel when Deric dragged the blade across his throat. Would he feel anything at all? The cold steel pressed against his neck, but Deric didn't cut him. Why did he hesitate? Leto opened his mouth to yell at him again, but Deric only grunted.

A moment later, his eyes fluttered and closed. The dagger fell from his hand, and he slumped forward across Leto's outstretched legs. The flight feathers of two arrows embedded in his back pointed to the treetops. The near-silent whoosh of more arrows filled the air, closely followed by light thuds as they hit their marks.

Several more bandits collapsed to the ground. Two Chins lay with his arms splayed, an arrow in his chest and two in his stomach. A couple of bandits emerged from a tent, swords at the ready, only to be pierced by multiple arrows. Sparks flew as one fell face first into the campfire, while the other stumbled back onto the tent, collapsing it.

The shouting and screaming died down as the bandits were either killed or escaped into the forest. Behind him, the sound of boots on dead leaves caused him to ignore the pain and turn, but the dead weight of the bandit on his legs limited further movement. A dozen fully armed soldiers appeared out of the forest to Leto's right. They all had their heads and faces covered. One of them approached Leto and Jacob. Leto flinched at the sudden appearance of another soldier from behind him. He groaned again as pain shook his body, and he dropped his head to his chest in exhaustion.

'The camp is clear, sir,' said the soldier.

'Thank you, Captain,' the well-dressed soldier said. 'Make sure that any who escaped into the forest don't come back and surprise us. If any are still alive, finish them off.'

He squatted in front of Leto as Deric had a few moments earlier.

'Now, who do we have here?'

He sounded young, not much older than Leto, but the other men deferred to him, so he must be the leader of this group. He recognised the emblem on the soldier's steel and leather armour, a white ship over water on a black background. Leto tried to form a smile.

'Look at me,' the leading soldier said.

Leto lifted his head and looked at the soldier. He still had his hood and face covering raised, but the soldier's eyes widened in recognition.

'Shit! Captain, help me untie them quickly.'

The leader unsheathed his dagger and reached above Leto's head as the captain who had spoken before hurried towards Jacob.

The soldier cut the ropes holding up his arms, and Leto gritted his teeth, his shoulders and back protesting as his arms dropped into his lap.

'We've been looking for you,' said the group's leader as he cut the rope binding Leto's hands. 'But we didn't expect to find you here.'

He had his suspicions about the identity of his saviour, however. Leto started to massage some life back into his now unbound hands.

'Which one are you ... Matteus ... Ewen?' he said.

'My apologies,' the soldier said.

He pushed back his hood and pulled down his face covering, revealing a much younger man than Leto expected. His face held a broad grin.

'Finn!' Leto exclaimed.

'At your service, cousin.'

'Help me up,' Leto said. 'And water, we need water.'

He glanced over at Jacob, who had been helped to his feet by Finn's captain and, like Leto, needed some aid in standing.

Finn Kirkwood, the youngest son of his Uncle Malachy, barked an order and led Leto over to the remnants of the campfire, where his men continued to drag away the bodies of fallen bandits. Leto sat on the log and looked at his cousin, whom he hadn't seen for over a year.

'Thank you,' he said.

The feeling had begun to come back into Leto's hands. They stung; he shook them, hoping it would lessen the pain.

A soldier handed a skin of water to Finn, who passed it to Leto. Leto and Jacob drank, spilling in their haste.

'How long have you been out here?' Finn asked.

'Long enough,' Jacob finally spoke, taking another swig from the skin.

Leto drained the skin and wiped his face with his sleeve.

'Your timing was impeccable. How did you find us?'

'We were patrolling the King's Road looking for you, and as we passed through Oldtown on our way back home, we were told that Cross, a notorious bandit in these parts, was in the local inn boning the innkeeper's daughter. We've been after him for ages.'

'Did you get him?' said Jacob, hopeful.

'No,' Finn shook his head, clearly disappointed. 'The informant neglected to mention he had friends. They alerted him as soon as we entered the inn. They nearly killed one of my men, but we killed one and captured another. He's a slippery bastard.'

'He had three with him,' Leto said.

'Yeah,' Finn said. 'The guy with the big scar across his face also got away.'

'Which one did you kill?' Leto said. 'Not the boy?'

'No,' Finn said. 'The big one, but he put up quite a fight before we got him.'

Leto felt relief.

'And it was pretty easy to convince the boy to lead us here,' Finn continued. 'We would have been here earlier, but he got us lost, and we had to backtrack a couple of times.'

'What have you done with him?' Leto asked.

'Nothing yet,' Finn said. 'But now we've killed the rest of this vermin and found you, it's his turn to pay the price.'

Leto remembered Lord Steffan's squire and the price he paid for being in the wrong place at the wrong time. 'You can't kill him, he's just a boy.'

'So?' said Finn.

'I forbid it,' Leto wasn't sure why he went against Finn, who had saved him from certain death.

'You forbid it?' Finn asked, incredulous. 'He's a criminal like the rest.'

'No,' said Leto.

'But-' Finn started to reply, but Jacob interrupted.

'Are you questioning the wishes of your liege lord?' he said, glaring at the young commander.

Finn gave Jacob a haughty look. Leto assumed that Finn had thought he was just arguing with his cousin from the capitol as he had done on countless occasions, not anyone of rank.

'As I was about to say,' Finn said. 'We can't just let him go. If we did, he'd grow up into another Cross, or worse, and that's not in the best interests of anyone.'

He did have a point. Left to his own devices, the boy would probably fall in with other criminals. He'd be lucky if he made it to manhood, especially if Cross found out who'd led Finn and his men to his camp.

'Bring him here,' Leto said.

Finn turned and signalled his captain, who stood nearby.

'You're right. We can't let him go,' Leto added.

'I'm glad you have seen reason, Your Highness,' Finn said, more deferential now. 'But if you don't want us to kill or release him, what do we do with him?'

'He's to be your squire,' Leto said.

'*My squire*? Surely, you're joking?'

'Remember to whom you speak, Sir Finn,' said Leto.

Giving orders like this didn't sit well with Leto, but he'd rather inconvenience his cousin than have the death of another boy on his conscience.

'Err … I apologise, sire,' Finn said. 'But I already have a squire.'

'Now you have two,' Leto said. 'And I expect you to treat him well and train him like any other boy under your charge. Ensure that by the time he's a man, he understands loyalty, knows right from wrong and respects the King's law. Do you understand?'

Finn couldn't hide his dismay but bowed his head in acceptance. 'Yes, sire.'

'I'm sure it won't be that bad, Finn,' Leto said, more conciliatory. 'If he grows up to be half the man you are, he will be well served.'

'I'll do my best,' Finn said as the Captain led the boy to the campfire. He'd been crying and wiped his nose on his sleeve.

'Gomer, is it?' Leto said to the boy, who nodded. 'How old are you?'

'Twelve, I think,' the boy blubbered.

Leto smiled at the answer. 'Gomer, from now on, you will go with Sir Finn and do everything he says. Do you understand?'

'Yes, sir,' Gomer replied and glanced at Finn.

'Good,' Leto said. 'If you behave, he'll treat you well.'

'You aren't going to kill me?' Gomer sniffled and wiped his nose again, this time on his other sleeve.

Leto looked to Finn, who took a moment to get the hint.

'No, we aren't going to kill you,' Finn said. 'Now go with Captain Canto. We'll discuss your new duties later.'

'Yes, sir,' Gomer said.

Leto wasn't the King yet. Time would tell, but he would accept being named as liege lord if Finn followed his first command, given to save the life of this ratty little boy.

'Now that we've sorted that out, do you have anything to eat? Those bastards weren't big on sharing their food.'

Finn glanced at Captain Canto, who nodded and led the boy away.

'How far to Anchorage from here?' Leto sat back on the log.

'Half a day's walk back to Oldtown. We can pick up the horses and ride through the night and be there by mid-morning,' Finn said, 'unless you want to stay at an inn tonight and rest. I can't recommend any of the ones in Oldtown, but I'm sure we could find something.'

Leto didn't want to spend another night on the road if he could help it, even if it meant losing a little sleep. He shook his head. 'We'll make straight for Anchorage.'

'As you wish, sire,' Finn replied. 'If there isn't anything else, I must see to my men.'

Leto nodded, and Finn walked off.

Captain Canto brought Leto and Jacob some dried meat.

'It's all we have, Your Highness,' he said. 'We didn't expect to be away from home for long.'

'This is fine, captain,' Leto said. 'Please let Sir Finn know we'll be ready to leave soon.'

Captain Canto nodded and left. The quicker we get out of this forest, the better, Leto thought as he tore off some of the dried meat. The simple fare tasted like a banquet after his lack of food, his hunger gratified at last. Jacob leaned a little closer to Leto.

'I don't think you're Sir Finn's favourite person right now,' he whispered.

Leto shrugged. 'Do you think you can make it? You don't look too good.'

'If you can, I certainly can.'

They had always competed against each other, in swordplay, archery and even with girls on occasion, and Jacob never liked to be beaten by Leto. However, the way he felt now, Leto wasn't sure he'd make it himself.

Captain Canto approached them again, this time carrying some blades. They had found their swords. Leto had given them up as lost.

'Thought you might want these,' he said with a smile, handing them to Leto and Jacob.

'Thank you, Captain.' Leto voiced his gratitude.

Their daggers and Jacob's crossbow weren't anywhere to be seen, but at least they had their swords. Leto knew that once you had found a good blade with the right weight and balance, replacing it always proved difficult.

After a short rest, they set off through the forest towards Oldtown. Leto and Jacob struggled to keep up, but if anyone noticed, they said nothing.

The group arrived in the town at sundown. Leto and Jacob were given hooded cloaks to keep them warm against the night chill and to cover their faces. Finn managed to find some extra mounts, courtesy of the owner of the Grey Stag, whose daughter his men had saved from Cross that morning.

'I don't think she wanted to be saved,' Captain Canto had said to Leto while they trekked through the forest, and they laughed. 'But I'm sure she won't be entertaining Cross again. In his hurry to escape, he knocked her on her arse. We found her sprawled on the floor, buck naked.'

'Was she alright?' Leto said.

'Didn't hang around to find out,' the Captain said. 'Still fed up he got away.'

They mounted the horses and started towards Anchorage and, hopefully, safety. They rode in silence, using only the moonlight to guide them. They travelled north through the night and most of the next day. Leto could hardly keep his eyes open, so tired that he only vaguely remembered their arrival in Anchorage and being shown to a bed.

Leto woke from his slumber bit by bit, almost as he used to back home, in a soft bed with warm blankets. He sat up, swung his legs off the edge of the bed and glanced around his room. There wasn't much to see: two or three wall-mounted torches that had nearly burned out, and no windows, just a small grate at the top of the opposite wall.

He stood, and his whole body protested as he stretched. He examined his naked frame; a lot of bruises and cuts. He knew his head and neck had copped the worst of the abuse, as it ached to move his head and jaw in any direction.

He relieved himself in the chamber pot, washed his hands and face in the water bowl, and began to dress in the clean set of clothes that had been neatly laid out over a nearby chair. He put on the breeches and pulled on the plain woollen shirt, turning at a knock on the door.

'Come,' he said.

The door opened, and a young man about Leto's age entered. Leto grinned and approached him.

'Egon!'

They embraced.

'It's good to see you, Your Highness,' Egon said.

'Don't give me that rubbish,' Leto said and smiled, pleased to see his cousin. 'You know to call me Leto when we're alone, or with family.'

'After recent events, I wasn't sure how things would be,' Egon said, 'or how you would be, either.'

'I'm still me.'

Leto didn't think he'd changed in the short time since he fled the capitol. He may have lost some weight, but that was about it.

'We all thought you were dead,' Egon said. 'Especially after you didn't show yourself, as expected.'

'I nearly was,' Leto said. 'Tell me what's been happening while I was stumbling around in the woods?'

'I've been instructed to bring you straight to Sir Ewen once you woke,' Egon said.

'Then let's not keep Sir Ewen waiting.'

As he slipped on his boots, which had been cleaned, Leto wondered why he wasn't being taken to his Uncle Malachy.

'How has Sir Ewen been treating you?' Leto said as they made their way through the stone corridors of the keep.

'He's a good knight. I've learned a lot. I'm fortunate to be his squire.' Egon said, clearly respecting his master. 'I never got to thank your father for arranging this for me.'

And now you never will be able to, Leto thought.

'And your sword skills?'

Before Egon became Ewen's squire, they used to practice together. Leto always won, but his cousin's perseverance impressed him.

'Much better,' he grinned. 'Sir Ewen has been teaching me some tricks. I may even be able to challenge you now.'

'We'll see.'

Leto wanted nothing more than to stay in Anchorage for some time, but he had a feeling he wouldn't get his wish. Cobwebs and a thick coating of dust lined the corridors. Before he could ask, Egon stopped, opened a nondescript door, and gestured for him to go through.

Leto entered the dimly lit room. Several men stood between the unlit hearth and a small table bearing a candelabra, the new candles only recently lit. The men turned to face him as he entered. Leto recognised all of them except one, but noted that his uncle was not in attendance. A familiar face came towards him, arms spread wide.

'He's awake, finally!' Jacob said, wrapping Leto in a quick embrace.

'How long did I sleep?'

'Nearly a full day,' another familiar voice said. 'I had Egon check periodically to ensure you weren't dead.'

Jacob stepped aside to reveal his uncle's eldest son, Ewen, a tall, muscular man ten years older and a head taller than Leto.

He moved towards him, and they clutched each other's forearm in greeting. 'Hello, Ewen.'

Leto felt the strength in his grip. Sir Ewen Kirkwood, a master swordsman, possibly the finest in Avaleen, and only bested with the bow by his younger brother, Matteus. Ewen used to spar with him on the rare occasions Leto visited Anchorage or when his cousins travelled to the capitol. Sometimes, Leto forced Ewen to yield, though as he got older, he realised his cousin had let him win.

'It's good to see you alive and well,' Ewen said with a smile, but concern furrowed his brow as he looked at Leto. 'You look like shit, cousin.'

After a few silent moments, Leto burst into laughter, with Ewen and the others joining in.

'And I'm sure I smell like a dog's arse,' Leto said.

He hadn't bathed for a while, so Leto knew he wouldn't be smelling good.

The laughter eventually died down, and Ewen turned to indicate the other two men in the room.

'You know our Guard Commander, Gurney Jansen, and this is my father's chief advisor, Jeremias Roberts.'

'Roberts?' Leto said to the old man, recognising the name. 'Sir Ramin's brother?'

'Yes, sire,' said Jeremias, bowing his head.

'My father held him in high regard,' Leto said.

Jeremias bowed his head again, acknowledging the compliment to his brother.

169

'Commander, what part of the castle is this? It's not the First Hall, that's for sure.'

The First Hall was the original and largest stone building built by the first fleet of refugees that arrived in Avaleen.

'Lord Malachy's orders, sire,' Gurney said. 'He thought that deception was better than a show of force. We are in one of the rarely used lower levels of Shorehaven.'

That explained the cobwebs and dust. However, someone had cleaned both his sleeping chamber and this room. It seemed his uncle had planned this ahead of time.

'Only the people in this room and a few select guards know you're here. Sir Finn and his men also know, but they've been sent out on patrol again, so there won't be any loose tongues in the city for the next few days.'

Leto accepted Gurney's explanation with a nod. 'Did he take his new squire with him?'

'He did,' Ewen said, chuckling. 'But he wasn't too happy about it.'

'Did he tell you why I did it?' Leto said.

'It doesn't matter why. You're now his liege lord above all others,' Ewen said. 'I just think you surprised him. You're no longer the cheeky royal cousin from the capitol who always wanted to spar with his older and significantly more skilled relatives.'

That brought a smile back to Leto's face.

'Would you like to bathe before we begin?' Ewen said. 'I can get Egon to draw you a bath.'

The offer tempted Leto. A long soak in a hot bath sounded appealing, but he wanted answers.

'If you can put up with my stench, I think that can wait.'

'I'm sure we'll manage,' Ewen said, gesturing to the table. 'We have a lot to discuss, it seems. Egon, fetch food and wine and be quick about it.'

Ewen indicated the head of the table for Leto. The others all waited until he sat before they took their seats. Is this how it would be now? Everyone watching his every move, always deferring to him and hanging off his every word? He wasn't sure whether he'd ever get used to it.

'We were all shocked by the events in the capitol,' Jeremias said. 'Young Jacob here has told us some of what happened. We'd like to hear the rest from you if you're able.'

Leto didn't particularly want to tell the story to anyone, but these men deserved to know. But first, he wanted to know why Ewen sat before him instead of the Lord of Anchorage, House Blackwater's closest ally in the north. He should be here.

'Where is Uncle Malachy? No disrespect to you, Ewen, but I expected him to be here.'

'None taken,' Ewen said, his tone, solemn. 'He's in the capitol for the King's funeral.'

'Oh.'

Leto hadn't even given a thought to a funeral for his father.

'It's probably happening even as we speak,' Ewen said.

'Does he even know I'm here?'

'We sent a coded message by bird as soon as you arrived. He'll know soon and will return here as soon as possible. I'm sure he'll inform Lord Owen if he can.'

'Have you heard anything of Melina? Jacob said that Lord Owen would try and get her out of Sisters End.'

Ewen shook his head.

'I'm sorry you aren't able to attend your father's funeral,' Jeremias said.

'It doesn't matter. I'm happy with the memories I have of him. Attending his funeral won't change them.'

Leto didn't see the point of funerals; he hated them. They didn't bring the dead back to life. And being his father's eldest surviving son, Leto would've been expected to lead the procession through the city streets from the Abbey to the crypt. He shivered at the thought.

'We can get the fire lit if you're cold,' Ewen said. 'We didn't know when you'd wake, so we were caught unawares.'

'Yes, this could take a while,' Leto said.

'I'll do it. They've already heard my part,' Jacob said.

His friend stood and headed to the stack of newly chopped wood near the hearth. Egon returned with a tray full of cheese, roasted meat, fruit and bread and a large jug of wine with enough goblets for everyone. He filled the goblets and handed the first one to Leto, who took a generous swig of the excellent wine.

Leto took a deep breath and began his story. It wasn't long before his throat became tight, and he fought back tears when describing his father's murder. No one dared interrupt, and Leto didn't stop, fearing he might be unable to start again. He recounted their slow trek through the Great Forest, up the North Road, their capture and interrogation by Cross and his band of outlaws, and their rescue by Sir Finn. After he'd finished, they all stayed silent for a while, contemplating his story.

'Now I understand why you spared that boy in the forest,' Jeremias said. 'Some men kill because it's easy. Some men kill because they don't know any better. And like you, some only kill when there is no other way. Your father would be proud.'

In his heart, Leto knew he wasn't the type of man who would kill on a whim.

'You can hide here for as long as you wish,' Ewen said, 'but Lord Regan will learn of your location, eventually.'

Leto had never thought he would remain here for long.

'Thank you, but I can't stay,' he said. 'I can't risk Anchorage being marched on by Greythorpe.'

'He wouldn't dare,' Gurney Jansen said.

'He might,' Ewen said, 'and we could hold out here in the castle for a while, but defending the harbour would be impossible. We're thin on allies up here.'

'So, I have to leave and keep the Greythorpes blind, or at least keep their eyes elsewhere,' Leto said.

'Where will we go?' Jacob said.

He looked at his boyhood friend, heartened that wherever he ended up going, he wouldn't be alone.

'I don't know.'

'Pardon me for asking, sire,' Jeremias said, 'but have you considered what you'll do when you stop running?'

A fair question and one to which he had no answer.

'I have no idea.'

'You can't run forever,' the old man said. 'You'll have to stop at some point and make a stand for yourself and the good of Avaleen. Granted, anywhere north of the capitol, including Anchorage, is not the place to do it.'

'Your brother was right about you,' Leto said. 'You are wise. Wiser than a young prince with no clue what's best for himself, let alone an entire realm.'

'He often tells my father things he doesn't want to hear, and they're constantly bickering,' Ewen said with a smirk. 'Truth be told, my father does all the yelling and screaming, and Jeremias waits until he's finished, then tells him what to do. I'm sure he sometimes relents because Jeremias frustrates him with wisdom, logic and stubbornness.'

'You flatter me,' Jeremias said. 'I only offer suggestions to His Lordship. He makes the decisions.'

'Do you have any suggestions for me?' Leto inquired now.

'As Sir Ewen alluded to before, we have too few supporters up here in the north to mount any defence against Lord Regan and his allies,' Jeremias said. 'We have to get you down to the Shadowlands.'

'How do we get there?' Jacob said. 'We can't go anywhere near the capitol. It'll be crawling with Greythorpe spies and patrols, from King Lake to the mountains, and it's pretty much Greythorpe's home territory all the way west to the sea.'

'He's right,' Leto said. 'And we aren't the best at sneaking around avoiding capture.'

Ewen grinned. 'This is the largest and busiest port in Avaleen, and we have one of the biggest merchant fleets, and of course, there's the King's fleet.'

'There's a King's fleet?'

Leto shouldn't have been surprised. He'd heard his father mention the royal fleet before, but he hadn't paid much attention.

'How many?'

'Only forty-three ocean-ready ships at the moment,' Jeremias said. 'We lost nearly a dozen in the past year through storms and misadventure.'

'And they just sit in the harbour waiting for a war?' Leto showed his surprise.

'They're usually used for patrolling the seas close to the harbour, hunting pirates, and occasionally escorting ambassadors or King's representatives to foreign lands,' Jeremias said. 'We even station a few at Cliffs End, but they're currently here for repairs. They were scheduled to return before the next full moon.'

Embarrassed that he had forgotten about the fleet, Leto realised he had much to learn and should have been learning it earlier. Why didn't his father push him harder?

'By ship then?' Leto said.

'You can sail out of the bay, around the peninsula and straight to Cliffs End,' Ewen said.

He made it sound so easy.

'Once you're in the south with allies and a significant army at your disposal, you should be able to force Lord Regan to treat with you,' Jeremias said.

'He wants me dead.'

'Are you sure about that, Sire?' Jeremias said.

Leto nearly reproached the old man, but when he thought about the scene in the throne room, he could only see his father lying there in a pool of blood. He tried to remember exactly what happened this time, going over it in his head several times.

'... and find the boy,' Lord Regan had said.

Leto naturally thought that meant they wanted him dead like his father. Maybe he didn't, and he had been running for no reason, but he found that hard to believe.

'He didn't say the words,' Leto said. 'But there's no way I'm going back to the capitol while he's there. What if he does want me dead?'

'I'm not saying you should go back,' Jeremias said. 'But we do need to know his intentions.'

'Has he declared himself King?' Leto said.

'No,' Ewen said. 'But he did get himself elected Steward of the Realm, which is like being King without actually being the King.'

'I've known Lord Regan for a long time and have dealt with him and his father on many occasions over the years,' Jeremias said. 'He may lust for money and power but he won't just take it. Any honours or titles he receives must be seen as legitimate.'

'Legitimate?' Leto said, incredulous. 'He murdered my father! I was there. I saw it!'

'He's not saying Regan is guiltless. Far from it,' Ewen said. 'But from what you have told us, he's played this politically rather well.'

'He's going to get away with it?' Leto said.

'Not if I have anything to say about it, I promise you that,' Ewen was reassuring. 'But we should wait for my father to return before we make any decisions. He'll know what's been happening and better understand the mood in the capitol. Until then, you should rest and recover your strength.'

Leto had slept for nearly a whole day, and he had only been awake for a few hours, but already he felt weary. Far from being a battle-hardened soldier like Ewen, he thought that by the time this ended, he would be a better soldier – or dead. It seemed daily swordplay with Master Alexi and horse riding hadn't been enough.

Leto had eaten his fill of the food Egon set out and had consumed more than enough wine. He yawned.

'You should go and rest,' Ewen urged him.

Leto nodded and got to his feet. The others stood again, reminding him of his new place in the world. Part of him wished he could be a simple farmer, and all he had to worry about, could be seen from his cottage door. The responsibility for the whole realm already began to weigh on him, and he wasn't even King. Not until the coronation, if that ever happened.

'Thank you, gentlemen,' Leto stifled another yawn.

'One last thing before you go,' Ewen said. 'I respectfully request that neither of you go wandering around the castle without one of us as an escort.'

Too tired to argue, he just nodded.

'Good,' Ewen continued. 'Egon, show the prince back to his chambers.'

Before Leto left the room, he took Jacob aside. They hadn't had a chance to talk since being taken prisoner by Cross.

'You should get some rest as well. You look as tired as I feel. We'll speak later, I promise.'

'We know how to get ourselves into trouble, don't we?' Jacob joked.

'True,' Leto agreed, patting his friend's shoulder. 'But this time, it's not of our own doing.'

He followed Egon through the dimly lit corridors of Shorehaven back to his room. His bed had new blankets, another set of clothes had already been laid out, and the torches burned brightly.

'If you need anything, just ring the bell or knock on the door, and the guard will fetch me or Sir Ewen to attend you,' Egon said.

Leto waved his hand in dismissal, and Egon closed the door behind him. He couldn't be bothered checking whether he had been locked in this little room. He did have a reputation for sneaking out, so it wouldn't have been a surprise, liege lord or not. He undressed and climbed into the freshly made bed. Grateful again for the soft, warm blankets, he felt safe for the first time since fleeing his home.

20

OWEN

The open-top carriage rumbled through the torch-lined streets of the capitol.

The sun had set over an hour ago, and an eerie quiet had settled over the bustling city of nearly one hundred thousand souls. Only the click of hooves against the cobblestones echoed through the streets, as the twelve white horses pulled the carriage bearing the body of King Caleb.

The funeral service had begun at the Abbey at high sun. The King, whose body had been expertly preserved by the brotherhood, had been dressed in a simple robe showing the Blackwater emblem. A plain gold-painted wooden crown, the crown of a dead King, had been placed on his head. He'd been laid out on a solid timber slab and placed on the large stone altar beneath the coloured arched windows in the Abbey's main hall. A dozen Noble Guards protected the body, six on either side of the altar. Abbot Alwen led the service, starting with a recital reflecting on King Caleb's life and accomplishments. Afterwards, the Lords of Avaleen and their families paid their last respects to their King, passing by the altar where his body lay, then the knights and nobles, and finally the commoners.

At sunset, the Noble Guards who stood near the altar unsheathed their ceremonial swords and inserted their blades into holes bored into the edges of the timber slab on which the King's body lay. They used the handles to lift and carry the King out of the Abbey to the waiting carriage, where he would begin his final journey to Riverview Castle.

Owen trudged along the street behind the carriage in which the dead King lay, escorted by the Noble Guard. Their swords remained drawn and would remain so until they reached their destination. They would use them again to lift the King from the carriage to the funeral pyre. Only then would they be sheathed. Owen couldn't see him, but he knew Sir Peyton Holmguard led the procession.

He still felt relief that the Noble Guard had been permitted to participate in the funeral, as tradition dictated. Owen wouldn't have put it past Regan to have replaced them with the Capitol Guard, especially since the official story still held members of the Noble Guard responsible for the King's death. As Steward of the Realm, he could have made the decision himself, but he had put it to a vote in one of the Ruling Council meetings. The vote passed, with only Clay White and Sir Baltair Drum voting against. Regan had abstained, as he usually did now, deciding to vote only on a deadlock. Keeping the Noble Guard from escorting their King to his final resting place would have been an unforgivable insult. Allowing them to take part likely avoided any bloodshed.

Owen would have preferred it if the new Steward of the Realm had nothing to do with the funeral. He walked in the rightful place for a Regent or Steward, just behind the carriage, only ten yards ahead of Owen. It burned him up inside seeing that murdering bastard in a place of honour. He would've liked nothing more than to plunge his dagger through that murderous prick's heart right now, but it would disrespect the memory of the King. It would also get him killed by one of the hundreds of Capitol Guards lining the route.

It had been a long, exhausting day, but thankfully, the castle gate had finally come into view. It would all be over soon. Ever since he had returned to Twin Falls at the start of the summer, a dark, empty feeling had slowly pervaded Owen. It was as though the capitol had sucked the joy of living out of him, and the feeling had worsened since his friend's death.

Unfortunately, he couldn't leave; otherwise, Regan and his cadre would be free to do as they wished. Regan Greythorpe may be the Steward of the Realm, but Owen represented the spirit of the now-absent royal family. When out in the city streets, the people's support for the dead King and concern for the missing prince buoyed his flagging spirits.

'King Caleb was a good man. He will be missed.'

'We pray for the prince's safe return, milord.'

Despite the people's obvious love for the Blackwater family and the King, no one openly disparaged House Greythorpe or Lord Regan. Either the people believed the official story of the King's death, or they feared retribution if they spoke up. Once Leto sat on the throne, Owen would return home as the Lord of Cliffs End again. The thought gave him renewed strength.

He glanced to his right. Abbot Alwen walked alongside him, albeit with a very slight limp, a malady he'd had ever since Owen could remember. Most people saw him as a doddering old fool, but Owen knew better and counted him amongst his closest friends in the capitol.

To his left, Malachy Kirkwood, the Lord of the Borderlands and brother-by-law of the King, seemed lost in his own thoughts. He had only arrived in the capitol that morning, just before the ceremony began; hence, they had not had any time to discuss the current situation, only learning that when Malachy had left Anchorage, the prince had not yet arrived. It didn't surprise Owen, but he had hoped for more.

After paying their respects to the King, the lords and their families gathered in the Cloisters of the Abbey and waited in relative comfort while the rest of the city filed past the altar to glimpse their monarch for the last time.

Even the Cloisters proved unsuitable for conversation for Owen; too many enemy ears. He now classed many of the aristocracy as enemies of Avaleen, with the most dangerous of them ruling unopposed. Yes, he voted for Regan to become Steward and urged his friends in the council to do so too because the result would've been the same anyway. They had been comprehensively outfoxed, and he hoped the unanimous vote would at least confuse Regan.

The procession made its way through the East Gate of Riverview Castle. From this point on, commoners weren't permitted, leaving only nobles and members of the Capitol Guard lining the rest of the route to the central courtyard. The carriage passed through the southeast arch into the castle's inner bailey, turned left and followed the torch-lined paved road that skirted the courtyard. No trees or large shrubs of any kind grew in the courtyard, being grassed apart from a large, paved area to the west and a road down the centre, which Owen thought a shame.

The followers peeled off as the carriage continued down the southern edge of the courtyard. They took their positions in front of the mourners on the western edge of the grassed area near the other Ruling Council members. Over a thousand people would be here now. Much to Owen's chagrin, he had to stand beside Regan Greythorpe and his wife. Thankfully, she'd dressed in a subdued manner today, not in her usual style of dressing like an upmarket brothel madam.

As tradition dictated, the Noble Guard lined the paved roads around the courtyard. No Capitol Guards could be seen, and only Sir Baltair Drum and those performing guard duty for nearby buildings were permitted within the inner castle. All others had to wait in the outer ring of the castle. Owen glimpsed Finnea Blackwater standing on the steps that led up to the royal residence holding the hand of her retarded son, Molan. He never knew what to make of the King's sister-by-law. Even before Lydall had been killed she had rarely been seen after the birth of her son. She hardly attended any family events and refused to appear in public with her husband. Finnea had only attended Leto and Cordelia's betrothal dinner because the King had ordered it. Addwyn had revealed that Finnea had no interest in helping with the wedding even though she had accepted the request for assistance at the betrothal dinner.

Rumours of Finnea's disenchantment with the Blackwaters had flourished. Even more so, since her husband's infidelity and subsequent fathering of two children with his mistress. Despite their illegitimacy, the children were welcomed by the royal family. Owen understood her bitterness towards her husband's family, and wondered again where her allegiance lay.

The carriage and its escorts made a wide arc and stopped near where Owen stood. A large stone structure about thirty feet high, was the only thing at the western end of the courtyard. Its primary purpose was as the base for the royal funeral pyre, but people also used it to take in the view over King Lake and the sunsets in the evening.

The Noble Guards escorting the funeral carriage turned to face the pyre, reinserted their swords into the slots of the timber block, and as one lifted it high, bearing the King's body above their heads. The carriage driver flicked the reins, and the white horses moved forward, heading down the paved road towards the other end of the courtyard. The honour guard, still holding the King above their heads, began walking towards the pyre, with Sir Peyton following. He still had his sword drawn, but now he held it upright with both hands.

As the honour guard carried the King's body to the top of the ramp, Owen again reflected on his friendship with Caleb. Early in their friendship, he had insisted Owen always be straight with him. Even after Caleb became King, Owen never lied to him or held back on his opinion. This irked the bureaucrats surrounding the King, but he didn't care. Sometimes, Caleb would get frustrated with him speaking his mind and admonish him, usually in private.

'Have you ever known me to be anything but direct,' Owen would say.

'Couldn't you be more tactful, at least?' Caleb had said on many occasions.

'Me, tactful?'

Owen would miss all of that.

The honour guard had reached the top of the final ramp, and the Knight-Commander held his sword high above his head. As he brought his arm slowly down, the Noble Guards lowered the King's body to the stone pedestal atop the pyre. They withdrew their swords from the timber slab, turned towards Sir Peyton, and ceremoniously sheathed their weapons. The Knight-Commander nodded at the honour guard, who stacked nearby bundles of dry kindling around the King. They then detached small skin pouches from their belts and poured the oily contents over the surrounding wood. Only then did the Knight-Commander sheath his sword and turn away from the pyre to face the crowd. With their final task for the King complete, the Noble Guard escort started back down the ramp.

A member of the royal family usually lit the funeral pyre, but with the King's children absent and Finnea's lack of interest, it fell to Owen. Even Regan and his allies acknowledged Owen as the most appropriate person to perform the task.

The honour guard reached the bottom of the ramp, made their way down the centre road, and halted in front of the group of mourners. Owen stepped forward, took the lighted torch offered by a Noble Guard, and started towards the timber and stone structure. He made his way up the ramp to the top and stood before the stone pedestal on which his friend rested.

'Goodbye, my friend,' he said quietly and touched the torch to the oil-soaked wood.

Owen turned away as the flames spread quickly around the pedestal and engulfed the dead King. Within moments he could feel the warmth of the fire on his back. With a deep sigh, he descended the ramp to the courtyard below.

He didn't return to his position in front of the mourners. Instead, he continued down the centre road, passed Sir Peyton and the honour guard and towards the stairs at the eastern end of the courtyard, with Archer several steps behind. On reaching the top of the stairs he headed for the wide open doors to the throne room. The guards recognised Owen and didn't move to stop him as he signalled to Archer to wait. He entered alone.

He trudged up to the dais. On the throne sat the King's crown. It was a simple design, fashioned of gold and a few precious gemstones, but devoid of any ornate patterns. Caleb was never an ostentatious King, and his crown reflected that. It would sit there on the throne until the coronation of a new monarch. Once the King's statue had been completed and placed in the crypt, the crown would be placed on its head. He stared at it for a time, watching the flickering reflection of the flames from the fire he'd just lit dance about its shiny surface.

Owen wasn't one for hate. It clouded your judgement, but right now, he could feel the thirst for vengeance growing inside him. He wanted the murderers of his friend dead and buried. He wanted them to feel the pain of his loss and he wanted to inflict it personally. Owen wasn't proud of these feelings, and with the responsibilities he now shouldered he couldn't act on them. So, with great effort, he pushed the loathing and hate aside. The time would come when his enemies would pay for their crimes, but revenge would have to wait.

He turned and strode out of the throne room. Stopping at the top of the stairs, he surveyed the crowd of mourners and the burning pyre beyond, from which flames now rose thirty feet into the air. He took the long way back to his quarters, Captain Archer close on his heels.

Later, he sat at the desk in his solar and gazed into his half-full cup of wine, swishing the scarlet liquid round and round. He'd already dismissed Archer and his body servant, Coen, but not before Owen had him bring the wine. Archer had seemed reticent to leave, but Owen had insisted. He didn't feel like talking to anyone. How many cups of wine had he drunk … five or six? He slugged down the last of the wine and went to refill his cup, but the jug was empty as well. He threw the empty goblet across the room, slumped back into his chair, and wept.

Caleb had been like a brother, and Owen didn't know how to grieve for him. The sobs wracked his body as he longed for Addwyn. He just wanted to hold her. She would know what to say to make him feel better. It had been over a week since his family had left the capitol, but he missed her so much. They'd be well into the Shadowlands by now and in a few more days, would be safely home.

Safe, but for how long? With Regan now ruling Avaleen, and Owen's allies few and far between, things did not look good for House Redstone. If the situation deteriorated further, he would have to either submit to Greythorpe's rule, or fight it. He relished neither choice.

The tears eventually subsided. Owen lifted himself out of the chair and wavered. He stumbled to his sleeping chambers, where he fell fully clothed onto the bed and didn't move. Maybe things will be better in the morning, he thought as he fell into a deep sleep.

Coen woke him up the following day.

'What is it?' Owen mumbled.

'Lord Malachy, my lord,' Coen said. 'He's been waiting nearly an hour.'

Damn! He'd forgotten about it.

'Yes, yes,' Owen said, sitting up.

His head felt like it had been kicked by a mule.

'Why didn't you wake me earlier?'

'You made quite a mess last night,' Coen said, not one to skirt the truth. 'I figured you may need some extra rest.'

He wasn't wrong.

Owen rubbed his temple. 'So why wake me now?'

'Lord Malachy threatened to come in and wake you himself.'

He felt guilty; he had asked to meet Malachy before he returned to Anchorage, and Owen had probably now delayed his departure.

'Tell Lord Malachy that I'm awake and will be out directly. And get me some food,' he added.

Owen made his way to the privy.

On returning to his chambers, he splashed cool water on his face. He attempted to straighten his crumpled clothes but gave up. He considered changing but didn't want to keep the Lord of Ships waiting any longer.

'I'm sorry for keeping you waiting, my friend,' Owen said as he entered his solar. 'I ... err ... had a rough night.'

Malachy approached Owen. They embraced.

'I understand. Yesterday was a trying day for you,' Malachy said.

'For all of us,' Owen said, gesturing to the nearby chair. 'Please.'

Malachy sat, and Owen went around his desk and gingerly seated himself. He still had a headache, and any sudden movements made it worse.

'Still no word?'

Malachy shook his head, his face solemn.

'He should have arrived days ago,' he said.

Even though they had yet to discuss it, Malachy knew the possible ramifications if Leto couldn't be found. Being the brother-by-law of the murdered King placed him on the wrong side of Regan Greythorpe, and Malachy Kirkwood wasn't one to desert his family or allies. Coen entered with a tray of meat, cheese, bread, and two jugs.

'Ale and wine?' Owen said, raising his eyebrows.

'Water and milk,' Coen said, placing the tray before Owen and filling a cup from each of the jugs. 'Would you care for anything, Lord Malachy?'

Malachy shook his head, and Coen left the room.

'He'll turn up,' said Owen, cutting a hunk of cheese from the block and slipping it into his mouth with a piece of bread.

'I wish I had your confidence,' Malachy said. 'The Great Forest isn't safe for those unfamiliar with it.'

Owen wasn't that confident either, but he wouldn't express that opinion out loud.

'There's nothing much we can do for the prince now,' Owen said. 'We'll just have to wait and hope Jacob can keep him alive long enough to get to Anchorage.'

'And if he doesn't?' Malachy voiced what they both thought.

'I honestly don't know,' Owen said. 'But no matter what happens to the prince, we must get the princess away from the Whites.'

'I've been thinking about that,' Malachy said. 'What about Gruffydd? He's the closest ally with any competence near to Sisters End.'

Owen and Sir Peyton had already dispatched a letter to Penn's daughter at Whitehall. It was coded with a message for Sir Fergus, the princess's bodyguard. There was no knowing if it would get through, so Malachy's idea had merit.

Being Addwyn's older brother, Gruffydd Greenwood, Lord of the Greenhavens, could be trusted with this delicate task. A small detachment of soldiers could travel from Forest Keep to Whitehall Castle in a few days.

'I'll draft a message as soon as we're done here. He should have it in a few days.'

'Now, if Leto and Jacob do make it to Anchorage undetected,' Malachy said, 'where do we stand with the heir to the throne under our protection and Regan still the Steward of the Realm?'

'Wherever Leto wants us to stand,' Owen said. 'Or we'd be no better than that Greythorpe.'

'But he's young.'

'He'll take good advice.'

Someone rapped on the door.

'Come,' Owen said.

The door opened, and Archer entered and offered Owen two scrolls. Both had the Steward of the Realm's mark on the wax seals, but one of the scrolls also had an X marked on it.

'What's this?' Owen asked as he took the scrolls, not really expecting an answer.

'The messenger instructed me that this one should be opened first,' Archer said, pointing to the scroll with the X.

'Seriously?'

'He was quite specific about it.'

Very odd, Owen thought, and that they both came at the same time gave him pause. He glanced at Malachy, who shrugged. It had to be unwelcome news. What other kind could there be from the office of the Steward? Owen waited until Archer had left the room before breaking the seal of the marked scroll. He unfurled it and began to read. The wording of the short message was self-explanatory and to the point, and he finished it quickly.

He sighed, passed it to Malachy, picked up the second scroll, and broke the seal. He unrolled it to find another short and to-the-point message. After he'd finished reading it, Owen chuckled to himself despite his headache.

'What's so funny? Malachy had finished reading the first scroll. 'Being kicked off the Ruling Council is no laughing matter.'

'No,' he said and handed the second scroll to Malachy. 'But being kicked out of the castle is mildly amusing, you must admit.'

He cut off a chunk of meat and bit into it.

Malachy finished reading the second scroll. 'Petty bastard.'

He'd only recently moved into these quarters and settled in, and now he'd have to move again. That's what annoyed Owen the most about this trivial directive.

'I hate moving.'

'I have a place in the north quarter. It's at your disposal for as long as you need,' Malachy said. 'I won't be using it any time soon.'

'Thank you,' Owen said. 'Though, given my new status, I don't know how long I'll need it.'

Malachy put the second scroll down on the desk. 'Not being on the council will limit your influence with potential allies, and we have few enough already.'

Apart from a few minor eastern and southern lords who happened to be in the capitol, allies of House Greythorpe surrounded and severely outnumbered them.

'I'm sorry to say it Malachy, but I may have to abandon the capitol.'

The words irked him. 'A Redstone never gives up' was a mantra Owen lived by and drummed into his children. He didn't want to leave House Kirkwood as the only major Blackwater ally in the north, but his choices had dwindled significantly.

'Staying could be risky for me, now that I'm an ordinary citizen again.'

'I understand,' he said, though Owen could see his disappointment.

'I'll wait as long as possible before leaving,' Owen said. 'We just have to wait and see when he turns up, but if the Greythorpes find him first, then –'

The door opened without so much as a knock. A tense Archer came into the room.

'What is it?' Owen barked, not in the mood for insolence from his men, even his loyal Captain of the Guard.

Before Archer could answer, Sir Peyton pushed past him and strode into the room.

'I'm sorry, my lord,' Archer said, embarrassed. 'He insisted.'

Archer left and closed the door, leaving a distressed Knight-Commander in the middle of the room.

'That bastard!' Sir Peyton trembled with anger as he approached the desk.

He held a scroll out in front like those Owen had just received. Sir Peyton wasn't easily riled, so what in blazes had Regan done?

'Peyton. What is it?'

Owen stood as Malachy took the scroll from Sir Peyton. The Knight-Commander tried to speak but couldn't form the words.

'By the gods,' Malachy said.

'What the hell has Greythorpe done now?' Owen demanded.

A shocked Malachy looked up from the scroll. 'He's disbanded the Noble Guard.'

Owen dropped back into his chair, stunned. Things had just become a whole lot more dangerous.

21

CEDRIC

They had left Oldtown at dawn, and their mounts required water and feed, but they first needed to find Wes.

Cedric and his men slowed to a trot as they approached High Pass, the natural gorge that cut through the Daylight Mountains. They reached the top of the pass and Sanctuary Cove, the harbour, and the city of Anchorage came into view. The sheer scale of the largest and busiest port in Avaleen impressed Cedric.

Atop the bluff, Shorehaven Keep had stood watch over the harbour for hundreds of years. House Kirkwood called it home, and if you had the name Blackwater or Redstone, you couldn't have a closer or more loyal ally. This meant that despite having a signed letter bearing the Steward's seal, Cedric expected little, if any, offers of aid. He would only show the letter as a last resort.

All but one of the soldiers accompanying Wes had returned to the capitol with a similar message. He followed the trail but had not yet found his uncle's killers. He had almost given up on the old tracker, half expecting him to stumble into Twin Falls empty-handed. However, two days ago, a simple message arrived by bird:

Found him. Grey Stag Oldtown. Ask for Bart.

After notifying his father, Cedric gathered his men and went north. They'd intercepted the last remaining soldier Wes had dispatched with a message that the trail had gone cold. Something must have happened in the intervening days.

Cedric had pushed his men and the horses hard, arriving in Oldtown late on the second day. He left most of his men with the horses at the stables on the edge of the town. Captain Kirby and three other soldiers escorted Cedric to the Grey Stag, a dilapidated timber structure in one of the less desirable parts of town. Cedric couldn't see anything desirable about the place. Even the cracked and faded sign hanging above the door looked as if it would fall to the ground at any moment.

Cedric entered the inn with Captain Kirby and a few of the soldiers. They passed a colossal bald man just inside the door and stopped in surprise. The neat, clean interior of the inn belied the decrepit crumbling facade of the building. It was much better than many places he frequented in the capitol.

'Move on,' the burly doorman said.

Cedric glared at the man, and his bodyguards prepared to draw their swords.

'You're blocking the doorway, sir,' he added, in a slightly more appeasing tone.

Cedric didn't appreciate being ordered around by anyone and had to fight the urge to teach the impudent doorman a lesson. He nodded to Captain Kirby, who went further into the inn and led him towards one of the few empty tables in the far corner. He couldn't see Wes anywhere, as he took a seat at the table, his back against the wall. Cedric liked to be able to see everything and everyone when in unfamiliar surroundings.

'Ale,' Cedric said to the busty young serving girl approaching the table.

'Certainly, milord,' she chirped and skipped away.

'Interesting place,' Captain Kirby noted as he sat across from Cedric.

Cedric now surveyed the inn more carefully, noticing plenty of unsavoury-looking characters. Some teased the serving wenches, others kept to themselves, and there were some rowdy types, arguing or singing. Even so, given the clientele, the place wasn't as loud as he'd expected. In the darker corners of the room, he could see women being groped by the men on whose knees they sat. The staircase near the entrance led up to a large mezzanine and into a corridor beyond. Rooms for rent by the hour, he assumed. The same serving girl placed their ales, large tankards overflowing with froth, before them.

'We're looking for Bart?' Captain Kirby said to her.

'Is he expecting you?'

'He'd better be.'

Cedric would be seriously put out if he wasn't.

'When he comes in, I'll let him know.'

He nodded and took a swig of the ale, which tasted surprisingly good.

'Anything else, milords?' the girl asked.

'What makes you think we're lords?'

Cedric felt his mood lighten, beginning to feel relaxed already.

'Handsome men like you dressed all noble-like,' she said with a smile. 'Don't get your kind in here much.'

Cedric looked her up and down. She had long dark hair and very noticeable curves. Not a classic beauty by any means, but still pretty in her own way. He suspected she may not even be of age.

'If you would like anything else, just ask for Rosie. That's me.'

She giggled and skipped off.

Cedric and Captain Kirby drank ale for a couple of hours, though Cedric suspected he consumed much more than the captain did.

'Where is he?' Tamar said to no one in particular.

The old tracker would turn up eventually, but Cedric did wonder about Bart and what he had to do with anything. He had already decided to spend the night in Oldtown and had sent one of the soldiers back to the stables to tell his men to arrange their lodgings. They would be happy. Cedric had driven them hard, so they'd appreciate a decent rest.

He may even stay here. He eyed Rosie, serving a nearby table. She seemed to get prettier as the night went on. She glanced over and gave him a quick smile. He tried to send Tamar away to be with the rest of the men.

'They need their Captain,' Cedric had said, not sounding too convincing.

'I'm the last person they want to see tonight, except maybe for you,' he said with a chuckle. 'And I'm not leaving you in this place alone.'

Sometimes, Tamar's loyalty could be downright irritating.

'I don't think I'll be alone,' Cedric smiled as Rosie approached the table with more ale. 'Young Rosie here will arrange a room for me. Won't you?'

'Certainly, milord,' she said, placing the ales on the table, 'whatever you need.'

'Excellent,' Cedric said, looking her up and down. 'Fetch me something to eat. The best you have. I don't ... umm ... sleep well on an empty stomach.'

'Yes, milord,' she said and disappeared through the door behind the bar, presumably into the kitchen.

Captain Kirby turned to Cedric. 'Is this wise, sir?'

'Don't try and spoil my fun,' Cedric said. 'And besides, if I don't have a woman now and then, I get in a bad mood, and you wouldn't want that, would you?'

'Err ... no.'

Captain Kirby finished his ale and stood. 'I'll go and arrange night guard duty then.'

'Yes, you do that,' Cedric said and waved him away, preoccupied with Rosie, who'd come out of the kitchen bearing a tray piled high with food.

'Have a pleasant evening, my lord,' Captain Kirby said and left.

Cedric ogled the young girl while she set the food on the table.

'Enjoy it,' she said. 'It's the best in Oldtown.'

She headed up the stairs, flashed him a cheeky smile and disappeared down the corridor. No longer distracted, Cedric turned to the platter of food, which contained fresh bread, roasted chicken, cheese and meat with a thick, dark gravy. He started eating, and before long, had demolished most of it, not realising how famished he had been. Cedric leaned back in his chair and regarded the place. An enigma, for sure, but being a little drunk, he didn't care to think too much about it.

Now, he needed to take a piss, so he got up, went out the front door. He acknowledged the men who'd been selected to guard him for the night with a nod. They followed him as he wandered around the inn to the rear of the building. It backed onto the forest, so he took a few steps into the trees, stopped and relieved himself on a small shrub.

Feeling much better, he made his way back inside. One of the soldiers followed him inside but stayed near the entrance. Cedric wandered over to his table only to find someone sitting in his seat.

'You're sitting in my chair,' he said, trying not to slur his words. 'So, fuck off.'

The stranger looked up at him. The older man, in his late forties or thereabouts, had leathery skin and tousled dark hair.

'Do you know who I am?' Cedric continued.

'You're Sir Cedric Greythorpe, twenty-six, eldest son of the Steward of Avaleen, Lord Regan Greythorpe, heir to House Greythorpe, and you're hunting the killer of your uncle.'

Cedric scratched his chin, taken aback by the stranger's accurate response and unsure what to say next. Damn it to hell, he'd drunk way too much ale, and this bastard took advantage. He turned to signal his bodyguard, Askall, who watched them intently from across the room.

'You won't need him,' the man said. 'I'm Bart. This is my establishment.'

Bart? Who the hell … oh shit, Bart!

'Where's Wes?' Cedric said, spouting the first thought that entered his head, and hoped he didn't sound like a complete idiot.

'He had to go,' Bart said.

'Where?'

'He paid me ten silver sovereigns to wait for you and pass on a message.'

'Well, here I am. Tell me where he's gone.'

Bart gestured towards the chair that Captain Kirby had occupied earlier, and Cedric sat.

'As a man in your position can appreciate, ten silver isn't a lot.'

Even half-drunk Cedric understood the innkeeper's insinuation. 'How much?'

'Your man promised me five gold,' Bart said.

'Five gold sovereigns?'

'He assured me you'd be able to pay.'

'Wes wouldn't agree to such an outrageous amount just to pass on a message?'

'He thought it was important enough,' Bart said. 'But I see you don't believe me.'

'You're a clever one, aren't you?' Cedric said.

The innkeeper seemed to ignore his sarcasm. Maybe Wes did make a deal, but five gold sovereigns sounded steep.

'Let me make you an offer,' Bart said. 'Give me the five that your man promised, and when you find him, if he says the deal was for less, return, and I'll give your five back plus five more for your inconvenience.'

'Ten?' Cedric didn't expect that kind of offer. 'If I find Wes.'

The innkeeper nodded.

'Who's to say you haven't killed and buried him out back somewhere?'

'If I began killing my patrons, my business wouldn't last long, would it?'

Cedric didn't have anything to lose.

'Sure, why not.'

'Let's drink on it,' Bart signalled the bar, and within moments, a serving girl delivered two cups of ale to the table.

They lifted their cups, saluted each other, and took a long drink.

'I'll send my captain to get the money in the morning, then we can conclude our business,' Cedric said.

'That will be fine,' Bart said and finished his ale.

'Good.'

Rosie descended the stairs and came up to Cedric.

'Your room is ready, milord,' she said.

'Well then. I must retire for the evening,' Cedric said. 'I'll see you around dawn.'

He jumped up and put his arm around the shoulder of the young girl.

'Rosie!' Bart barked. 'Are you showing this gentleman to his room tonight?'

Her smile disappeared, and she glared at the innkeeper. Cedric suppressed a smile at Bart's obvious disapproval. The jealous bastard probably didn't want her to fuck anyone except him. Understandable, Cedric thought as he cast his eyes up and down Rosie again.

Bart sighed. 'This one's highborn, at least.'

Rosie turned back to Cedric, and her smile reappeared. 'Follow me, milord.'

He followed the buxom young wench upstairs, but not before his bodyguard intercepted them and led the way. Askall inspected the room Rosie pointed out and deemed it safe.

'I'll be downstairs if you need me, milord,' Askall said and left.

Cedric wore his light leather armour, so removing it didn't take long, especially with Rosie's help. He sat on the edge of the bed in only his boots, breeches, and shirt. The neat room wasn't huge but had a large rug, and the bed seemed comfortable with clean blankets and feather pillows. The Grey Stag continued to surprise him. Cedric beckoned Rosie to the bed,

She knelt before him and removed his boots, tossing them in the corner where he'd dropped his armour. She went to undo his belt, but he stopped her.

'You first,' he said.

Rosie smiled and stood, and before he could take two breaths, she'd pulled her dress over her head and cast it to the floor. A moment later, the slip also disappeared, thrown carelessly in the direction of her dress. She wore no underwear, and he gazed upon her nakedness. Her full breasts hung down with their large dark pink nipples pointing at his feet. His gaze moved down as he admired her curvy hips and mess of dark curls below her small belly. She had milky white skin, marred by only a few small scars, but this didn't bother Cedric in the slightest.

Rosie grinned. 'Your turn, milord.'

He smiled and stood as she approached him and removed his belt. This time, he didn't stop her. She knelt, undid the buttons on his breeches and pulled them down. She looked up at him and smiled.

He woke just before dawn and rolled over to find her still in his bed, lying on her side facing away from him. He rested his hand on her shoulder, and slid it down her arm, pushing aside the blanket, exposing her arse. A couple of huge bruises on her hip and buttock tarnished her otherwise pure white skin. He wasn't surprised he hadn't noticed them before; half-drunk with only one thing on his mind. He rubbed his hand over the bruise on her arse. She stirred and pushed her hips back against him. He felt a rousing in his loins and, with the bruises forgotten, took her once more in that position.

Afterwards, she dressed almost as fast as she had removed her clothing the night before. She pointed out the privy door in the corner of the room for his use and left the room, promising to return soon.

He dressed, with Rosie bouncing back into the room just as he finished lacing up his last piece of armour.

'My father's waiting for you downstairs, milord,' she said.

'Your what? Father?'

'Weren't you meeting with him this morning?'

'Err … yes.'

Shit! He had just spent the night with the innkeeper's daughter, and it wasn't like he had made a secret of it.

'Why didn't you tell me this last night?'

Bart may demand more than five gold sovereigns for that message now.

'I didn't think it was important,' she said with a smile. 'Would it have made a difference?'

He may have been a bit more circumspect, but probably not. 'Do you sleep with any man who comes through the front door?'

'I like having fun, is all,' she said, 'but I'm very selective.'

'I should go and see your father.'

Rosie led him downstairs to the table he had used the night before, already occupied by Bart and Captain Kirby.

'Milord,' Tamar said.

'Did you have a restful evening?' the innkeeper said.

'Err … yes,' he didn't know what else to say. 'Thank you.'

Yes, thank you for letting me have my way with your daughter.

'I hope you can return sometime,' Bart said, sounding sincere.

'So do I,' Rosie chimed in with a grin.

Captain Kirby suppressed a smile as Bart stood.

'Now that our business is complete, I'll take my leave,' the innkeeper said. 'Rosie, let's leave these gentlemen in peace.'

But I only just got here, Cedric thought as Bart and Rosie left. Captain Kirby informed him that he'd had dealings with Bart in the past and their business was now concluded without paying any more than what Cedric had agreed. If the innkeeper lied, they would return to make him pay. The gold didn't worry him much, but he didn't appreciate being lied to. He might come back anyway, just for a second round with young Rosie.

Cedric's horse came to a sudden halt, interrupting his daydream. Ahead, Captain Kirby was talking to a skinny little boy on the side of the road. The dirt couldn't hide his olive complexion, and his simple clothes were filthy and threadbare, like a little slum rat.

'What is it?' Cedric said, irritated.

'A message from Wes, my lord,' Captain Kirby said.

Cedric sighed. 'Where do we have to go now?'

'Lucky Shag tavern,' Tamar said, 'at the north end of the harbour.'

'He'd better be there.'

Cedric didn't want to be chasing Wes across Avaleen.

Captain Kirby turned back to the boy. 'Well?'

The boy glanced at Cedric and nodded.

'Mr Wes said to bring the lord with the hair like fire to him,' he said.

'How much is this going to cost us?'

If the boy asks for five more gold, he'll cut off the old tracker's balls.

The boy shook his head.

'Mr Wes said I get nothing until you are sitting in front of him,' he said.

'Then you better make sure we find him,' said Cedric. 'Do you have a horse?'

The boy shook his head, and Cedric gestured to Captain Kirby. The boy yelped as the Captain picked him up by the scruff of the neck and lifted him onto the horse, sitting the boy behind him.

By mid-afternoon, they had ridden down the scarp to the outskirts of Anchorage. They stopped at a stable near the harbour, and Cedric, Captain Kirby and a dozen men followed the boy on foot into the docks.

Anchorage Harbour is the busiest port in Avaleen, with scores of vessels of various shapes and sizes docked at one of the dozens of piers.

Cedric's soldiers resorted to shouting and pushing through the throng.

'Make way!' his sergeant yelled continuously.

Sergeant Mason Tolas, a young soldier around Cedric's age but taller, stronger, and meaner, cleared a path, shouting and shoving people aside.

'Move, you dirty bastard,' he shouted at a few who took their time getting out of the way.

Some took exception to being bullied and turned to confront them but rapidly changed their tune when they saw the group of armed soldiers. However, one rude merchant and two drunken sailors ended up in the water after not moving quickly enough for the Sergeant's liking.

They arrived at the Lucky Shag, a dilapidated wooden structure that sat on the edge of one of the outer piers. Cedric, Captain Kirby and Sergeant Tolas followed the boy into the tavern, leaving the others outside.

Unlike the Grey Stag, the Lucky Shag looked as shitty on the inside as it did out, and there seemed to be twice as many people in it than there should be; sailors, merchants, whores, dock workers, soldiers, and no doubt, criminals as well. Cedric scanned the room. A scantily clad woman caught his eye. She led an old sailor behind one of several curtained-off booths at one end of the tavern. Unfortunately, the thin, shabby curtain stopped a foot short of the floor. The sailor's pants dropped to the floor and the whore knelt before him, leaving little to the imagination.

'My lord!' Captain Kirby touched Cedric on the shoulder.

Cedric looked in the direction his captain pointed, towards the opposite end of the room. He nodded and his soldiers began muscling their way through the crowd until they arrived at a small table. The boy broke free from Captain Kirby's grasp and approached the man at the table.

The man blinked several times before looking up at Cedric and across to Tamar. The old tracker looked gaunt and dirty as if he hadn't slept for days.

'Mr Wes, Mr Wes,' the boy said. 'I brought the red-haired lord.'

'Good boy, Turo,' Wes said and fumbled with a small bag, retrieving five silver coins from it and handing them to the boy. 'Make sure you give two to your brother and then get some sleep. Take Bata's place on the lookout at dawn.'

Turo turned, squeezed past Cedric and his men, and disappeared into the tavern crowd.

'Milord,' Wes said. 'Excuse my appearance, but … umm-'

'What do you have for me?' Cedric interrupted the tracker as he took a seat at the table.

'I saw him,' Wes echoed the message he had sent.

Captain Kirby leaned forward in anticipation. 'Lord Steffan's killer?'

Wes thought for a moment. 'No … no, no … not him, though it's possible. But no, I saw his sword.'

Wes closed his eyes. Did he just go to sleep? Cedric grabbed his shoulder and shook him awake.

'Wes! Who have you found?'

'The man had his sword,' Wes mumbled.

'Whose sword?' Cedric began to get frustrated.

'Lord Steffan's, of course,' the old tracker said, as if it could be anyone else's sword.

Now, they were getting somewhere.

'You found his killer? Where is he?'

'I don't know,' Wes said.

Cedric sighed. He could have belted the old man, but he knew it would be a waste of time to question him in his current condition.

'Captain, make sure he has a decent rest tonight. Hopefully, he'll make more sense in the morning.'

Cedric went to leave.

He didn't want to stay in this shithole any longer.

'But I found the prince,' said Wes.

'Prince Leto?' Cedric said and sat back down. 'You saw him?'

The old man could have hallucinated but Cedric needed to know whether he meant the prince of Avaleen or a visiting prince of fucking Tunai.

'Yes, milord,' Wes nodded.

'Tell me –'

Cedric stopped as Captain Kirby put a hand on his arm.

'My lord, I know Wes isn't quite himself at the moment and he may be talking a pile of horse shit, but just in case he isn't, shouldn't we discuss this somewhere more private?'

Tamar had a point. Cedric thought about it for a moment and nodded his assent.

'You and Mason take Wes and find a room in a more respectable establishment, if there is such a thing around here,' Cedric said. 'The quieter, the better. I'll return to the men and tell them what's happening. Once you've found a suitable place, send Mason to fetch me.'

'Yes, my lord,' Captain Kirby said.

Cedric left the captain and the sergeant with Wes and headed out of the inn.

Sergeant Tolas arrived at the stables at dusk and led Cedric back to the docks, but this time, they headed toward piers one and two, the royal docks. Unlike most of the harbour's docking facilities, the royal docks had been constructed of beautifully carved stone and timber and dwarfed everything around them. The Royal Inn, which stood between the two royal piers, sat at the opposite end of the spectrum from The Lucky Shag. The large upmarket three-storey building was frequented only by those who had business at the royal piers, or enough coin. It also had the distinction of being the oldest lodging in Avaleen, trading constantly for over two hundred years in various forms.

This place would cost a fortune, Cedric thought as he and the sergeant climbed the marble stairs to the large entry. He had his father's attitude towards money and would typically have baulked at staying at a place like this. His first thought had been to drag Captain Kirby and Wes out of The Royal and find a less ostentatious place. But he was on an assignment for the ruler of Avaleen, so why shouldn't he afford himself a bit of luxury? Now his task had also become much more important than finding a simple killer, so Cedric decided not to concern himself with money. His father would understand, he hoped.

Cedric followed the sergeant up the main staircase to the first floor and to a room at the end of a long, wide corridor where Captain Kirby sat near the roaring fire.

'Do you know how much this place will cost me?'

The captain jumped up and turned to Cedric.

'You wanted somewhere quiet,' he said, 'and more respectable.'

'Bloody hell, Tamar, look at this place.'

You could fit a small house into this one room, and it had polished timber furniture, lush rugs and elegant candelabras. He could see doors off the main room, probably sleeping chambers, which would no doubt be as luxurious. He could also see the entire harbour through the open shutters, which began to glow with hundreds of lanterns and torches as night descended on the city.

'Given what we need to discuss, it's a relatively small price to pay,' the Captain said.

'It'd better be, or it'll come out of your pay.'

'We can leave and go elsewhere if you wish, my lord.'

The Captain appeared sincere and would pack up and leave if Cedric ordered it.

'No, no,' Cedric relented. 'It's dark now, and I don't want to be wandering the wharf at night. Where is Wes anyway?'

'Already asleep,' Tamar pointed to the nearest closed door. 'The poor bastard had been awake for three days straight. No wonder he was a gibbering mess.'

'Let's hope he remembers what we need to know. If we can get the prince, it would be perfect for me … for us.'

He still felt that his father didn't fully trust him yet, and he had been given a huge opportunity to prove his worth.

Now that he wasn't on the go, he began to feel weary. It had been a long day, and if the old tracker wasn't talking shit, he'd need his wits about him tomorrow. Tamar directed him to the spare sleeping chamber.

'Wake me at dawn,' Cedric yawned, 'or whenever Wes wakes.'

He shut the door behind him, closed the shutters and after removing his armour, lay down and let out a long sigh. He found the bed comfortable, even more so than the one at the Grey Stag, but no Rosie to keep him warm. He drifted off to sleep thinking about the buxom young girl from Oldtown.

Wes didn't rise until well after dawn, much to Cedric's frustration, who had woken and eaten before the sun had risen. He tossed up whether to wake Wes earlier, but Captain Kirby counselled against it. Instead, Cedric filled his time with a walk around the harbour, with only Sergeant Tolas as an escort. As he took in the sheer size of the place, he thought of their small port at home in Hillvale, barely a tenth of the size. When Cedric eventually returned to The Royal, he found Wes awake and eating. The old tracker stood when Cedric entered the room.

'Milord, I apologise for my condition yesterday,' he said, quite distressed.

'If you have the information you claim, all will be forgiven,' Cedric said. 'Now sit and finish your meal. You can talk and eat.'

'Thank you, milord,' Wes said, and sat back down.

Cedric took his place at the table opposite the old tracker and urged Captain Kirby to do the same. 'What makes you think you've found the prince?'

'I saw him, milord,' Wes said through a mouth full of bread.

'Where?'

'Back in Oldtown where I saw Lord Steffan's killer, or at least I thought he was,' Wes said.

'You aren't making any sense,' Captain Kirby said. 'Just tell us everything from when we left you at the site of the killings.'

Wes looked across to Cedric for approval, who nodded.

He swallowed the last of his mouthful and drank his goat milk. 'The day after you left, I found where the killers had gone into the forest. I followed their trail for a while, but tracking someone in the woods is difficult. It took longer than I would have liked, but I eventually found where they camped for the night.'

'They?' Cedric interjected. 'There was more than one?'

'Two,' Wes said. 'And they were heading northeast towards the North Road with the two horses they stole from Captain Wever and the squire. I tracked them south of Riverside but lost the trail.

'I ended up in Oldtown at the Grey Stag. Bart and I go back a long way, so he didn't mind me hanging around. I'd just sent away the last soldier you assigned to me … ummm … his name escapes me now. Anyway, I'd just sent him on his way with the message that I had lost them. I could have returned with him, but I was too disappointed in myself and decided to stay in town a couple more days and see if I could pick up their trail.'

Wes sounded embarrassed as he related that part of his story, but his eyes widened, and a smile appeared.

'Then I got lucky. I was still at the Grey Stag, and a group of men came in with a boy. One of them was huge, and another had a big scar across his face. The third one seemed kind of ordinary, but you could see he was the leader, and that's when I saw it.'

Wes paused and gazed at nothing in particular.

'Saw what?'

'Blood Mercy, milord,' Wes said, his attention flicking between Cedric and Tamar. 'Lord Steffan's sword.'

Cedric didn't care for giving weapons names, so he gave them scant regard. He did appreciate quality weapons, but he thought of them as just tools for combat. He could handle himself in a sword fight, better than most by his reckoning, but he preferred the longbow or crossbow. If you can kill your enemy before they can get near, you'll live longer. A fine mantra to live by, Cedic thought.

'You recognised the sword from across the room?' Captain Kirby said.

'The blue jewel in the hilt was the giveaway. I served with Lord Steffan for over ten years before coming to Lord Regan's service, and he's had the sword for as long as I can remember.'

'How does this relate to the prince?'

Cedric's belief in Wes's claim began to falter. He'd heard that Leto had gone south towards Redstone territory, even though Lord Owen denied it.

'I thought my luck had changed,' Wes said, ignoring Cedric's question. 'A man with Lord Steffan's sword had just come in. At worst, he'd know who gave it to him or who he stole it from; or, he was the killer, and there he was, not thirty feet from me. I watched him, I did. He argued with Bart. I don't know what about, but whatever it was, Bart was furious, and it takes a lot to make him mad. Then this guy went upstairs, and his men sat at a table near the stairs, and before long, they were drinking and carrying on.'

The tracker put down his cup, wiped his sleeve across his mouth, and picked up another chunk of bread.

'I waited and tried to devise a plan to catch him,' Wes continued, 'but less than an hour passed, and some Anchorage soldiers burst in. It was chaos. The guy with the scar shouted a warning and rushed up the stairs, and the big guy attacked them. He knocked a few of them about, but they eventually killed him and rushed upstairs. I heard some commotion, and the soldiers came back down after a while. They were quite irate, so I assumed the others got away, along with the sword. They grabbed the boy and took him outside. I followed them, discreetly, of course. I didn't see their commander, but they were definitely from Anchorage. I overheard some of their interrogation of the boy. He was part of a larger band of outlaws camped about half a day's walk east into the forest and had some rich merchants they would ransom. The soldiers were going to rescue these merchants, it seems.'

'Did you follow them?' said Captain Kirby.

Wes shook his head. 'No point.'

'Why?'

'They had to come back for their horses. If they wanted to be silent, they couldn't take them into the forest. So, I returned to the Grey Stag for some sleep.'

The tracker finished his drink and bit off more bread.

'You're telling us you lost the killer's trail, saw my uncle's sword on someone who was possibly the murderer, lost him as well and then you fucking went to bed?' said Cedric, incredulous.

Wes nodded. 'They returned to Oldtown late the next night, as I knew they would, but with two others. They were hooded, but as they mounted their horses, the hood briefly slipped from one of them, and I got a good look.'

'The prince?' said Captain Kirby, hopefully.

'No.'

'Fuck!' Cedric exclaimed, his patience wearing thin. 'Get to the damn point!'

'But … but the Captain said to tell you everything,' Wes said, confused.

Cedric sighed, his patience nearly at its end.

'Right, fine. If it wasn't the prince, who did you see?'

Wes grinned. 'Jacob Rivers.'

'Are you sure?' Captain Kirby asked.

'I'm certain of it,' Wes said with confidence.

Finally, a piece of solid information they could use. Cedric could hardly contain his excitement at hearing that name. The stable boy and the prince were practically joined at the hip.

'Good man.'

Cedric would catch the snotty little prince and drag him back to the capitol, whether he wanted to go or not.

22

CONSTANCE

A crack of thunder rattled the wooden shutters as Constance tried without success to sleep. The first major storm of the coming winter had arrived earlier than usual, and it had been raining non-stop for days.

She turned her head and looked across at the still-sleeping form of the princess. After receiving the news of her father and brother a week ago, she seemed to have given up and had been inconsolable ever since. She'd hardly eaten or left her bedchamber, and Constance had to practically force her to bathe. She spent most of her time in bed but didn't sleep. The rest of the time, she sat on a chair in the living room in front of the hearth, staring at the fire, hardly speaking to anyone. Constance received the occasional utterance, but neither Sir Fergus nor Nerys could extract anything from her.

Constance had taken to sleeping in the princess's bed, hoping she could encourage her to sleep. Constance tried everything she could think of. She told her stories, sang to her, and even held and rocked her gently, but nothing helped. Finally, Constance convinced her to take the sleeping draught. Now, if only she could go to sleep herself.

She'd managed to get some rest when Nerys had come in and watched over the princess, but her grief and concern for Melina had made for a fitful slumber. She considered taking some of the sleeping draught herself, but Constance wanted to be ready to attend to Melina the moment she woke. The Maester had said the princess would sleep for a whole day, but Melina had slept the rest of that night, through the next day and now another whole night, and had barely moved.

Constance sighed, opened her eyes and got out of bed. The cold air caused her to shiver, so she slipped a dress over her nightshirt and stoked the fire in the small hearth. She glanced back at the princess and quietly closed the door on the way out.

The coals in the living room hearth still glowed a bright orange, so she added a couple more pieces of wood and left the apartment.

Four guards had now been assigned to guard the princess, and she instantly felt their gaze as she stepped out into the corridor. Neither she nor the princess trusted them, but Sir Fergus had to sleep sometime, so they had to rely on the goodwill of House White for at least part of the day. She descended the stairs to the kitchen, deciding to get something for herself and the princess.

The kitchen buzzed with activity. The staff had the no small task of preparing the morning meals for a castle full of people, so they started very early, with preparation for the midday and evening meals following. They also had to be ready to serve their lord and his important guests any time of the day or night. When she thought about it, Constance realised the kitchen never really closed.

Orvar, the head cook, already barking orders to the kitchen hands, didn't care for her that much, so Constance went straight to one of the other cooks, an older woman with whom she had struck up a friendship.

Elke grinned as she approached.

'You're up early, dear,' she said. 'Hope everything's good with the princess.'

Some didn't care for the Blackwater family in these parts. False rumours began to spread, such as the princess had the black spot, the devil rash, some other exotic fever, or was even at death's door. While gossip about the King's death and the princess's sorrow became the talk of the castle, others, like Elke, always asked after her when they could.

'She's been sleeping, which is good,' Constance said. 'But she should be waking any time now.'

'That's good,' said the older woman. 'Now, what can I get you? I assume you didn't just come down here to chat with old Elke.'

'You aren't that old,' Constance said, enjoying the banter with the woman.

'Look at these wrinkles. They didn't just appear overnight, you know,' Elke chuckled. 'Now hurry and tell me what you want, or Orvar will wonder why I'm talking and not working.'

Constance asked for some meat, bread and cheese, nothing too rich, so early in the morning.

'Just between you and me, I think he's sweet on me, but that doesn't mean I want to be on the end of one of his tirades,' Elke said, laughing as she shuffled away, returning with a tray covered by a white cloth.

She handed it to Constance and leaned a little closer. 'Don't tell Orvar, but I've put one of my special pies in there for you and the princess.'

'Thank you.'

'And make sure that princess of yours eats,' Elke said a bit louder. 'We can't have her wasting away to nothing.'

'I'll do my best,' she said, leaving the kitchen.

With the food tray in hand, she started back up the stairs to the princess's apartment. She took her time, careful not to drop the tray. She thought about what Elke had put under the cloth, and her mouth began to water. Her pies never failed to disappoint, always good no matter what she put in them, whether it be boar, chicken, lamb or even aurochs. Melina had mentioned she may offer the old woman a place in the royal kitchen back in the capitol.

Constance stopped to yawn and continued up the stone staircase, carefully keeping the tray level. She reached the top, turned into the corridor, and yelped in surprise as the tray was knocked from her grasp. It hit the stone with a loud clang, and the food scattered across the floor.

'I'm so sorry, Lady Constance,' a deep, familiar voice said.

She glanced up at her assailant. She usually smiled when Sir Fergus called her a lady. This time, Constance just looked down at the floor and gasped. At her feet lay Elke's pie, upside down but still in one piece. She squatted down and tried to pick it up. She had nearly lifted it to the nearby tray, but it fell apart, splattering on the floor and leaving her with a small piece of crust in each hand.

Constance burst into tears. The King had been murdered, the prince couldn't be found, the princess fell into a melancholy, and now she had dropped this beautiful pie.

'It's just a pie,' he said. 'We can always get another one.'

A Whitehall guard appeared from around the corner.

'What's going on here?' he barked.

'Nothing!' Sir Fergus snapped back. 'Go back to your station.'

The Noble Guard did not like the Whitehall guards either. He found them inept and rude, but he had a well-earned reputation and played on that whenever possible. The guard nodded and disappeared back around the corner.

Constance stood and tried to stop crying, but she couldn't.

'Lady Constance,' the Noble Guard said, placing a light hand on her shoulder.

She stepped forward and hugged him. Being quite a tall man, she barely came up to his chest.

'I'm sorry,' she blubbered.

Caught off guard by her familiarity, he held her awkwardly. Her sobs eventually abated, and she stepped back, wiping away the tears with the sleeve of her dress.

'You must think me a foolish little girl.'

'Far from it. You have been a wonder looking after Her Highness,' he said and paused for a moment, 'but we have a grave problem that we need to discuss with her.'

At the mention of the princess, she stifled another sob and looked up at the old knight. 'What is it?'

'Not here,' he said and glanced down the corridor.

'She's still sleeping.'

'We'll have to wake her.'

It must be serious if Sir Fergus wanted to wake the princess.

She glanced down at the mess on the floor.

'But she'll need something to eat when she wakes.'

'Then let's fix that.'

Sir Fergus escorted her back down to the kitchen, and he went straight to Orvar.

'Lady Constance requires some food prepared for herself and the princess,' he said. 'What do you have?'

Sir Fergus had been a Noble Guard for many years, being older than most knights in Avaleen, but he still had a presence that made others who didn't know him uneasy.

'Err … certainly, milord,' the head cook said.

Knights and nobles rarely came to the kitchen, so a dumbfounded Orvar seemed eager to please.

'And don't forget one of those pies the –,' he turned to Constance.

'Elke,' she said.

He turned back to Orvar. '– the Elke woman makes.'

'Certainly, sir. I won't be a moment.'

The head cook hurried off. He soon returned carrying a silver tray with a matching cover.

'I've even put an extra pie in for yourself, milord,' said Orvar.

'Thank you,' Sir Fergus said. 'You are most generous.'

'Err … a pleasure, milord,' the politeness of the Noble Guard confusing the head cook.

Constance doubted that no lord or knight had ever thanked him for anything, especially not in his kitchen.

'And there's a mess at the top of the stairs. Arrange for it to be cleaned up,' the Noble Guard added.

He picked up the tray and headed out of the kitchen with Constance in tow.

'Let's get back to Her Highness,' he said as they left the kitchen.

'You're up early,' Constance said as they ascended the stairs. 'I didn't expect you until mid-morning.'

It seemed he had been awake for a while.

'I'll explain soon.'

His serious tone halted further enquiries, and she followed him in silence. As they approached the princess's quarters, all the Whitehall guards turned towards them. They recognised them but only partially relaxed. Constance nearly collided with Sir Fergus when he stopped a few yards short of the door and waited.

No one moved.

After a few moments, he turned to face the nearest guard who stood there, his unease increasing the longer the Noble Guard stared. Constance waited in silence. Sir Fergus's gaze flicked to the tray he held, and back to the guard. A few more moments passed, and the guard figured it out and opened the door to Princess Melina's quarters.

'Sorry, sir,' he said, stepping back to allow them through.

Sir Fergus entered the room without a word, and Constance followed. The guard closed the door behind them.

'We need to wake her,' he said, placing the tray on the table.

'She's been sleeping nearly a whole day,' Constance said, 'but I still don't want to wake her.'

'I have word from the capitol,' he said.

'What word?'

'We have to leave,' his voice had lowered to a whisper.

'I don't understand.'

Beckoning her closer, he gestured to a seat at the table. She sat at the proffered chair at the head of the table, and he sat across the corner from her. He leaned closer and spoke in a hushed tone.

'I ... we have to get the princess out of Whitehall and away from Sisters End.'

'Is this something to do with the King's death?' she whispered back.

'It's possible,' he agreed. 'I received a message yesterday evening ordering us to leave.'

Even Constance knew that any messages they received were most likely read by the Whites except for hand-delivered messages.

'How?'

'I received this message through Lady Nerys.'

'Nerys?' she exclaimed.

The Noble Guard raised his hand to quieten her, and she winced at her outburst.

'Nerys, how?' she whispered this time.

'My superiors and I agreed on a code if circumstances arose that required secrecy and it seems that time is now.'

'From the Knight-Commander?'

'Not directly,' he said, shaking his head. 'It would be rather strange for him to send Nerys a message of any kind. I guess her father or Lord Owen sent the warning in cooperation with Sir Peyton.'

'But why Nerys? Why didn't they get Lady Finnea to send a message directly to the princess?' she said. 'Surely, that wouldn't be out of the ordinary. She's her only surviving relative, apart from the prince.'

'I don't know.'

'Are we truly in danger?'

'The Whites are no friend of the Blackwaters, or the Redstones for that matter, and with them being close allies of Lord Regan ... '

He left the rest of the sentence hanging.

'I know. Lord Rainer's bothersome daughter is betrothed to his son,' she said and made a shuddering sound. 'He makes my skin crawl.'

They deserve each other, she thought.

'Be that as it may, House Greythorpe and House White are now bound more tightly than ever. It does not bode well for us.'

'When do we have to leave?' Constance said. 'The princess is not well.'

'Soon, and she won't have a choice. Her life is in danger, and we've already been delayed.'

Guarding the princess could be quite a boring task, even tedious. Princess Melina had a strong will, and she and Sir Fergus had butted heads on many occasions, but usually over insignificant issues with little lasting impact. With her life now at risk, Constance could see the strain beginning to show from the weight of the responsibility he carried.

'Let's wait a little longer before we wake her,' said Constance. 'Then we'll talk to her together.'

'Thank you,' he said. 'Her Highness is more likely to listen to you than a grumpy old man like me.'

She dragged the food tray closer to herself and removed the lid. The smell of the fresh bread and pies assaulted her senses.

'Eat something. If what you say is true, we will both need our strength. And one of these pies is yours anyway,' Constance said, managing a grin.

He chuckled despite the seriousness of the situation.

'You are a gem, young Constance. Her Highness is lucky to have you.'

She and the old knight skipped the bread and cheese and went straight for the pies, taking one each, leaving one for Melina.

They ate in silence, savouring the taste of the excellent food. Constance wasn't a big eater, so she surprised herself when she consumed the whole pie. About to take a sip of her wine, she burped instead.

'Oh my,' Constance said, embarrassed. 'I must have eaten too fast.'

Sir Fergus laughed. 'More women should enjoy their food like that.'

They washed down their food with wine, and he suggested Nerys be present when they talked to the princess. Constance offered to fetch her, but the Noble Guard shook his head.

'It won't look out of place me doing it,' he said. 'I'll just be doing my lady's bidding. You wake Her Highness.'

Constance wasn't looking forward to it, but she nodded her assent, and Sir Fergus stood and left. Dawn had not yet come, so he may even have to wake Nerys, and assuming Melina woke at all, it would still take time to get her presentable. Constance entered the princess's sleeping chambers. She retrieved some clean underclothes and a dress for Melina to wear and poured clean water into the wash basin.

She caught herself creeping around the bedchambers to the side of the bed where the princess lay, and felt a little foolish. She didn't need to be quiet now, she thought. There may be a better, less direct way of waking the princess, so she turned and went to the window. She couldn't hear any rain, so she lifted the latch on the shutters and opened the left side, ready to close it quickly if the wind gusted too strongly.

The faint light of the approaching dawn filled the bedchambers and she felt the cool early morning breeze brush passed her. It wasn't too cold, so she opened the other shutter. Dark storm clouds still hung in the sky, and she could see flashes of lightning far out to sea, but she was satisfied that she could safely leave the window open, at least for the moment.

'The storm has passed,' Constance said aloud and returned to the bed. 'It's going to be a beautiful day.'

Melina didn't move.

'Time to wake up.'

She moved towards the bed.

'We must get you up and dressed. Sir Fergus has some news from the capitol.'

The princess stirred but did not wake. Constance regarded the princess. Her serene look couldn't disguise her pale skin and drawn cheeks. She took a deep breath, placed her hand on Melina's exposed shoulder and gave it a short, sharp shake.

'Your Highness. You must wake.'

Melina stirred and mumbled something incoherent.

'Mellie!' she shook the princess again, this time with a little more force. 'Please wake up. We're in danger.'

Maybe the urgency in her voice or what she said got through to her, but Melina's eyes fluttered partially open, still barely slits.

'Connie,' she said, still very sleepy. 'What is it?'

'You have to get up, Mellie. Sir Fergus will return soon. We're in danger.'

'Danger?' the princess's eyes opened wider, beginning to understand what her cousin had told her.

'Yes. We must leave.'

That got Melina's attention. 'Whatever do you mean?' she said as she sat up and rubbed her eyes.

'Sir Fergus has gone to fetch Nerys. They'll be here soon.'

'Nerys?'

Melina yawned.

'He'll explain everything, but you must get ready. You can't receive him in your night clothes.'

The princess gave Constance a sleepy stare.

'Very well,' Melina said and swung her legs over the edge of the bed.

She slipped off the bed onto her feet and stretched. Constance waited only a step away, in case the princess stumbled.

Melina gave her a weak smile and headed for the privy. Constance double-checked the water bowl and grabbed a suitable dress. Melina returned to the wash bowl, glancing across at the open window.

'Close the shutters, Connie,' the princess said as she washed her face. 'It's cold in here.'

After attending to the shutters, Constance lit a couple of the sconced torches and straightened the blankets on the bed.

'How're you feeling?' Constance asked as Melina patted her face with the drying cloth.

The princess stepped closer to the hearth and yawned again. 'Tired.'

She removed her nightshirt, letting it drop to the floor, and Constance choked back a gasp. She'd seen the princess in various stages of undress on many occasions, so seeing her naked wasn't a shock. Melina had always been small but had always eaten enough to keep her developing womanly figure intact. It had been just over a week since she plunged into despair, but in that brief time, her beautiful curves had all but disappeared. Even her arms and legs seemed skinnier.

Constance put aside her dismay at how gaunt Melina had become and handed her some underclothes.

'I hope you're hungry. We have one of Elke's pies waiting for you.'

'I am feeling a bit peckish,' Melina said as she slipped the chemise over her head and brought it down over her thin frame.

Constance held the dress's bodice and knelt in front of the princess. Melina stepped into it and put her arms through the long sleeves as Constance stood and lifted it up and over her shoulders. She moved behind the princess and began to tie the laces on the bodice. She could already see the dress wouldn't fit as it should, but she'd do her best.

'Has something else happened?' Melina said, yawning.

'I don't know,' she replied, relieved that Melina seemed to be taking this situation seriously.

Constance tied the last lace and collected the comb.

The princess sat on the nearby chair, and Constance did her hair. She decided to keep it simple today, a single braid that would reach down to the small of her back. Constance had done this hundreds of times and made short work of it.

'I hope Leto is safe,' said Melina.

They both looked up towards the door at the sound of people entering the living room beyond.

'Let's go and find out,' said Constance and started towards the door, but Melina grabbed her hand.

'Connie, I know I haven't been very easy to be around. I don't know how long it's been since … you know … but thank you for being here for me.'

'I was worried for you, Mellie.'

'I'm sorry,' Melina said as she embraced Constance. 'I love you.'

Constance cared for her royal cousin so much and would do anything for her. 'I love you too.'

They held each other for a little while. Constance broke the embrace and stepped back. She wiped her tears with the sleeve of her dress and attempted a weak smile.

'We had better go, or Sir Fergus will begin to wonder what's taking so long.'

They took a few moments to settle themselves, and Constance opened the door. The princess straightened up, raised her chin, and walked out.

Sir Fergus stoked the fire as Nerys looked on. He put down the fire iron when Melina and Constance entered the living room.

'Your Highness,' he said and bowed. 'I trust you are well.'

'I am, Sir Fergus,' Melina said. 'Thank you for your concern. Nerys, it's good to see you.'

'Your Highness,' Nerys curtsied. 'I'm glad to see you up and about.'

Constance led the princess to the chair at the head of the table and pulled it out for her. She sat and looked expectantly at Sir Fergus, who sat across the table to her left; Nerys sat next to the Noble Guard. Constance placed the tray of food in front of the princess.

'I suggest you start with some plain bread and cheese, Your Highness, before having some pie,' Constance suggested.

Melina ignored her but broke a piece of bread from the small loaf.

'Sir Fergus, could you now tell me what is so important that I had to be woken,' Melina said.

Sir Fergus began to say something but stopped as the princess put the bread in her mouth.

'Well?' the princess said. 'Don't let my eating stop you. We're all friends here.'

'Yesterday evening,' he began, 'I was walking the halls as I do most nights. By chance, I passed Lady Nerys in one of the corridors. We exchanged pleasantries, and as I was about to walk away, she said something that attracted my attention.'

Sir Fergus glanced at Nerys. 'She told me my father sends his regards to you and the princess.'

The princess frowned.

'Is that it?' she said, her mouth full of bread.

Constance had the same thought, expecting something more substantial.

'Your Highness,' he said, 'The Knight-Commander, your father and I came up with a way to secretly pass simple orders if there was no way of sending a message by direct means. One was *Give my regards to Sir Fergus*, which means danger, get the princess away at once.'

Melina stopped eating and sipped her wine.

'As you said, the arrangement was between yourself, Sir Peyton, and my father. My father is dead, so who sent this coded message to you and why send it to Nerys?'

The princess's mention of the King instantly put everyone on edge. Constance glanced at her cousin. There were no tears, just a look of resolve.

'I would guess that the Knight-Commander used Lord Owen or Sir Penn to deliver the message,' Sir Fergus said.

'Do you have the letter?' Melina said.

Nerys nodded and handed a tiny scroll to Sir Fergus, who passed it to the princess.

'It came by raven?' Melina seemed surprised.

'Yes, Your Highness,' Nerys said.

'Lady Nerys, explain to Her Highness about the writing,' Sir Fergus.

'It's not like my father's usual writing style, Highness,' Nerys said. 'It was like he was in a hurry, but he did say he'd write a proper letter soon.'

The princess unfurled the tiny scroll and began reading the letter. Barely three inches wide, it unrolled to about six inches long.

'Don't you see, Your Highness?' Sir Fergus said. 'We must get you and Lady Nerys out of Whitehall immediately.'

'Me as well?' Nerys blurted out.

Melina rolled the letter up and looked up at Sir Fergus. 'Is it strange that Nerys's father would pass his regards on to a princess of the realm who happens to be a personal friend of his daughter?'

'No, Your Highness,' Sir Fergus said. 'But why would I be included in the message? I'm a simple soldier and don't know Lord Owen or Sir Penn. We've met a few times over the years, and I have the deepest respect for them both, but we are not friends.'

The princess had another look at the letter. She rolled it back up and handed it to Sir Fergus.

'You're in grave danger, Your Highness,' he said, returning the scroll to Nerys.

'From what?' Melina said. 'From whom?'

'I don't know,' he said. 'But I trust the Knight-Commander implicitly. He wouldn't send this order lightly.'

'So, what do we do now?' Constance asked.

'Prepare to leave as soon as we can,' he said. 'Unfortunately, Lady Nerys had the letter in her possession for several days before she said anything to me.'

'I'm sorry,' Nerys said. 'I didn't –'

Sir Fergus raised his hand. 'I'm not blaming you, my lady. I'm just laying out the situation as it is.'

'Sir Fergus is right,' Melina said to Nerys. 'You weren't to know.'

Constance stood and refilled everyone's cups with wine.

'Do we just pack up and leave? Where would we go?' Melina said.

'Hampstead Heath,' Sir Fergus said. 'The Greenwoods are close allies of the royal family and the Redstones. Both Lord Owen and Sir Penn married Greenwood women. We could go there and then decide our next step. However, we can't just up and leave, or it would raise suspicions. We'd have to inform Lord Rainer of our plans.'

'We could just say the princess was returning to the capitol to be with her family,' Nerys said. 'That wouldn't seem strange, would it?'

'But Lord Rainer may not let us go,' said Sir Fergus.

'He has to!' Melina barked. 'I am a member of the royal family. He can't order me around like a common kitchenhand.'

'Ordinarily, I'd agree, but Lord Regan is now Steward, so he effectively rules Avaleen. If he has decreed that you are to stay here, Lord Rainer is obliged to obey. And given the relationship between their houses, he would carry out the Steward's order.'

'But I'm a princess of the realm!'

Constance hadn't seen the princess this riled up for a long time. She rarely let her temper show.

'And my brother will be King. The lord of this little backwater will listen to me!'

Constance hoped Leto would be found alive, but there had been no news.

'I hope you're right, Your Highness, I sincerely do,' Sir Fergus said. 'I'm just saying what may happen and why.'

Melina stood. 'Then we'll go and see Lord Rainer.'

Constance stood along with Nerys and Sir Fergus.

'Right now?' Sir Fergus said. 'Are you sure, Your Highness?'

'I'm still a princess, so he will see me now,' Melina said.

Constance fetched their cloaks, helped the princess into hers, and started putting on her own.

'Connie,' Melina said. 'You stay here. Sir Fergus and I will handle this.'

'But –' Constance began to plead.

'Look at you. You can hardly keep your eyes open,' Melina said. 'If we must leave in a hurry, I'll need you awake.'

Constance had slept little the last few days, and now that it had been said aloud, she felt the weariness wash over her. At least Melina was awake and acting more like her usual self now, so she herself might be able to rest.

'Yes, Your Highness,' she said.

'Sir Fergus, we should go and pay Lord Rainer a visit,' Melina said. 'We'll take Nerys back to her room on the way.'

Sir Fergus followed the princess to the door.

'Good luck,' Constance said, hopeful, despite knowing the likely outcome.

Sir Fergus acknowledged her wishes and opened the door. Melina and Nerys walked out, and the Noble Guard followed, closing the door behind him. Constance stood in the middle of the room, holding her cloak. It was so quiet now. She entered her sleeping chambers, a small room near the princess's and closed the door. It was dark, but she didn't bother to light a candle. Still clothed, Constance lay down on the bed and closed her eyes. Maybe she would sleep after all.

23

LETO

Leto couldn't hide his dismay.

'He arrived two days ago,' Ewen said. 'He and his men caused some commotion at the docks, but nothing to worry about. The arrogant bastard finally requested an audience this morning.'

It had been nearly a week since he and Jacob had arrived in Anchorage, hiding in the bowels of Shorehaven Keep. He had just started feeling safe in the care of House Kirkwood and no longer like a hunted animal, when his cousin gave him the news that Cedric Greythorpe had been sighted in the city.

Leto turned from the hearth where he had been warming his hands. 'Two days? You should have told me of his arrival as soon as you knew.'

'I didn't want to alarm you,' Ewen said.

'Does he know I'm here?'

Leto sat back at the table next to Jacob, who had finished yet another plate of food.

'No,' Ewen said.

'The Greythorpes will turn Avaleen upside down to find the prince,' Jacob said, 'and if the son of the King's murderer is in the city, then we should have been told.'

'He doesn't know you're here,' Ewen said.

'It can't be a coincidence he arrived a few days after we did,' Jacob said.

His friend had been taking his responsibility of protecting Leto more seriously than ever, but Leto didn't need his friend and his cousin at loggerheads.

'I thought you might like to enjoy our hospitality unencumbered by worry for a little while longer,' Ewen directed his explanation at Leto. 'At least until I had ascertained the reason for his visit.'

'And?' Leto said before Jacob could direct another uncomfortable question at his cousin.

'He informed me he was here searching for his uncle's killers.'

'But that was us!' Jacob said.

'There's no way he could know that,' Ewen said. 'The rumours say you were headed south, and your encounter with Lord Steffan happened north of the capitol.'

'How can you be sure?' Jacob said.

'Unless you left a letter saying I, Jacob Rivers, killed Lord Steffan, there's no way he could know,' Ewen said, unimpressed.

This had to happen eventually, Leto thought.

'Whether he knows or not, I think it's time we left,' he said.

'But my father will be returning any day now,' Ewen said. 'He'll be able to counsel you better than I on your next move.'

Leto would have loved to see his uncle if only to get news from the capitol, but he had to leave the Borderlands.

'I can't risk it,' Leto said. 'Arrange for a ship to be ready to leave tomorrow night. We'll be on it if your father hasn't returned by dusk.'

'But sire –' Ewen stopped short at Leto's raised hand.

'I've made my decision.'

Sir Ewen suppressed any further objection and nodded his assent.

'Good.'

'Will you go south?' his cousin said.

They had discussed Leto's plans just after he arrived at Shorehaven Keep, and proposed he should sail south, with Cliffs End in the Shadowlands the popular choice. They also considered Greenhavens or

Oakwood at the foot of the cliffs in the northern highlands. All good suggestions, Leto thought, but he had come up with an alternative option.

'Ewen, ensure the ship is a proper ocean-going vessel,' Leto said.

'But we don't need one to get to Cliffs End,' Ewen said.

'We're not going to the Shadowlands.'

'We aren't?' Jacob said, surprised.

'No.' Leto hadn't discussed his choice with anyone, not even Jacob. 'I'm going to the Diamond Isles.'

'Leave Avaleen?' Ewen said, stunned.

'Yes.'

He glanced at Jacob, who stared at him in surprise and confusion.

'You said I, not we,' Jacob said, eventually, 'Don't you want me along?'

'I don't know how long I'll be gone. I didn't want to speak for you.'

Jacob stood without taking his eyes off Leto.

'After all we've been through, you want to cut me loose?'

'No ... no, that's not it. I just want you to have a choice.'

'I'll go anywhere with you, you know that,' Jacob said, almost in tears. 'I'm nothing without you.'

Leto stood and placed a hand on Jacob's shoulder.

'You are far from nothing, and I'd certainly be dead by now if it wasn't for you.'

They embraced.

'I'm glad you'll be with me,' Leto said and stepped back from his friend.

'I doubt anyone could separate you two for long even if they tried,' Ewen said, trying to lighten the mood.

'Ewen, I'll need a list of contacts in the Diamond Isles along with letters of introduction addressed to those who would be considered approachable,' Leto said.

'That depends on your reasons for approaching them,' Ewen said. 'If you want a safe place to ride out the winter, that should be straightforward. My father has built many relationships across the Dividing Sea, in Amberfall, Pinespell, and even further north in the floating cities of Edreyon and Driftview.'

'I don't have enough allies here in Avaleen to challenge Greythorpe,' Leto said as he moved back to the hearth to warm his hands again. 'I need more.'

'You're looking for an army?' Ewen asked, shocked.

Leto glanced at his cousin. 'You don't approve?'

'There hasn't been a foreign army in Avaleen for over five hundred years.'

'If I remember my history lessons, they were invaders,' Leto said, not in the mood to be lectured. 'Any army I bring back will be fighting for me … if I bring one back.'

Leto's plan may not even eventuate, but he had to try.

'You may go,' Leto said to Ewen.

'Sire,' Sir Ewen bowed and left.

Jacob came up to the hearth next to Leto. 'I'll follow you to the end of the world, but are you sure you want to leave Avaleen?'

'Are you afraid?' Leto asked.

'No, I'm not afraid,' Jacob said with somewhat forced bravado.

'I am,' Leto said. 'Afraid I will fail, afraid of making the wrong choices, afraid I'll die without seeing my home again. In answer to your question, I'm not sure, but it's what I've decided.'

'Well, you're pretty new at making real decisions,' Jacob said, forcing a grin. 'You're bound to make a few mistakes.'

Leto just hoped any wrong decisions didn't cost them too much.

'I'm glad you're here. I'll need you to extricate me from any situations my bad decisions get me into.'

Leto smiled back at his friend.

'So, nothing has changed then,' Jacob yawned.

Plenty had changed, but Leto felt reassured that Jacob would be with him on this journey.

As Leto lay in bed trying to sleep, thoughts of the impending journey occupied his mind. Would it be a success? How long would he be gone, and how far would he go? When he had sailed to the Shadowlands as a young boy, it had been his first time on a ship and the furthest he'd ever been from his homeland. Leto had only sailed on the rivers and within

Sanctuary Cove. Now, he had decided to leave Avaleen and sail across the ocean, far away from home and out of sight of land for weeks.

After a restless night, Leto rose before dawn. Now that he'd decided on a course of action, he wanted to get started, but the day seemed to last forever.

It wasn't until mid-afternoon when Leto and Jacob had completed their sparring session up on the northern ramparts, that Ewen finally came to him with arrangements for a ship. Leto lowered his weapon as his cousin approached.

'I thought I was going to have to go down to the harbour and find my own way,' Leto said.

'It wasn't easy to find a ship that would leave at such short notice and with a captain I trusted,' Ewen said, his frustration evident. 'Now, as far as this captain is concerned, he'll be transporting two people to Amberfall as a favour to the Lord of Anchorage, no questions.'

Leto nodded his approval.

'You can board any time after sundown,' Ewen continued. 'However, the captain insisted they won't set sail until just before dawn tomorrow.'

'I want to leave tonight,' Leto said.

'It's too dangerous to sail out of the harbour in complete darkness,' Ewen said. 'Too many ships anchored around the harbour, and if they can't see where they're going … '

'No moon tonight,' Jacob said a few moments later.

'Very well then,' Leto sighed. 'Tell the captain we'll be there an hour before sunrise, and I'll want to be underway immediately.'

'I'll inform him of your plans,' Ewen said, his manner more formal than usual.

Ewen left Leto and Jacob to continue their sparring.

His cousin had insisted that Leto and Jacob dine with him that night. At the nominated hour, Egon came to fetch them from Leto's room, where he'd just taken a hot bath. It could be his last for a while.

'Is it true you're going to Amberfall?' his young cousin said as he led Leto and Jacob through the corridors.

'Good news travels fast.'

'Can I come with you?'

Leto shook his head.

'I don't know how long we'll be gone, and it's a dangerous voyage.'

He didn't want to be responsible for anyone else and glanced at his young cousin.

'I'm not scared,' Egon said.

'Your bravery isn't in question,' Leto said. 'But you've sworn an oath to Sir Ewen.'

'He would release me if you asked.'

'No, Egon. I can't take you with me.'

'Oh,' his cousin's obvious disappointment gave way to nervousness. 'Please don't tell Sir Ewen I asked.'

'Your secret is safe with us,' Leto said and turned to Jacob. 'Right?'

'Not a word,' Jacob said, smiling.

Yet again, they had been hidden away from everyone else, though this time they dined in his uncle's private quarters, with Jeremias and Gurney Jansen joining Leto, Jacob and Ewen for the evening meal. As usual, Egon served them all, including Jacob, filling their cups and fetching the food.

'Eat up,' Ewen encouraged Leto and Jacob. 'It could be your last proper meal for some time.'

Now that everything was organised and he had a plan, his appetite had returned, and he took full advantage of the sumptuous meal.

'Are you certain you won't change your mind, sire,' Jeremias said. 'At least until Lord Malachy returns.'

'Yes,' Ewen chimed in, more hopeful than anything. 'Please reconsider.'

Leto had been expecting another plea to delay his departure, but he wasn't angry with them for trying.

'I would have liked my uncle's counsel, but I'm certain the appearance of Cedric Greythorpe in Anchorage isn't a coincidence.'

Leto finished his cup of wine and stood; everyone else did the same. He wasn't sure if he'd ever get used to that.

'I trust I'll see you before I leave?' Leto said.

'Of course,' Ewen said. 'Goodnight, Your Highness.'

Leto woke to a knocking at the door.

'Leto, are you awake?' Egon called out. 'It's time.'

Leto rubbed his tired eyes.

'Come in.'

He got out of bed as Egon entered the room.

'Did I sleep too long?' Leto said.

'It's about two hours until dawn,' Egon said.

For a few moments, Leto thought he had slept through and missed his own boat. After a quick visit to the privy, he dressed.

'Your things have already been taken to the ship,' Egon informed him. 'Sir Ewen says the ship will leave the pier the moment you're aboard.'

'Let's go, then,' Leto strapped on his sword and took the cloak Egon handed him.

He followed his young cousin out of the keep to the stables where Ewen and Jacob were already waiting. Ewen held the reins of a chestnut steed while Jacob checked his mount's saddle. As Leto approached, the dim light of the lanterns revealed another man, one he didn't recognise, who stood waiting beside a third horse. He glimpsed a simple tunic and plain leather armour beneath the cloak. Leto shot a glare at Ewen,

'This is Granger,' Ewen said, 'one of my most trusted lieutenants. He'll safely escort you to the ship.'

Granger acknowledged Leto with a nod. He returned the nod, relieved to know the stranger's identity.

'I guess this is goodbye,' Leto said and embraced Ewen. 'Thank you for everything.'

'Anything for my little cousin,' Ewen said and glanced at Jacob. 'Make sure he gets back in one piece.'

'I will, my lord,' Jacob said, nodding.

Jacob and Granger mounted their horses.

'All going well, we'll be back in the summer,' Leto said.

'Take care,' Egon said.

'I will.' Leto embraced his younger cousin.

229

Ewen handed the reins to Leto, who mounted the horse.

'Good luck,' Ewen said.

The three riders pulled the hoods of their cloaks over their heads and, without a word, directed their mounts out of the stables, Granger in the lead, followed by Leto and Jacob. It took nearly an hour to get to the harbour stables, where they left the horses. From the stables, Leto and Jacob followed the lieutenant to one of the northern piers.

Despite the early hour, people were already milling around, going about their business, though none paid them any attention. Granger pointed to the ship at the end of the small pier onto which they had just turned. They heard yelling and cursing as they neared the ship. Moments later, a small, skinny boy rushed past them.

'And I don't want to see you around here again, you little shit!' a man at the top of the gangway shouted.

The boy sprinted down the pier and disappeared into the morning haze.

Granger signalled to Leto and Jacob to wait as he approached the ship. A sailor met the lieutenant at the bottom of the gangway. Leto could just see the ship in the pre-dawn light; over a hundred feet long, with raised platforms at each end. Jacob nudged him, interrupting Leto's inspection of the vessel. Their escort beckoned, so they headed towards the ship.

'This is Quartermaster Tibbet,' Granger said, gesturing towards the sailor. 'He'll take you aboard and get you settled in. The captain will meet with you once you're underway.'

Leto nodded his acknowledgement, and Granger started back down the pier. The quartermaster stepped back, allowing Leto and Jacob to board the ship.

'Welcome aboard the *Silver Sparrow*, good sirs,' he said as they passed him. and ascended the gangway to the main deck.

From there, Tibbet led them to a small door under the raised aft deck. 'I'll show you to your cabin.'

They followed the quartermaster below deck.

'I hope you don't mind sharing,' Tibbet said. 'We don't usually cater for passengers.'

'That'll be fine,' Leto said.

The quartermaster stopped and opened a small door. 'The captain will see you once we've cleared the harbour.'

They entered the small cabin. It had a double bunk on one side and a chest on the other, which Leto assumed held what few belongings they had.

'Cosy,' Jacob said, clearly unimpressed.

At about five by eight feet, Leto didn't relish staying here for any length of time during the voyage, except maybe to sleep.

'I think we'll be spending a lot of time on deck,' Jacob added, and Leto had to agree.

He didn't want to wait for the captain in the cabin either, so they hid their swords in the bunks, keeping their daggers on them, and made their way up on deck. Some of the sails had been lowered, and sailors rushed around performing various tasks. Leto didn't know much about boats or sailing, but it seemed that whatever the sailors were paid, they worked hard for it. Quartermaster Tibbet intercepted Leto and Jacob and, with an exasperated sigh, ushered them up to the forecastle, out of the way of the working sailors.

The *Silver Sparrow* slipped by the other ships anchored in the harbour. It wasn't long before they had cleared the port and were into the deep water of Sanctuary Cove.

'I can't believe we're doing this,' Jacob said.

Leto looked back towards Anchorage.

'Me neither.'

Leto pushed back his hood once they cleared the outer harbour. Jacob did the same, and they watched the sun rise over Shorehaven Keep in silence. With a tinge of sadness, Leto realised it would be the last time he'd see an Avaleen sunrise for a while. He leaned on the railing and looked forward. The Sand Cliffs loomed large to the north, and in the distance, he could see the top of The Cut, where the bay opened into the ocean. It would take the best part of a day to reach it, depending on the wind, and from there, the sunsets would look different.

They stayed on deck, remaining on the forecastle out of everyone's way for another hour before the quartermaster came up to them. A slight man followed him, a shade taller than Leto, with black hair to his shoulders and a wispy beard.

'Good morning, sirs. This is Lars Mellek, Captain of the *Silver Sparrow*.'

Lars Mellek seemed far too young to be a merchant captain.

'Thank you, Jon. You can go now,' his strong, deep voice belied his youthful appearance.

The quartermaster left them alone.

'Thank you for taking us aboard at such short notice, Captain,' Leto said.

'I'll be honest. I wasn't wild about the idea,' Captain Mellek said. 'I rarely take passengers, and I had only half-filled my hold with cargo.'

'What made you change your mind?' Jacob said.

'Our … err … a mutual friend bought everything I had not yet loaded,' the captain grinned. 'Paid a premium price, too. He and my father go back a long way, but this surprised me. You must be very important to someone.'

'Something like that,' Leto said, wary that the captain may ask him for additional compensation.

'Anyway, three extra bodies don't weigh much, and with only half a load, we'll sail through the Torch Gate two days early,' Captain Mellek said, smiling. 'Maybe more if the wind is with us.'

'Three bodies?' Leto's guard immediately went up, and he automatically reached for the pommel of his sword, which wasn't there. 'Who's your other passenger?'

'Why, our mutual friend, of course.' If the captain noticed Leto's discomfort, he didn't show it.

They'd left Ewen and Egon at the stables in Shorehaven. Who could be this mutual friend? Out of the corner of his eye, Leto spied a robed figure ascending the stairs to the upper deck.

Jacob moved between Leto and the two other men.

'Who are you?'

232

'No need to be concerned, Master Mort,' the man pushed back his hood, revealing Jeremias, his uncle's chief advisor.

'What are you doing here?' Leto said as he stepped around Jacob.

'I'll be conducting business in Amberfall for my lord, visiting some merchants, including Captain Mellek's father, if he'll see me.'

'I'm sure he'll make time for you,' the captain said cheerfully, turning to Leto and Jacob. 'I'll leave you now. Enjoy the voyage.'

The captain descended the stairs to the main deck and Jeremias turned to Leto.

'I apologise for alarming you,' Jeremias said. 'My lord sends me on these errands occasionally.'

'Your lord wasn't even in the city … err … ,' Leto didn't want to give away his identity.

'Master Callum,' the old man smiled. 'I've known Captain Mellek since he was a boy, and his crew all know who I am.'

'What are you doing here?' Leto repeated.

'As I said, I'll be meeting with various merchants and traders in Amberfall, and Sir Ewen also thought it prudent to send me to aid you in your negotiations. I have some experience dealing with cities of the Diamond Isles.

Leto wasn't unhappy that Jeremias had come aboard with them. He certainly didn't have any experience in serious negotiation himself, let alone with wealthy merchants or foreign heads of state. He had been so anxious to get out of Anchorage that the thought hadn't even occurred to him.

'Why didn't Sir Ewen just tell me you were coming?' Leto said.

'He was afraid you would reject his offer,' Jeremias said,' and then he would have been forced to go against your wishes and send me anyway.'

Leto shook his head and smiled at his cousin's subterfuge. Perhaps he did need an advisor, though he'd try to remember to have words with Ewen when he returned to Anchorage.

'Ewen is right,' Leto said. 'I'm sure we'll need your help.'

The *Silver Sparrow* continued to sail north towards The Cut. The ungainly formation looked as if the middle part of a mountain had been sliced away, leaving monstrous cliffs on either side of a mile-wide gap of water that spilled out into the sea. It could be intimidating, to the uninitiated. A permanent lookout had been stationed at the top of the overhang on the southern side, known as The Eye of Avaleen, or simply The Eye. It jutted so far out over the water that people believed it would fall at any moment, but it had stood for as long as these lands had been inhabited.

That evening, Leto, Jacob and Jeremias dined with Captain Mellek in his cabin, and to his surprise, they dined well, with quality food and an excellent selection of wine.

'Do you always eat this well, captain?' Leto said.

The captain smiled and finished off his cup of wine.

'Not usually, but Jeremias arranged for some extra special supplies for my inconvenience. Needless to say, the quartermaster was quite pleased.'

'I'm sure the benefit of our being here has more than outweighed your inconvenience,' Jeremias said.

'Hmmm, I don't know,' the captain refilled his cup. 'The girls at Lady Janes are quite beautiful, and I didn't have time to visit.'

Jacob leaned towards him.

'It's a whorehouse,' he said to Leto in a loud whisper.

The others laughed at Leto's perceived ignorance.

'I knew that,' Leto said, laughing along with them.

He had never visited a whorehouse, but he wasn't that naïve. However, it did make him realise that, despite having anything he wanted at his fingertips, he had led a very sheltered life.

With their stomachs full and their thirst well and truly slated, Leto and Jacob bid the others goodnight and returned to their tiny cabin. Leto rolled into the lower bunk and drifted off to sleep before Jacob had barely climbed into the bunk above.

Leto woke to the cabin door being opened with a loud crash.

'Wake up!'

'What?' Leto mumbled.

'Something's happening.'

What could be happening? They weren't expected to sail out of the bay until sometime that evening. Not even the boldest pirate would dare operate this close to Avaleen. Leto listened, hearing only mumbled voices. Probably the crew having an argument or something, he thought.

'Get up!' Jacob shouted.

He fished his sword out from under the bedding and strapped it around his waist.

'Hurry!'

Leto clambered himself from the bunk and rubbed his eyes. Jacob retrieved Leto's sword and handed it to him.

'What's going on?' Leto said as he accepted the sword and began to strap it on.

'We have visitors.'

Leto finished buckling the belt and followed Jacob out of the cabin. They rushed onto the deck to find it full of men, armoured soldiers and unarmed sailors. A sailor's body lay at the feet of one of the soldiers near the forward mast. The soldier now pointed his crossbow at Captain Mellek as more soldiers jumped across the six-foot gap from the other ship, now grappled to the *Silver Sparrow*.

'Now don't do anything stupid, Captain, or you'll end up like your friend here,' the soldier said.

'I'm sure we can come to some sort of arrangement,' the captain said, staying calm.

'Follow me,' Jacob said, pulling Leto up the stairs to the stern railing.

'Hey, you two,' a voice called after them. 'Stop!'

Leto and Jacob reached the ship's stern and quickly realised they had nowhere to run. They turned, and with their backs to the railing, unsheathed their swords and readied themselves. Six soldiers scrambled up the stairs, weapons drawn, but stopped fifteen feet from them and waited.

'Three each,' Jacob said to Leto. 'Sounds fair.'

Leto couldn't tell whether or not Jacob had made a joke. Leto knew he could successfully take on one enemy, probably two since he had forewarning and had his sword ready, but three? Whatever happened, Leto would go down fighting, unlike his father, who had never been given a chance to defend himself. That thought aroused the pent-up fury at his father's death, and he stepped forward.

'Which of you wants to die first?' Leto hissed.

The soldiers didn't move, and he glimpsed another man ascending the stairs to the rear deck.

'I don't want to kill you, Your Highness,' the man said.

He knows!

The soldiers let the man pass and Leto's heart sank at the sight of the shock of red hair. Cedric Greythorpe stopped just in front of the soldiers and held a loaded crossbow at his side.

'I'm here to escort you back to the capitol.'

'He's not going anywhere with you!' Jacob said, stepping between Leto and Cedric, his sword and dagger ready.

'Ah, the stable boy,' Cedric said. 'I've been tasked to bring the prince back to Twin Falls alive, but you … '

Cedric glanced back at one of the soldiers.

'Kill him.'

'No!' Leto screamed and grabbed at Jacob.

With a yell, his boyhood friend lunged forward out of his grasp, but a crossbow bolt thudded into his chest, stopping him in his tracks. He stumbled and dropped his sword as a second bolt pierced his side. Jacob stumbled back against the railing and crumpled to his knees. Leto rushed to his aid, but many hands grabbed him and yanked him back. In moments, the soldiers had disarmed him and held him tight, leaving an injured Jacob at the railing, unprotected.

Jacob managed to stand, supporting himself on the railing. He still held his dagger, defiantly pointing it at Cedric, but blood had begun to appear on his lips.

Cedric raised his crossbow.

'No, don't!' Leto said.

'Coward!' Jacob spat, blood spraying onto the deck.

'I'll do anything,' Leto pleaded. 'I'll come with you.'

'I know you will,' Cedric sneered at Leto and fired his weapon.

The bolt struck Jacob in the shoulder. The force spun him around and he toppled over the railing. The splash as the sea swallowed his boyhood friend could barely be heard.

'Nooooo!' roared Leto. '*Jacob!*'

He would have collapsed right there, but his captors held him upright.

'Too easy,' Cedric said, 'Let's go.'

The soldiers carrying Leto followed Cedric down the stairs to the main deck.

'You don't need to do this,' Jeremias stood in his path. 'Leave the prince here, and nothing will come of this.'

'Get out of my way, old man,' Cedric sneered, shoving Jeremias aside.

'The lords of Avaleen will hear about your actions here tonight,' Jeremias said. 'The Greythorpes will be outcasts again.'

Cedric turned and glared at Jeremias.

'Sergeant, shut him up, permanently.'

A soldier stepped up behind Jeremias, grabbed his head and yanked it back. He dragged his dagger across the old man's exposed throat and blood spurted across the deck. The soldier let Jeremias go, and the old man slumped to the deck.

'How dare you come aboard my ship and perform murder,' Captain Mellek said.

'My advice to you, captain, would be to sail your little ship to wherever you're going and don't come back,' Cedric said. 'And just so you know how serious I am … Sergeant, break one of his legs.'

'You wouldn't dare!'

Several sailors stepped forward to protect Captain Mellek but retreated when the Greythorpe soldiers raised their crossbows. Two of Cedric's men grabbed the captain and held him.

'Do you know who I am?' Mellek yelled.

'I don't care,' Cedric said.

The same soldier who killed Jeremias stepped up and struck the back of Captain Mellek's legs with his sword. The captain crumpled to the deck, and two other soldiers rushed to hold him down.

Cedric stood over the fallen captain, who glared up at him.

'If I see you anywhere in Avaleen again, I'll have you killed.'

'You'll pay for this!' Captain Mellek said.

'I've changed my mind,' Cedric said. 'Sergeant, break both of his legs.'

Leto, so distraught he could barely stand, offered no resistance and the soldiers dragged him across to the other ship. As they hustled him below deck, he heard the muffled screams of Captain Mellek.

He sank to the floor of the tiny, dank cabin, and brought his knees up to his chest. Sobs racked his body.

24

DARIAH

Dariah held her arms out from her sides. 'Tighter,' she instructed her new handmaiden.

'Yes, ma'am,' the girl said and worked on the laces down the back of Dariah's new dress.

Being a lady-in-waiting, the expectation to dress more like her mistress had been made clear to her, so now she required help to get dressed. Gretchen had been promoted to be Lady Greythorpe's handmaiden, so, for herself, Dariah had selected Jane, a recent addition to the Governor's household staff. The thirteen-year-old needed more training, but she learned quickly.

'That better, ma'am?' Jane enquired.

Being referred to as ma'am still felt strange, Dariah thought, as she looked in the mirror. The short-sleeved, low-cut dress, one of the many that Lady Greythorpe had arranged to be made for her over the past weeks, felt so tight she could hardly breathe. However, it did show off her slim figure, and even though she had small breasts, the dress gave her a modest cleavage. She wasn't entirely comfortable showing so much flesh, but she felt obliged to, since Lady Greythorpe wore dresses of similar style.

'Yes, thank you,' Dariah said.

She still preferred combing her own hair, but she let Jane do it on this occasion. The girl needed to learn how to perform her duties, but couldn't if she wasn't allowed. When her hair was done, Dariah left the girl to clean up the room and went to Lady Greythorpe's apartment.

Dariah opened the door without knocking as she usually did and entered the living room. Her mistress wasn't in the main living room, so she headed towards her sleeping chambers. She reached for the door but stopped at the sound of voices from within. Usually, it wouldn't have concerned her, but one of the voices came from a man. Dariah put her ear to the door.

'On my honour, she'll never return to the capitol alive,' the man said. 'But do I have your word?'

'Don't worry,' said Lady Greythorpe. 'You'll be well rewarded, as promised.'

'I'd like a taste of my reward now.'

'I can't. She'll be here soon.'

'Then I can sample you both.'

'She's an innocent one, so I'll need to prepare her,' her mistress said. 'You should go.'

Dariah raced back to the entry door and began to open it. However, the door to the sleeping chambers opened before she could get out, so she closed the door, pretending she'd just arrived. Lady Greythorpe had already led the man into the living room.

'Oh, Dariah,' her mistress sounded flustered. 'You're here.'

'Mistress,' Dariah acknowledged her and glanced at the man standing beside her. 'I can come back later if you wish.'

The man stood over six feet tall, with long, straggly hair and leather armour so poor even Dariah recognised its low quality.

'Is this the one you were telling me about?' the man said, licking his lips.

'Dariah, this is Sir Masten Checker,' Lady Greythorpe said.

'Sir Masten,' Dariah said and curtsied. 'A pleasure to meet you.'

She didn't like the way he was leering at her.

'Oh no,' he exclaimed with a lop-sided smile. 'The pleasure is all mine.'

'Sir Masten,' her mistress said. 'We shall speak again when you return.'

'Yes, we shall,' he said, continuing to ogle Dariah as he spoke.

Dariah shuddered and hoped her revulsion wasn't obvious. His eyes never left her as he headed to the door. Dariah stepped aside to allow him to pass, but he stopped.

'My lady,' he said with a nod.

'Sir Masten,' she said, hoping he wouldn't try and touch her.

Thankfully, he opened the door and disappeared. Dariah shut the door behind him and turned to face her mistress.

'Thank the gods he's gone!' she exclaimed. 'The lecher could barely keep his hands off me. I'm glad you came when you did.'

'You're the wife of the Steward,' Dariah said. 'He wouldn't dare.'

'I require Sir Masten to perform a delicate task for me, so he thinks he's in a position to take liberties.'

'Liberties, my lady?'

'Let's just say I've made some promises I'm hoping I won't have to keep, for your sake as well as mine.'

'I don't understand.'

'Did you see the way Sir Masten looked at you?'

Dariah nodded as she remembered, and it made her skin crawl. A few moments passed, and it dawned on her.

'You promised he could ... ' Dariah said, unable to hide her revulsion, ' ... with me? Why would you do such a thing?'

She had never questioned Lady Greythorpe before, but this ... her stomach turned at the thought of him even touching her. Aside from the fact that she had never been with a man, she was not a slave or a whore who could be ordered to bed someone against her wishes.

'He wants me as well,' her mistress said. 'He drove a hard bargain, but don't worry, I'll do my best to see it doesn't happen.'

'What is Sir Masten doing that would require such a promise,' Dariah said, struggling to keep the disgust from her voice.

'Nothing you need to worry yourself about. But if he is successful, it will cement my husband's position as ruler of the realm, which will be good for both of us.'

'Surely Lord Regan wouldn't approve if he knew what … err … liberties Sir Masten wants to take?'

Her mistress took a step towards Dariah. 'Lord Regan doesn't know, and he must never know. Do you understand?'

'Yes, my lady,' Dariah said under Lady Greythorpe's steely gaze.

'It's a surprise for him,' she said, her tone lightening. 'Sir Masten's visit has to stay between us.'

'Of course.'

Her mistress's smile returned. 'You're a good girl, Dariah. Now, let's go for a walk. I need some fresh air.'

Dariah enjoyed the afternoon sun as she and Lady Greythorpe wandered amongst the trees and hedges in the Queen's Gardens. Eventually, they came upon a small open courtyard near the edge of the cliff overlooking Queens Falls, and sat on a stone bench.

'It's beautiful,' Dariah said. 'So peaceful. It's like the city doesn't exist here.'

'You don't like it here in the capitol?'

'It's not that. I've been blessed and I'm most appreciative of everything you've done for me,' Dariah said. 'It's just that the city seems to be so anxious, even angry, since the King's death.'

'That's understandable, but that should change soon. The prince is on his way to the capitol even as we speak. The people will settle down once he returns.'

'Prince Leto has been found?'

Like most people, Dariah had thought he would be found dead, killed by the same criminals that had murdered the King.

'That's wonderful news,' Dariah added.

'It is, but you mustn't tell anyone just yet. Not until he's safely back under our protection. He has many enemies who would stop at nothing to destroy him, like they did his father.'

Dariah noted that she had been asked to keep a secret for the second time today. Did her mistress trust her more, or did the circumstances just require it, as with Sir Masten?

'And Princess Melina?' Dariah asked. 'Will she return to the capitol as well? I'm sure she and the prince would want to be together at a time like this.'

'Plans are already underway to retrieve her. The prince will be surprised when his sister arrives.'

'His Highness will be grateful, I'm sure,' Dariah said. 'I hope she returns safely.'

'Sir Masten is part of the company that will be fetching the princess and assured me he would take care of her.'

'That's good to know.'

Dariah shuddered again at the mention of his name. She had only met the man briefly but had taken a severe dislike to him and felt uneasy about the promise her mistress had made. Something didn't feel right. Why Lady Greythorpe had included Dariah as part of her depraved agreement with that ghastly knight, she didn't know. Whilst this disturbed her greatly on many levels, something else nagged at her, but she couldn't figure out what it was.

They stayed at the overlook a while longer, then returned to the castle to find Gretchen waiting for them, ready to aid Lady Greythorpe with whatever she needed for the evening. The young handmaiden did most of the hands-on work now. However, Dariah still needed to oversee her to ensure she did everything right, especially until Gretchen became familiar with their mistress's idiosyncrasies. Soon, Dariah wouldn't even be needed for that.

Gretchen fussed over their mistress, but Dariah couldn't stop thinking about the conversation she'd overheard. Her mistress turned away from the mirror to face her.

'You look beautiful as usual, my lady. Lord Regan will be pleased.'

'I hope so.'

Dariah tried to put the conversation with Sir Masten out of her mind and instead turned her thoughts to the prince. Many would celebrate his return to the capitol, especially the common folk who loved the Blackwaters.

'Will Lennore be accompanying you tonight?' Dariah said.

She hadn't seen the young girl for a few days now, which was unusual. The only daughter of her mistress regularly attended the evening meal with her mother, but she knew her father practically ignored her. Dariah felt a semblance of pity for the young girl.

'Definitely not!' her mistress said. 'This isn't a gathering for children.'

Her tone seemed harsh and Dariah took the rebuke in her stride and changed the subject.

'Would you like some wine before you leave?' Dariah said.

'Yes, I'll need it. My husband is entertaining members of the Ruling Council tonight. They can be such a bore.'

Dariah went to the sideboard and began pouring a cup of wine. She had never met Prince Leto. The time he fell through her roof and the later audience with the King where he had been in the same room could hardly be construed as having met him. Dariah had not met the princess either, but had heard nothing but good things about her.

All of a sudden, her misgivings all came together. The princess ... Sir Masten ... and her mistress. Unable to suppress a gasp, the wine goblet slipped from her hands, clanging against the stone floor.

'Dariah,' Lady Greythorpe said. 'What are you doing?'

Dariah poured another goblet of wine and faced her mistress.

'It's nothing, my lady. Just clumsy,' Dariah said and held the cup with a trembling hand.

It couldn't possibly be true, Dariah thought as she poured wine into another goblet and took it to her mistress.

'Be more careful,' Lady Greythorpe scolded her and took the offered wine. 'This is expensive.'

'Sorry, my lady,' Dariah tried to hide her astonishment at the conclusions she had drawn.

She pondered further as she grabbed a cloth and mopped up the spilt wine. No matter how she looked at it, the pieces fell into the same place. Dariah could feel her heart beat faster and she broke into a sweat. Lady Greythorpe continued to sip her wine as Gretchen checked her dress.

Thus far, Dariah had given Abbot Alwen innocuous information about the Governor and his wife, but she had come to care for her mistress and began to feel a level of guilt at passing on any information. Lady Greythorpe acted like most nobles; self-important and prone to outbursts of anger. Still, she had been very generous and had treated Dariah well. If her patron had never summoned her again, she would have been happy, but this … this felt different. Maybe her mistress wasn't the person Dariah thought.

'Dariah,' Lady Greythorpe glared at her. 'You look pale. Are you unwell?'

She felt betrayed.

'Just a little lightheaded, my lady,' Dariah said. 'Probably haven't eaten enough today.'

'I'll be gone for most of the evening. Go and get something to eat and rest. I want to go riding down to Crystal Pool tomorrow.'

'Yes, my lady.'

At least Dariah wasn't expected to attend Lady Greythorpe this evening.

'I'll alert the stables.'

After Dariah had escorted Lady Greythorpe to the Governor's tower, she returned to her room, grabbed her cloak and made her way down to the stables. She notified the Stable Master of Lady Greythorpe's plans for their ride tomorrow, then set out for the Abbey.

Dusk always brought more people out into the streets of Twin Falls, with everyone busy trying to finish up their business before dark. As a consequence, it took Dariah a little longer than usual to reach her destination. Eventually, she stood before the open doors of the Abbey. Even when commanded to do so, Dariah always worried that the Abbot would not see her. This would be the first time she attempted to see him without being summoned, and she was anxious. She took a deep breath and entered the Abbey's large main hall, then headed towards the cloisters, looking for a monk she recognised from her earlier visits. Unfortunately, she didn't see a familiar face among them.

'Milady,' the voice came from behind her.

Dariah turned, shocked to see Prior Fren addressing her.

'Oh, it's you,' the Prior said.

Dariah didn't know what to say. Their last conversation hadn't ended well, so she began to turn on her heel, ready to walk out. His eyes narrowed briefly, and he broke into an awkward smile.

'Miss Winnie,' he said. 'I apologise for my reaction. I didn't expect to see you here today.'

His somewhat friendly tone seemed forced, but maybe it could be his attempt at making amends for his earlier rudeness.

'I didn't expect to be here either, Prior Fren,' Dariah said politely. 'But I have urgent news for the Abbot.'

'I see.'

Dariah hoped he wouldn't stymie her efforts to see the Abbott this time.

'I promise it won't take long,' she said. 'I wouldn't be here if it wasn't important.'

'I'll find Abbot Alwen and tell him you are here,' the Prior said, 'but I can't guarantee that he'll see you.'

His voice grated, but at least he wasn't refusing her this time.

'Thank you,' she said.

'Think nothing of it,' he said. 'Now, follow me. I'll show you to the library where you can wait. It'll be more comfortable than out here.'

Without another word, the Prior walked towards the cloisters, and Dariah followed. He held the door open for her.

'Thank you,' she said as she passed the monk and entered the cloisters.

Surprised but pleased with the change in the prior's behaviour, Dariah felt a tiny pang of regret at her own earlier behaviour. Everyone has difficult days, she thought. He may have been more cooperative had she been more polite.

She stopped and admired the stained-glass window again as the Prior moved to the other end of the room and opened the door to the library.

'Miss Winnie,' the Prior said and disappeared into the room.

Dariah stopped gazing at the window and entered the library, a room familiar to her, with the simple wooden table at its centre, where she and the Abbot had sat several times before.

'Take a seat, and I'll fetch the Abbot,' Prior Fren said as he fumbled in one of the chests.

Dariah turned away from the Prior and sat on a nearby chair.

'I appreciate the kind –'

A sudden pain exploded in the back of her head, and the tabletop rushed towards her. She tried putting her arms out to stop her fall, but they wouldn't respond, and her face hit the table.

25

OWEN

Owen reached into the large wooden chest, brushing his fingers across the armour. The metal felt cool to the touch. He caressed the image of the prancing horse incorporated into the chest piece. Most soldiers wore painted armour and displayed the symbols of their house or that of their lord on their tabards, but the Redstone prancing horse had somehow been imprinted on the metal itself. It was a work of art made by the Grand Master Armourer of Wolfden, a village east of the capitol at the base of The Pinnacles. King Caleb had given it to him to celebrate his becoming Lord of Cliffs End.

It had been many years since he'd worn full battle armour, and he certainly wouldn't be wearing it today. There was already enough scrutiny of him and his men without parading around in full battle armour. He'd get Coen to pack it ready for their morning departure, he thought as he closed the chest.

Owen surveyed the room. Lord Malachy's residence in the north quarter would suit his needs, being quite large and comfortable, and it had a sizable stable. He had unpacked some of his belongings after moving out of Riverview, but most were still packed in chests. He didn't anticipate needing to stay much longer, and the disbanding of the Noble Guard meant the capitol could no longer be considered safe for Owen and his allies.

Sir Peyton had not taken it well. When the initial shock had dissipated, fury had set in, and he would have stormed into the Governor's Tower and taken Regan's head himself had not Owen and Malachy managed to convince him otherwise. Eventually, the anger subsided, and he slumped into the nearest chair.

'What will we do?' Sir Peyton had said. 'We have nothing.'

Owen could see the Knight-Commander's pain, both for himself and the men under his command. Noble Guards usually had few possessions beyond their horse, armour, and weapons.

Owen had considered offering them a place at Cliffs End but he wasn't ready to leave the capitol just yet.

'Sir Peyton,' Malachy said. 'You and your men should return with me to Anchorage.'

'And do what?' Sir Peyton said.

'I don't know yet,' Malachy said, 'But it would be best if you all left the city as soon as possible.'

Owen agreed. Despite the restraint of those who wore the black cloak, blood would be shed if they stayed in the city for much longer.

'He's right, Peyton,' Owen said. 'Once Leto is crowned, you'll return to the capitol and guard a King again.'

'What if the prince isn't found?' Sir Peyton said, unconvinced.

Owen and Malachy had talked him around, taking advantage of the Knight-Commander's deep loyalty to the Blackwaters and members of the Noble Guard. Malachy had planned to leave the city and return home straight after the meeting with Owen, but had delayed his departure to allow Sir Peyton time to organise his men. However, he didn't have to wait long as the Noble Guard had not wasted time making ready to depart before high sun.

Owen accompanied Sir Peyton and his men as they left their barracks. With Sir Peyton and Owen at their head, eighty-six members of the former Noble Guard, resplendent in their white, gold and black armour, rode single file out of Riverview.

As they passed under the great arch of the main castle gate, the Knight-Commander removed his black cloak and, with exaggerated ceremony, dropped it at the feet of the Chief Watcher. The black cloak signified their membership of the elite group, each man receiving it from the King himself, so this bold statement by Sir Peyton sent jaws dropping and tongues wagging. The next man in line did the same, casting his cloak to the ground as he passed beneath the arch, the act of protest being repeated until all members of the former Noble Guard had exited the castle, leaving a great pile of cloaks in front of the dumfounded Chief Watcher.

Word of the disbanding had spread like wildfire throughout the city. Before long, thousands of people had come onto the streets to watch Sir Peyton and his men make their way to the north quarter. They joined Lord Malachy's retinue in the north quarter and headed out of the city. Owen had ridden with them as far as the North Gate and watched them until the last rider had disappeared over the hill.

The morning after Malachy's departure, Owen had finally received word of the prince's arrival in Anchorage, though the message was dated three days earlier. He debated sending a message after the Lord of Ships but decided against it. He'd learn of the good news soon enough. The prince was now in the care of Blackwater allies, so maybe all wasn't lost. He waited and tried to formulate a plan to get Leto crowned without being exposed to Greythorpe and his cadre in the capitol.

Unofficially, as the eldest living offspring of King Caleb, he automatically became King, but a coronation was the traditional way to seal an elevation to the throne. Abbot Alwen could perform the coronation at Shorehaven Keep in Anchorage. Leto could also simply ask the lords to kneel before him and pledge allegiance. It would be Leto's decision as to which way he wanted it.

Owen decided not to return home just yet, but he had to get out of the city, even if for only a few days. Either that or stay indoors and drink himself into a stupor; instead, Owen went hunting.

Leaving half a dozen soldiers to guard Malachy's residence, he and the rest of his men rode into the Kingswood, southeast of Southern Brook.

Even though they hunted some large and dangerous game, he felt safer in the woods than in the capitol.

They returned to Twin Falls four days later with a deer, a boar and half a dozen hares, of which Owen had killed none. Archer felled the boar, and another of his men killed the deer after Owen had missed the kill shot, and it nearly escaped. He needed to brush up on his bow skills, but he had enjoyed being outdoors, away from the city.

During the ride back, Owen had again decided to leave Twin Falls. He'd send Malachy a message recommending that the prince sail to Cliffs End. That way, Owen could look after the prince from a place of strength, surrounded by allies. The retinue re-entered the city from the East Gate and made for the north quarter.

'We'll take the game to the Brothers,' Owen said to his captain. 'And I want to say farewell to the Abbot. We'll be travelling home tomorrow.'

'Certainly, my lord,' Archer smiled.

There had been a significant deterioration of morale amongst his men over the past weeks, though none had complained. Like Owen, they all wanted to go home.

He left most of his retinue at the residence and picked up his messages, one of which was from Anchorage, before continuing to the Abbey with only Archer and two other guards. They arrived at the Abbey just before sundown and Archer went with Owen into the main hall while the others took the game to the Monastery next door.

As expected, Owen was recognised and led into the cloisters to wait for the Abbot. Owen sat and pulled out the scrolls. He found the one from Anchorage, broke the wax seal and unfurled it. He read the message and quietly cursed. What in blazes was the boy thinking?

'Problem?' Archer said.

'I'm not sure,' Owen said as Abbot Alwen came into the cloisters.

'Lord Owen,' the Abbot said. 'A pleasant, if unexpected surprise.'

'Good evening, Alwen,' Owen said, shoving the messages into his coat as he stood and shook the old monk's hand.

The monk nodded to Archer. 'Captain.'

'Abbot,' Archer replied, nodding back.

252

'I had originally come bearing gifts,' Owen said, 'and to say goodbye.'

Owen told the Abbot about the game his men were delivering to the monastery.

'Your generosity is always appreciated,' the Abbot said, 'and the goodbye, is it still a goodbye?

Owen gave him the news he'd just received in the message from Anchorage.

'He's sailed for Amberfall? He didn't wait for Malachy to return?'

'It doesn't seem so,' Owen said. 'If he had, I'm sure Malachy would have talked him out of this foolishness.'

'He is our liege lord, and he can do as he wishes,' the Abbot reminded him, 'but he should have waited for his uncle before making such a decision.'

Owen voiced his thoughts about returning home anyway, but Abbot Alwen turned for the door to the library.

'Let's discuss this further,' the Abbot said.

'Stay here,' Owen said to the Captain. 'We shan't be long.'

Archer nodded as Owen followed the old Abbot to the library. Alwen opened the door and stopped dead in his tracks, causing Owen to bump into him. He stepped aside and sucked in a breath at the appalling scene before him.

A girl was bent over the table with her arms splayed and legs hanging to the floor. Her dress had been thrown back over her torso, covering her face. Her undergarments had been removed exposing her bare legs and buttocks. Directly behind her, an ugly little monk held his robes above his waist, ready to violate her.

'Prior!' the Abbot cried.

The monk instantly dropped his robe and glanced towards the door. His surprise turned to fear as Owen pushed past the Abbot and grabbed at him. The monk ducked out of his way with unexpected speed and scurried around the other side of the table. Owen gave chase, but the little monk bolted out of the room, knocking the Abbot to the floor.

Owen rushed into the cloisters to find his Captain with Prior Fren firmly in his grasp.

'I've got him,' Archer said.

'Don't let go of the little bastard.'

'He's not going anywhere,' Archer said, tightening his grip on the monk, who yelped. 'Shut up, or I'll squeeze harder.'

Owen turned back to the library.

He bent down to help Alwen. 'Are you hurt?'

'No, no. I'm fine,' the Abbot said, unsettled.

'I knew he was a troubled one,' the Abbot got to his feet with Owen's aid and looked across at the monk, who struggled against Archer's iron grip. 'But it seems I wasn't given the entire story.'

'This is hardly your fault, 'Owen said.

Owen re-entered the library. The half-naked girl had not moved. He pulled the dress back over her exposed body and noticed a trickle of blood down the back of her neck. He carefully lifted the unconscious girl and laid her gently on the table.

'Do you know this girl?' Owen said as the Abbot entered the library.

'Oh dear,' he said. 'She's our observer in the Steward's household, though I have no idea why she's here today.'

He glanced at the Abbot.

'This is she?'

Alwen nodded.

'Her name is Dariah Fields.'

Owen had quite a large web of spies and informers throughout Avaleen, but he rarely met them face to face. Abbot Alwen proved such a boon as no one considered it unusual when people went to the Abbey.

'Watch her for a few moments,' he instructed the Abbot. 'I'm going to sort out this prior of yours.'

'What're you going to do with him?'

'We can't give him to the Capitol Guard,' Owen said.

'No, I guess not,' Alwen conceded.

'He's a rapist,' Owen said. 'We can't just let him go, either.'

The Abbot seemed torn and gave Owen a pained look.

'Behind the centre tapestry, there's a door. It leads out to the alley,' the Abbot sighed. 'Just ensure he doesn't suffer.'

Owen returned to the cloisters. The monk had stopped struggling.

'Take him outside,' Owen said. 'Don't kill him yet.'

'No … wait … you can't do that,' Prior Fren said.

'Through the Abbey?' Archer said, ignoring the monk.

'No,' Owen pulled back one of the tapestries and revealed a small wooden door, which he opened.

'You can't do this!' the prior squeaked. 'I'm a monk of the Brotherhood!'

'Then maybe one of your gods will forgive you for your sins,' Owen said.

Archer nodded and dragged the prior through the door. The monk's continued protests faded as Owen closed the door, straightened up the tapestry and returned to the library.

The girl had come round, and Abbot Alwen helped her sit up.

'Careful,' the Abbot said. 'You've had a nasty knock.'

'What happened?' she said.

Her eyes darted around the room, finally resting on Owen. She looked at him momentarily.

'You're … ' was all she managed before grimacing and putting her hand to the back of her head.

She pulled her hand back and blanched at the blood, panic rising as she realised what had happened to her.

'The prior!' she said, reaching down in dread.

She felt her hips and rubbed her hands along her legs.

'It's alright,' Owen reassured her. 'He didn't get a chance to do anything.'

Tentatively, she looked up at him again and across to the Abbot. He saw a few tears trickle down her cheek, but she didn't cry.

'You're safe now,' Alwen said and turned to Owen. 'Now, if you can watch over the young lady, I'll get something for her wound.'

Owen nodded, and Alwen made a hasty retreat from the library. Owen closed the door behind the Abbot and turned back to Dariah.

'Dariah, do you know who I am?' Owen asked.

She nodded. 'You know my real name?'

'Abbot Alwen told me everything about you.'

'He has?' she looked baffled for a moment. 'You ... you're my patron?'

Patron? Is that what the Abbot had called him? Owen was bemused.

'I am, but he said he hadn't summoned you today.'

Dariah lowered her gaze, gathered her thoughts, and looked back at Owen.

'I wouldn't usually come unannounced, but I have urgent news for the Abbot ... for you, my lord.'

Owen sat on the nearby chair as the Abbot returned.

'One of the sisters will be along in a moment,' he said and sat beside Dariah.

Dariah told them about Lady Greythorpe's plan to have Sir Masten kill Princess Melina.

'Why would he do such a thing?' exclaimed the Abbot.

'My mistress promised he could do things with her ... ' she said with undisguised revulsion, ' ... and me.'

Owen wasn't surprised by this revelation. That woman belonged in a whorehouse. He was glad he'd already arranged to get the princess out of Whitehall, though with the stakes now much higher, he hoped both Lord Gruffydd and the Noble Guard protecting the princess had received his instructions.

'Don't concern yourself,' Owen said. 'The princess will be safe.'

'That's good to hear,' Dariah said. 'Prince Leto will be happy to hear his sister is safe when he returns to the capitol.'

'How do you know about the prince?' Owen asked.

'My mistress told me Lord Regan's son is bringing him back even as we speak.'

That Prince Leto had fallen into the hands of the Greythorpes disturbed Owen, but at least he still lived.

'Did she say when?'

'No, my lord, but soon.'

Owen considered what the girl had said and saw an opportunity. He hesitated, realising what he'd be asking of her, but thought it would be the best chance he had of getting word to the prince.

'Dariah, wait here for a few moments,' Owen said.

She nodded, and Owen ushered the Abbot out to the cloisters.

'What's this girl like?' Owen said in a hushed tone. 'Is she reliable?'

'Oh yes. She's quite a smart young lady.'

Owen explained his plan.

'Are you serious?' the Abbot said, clearly unimpressed.

'Can you think of a better way to disrupt the workings of the Greythorpes?' Owen said. 'And as for Leto, Regan will keep him isolated when he returns to the capitol. It'll be impossible to contact him.'

'What about me?' Alwen said.

'Anyone who has contact with the prince and is seen as a possible ally of mine will be watched,' Owen said. 'I'd be surprised if you were allowed to be alone with him.'

'But it could be a death sentence for her.'

Owen understood the risks, but he didn't have many options left.

'We'll let her decide.'

'Lord Owen, I don't like this. Not at all. I am quite uncomfortable with it.'

Abbot Alwen had been an excellent spymaster, but because of his pious nature, he cared about those in his charge; nonetheless, Owen wouldn't be swayed.

'I'm sorry you feel that way,' he said, 'but this is more important than the safety of one girl. The heir to the throne is in the custody of murderers, and the safety of the whole realm is at stake. She's the best chance we have.'

'Fine. I see your point,' Alwen grumbled. 'But promise me you won't pressure her.'

'Agreed.'

Owen and the Abbot returned to the library.

'Dariah,' Owen said. 'In addition to your normal duties, there are some tasks I need you to perform for us.'

'But you're under no obligation to accept,' the Abbot added for him.

Dariah's brow furrowed, but she nodded, and Owen told her what he needed. He explained the dangers, and he had expected some resistance, but she readily agreed.

'I'll do my best, my lord. But what if I fail?' she said and gave Owen a fretful look. 'What happens to my family if I can't do as you ask?'

She shifted her gaze to the Abbot and back to Owen.

'They'll be looked after regardless, my dear girl,' Alwen said before Owen could reply.

Her concern for her family made Owen think of his own wife and daughters, who should now be well and truly back home. Unfortunately, it would be a while longer before he saw them again. With these new developments, it didn't look like he'd be returning home tomorrow after all.

'Do you think she knows what she's getting into?' Owen said to the Abbot after the girl had left.

'I hope so. She'll have to step very carefully. I'm afraid you may have asked too much of her.'

Part of him wanted to thank the girl for her service and get her out of the city, but considering what was at stake, he couldn't pass up this opportunity. However, he thought about his twin daughters, only a few years younger than Dariah, and couldn't imagine deliberately putting them in harm's way as he had just done with Dariah. He almost felt ashamed.

26

CONSTANCE

At last they had finished.

Constance stood back and looked at the girls in front of her. If no one had met them before, they shouldn't be able to tell one from the other.

'Turn around,' she instructed.

The girls complied and faced the other way. If Constance hadn't dressed them herself, even she couldn't have picked between them.

'And back,' she said, and the girls turned and faced her again.

Similar in height and, since Melina's recent weight loss, she and Nerys also had a similar build. Even though Melina had slightly longer, fairer hair, there wasn't anything to worry about. Most men wouldn't even notice the difference in the colour of a woman's hair, but their faces could cause a problem. They each had a distinctive look, which would be obvious to anyone who had met them.

'The hood,' Constance said, and the princess raised the hood on her cloak.

Much better, she thought. The hood concealed most of the princess's face and cast shadows on the rest.

'Well?' Melina said as she pushed back the hood.

'As long you keep the hood up, it should work,' Constance said.

'Let's see what Sir Fergus thinks,' Constance said, leading the two girls into the living room of Melina's apartment.

The three girls entered the room. Melina and Nerys stood in front of the hearth and faced Constance and Sir Fergus, who had moved to the centre of the room. Sir Fergus looked at them for a few moments. Constance signalled them to turn around.

'Good,' he murmured, nodding his approval.

Melina and Nerys turned back to face them, and Constance asked Melina to raise the hood. The princess did so, and the Noble Guard silently scrutinised the girls for a few more moments.

'Excellent,' he said. 'Just remember, Your Highness, keep the hood on at all times, even after you've left the castle.'

'Yes, I know.'

Sir Fergus had wanted to leave earlier, but it had taken longer than expected to implement their plan. But the day had finally come, and Constance had been getting increasingly anxious. Sir Fergus had told them that it would be at least a two-day ride to the relative safety of the Greenhavens. The princess's mind remained strong, but her body had not yet recovered. Constance wasn't confident she would be able to make it, but Melina remained stubborn, declaring she could ride.

The princess had been unsuccessful at convincing Lord Rainer to let her return to the capitol, and they wanted to all leave together but couldn't figure out a safe way to do so without alerting the Whites. In the meantime, the guards had been increased all around Whitehall, which meant when Melina did go outside to walk around the grounds, she had an escort of at least two guards. Lord Rainer ignored her protests and complaints, spouting orders from the Steward and concerns for her safety as the reasons for the increased security and not allowing her to leave.

Constance again suggested Hamlin could help, but Sir Fergus wouldn't entertain the idea, even when they had reached an impasse. Getting all four of them out of Whitehall posed a bigger problem than they had first thought. Ironically, an off-the-cuff remark by the Noble Guard had led to the answer, but it wasn't something any of them would have imagined.

'If only there was a way to convince them that Her Highness was still here when we slip away,' a frustrated Sir Fergus had said.

Constance had thought about it. The soldiers who guarded them weren't very bright, so tricking them shouldn't be difficult. They just had to ensure the guards would not see the princess leave her quarters. It sounded simple enough, but how could they do it, or who could do it? Constance had an inspired idea. She considered it as the others discussed their options, though Sir Fergus and Melina did most of the talking.

'I'll stay,' said Constance, interrupting their conversation. 'I'll pretend to be the princess.'

Sir Fergus, Melina and Nerys stopped as one and stared at her in disbelief.

'Connie!' Melina said. 'I'm sure Sir Fergus didn't mean one of us should stay.'

'Her Highness is correct,' he said. 'We're all leaving this place.'

'No,' Constance said. 'You can escape with the princess and Lady Nerys. I'm not important.'

Melina opened her mouth to protest again, but Sir Fergus got in first.

'That's a courageous offer.'

Constance didn't think of it as courageous, just something that had to be done.

'But Lady Constance,' Sir Fergus continued. 'You don't look anything like Her Highness.'

'Does it matter?'

Constance hadn't thought of that. She just wanted Melina to be safe.

'Sir Fergus is right,' Melina said. 'I'm sure we'll come up with another way.'

'But there is no other way,' Constance said. 'We've run out of ideas and can't wait much longer. And unless we involve Hamlin or someone else, it's all we have.'

'What you say is true,' he said with reluctance.

'But Connie, you can't –'

'I'll do it,' Nerys said, interrupting the princess.

All eyes turned to the young girl from the Shadowlands.

'Nerys?' Constance said.

'As you said, we've run out of time,' Nerys said, 'and I look more like Princess Melina than Constance does.'

'Lady Nerys, my orders are to get you out as well,' Sir Fergus said.

'I don't care. This is the only way,' Nerys said with conviction.

After a few moments of silence, the Noble Guard spoke again.

'Do you know what it'll mean?'

Nerys shook her head. 'It doesn't matter. The important thing is that the princess escapes.'

'I can't guarantee that Lord Rainer will treat you well once we're discovered missing,' he warned.

'Nerys,' Melina said. 'Are you sure you want to do this?'

She nodded, and Melina reached across the table and gripped her hand. Constance could see Nerys holding her emotions in check, trying hard not to cry.

'I won't forget this,' Melina had said.

Now, the time had come to leave.

'Your Highness,' Sir Fergus said. 'Have you eaten this morning? You will need your strength, and we may have limited time for rest over the next few days.'

'Yes,' she said. 'Just as you asked.'

Constance didn't feel very hungry this morning. Nervousness had blunted her appetite, but she ate anyway. Although she urged Melina to eat, the princess had only picked at the food on her plate, barely eating anything; however, she wasn't about to dispute the princess's version of events. Sir Fergus gave a questioning glance at Constance, who shrugged.

'It's time, then,' he said.

Melina turned to Nerys and hugged her.

'We'll see you soon, I'm sure of it,' Melina said.

Tears began to roll down the young girl's cheeks. 'I'll look forward to that day, Your Highness.'

Constance went up to the young girl and embraced her.

'Goodbye, Nerys.'

'Lady Nerys, I will ensure that your father is made aware of your sacrifice,' Sir Fergus said. 'You're as courageous as any Noble Guard.'

He bowed his head in recognition.

'Thank you, sir,' she stammered. 'You ... you should go now.'

Constance and Sir Fergus went to the door. The Noble Guard looked back at Melina, who nodded and pulled the hood over her head. He opened the door a few inches.

'Have a pleasant time, Nerys,' Melina said louder than usual. 'I wish I could join you.'

'Goodbye, Your Highness,' Nerys said.

Melina joined Constance and Sir Fergus at the door as he opened it.

Here we go, Constance thought as she and Melina entered the corridor. Sir Fergus closed the door behind them and led the two girls towards the stairs.

'I'll be back once I have these ladies safely on their way,' he told the guards at the top of the stairs.

His tone suggested a warning not to disturb the princess more than telling them his whereabouts. Under normal circumstances, he would not have said anything to them, but the circumstances were far from normal. They continued down the stairs and to the courtyard in silence.

'Good morning, Maester,' Constance greeted her teacher, who had already taken his seat at the front of the small wooden cart.

Next to him sat the driver, a stable hand Constance had never met. The driver, was disinterested, simply looking ahead and waiting for the signal to begin their journey. Two mounted soldiers had also been assigned as an escort. They had hoped it would be only a single soldier or none, but a glance at Sir Fergus reassured Constance that he didn't seem concerned. She recognised the guards. The older one, Swayne, a sergeant and the other, a regular guard called Cirroc.

Two other passengers had already arrived and been seated in the cart. Melina had requested only Nerys and Constance go on this trip, but Maester Arkham wouldn't have it. He couldn't be seen to favour her too much. Thankfully, only Gaylene and Willem had accepted the invitation for the day's trip to Moon Cove, a small crescent-shaped stretch of beach about fifteen miles east of Whitehall. They had visited it several times since being at Sisters End, so it seemed an excellent place to request a last trip before winter confined them to the castle.

'Lady Nerys, Miss Constance,' Maester Arkam greeted them as Sir Fergus helped Melina onto the cart. 'Glad you could join us.'

'My apologies, Maester,' Constance said. 'Her Highness kept us longer than expected. She's a mite envious she can't go with us.'

'No doubt,' the Maester said. 'Come on then, up you get so we can start this little adventure. We certainly have a lovely day for it. Let's hope it stays that way.'

'Any idea when you'll return?' Sir Fergus asked the Maester.

'Late afternoon, I expect.'

'Good. Lady Nerys is feeling a bit poorly, but she insists on coming. I think she wanted out of the castle one last time before it gets too cold,' Sir Fergus said.

'I know the feeling,' Arkam said. 'I don't fancy being cooped up in here either. We'll be back before dark.'

'I'll make sure Lady Nerys keeps warm,' Constance said to the Noble Guard, hoping that even though the day was clear with hardly a cloud in the sky, no one would question Melina keeping her hood up.

'Thank you, Lady Constance.'

Sir Fergus held out his hand to help her onto the cart. She reached for his hand but stiffened when a familiar voice shouted.

'Maester Arkam!'

Constance turned as Hamlin White slowed to a walk.

He approached the cart and stopped. 'Maester, I've been instructed to tell you that Lady Margot now wishes to join your outing.'

Arkam glanced down at the single space available reserved for Constance.

'Does she now?'

This would mean a considerable delay as a bigger wagon and extra horses would have to be organised, and more time for their ruse to be discovered. Arkam sighed.

'But I can see your cart is full,' Hamlin glanced at Constance and smiled. 'I'll tell my cousin you have already left.'

'Thank you, Master Hamlin,' Arkam said, nodding his approval. 'Then we had better leave now.'

Sir Fergus helped Constance into the seat opposite Melina. Hamlin stepped closer to the cart near her. He glanced at Melina.

'Have a good trip, Lady Nerys,' Hamlin said.

Melina nodded as Hamlin gave Constance a gentle smile.

'Goodbye, Lady Constance.'

He knows, she thought, and smiled back. She would miss him.

'Goodbye, Master Hamlin.'

Sir Fergus gave her a stern look, but she knew Hamlin posed no danger to them. Constance felt the cart begin to move, and she watched Hamlin as their mounted escort led the cart out of the courtyard.

'That was mighty odd,' Willem said.

'What was?' said Constance a little too fast.

'Master Hamlin,' the young monk said. 'He talked like … umm … like he wasn't going to see you again.'

'Hamlin has always been a bit dramatic,' Constance said, trying to downplay Hamlin's actions.

'Do you and Master Hamlin have something going?' Gaylene asked, always interested in castle gossip. 'He is rather handsome.'

'Don't be silly,' Constance said. 'He wouldn't be interested in someone like me.'

'He obviously cares for you,' Gaylene said.

He does, and I care for him too, she thought. But it would have never worked.

'Let's talk about something else,' she snapped, instantly regretting her harsh tone.

Gaylene nodded but didn't reply.

'I'm sorry,' Constance said to the young girl. 'I guess I feel a bit poorly myself. I think a day out will be beneficial for us all.'

Despite her apology, they continued in relative silence, the cart rumbling over the cobbled streets and through the main gate. Constance looked straight ahead as they passed over each of the bridges, which spanned the plunging cliffs and crevasses leading up to Whitehall, functioning as a natural protection for the castle. They approached the last bridge. The largest and longest, it spanned a crevasse more than a hundred feet wide. The unwanted escort turned out to be a blessing in disguise, with no one questioning them along the way as they crossed the bridges. Constance breathed a sigh of relief as they passed under the final gate onto The Narrows without incident. Constance gripped Melina's hand and squeezed it as they left Whitehall behind. The rest of the plan depended upon Sir Fergus.

The time passed slowly, with only sporadic conversation from Willem and Gaylene. They only passed a couple of farmers going in the opposite direction. Even Maester Arkam had stayed quiet instead of telling his students some fanciful tale.

'Maester,' Constance finally said, 'could you please tell us a story?'

The teacher glanced back at her with a grin. 'What would you like to hear, Miss Constance?'

'Something about your homeland,' she said, always enjoying tales of places outside of Avaleen.

'Well then,' the Maester said, cocking his head thoughtfully. 'When I was a lad, my mother took me to the greatest store of knowledge in the known world, The Etrutian Sanctum. She knew I adored reading and loved books. This was her gift to me for my thirteenth name day. It took us nearly a –'

'Stop!' barked Sergeant Swayne.

He pulled his horse around and trotted to the rear of the cart. He halted about ten yards behind it and stared back along the road. He beckoned to Cirroc who joined him.

'What is it, Sergeant?' the Maester said, disappointed his story had been interrupted.

'Be quiet,' Swayne said and continued to gaze back down the road.

Constance tensed up. She knew who was coming up behind them. She had been expecting it.

Cirroc loaded his crossbow and raised it at the approaching horses. The guards' horses blocked her view, but she could now hear hooves on the hard ground.

'Lower your weapon,' the Sergeant said.

After a moment's hesitation, Cirroc obeyed.

'Sir Fergus,' Sergeant Swayne continued. 'This is most unexpected.'

'I have orders from Her Highness to return Lady Nerys and Lady Constance to Whitehall immediately.'

'But we've only been gone a couple of hours,' Swayne said.

Sir Fergus pulled up beside the cart and dismounted.

'I don't question my orders, Sergeant. I just carry them out.'

The two guards moved their horses closer, barely ten feet from the cart.

'Why the extra horses?' said Sergeant Swayne.

'Only Lady Nerys and Lady Constance must return to the castle. The others can continue as planned,' Sir Fergus said, looking up at Sergeant Swayne. 'Do you have a problem with that?'

'Err … no sir,' he said.

'Good,' Sir Fergus turned back to the cart and assisted Constance from her seat.

'Did Her Highness give a reason why she wanted us to return?' Constance asked.

'No, my lady,' he said. 'I didn't ask, and neither should you.'

Constance wasn't sure whether he warned her as part of the ruse or if he just wanted her to be quiet. She accepted the rebuke and nodded her understanding.

'My lady,' Sir Fergus held his hand out to the princess.

Melina held the proffered hand and went to step off the cart. As she descended, her cloak snagged on the corner of the cart, and when she stepped to the ground, the hood was pulled from her face. A collective gasp ensued at the revelation of their deception.

'What's this?' Sergeant Swayne said, drawing his sword.

Cirroc nudged his horse closer to the cart and raised the crossbow again, aiming it at the Noble Guard.

'Sergeant,' Sir Fergus said.

Melina's face showed alarm at being discovered, and Constance held her breath.

Sir Fergus stood still, his back to the mounted soldiers. 'I'd advise you to put away your weapon and let us on our way.'

'I don't think so,' Swayne said. 'Step away from the cart.'

'I go where I please!' Melina finally found her voice.

'I'm sorry, Your Highness, but I cannot allow that,' the Sergeant said. 'Please get back on the cart, and we'll return to Whitehall immediately.'

Constance's gaze flicked from Melina to Sir Fergus. He looked grim and seemed to be staring at the princess who returned his gaze.

'I'll do no such thing,' she eventually said, marching between Constance and Sir Fergus towards the waiting horses.

The soldiers' gaze followed the princess.

'Please return to the cart, Your Highness,' Sergeant Swayne said.

'And what if I don't?' Melina said as she stopped and faced the Sergeant. 'Will you manhandle me back into the cart?'

'I will if I'm forced to –' the sergeant glanced back as a grunt of pain sounded behind him.

There followed a clatter as the crossbow hit the ground and Cirroc held up his arms, his pale face registering in shocked silence the bloody stumps where his hands used to be. Constance looked down to where the crossbow had fallen, one hand still gripping the butt of the weapon. The other had hit the ground and rolled across the dirt, stopping near her feet. She yelped and leapt back towards the cart.

'Drop your weapon, Sergeant.'

The Noble Guard had brandished his sword, but the dagger pressed into his inner thigh caught Sergeant Swayne's attention.

'And if I don't?'

There was a dull thud as Cirroc fell from his horse and hit the ground.

'Surely you aren't that stupid,' said Sir Fergus.

Swayne glared at the Noble Guard before dropping his sword. It hit the ground in front of Melina.

'Wise decision.' Sir Fergus removed the blade from the Sergeant's thigh.

Then the Noble Guard suddenly arched his body and tossed back his head, narrowly avoiding the knife which slashed at his throat. Within the space of a single breath, Sir Fergus had stepped forward and plunged his sword into the Sergeant's side and the dagger into his thigh. Sergeant Swayne screamed in agony and dropped his knife. Sir Fergus pulled both blades out of his body, and the Whitehall soldier slowly slipped from the saddle. He fell to the ground.

'Idiot!' Sir Fergus spat.

The Noble Guard went around to Sergeant Swayne. He still breathed, but the blood already soaking into the dirt showed he wouldn't much longer. Sir Fergus wiped his sword and dagger clean on the sergeant's tabard and sheathed them.

'Are you alright, Your Highness?' the Noble Guard said.

'Yes … yes,' Melina stammered.

Like Melina, the outburst of violence right before them had shaken Constance, being the first time she had ever seen anyone killed.

'My apologies Maester,' Sir Fergus said. 'I had no wish for you and your young charges to witness the death of these men.'

'Just do me a favour and ensure it's worth it,' Arkam said.

Sir Fergus helped Melina and Constance onto the spare horses he had brought with him. 'I'd suggest you return to Whitehall. I wouldn't want to give Lord Rainer any reason to think any of you were part of this deception.'

The Maester nodded his agreement.

'Thank you, Maester,' Melina said. 'Thank you for everything.'

'It was my humblest pleasure, Your Highness,' Arkam said. 'Good luck.'

Constance waved at Gaylene and Willem, who gave rather half-hearted waves in return.

The three set off at a trot, Sir Fergus in the lead, followed by Melina and Constance. Before long, she could no longer see the cart when she looked back. They increased their speed to a slow canter. Sir Fergus had explained they needed as much distance between them and Whitehall as possible, so the sun had reached its peak before he allowed them to stop and rest.

'The Maester should have arrived back at Whitehall by now,' Sir Fergus said. 'I was hoping for at least a full day's head start. We'll have to ride swiftly for the rest of the day.'

The original plan had been straightforward without the need to kill anyone, and it would have also given them at least half a day's head-start on any pursuit. How quickly things could be turned upside down, Constance thought.

'If we can make it to nightfall without being seen,' Sir Fergus continued, 'we'll stand a good chance.'

Rocks and low shrubs littered the landscape as it had most of the morning. The Narrows provided little cover, but to the east was the Graveswood. If they could reach it, they would be safer.

Constance rubbed her aching back and looked at Melina. The princess barely had hold of the reins as her horse drank from a rocky pool. Constance led her mount over to where the princess stood.

'Mellie, how are you doing?' Constance said, suspecting that Melina was also hurting.

Melina straightened up at the sound of Constance's voice.

'I'm fine,' she said.

Constance wasn't convinced, but they soldiered on, making their way east. Sir Fergus drove them as hard as he dared, fully aware of Melina's deficient physical condition, but neither of the young women complained. Constance could see the beginnings of the Graveswood now, but her heart sank when she glanced behind and glimpsed movement in the distance.

'Sir Fergus!' she said. 'Behind us!'

They brought their mounts to a rapid halt and looked west.

'At least a dozen, if not more,' he said matter-of-factly and turned to Melina. 'Your Highness, if we ride hard, we can make it to the woods. If not, we'll just wait for them. The choice is yours, Your Highness.'

Melina was struggling, and Constance wanted to find somewhere they could rest properly, but she couldn't believe that Sir Fergus offered to surrender them all back to the Whites.

'I'm not going back,' the princess said.

They took off at a gallop. However, this time, Sir Fergus brought up the rear, and Melina lead the way. They managed to keep ahead of their pursuers; the Graveswood beckoned, now only a few miles distant.

Melina had begun to sway in the saddle, and her mount slowed. Constance turned in her saddle to call out to Sir Fergus, but he had already kicked his mount forward, overtaking Constance and pulling up alongside Melina. He reached across and pulled on her reins, eventually bringing both mounts to a stop about half a mile from the trees. Constance pulled up on the other side of Melina. Sir Fergus had his hand on her shoulder, stopping her from sliding off.

'Mellie?' Constance said.

The princess did not respond. She could barely keep her eyes open.

'What are we going to do?' Constance said to the Noble Guard.

She risked a glance behind. The band of Whitehall soldiers had closed on them, now less than a mile away. Their situation seemed hopeless, despite the short distance to the forest.

'We'll be taken, won't we?' she said.

'Not necessarily,' Sir Fergus said, grabbing the princess with both hands and dragging her over to his horse.

Once Sir Fergus had Melina seated in front of him, he wrapped one arm tight around her tiny waist. She looked like a child leaning against the Noble Guard.

'Go!' Sir Fergus ordered. 'And don't look back.'

Constance kicked her mount forward. The horse was breathing heavily, its nostrils flaring, but it still took off at a gallop. They raced towards the trees and covered the last few hundred yards in no time. But as they approached the forest, a group of horsemen appeared from the trees, blocking their path to safety.

No ... no ... they were trapped!

Constance brought her horse to a stop about twenty yards shy of the riders blocking the road. They didn't look like typical bandits, to Constance. She glanced behind. Sir Fergus slowed his mount as he approached. Since they had stopped, their pursuers had closed the gap too fast for them to escape in any other direction. At the edge of the forest, ten men had spread across the road.

'Sir Fergus?' said the man in the centre.

Noble Guard nodded his assent. 'Greenhavens?'

'At your service,' the man said. 'Is that Her Highness?'

'Yes, and she's not well.'

'Please move behind us,' the man said. 'We'll take care of your friends.'

Constance and Sir Fergus wasted no time. They rode beyond the Greenhavens riders. The Noble Guard still held the princess, ready to race into the trees if needed.

'Mellie?' Constance probed.

'I'm fine,' Melina gave Constance a weak smile as twenty Whitehall soldiers, led by Captain Childs, stopped just inside the edge of the woods.

'Sir Kyle Greenwood, these are the lands of Lord Rainer White,' Captain Childs shouted across the thirty-yard gap. 'You are ordered to retreat, leaving Her Highness to return with us. You can keep the others.'

Sir Kyle Greenwood? He must have been looking for them. Why else would he be outside of his father's lands? But how did he know where they were?

'We'll leave,' Sir Kyle said. 'But Her Highness comes with us.'

'You will be defying a direct order from the Steward of the Realm!' the captain said.

'I have my orders, Captain,' Sir Kyle said.

'We could easily take her by force,' said Childs.

'You could try,' the young knight said. 'My men would certainly give a good account of themselves, I'm sure, but it's not these men you see here that should concern you.'

The Whitehall soldiers glanced at the trees on either side of them.

'You're bluffing,' Captain Childs said.

'Would you like an example?' Sir Kyle raised his hand high. 'Lieutenant! On my signal, put an arrow through the man to the Captain's left.'

'His left or mine?' a voice came from the trees.

'Take your pick,' the young knight grinned.

A few Whitehall riders raised crossbows and aimed blindly into the trees, while a furious Childs glared at Sir Kyle.

'This isn't over,' Childs said. 'There will be repercussions, I assure you.'

Sir Kyle remained silent; his hand still raised. This angered Captain Childs still more, but he and his men eventually pulled their mounts around and cantered away back towards Sisters End. Sir Kyle lowered his arm, but no one moved until Childs and his men had disappeared into the distance. The young knight trotted back, stopping near Sir Fergus.

'Your arrival was unexpected, but timely,' Sir Fergus said.

'I could say the same for you, but we should start back to Forest Keep. Captain Childs may change his mind, and I'd prefer not to fight if we can avoid it. I may not be able to fool him a second time.'

'How many archers do you have?' Sir Fergus said.

Sir Kyle grinned. 'Everyone, mount up. Let's head home.'

The Greenhaven's men formed up behind Sir Kyle, and a few moments later, three men came out of the trees, two from the left and one from the right.

'I don't want to push my luck twice in one day,' Sir Kyle glanced at Melina. 'Will you be right to ride until dark, Your Highness?'

'Yes,' she said, nodding. 'Sir Fergus will look after me.'

The young knight acknowledged her decision with a short bow, then turned to Constance.

'You are not the Lady Nerys.' His voice was firm.

'No.' She didn't know what else to say.

'Nerys stayed behind so I could escape,' Melina said.

The Greenhavens knight glanced at Sir Fergus, who nodded, confirming the princess's brief explanation. He seemed to think about it for a moment, then turned to one of his men.

'Captain Floris, take three men to scout our rear. I want to ensure that Childs doesn't double back.'

'Yes sir,' the rider nearest him said.

'Once we're safe, I want to hear exactly why my cousin isn't with you,' Sir Kyle told Sir Fergus.

The Greenhavens knight led the group east at a slow canter. His challenge deepened Constance's guilt at leaving Nerys behind. Her thoughts stayed with the young girl for a while, now surrounded by the enemy with not a friendly face amongst them. She prayed that Hamlin would look after her. At least their group was safe now, Constance thought, as they rode deeper into the Graveswood.

27

REGAN

Everything had begun to fall into place.

With Twin Falls now firmly under his control, the prince's arrival due any day and the Ruling Council his to command, he could practically taste the victory. He'd also considered removing the Abbot from the council but felt this would be seen as petty, even by his allies.

One of his biggest concerns had sorted itself out when the Noble Guard left the capitol of their own accord. Regan had contemplated having them all killed but had erred on the side of caution. Sir Baltair had crowed that his men would triumph over the Noble Guard, if those had been Regan's orders. But he had no doubt the Capitol Guard would be decimated.

To Regan's constant annoyance, Owen Redstone stubbornly refused to leave the capitol despite he and his allies being made unwelcome. The longer he remained, the more chance he had to interfere and cause trouble. As with the Blackwater family, the ordinary folk liked the Redstones; Regan couldn't have Owen killed outright, not yet anyway. Just thinking about the man irritated him.

A knock sounded at the door, and he looked up from the letter he held, another pledge of loyalty from yet another minor lord. They'd been steadily arriving ever since the King's death, which showed that no one suspected his involvement in the murder of the King, and these new allies knew who now wielded the power in Avaleen.

'Come.'

The door opened, and Harrow stepped in.

'She's here.'

Regan had almost forgotten. He thought for a moment and considered sending her away again. That this young girl wanted to see him had slipped his mind, but he needed a break from his paperwork anyway. It had increased markedly since he'd become Steward, but even now, Regan didn't trust anyone enough to delegate any of the responsibilities.

'Fine, show her in.'

Regan leaned back in his chair as the girl entered his solar. Harrow leered at her before he left the room, closing the door after him. She stopped a few steps inside the room, but he beckoned her closer.

'Sit,' Regan said, gesturing to one of the chairs opposite him.

'Thank you, my lord,' she said quietly, sitting with her hands cupped in her lap and her gaze lowered.

'I don't enjoy having my valuable time wasted,' Regan said, 'so this better be important.'

The girl exuded innocence and beauty, and he understood why his wife had taken a shine to her. He'd become aware of Lennane's dalliances with female members of her household long ago. As long she stuck to her own gender, he didn't care.

'Yes, my lord,' she said, her eyes still lowered.

'Look at me when I talk to you, girl.'

It was much easier to detect lies if people looked him in the eye when they spoke, even servants.

She lifted her head. 'Sorry, my lord.'

'Why did you wish to see me?'

'I … I have some ill news,' she said.

'And this ill news is what?' he said after a few moments of silence.

'Someone is going to kill Princess Melina!' she blurted out.

He had expected her to try and ingratiate herself by reporting the failure of another one of his staff or to offer herself to him to gain favour. Not that he would necessarily turn her down, but this unexpected information intrigued him.

'How do you know?'

'I overheard a conversation, my lord.'

'Where?'

'Err ... in my lady's apartment.'

The girl began fidgeting.

'You heard a plot to kill the princess in my wife's apartment?'

He wanted to make sure he heard her correctly.

'Yes, my lord,' she said.

'A conversation between whom?'

She bit her lip at the question and began to tremble.

'Sir Masten and ... and Lady Greythorpe,' she began to cry. 'I'm sorry, my lord. I didn't know what to do, who to trust, but I –'

'It's alright,' Regan said. 'Stop crying and tell me everything.'

He listened intently as the girl told her story. It didn't take long, even with the girl's constant blubbering, but her story both surprised and disappointed him.

Regan knew of this Sir Masten Checker, a lordless hedge knight who had recently offered his undying fidelity if Regan would accept him as a vassal. Although a bit of a fop, Regan had considered taking him on but hadn't yet made a final judgement. However, he had already decided to send Sir Masten with Cedric to escort the princess back from Whitehall. Of course, that would now change.

His anger began to grow towards Lennane, and himself. He'd brought her back into the fold because he thought they shared the same ideals and that she would do as instructed. It irked him that he had been proven wrong. Her insight and ideas had proved useful, but he couldn't have anyone making plans behind his back.

He did not doubt that the girl told him the truth. She had no reason to lie. Regan had a mind to order Harrow to fetch his wife and drag her down to the dungeons, something his bodyguard would relish. However, now he knew of her deceit, he could work around it and possibly use it. The hedge knight would be easily taken care of, but he would have his wife constantly watched to see if any others had been drawn into her web. The girl's sobbing had ceased, but tears still trickled down her face.

'You are a loyal and trustworthy servant looking out for my interests, so now I need you to do something for me.'

She nodded her agreement.

'Anything, my lord.'

'I need you to go back to Lady Greythorpe.'

'Go back?'

'Yes.'

'But what she did —'

He raised his hand.

'It is crucial that you continue to perform your regular duties, whatever they are. Look and listen and report anything unusual, such as this situation with Sir Masten. Do you understand?'

'Y … yes, my lord,' she nodded. 'I'll do as you ask.'

'Good.'

Regan already had spies in his wife's household, but not this close. If this girl proved her loyalty, she would be suitably rewarded. He had plenty of tasks a pretty young woman could perform. He dismissed her, and she left, hurrying out the door.

Spending a lot of time indoors went with the position of Governor, but Regan liked to get out into fresh air at least once a day. He went to the door, and as he opened it, a messenger arrived and handed him a small scroll. He unfurled and read it. Excellent, Cedric would arrive in the capitol with the prince in a few days. Maybe his eldest son wasn't the idiot he thought him to be.

Regan decided to dine with his wife that evening. He'd dismissed her request for an intimate dinner, but considering the recent revelations, he now changed his mind. He wanted to learn her motives, trip her up, then throw her into the dungeon. He found the idea quite appealing.

Lennane arrived at his private quarters at the appointed hour. At least she feared him enough not to be tardy. The conversation started pleasantly; she behaved as expected, being her usual glamorous self. She gave him all the capitol news, some of which he already knew, some he didn't. After the main meal, she brought up a subject more serious than the castle gossip.

'I understand the prince will arrive soon?'

She phrased it as a question. Regan confirmed with a nod and wondered whether she'd also try to have the prince killed. Anyone could arrange the murder of someone whilst they travelled through the countryside. He'd done that himself only last year, but to have someone killed in Riverview took planning and fortitude. Surely, she didn't have that type of influence or skill.

'He'll be difficult to control,' Lennane said.

'I don't think so,' Regan replied. 'If he cares for his sister's well-being, he'll behave.'

'Yes,' she said, hesitating, 'but if that's not successful, there may be another way to make him more amiable. We can't have him interfering with our plans.'

Regan suppressed a laugh. Our plans, indeed.

'What do you propose?'

'He's a young man, prone to a young man's yearnings,' she said. 'And we know he likes women, so ... '

She left her sentence unfinished, but Regan stayed silent, forcing her to explain herself fully.

'We can try to get someone close to him to report back to us and possibly try to make him see things from our perspective,' she continued. 'Plenty of lords would be willing to allow their daughters to assist us this way.'

'It could work,' Regan said, thinking it a more direct approach than he would normally have recommended. 'She'd have to be quite a beauty. He is a prince, after all.'

'Of course,' Lennane smiled.

Regan assumed she already had someone in mind.

'Your Lady-in-waiting, perhaps?' Regan said before she could suggest anyone else.

'Err … yes,' Lennane's smile disappeared. 'Though I was thinking of one of the ladies of the court, someone with good breeding, more suited to royalty.'

He wasn't surprised at her reaction. She didn't like sharing her lovers.

'We want him to bed her, not marry her,' Regan said, enjoying riding roughshod over his wife's opinions. 'And it's much easier to order a servant than a noble, wouldn't you agree? Besides, she's already loyal to you, is she not?'

After a few moments, her smile returned.

'As always, you have the best ideas, my love. Dariah is beautiful and has the added attraction of never being bedded.'

'By a man?' Regan wanted Lennane to know that he knew.

'Yes,' she said, straight-faced. 'Of course, by a man.'

'It's settled, then, and since you know more about this type of thing than I do, I'll leave the details to you.'

'Thank you,' she said. 'Dariah may or may not garner his cooperation right away, but I know how to bind him to us on a more permanent basis.'

'You're positively full of ideas tonight.'

'What's the best way of uniting two warring families?' she asked, ignoring his mockery.

Regan had already considered the longer-term situation of binding Leto to him. Blackmail would only work for so long, and one never knew what would happen in the future, so he always liked to have alternative plans.

'I've already decided,' he said. 'He'll wed Lucy.'

'Lucy?'

'Do you have a problem with that?'

'No … no. Lucy is a good choice,' Lennane said. 'But I thought that Lennore would be better suited.'

'She's too young.'

'But she is mature for her age and would be able to marry. She's already bled, so she's able to bear children.'

Lucy, his daughter by his first wife, was rather plain, but there was no shortage of suitors for her hand. Offers of betrothal had already begun rolling in for Lennore as well. However, he always had a soft spot for his eldest daughter, and with Lennane's deceit revealed, his choice had been made easy.

'No,' Regan said. 'The prince will wed Lucy, and Calvin will be betrothed to Princess Melina. That way, there will be twice the bond between the families.'

For once, Lennane didn't have anything to say, at least not immediately. She licked her lips, and her eyes darted around, looking everywhere except at him.

'Whatever you think is best,' she managed to say. 'I should be going. I know you always have a lot of work to get through.'

He did, but he found that he wanted something else. It might have been the wine, but seeing his wife squirm this evening had aroused him.

'I thought we might retire to my chambers,' he said.

She looked astonished for a moment, and Regan couldn't blame her. He couldn't recall the last time he'd instigated sex. Usually, she had to ask, and he declined more often than not. He knew she couldn't refuse, and this excited him more.

'Of course, my love,' she said.

They went upstairs to Regan's sleeping chambers, and he helped her out of her dress, ripping at the last few laces in his impatience.

She turned and stood in front of him with a mischievous smile. He gazed at his wife's naked form, his eyes lingering on her full breasts and curved hips. He couldn't deny her beauty.

'No,' Regan commanded as she began to kneel.

He turned her around and she obediently bent over, her hands on the edge of the bed. He untied his breeches and let them fall to his knees. Usually, she'd need to use her bedroom skills to prepare him, but he couldn't have been more ready. He ran his hands over the soft cheeks of

281

her arse and spread them apart, exposing her womanhood. Yes, she was beautiful, he thought and plunged in without a second thought.

Lennane screeched at the sudden invasion.

'My love!' she exclaimed and reached back with her hand to hold him off,

He slapped it away and began thrusting.

'Please,' she whimpered and let out another yelp of pain.

Her protestations only made him drive into her faster. He gripped her hips and pulled her hard towards him, and, oblivious to her screams, forced himself deeper. She began to fall forwards but he held her to him and continued to thrust even harder. With a final lunge, he shuddered and climaxed. Remaining fully inside her, still gripping her hips, he took several deep breaths and waited a few moments, amazed at how quickly he'd finished.

Releasing her and pulling out, Regan looked down at his wife. She had fallen and sprawled face down on the bed, making soft wailing noises. He debated whether to tell her to stay. He liked the idea of asserting his authority over her again later, but now that he'd finished, he found he couldn't stand the sight of her.

Regan hitched up his breeches and left without a word. He returned to his solar and poured himself some wine. He tried to work for a while, but after only an hour, he began to yawn. With reluctance, he went back upstairs. Thankfully, his wife was nowhere to be seen.

The following evening, Prince Leto arrived in a fully enclosed horse-drawn wagon with only a few slots around the top to allow the air to circulate. No one could see in, and he couldn't see out. Cedric seemed quite content, and for good reason. Regan had been pleased with what his son had accomplished, although Cedric still had a way to go before he earned his unqualified trust.

Bound and gagged, the prince had been taken up to his apartment, provided with clean clothes and a bath, and left to his own devices. Regan wanted to begin building some semblance of a relationship with the boy, so he hoped putting him in familiar surroundings would help. He did, however, post over a dozen guards at various points throughout the royal apartments. Leto wasn't getting out undetected this time.

Cedric reported on the events leading up to the prince's capture, and Regan's good mood soured.

'You killed his best friend right in front of him?' Regan said.

'He wouldn't surrender.'

'You could have just left him injured and then taken the prince. Do you realise it'll be much more difficult to control him now?'

Cedric started to say something, but Regan cut him off.

'And breaking the captain's legs like that was thoughtless,' he continued. 'The sensible thing to do would have been to kill them all and burn the ship to the waterline. Then it would've been put down to pirates or an accident, and not traceable to me. When word of this gets to our trading partners in the Diamond Isles, only the gods know how much damage it'll do.'

'I'm sorry. I didn't know.'

'It was reckless.'

Regan did realise that with his brother dead and his wife scheming behind his back, Cedric could be the only one he could depend on for absolute loyalty, even if he wasn't reliable.

'You did well in finding the prince,' his tone softened. 'You just need to think things through more before you act. Everything has consequences.'

'I'll do better next time.'

'Now go and do … whatever it is you do. You'll be leaving for Sisters End in a few days,' Regan said, dismissing his son with a wave of his hand.

He knew it wouldn't be easy to sway the young prince, especially considering his son's actions, but he had time and several incentives he could employ if the prince needed convincing to be cooperative.

His first meeting with Prince Leto didn't go as expected, although the prince did impart some enlightening, but disturbing information.

'I saw you,' Leto accused, 'and once everyone finds out, you're a dead man!'

This revelation troubled Regan and that he had overlooked the viewing gallery also concerned him. That was a detail he shouldn't have missed. It also meant that the Kirkwoods and those in the north knew of his complicity in the King's death. If the story hadn't yet reached the capitol, it soon would, so the long-term approach had to be abandoned.

'Let me remind you, Your Highness, that your sister is still under my protection.'

'Don't you dare hurt her,' Leto said with bravado.

'Don't test me,' Regan warned. 'If you cooperate, you'll be King, as is your birthright. I won't interfere with the day-to-day workings of your court. You will only need to accept some direction, and together, we'll rule Avaleen how it should be; with a strong hand.'

'And if I don't?'

'Do you really want to go down that path, boy?'

The prince glared back at him, undisguised hate in his eyes. Regan didn't need Leto to like him for this to work, but he needed him more receptive, calmer. He'd give him more time to recover from his ordeal. He made to leave, but the prince gave him a crooked smile.

'I killed your brother.'

Regan said nothing, but stood frozen on the spot for a few moments. The boy was baiting him, but he wasn't going to be goaded, so he started for the door.

'If you don't believe me, I can tell you exactly how he died,' Leto said, matter-of-factly and tapped his heart. 'His bodyguard too.' He poked his tongue out a bit as if coughing and pointed to the side of his neck.

Regan's face clenched, barely able to control himself. He knew he shouldn't engage in this conversation, but he couldn't help it. His brother was dead and this … this boy was responsible.'

'Is that so?' he said through gritted teeth.

The prince nodded, giving him a humourless smile.

'He tried to run away like a coward, but we got him.'

Regan seethed at the prince's confession and his hand moved to the pommel of his sword.

Leto scoffed. 'You going to kill me too?' his eyes flicking to the sword

You are so lucky I need you alive, boy, otherwise … he pushed the thought aside and lifted his finger.

'Think about everything I've just said.' Regan turned for the door.

'He was a coward!' the prince yelled as the door to the apartment closed behind him. 'Just like your son!'

Regan returned to his solar to find a messenger waiting. He took the small scroll and dropped it on his desk and poured himself a cup of wine, gulping it down in the hope it would settle his nerves. He closed his eyes and rubbed his temples. Whether the prince had told the truth or not, he shouldn't have let it get to him. Getting angry wouldn't bring his brother back, and the prince would be made to fall into line, eventually.

He opened his eyes and grabbed the small scroll. The wax seal revealed the sender, Whitehall. He broke the seal and unfurled the parchment. He read it, and his blood began to boil again. Damn it all to hell, Rainer White! How difficult is it to confine a young girl?

This was the first outright opposition to his position as Steward. It was treason, and if he allowed the Greenwoods to get away with it, others may follow suit.

He sent for Cedric at once. Regan had originally planned to send a token force to Sisters End to escort the princess back to the capitol. Not now. Now he would get his son to leave for the Greenhavens today, with a hundred and fifty soldiers at his command. He decided to send Harrow along as well. As he had reminded his son earlier, everything had its consequences.

28

DARIAH

She sat in silence, not daring to say a word.

Lady Greythorpe talked and talked, but the prince refused to respond. He paced around the room, stopping and occasionally gazing out over the balcony, ignoring anything her mistress said, but she persisted.

'– and I was most distressed to hear of your treatment at the hands of my stepson, Your Highness,' she said. 'He's always been somewhat of an imbecile.'

The prince poured himself a cup of wine and continued to ignore her.

'Personally, I think it would have been better if Jacob had killed him instead of –'

'Stop!' the prince barked, spilling wine as he turned on them.

Dariah flinched, startled at the unexpected outburst.

'Neither you nor any of your family are worthy to speak his name,' he said.

'I ... I'm sorry, Your Highness,' her mistress said, her tone deferential.

The sudden movement brought back her headache, and she rubbed the back of her head where she had been struck a few days before.

'Why are you here?' he demanded.

Dariah had wondered the same thing. Her mistress hadn't given her a reason.

'Dress as if you were meeting the King,' her mistress had said to Dariah that morning, and that was all.

Later that afternoon, she had followed Lady Greythorpe from her apartment and into the royal residence. Dariah had never been to this part of the castle, but now she sat across from the future King and he did not seem happy. The request from Lord Owen sat foremost in her mind, but she couldn't do anything about it with her mistress nearby.

'Since you have now returned to the capitol, we thought we should get to know one another better,' Lady Greythorpe said.

'Are you serious?' he said, incredulous. 'I want you and your family out of Riverview. I certainly don't want to see more of you.'

'I realise our families have not always seen eye to eye.'

'Huh, you're smarter than I thought,' the prince said.

'May I speak plainly, Your Highness?'

'Are you going to threaten me as well?' the prince spat.

'I'm not my husband,' she said.

Had Lord Regan threatened the prince? He had expressed dismay at his wife's plot to kill Princess Melina, so it didn't make sense. Dariah began to feel out of her depth. Less than a year ago, she was a farmer's daughter. Now, she stood in the centre of a feud between the most powerful families in Avaleen. With the Steward, his wife and Lord Owen all pulling her in different directions, she had begun to feel overwhelmed by it all. She also questioned her decision to return to Riverview after the Prior attack, thinking she should have gone home to her mother and father instead.

'Sure, why not,' the prince said after a moment. 'Speak.'

'You're alone here,' Lady Greythorpe began. 'Your father and best friend are gone, and your sister is hundreds of miles away. Your aunt hasn't even asked to see you. You have no one, so I thought you may need a friend.'

He scowled at Lady Greythorpe but said nothing. Dariah shifted in her seat at the uncomfortable silence.

'Your Highness, I –' she finally spoke, but the prince cut her off.

'Get out!'

'But –'

'Get ... out!'

Lady Greythorpe nodded 'I apologise, Your Highness. Let's go, Dariah.'

The prince turned his back on them and walked away. The door to his bedchamber slammed shut as Dariah followed Lady Greythorpe out into the hall, almost bumping into her when she stopped in the centre of the grand foyer.

'Why won't the boy see reason?' her mistress exclaimed.

Dariah wasn't surprised that Prince Leto had told them to leave. One doesn't speak to a member of the royal family in such a tone, even if you're in a family as powerful as the Greythorpes.

'Dariah, dear,' she continued. 'I left my veil in the prince's quarters. Go and fetch it for me.'

'Yes, my lady.'

'While you're there, see if you can engage him in conversation.'

'But he hates us.'

'He hates me, not you, and you're a beautiful young woman, a lady. He may talk to you.'

Dariah realised she may have the opportunity she needed.

'But what would I say?'

'Try to be his friend. You'll think of something. He's a man, so use your feminine wiles.'

'Seduce him?'

The suggestion stunned Dariah. She had never known a man before, and he was a prince, someone way above her station. She wouldn't know how.

'Yes, just like you did with me, only be more obvious. Men aren't very perceptive.'

She had hardly seduced her mistress. Lady Greythorpe had always been the dominant one and not subtle about it.

'Err ... Yes, my lady.'

Dariah didn't think she would succeed at beguiling the prince, but it would allow her to be alone with him.

'I'll do my best.'

'Good girl. Come and see me when you're done, whatever the hour.'

She turned, leaving Dariah alone in the middle of the foyer. She collected her thoughts and headed back to the royal residence.

'My lady left something in His Highness's quarters and has sent me to retrieve it,' Dariah said as she approached the guards outside the prince's apartment.

He ogled her, up and down.

'I'm sure she did,' the taller one said but opened the door.

Dariah went in, her eyes flicking around the room, looking for the prince. She had half expected him to suddenly appear and shout at her to leave.

'Hello,' she said and moved further into the living room.

He must be somewhere. He couldn't have just disappeared. Dariah picked up the silk scarf from the chair near the hearth and turned towards the door of the prince's sleeping chambers.

'Your Highness?'

She approached and prepared to knock, but the door burst open before she could touch it, and she jumped back in surprise.

'I said get out!' Leto stood at the door.

'My lady left her scarf behind,' Dariah bumbled and held up the length of silk to show him.

'You have it, now leave,' he said and shut the door, leaving Dariah holding the veil in the air.

Embarrassed, she lowered the cloth and stepped up to the door.

You can do this, she said to herself and knocked.

Again, the door jerked open, but this time she stood her ground.

'Are you stupid?' Leto growled.

Her chest heaved as she took a few large breaths.

'Well?'

The prince stepped back, about to slam the door closed.

'Lord Owen sends his regards,' she said before her courage deserted her.

He stopped but didn't remove his hand from the door.

'Owen Redstone?'

'Y … yes, Your Highness.'

'Why should I believe you? You're just Lennane Greythorpe's sidekick. You even dress like her.'

'No … no, Your Highness. Please let me explain,' she pleaded.

His anger had subsided a little, but he still didn't believe her.

'Please?'

He glared at her for a few moments.

'Make it quick,' he demanded.

'Thank you, Your Highness,' she said, taking another deep breath. 'Lady Greythorpe did send me here to try and befriend you and to … err … seduce you.'

Dariah thought the truth would be best, though she felt uncomfortable admitting it.

'I assumed as much,' he seemed more disappointed than angry. 'So why should I believe anything you say?'

'But … Lord Owen is my patron, and I've been his observer in the Steward's household since mid-summer,' Dariah said.

'Observer?'

'That's what Abbot Alwen calls it,' she said. 'It sounds better than a spy.'

'The Abbot?'

He seemed surprised.

She nodded. 'I met with them both a few days ago, Your Highness.'

The prince stared at Dariah.

'And Lord Owen said to tell you he's currently staying in Lord Kirkwood's residence in the north quarter,' she added.

Leto glanced around the apartment, stepped back into his chambers and beckoned her in. Dariah felt his gaze as she entered his chambers. The room, nearly as big as Lady Greythorpe's entire apartment, had doors that opened onto a huge balcony. She turned as he closed the door. The prince strode past her out to the balcony, grabbing two goblets from a table as he passed.

'Grab the jug and follow me.'

She picked up the jug from the sideboard and rushed to follow.

He directed her to one of the chairs on the balcony. The view of King Falls and the lake beyond took her breath away, and the imminent sunset made it even more beautiful, but it did little to settle her nerves.

'We have a lot to discuss,' he continued, filling both wine goblets and offering one to her.

She accepted it without comment. Maybe the wine would help, she thought. The prince moved one of the chairs closer and sat facing her.

'Dariah, isn't it?' he said, and she nodded. 'I need you to convince me I shouldn't throw you off this balcony.'

'Your Highness?' Dariah said, stunned at the sudden threat. 'I ... I don't –'

'I'm not convinced you are who you say,' he interjected.

He had to believe her, he just had to. So, before he could change his mind, Dariah launched into her story; how she came to be in the Abbot's service, her relationship with Lady Greythorpe, the plot against Princess Melina's life and her betrayal of her mistress to Lord Regan. She even told him about the attack by Prior Fren, her rescue by Lord Owen and the Abbot, and her return to the Greythorpe household. The prince stayed silent throughout.

'That's quite a tale,' the prince said after she'd finished. 'I want to believe you.'

'It's all true,' she said, her eyes flicking from the prince to the balustrade and back. 'I promise.'

He watched her for a few moments, his face grim.

'Don't worry,' he said, his stern face softening. 'I wouldn't have thrown you off the balcony.'

Dariah took a sip of her wine.

'I'm not like them,' he added.

'That's good to know, Your Highness'

'My father thought your mistress was a social climbing harlot,' he said. 'I'm sorry if that offends you. I know you are … close.'

Dariah's mind returned to the night in the servants' quarters when the prince and his friend had witnessed their midnight tryst, undetected until he fell through the roof. She visibly blushed and took another, longer drink.

'I'll admit I have been conflicted in my feelings towards her recently,' Dariah said. 'She has treated me very well, but ever since this situation with Sir Masten, I'm finding it much easier to justify my betrayal of her to the Governor.'

'You do realise that he's no better than his wife?'

Dariah gave the prince a questioning look. 'But he stopped the attempt on your sister's life. He said he would deal with Sir Masten.'

'If Melina was dead, he couldn't use her against me. That's the only reason he wants her alive.'

'Why would he do that?'

'That's what he does. He murders my father and then threatens my sister's life unless I do what he wants,' Leto said, his anger rising.

'Lord Regan killed the King?' Dariah gasped.

'With his own hand. I saw it myself. And his son killed my best friend, and now he wants to control Avaleen through me.'

Surely, she couldn't be that naïve … that stupid.

'I don't understand.'

'Then let me enlighten you,' said Leto, and told her his story, from when he saw his father's murder to the death of Jacob and his return to the capitol.

'I'm … I'm so sorry, Your Highness,' she said after he finished. 'I never knew.'

'You're a brave girl, spying on the Greythorpes,' Leto said. 'You have my eternal gratitude. Now I know I have friends in the capitol, despite what the Greythorpe woman says. If you see Lord Owen before I do, tell him I'll be in contact.'

She nodded.

'Will you visit me again?' he said.

'Certainly, Your Highness,' she replied, perhaps a bit too quickly.

'Good, and don't forget to tell your mistress about your success with me.'

'What?' she said. 'I won't tell her anything. I'm not –'

'If she thinks you've failed, she may not allow you to return,' he said.

Dariah flushed with embarrassment.

'Of course. I should have realised.'

'Even though I hate it, I understand the machinations of the nobility and the way to get what you want,' he said.

'My mistress said I'd make a fine lady of the court, but I'm beginning to doubt that,' she said, managing a weak smile.

'We'll discuss the nature of the nobility another time, but now you should go back to your mistress and tell her everything except about Lord Owen and what you know about my father's death.'

Dariah nodded. 'When should I return?'

'Tomorrow afternoon.'

'That would be wonderful,' Dariah said.

She hadn't expected to be invited back so soon and was delighted at the prospect. Leaving the royal residence, Dariah felt as happy as she had been in a long while. The prince had been through so much, all at the hands of the Greythorpe family, yet he treated her with respect. And he'd made her laugh.

Her happiness began to dissipate, and her heart sank. What had she gotten into? She had worked herself into a state by the time she arrived at Lady Greythorpe's apartment. She had to continue with this fabrication, keeping information from her mistress, reporting to Lord Regan about his wife, and telling everything to the Abbot and Lord Owen, all while knowing Lord Regan had murdered the King and blackmailed the prince. Dariah would inform her mistress of her apparent success, but when she approached the door and went to enter, one of the guards raised his hand to stop her.

'She's not here, ma'am,' he said.

'You will refer to Lady Greythorpe as the lady or Lady Greythorpe, not she,' Dariah said, probably harsher than she should have.

294

'Err … Yes, ma'am,' he apologised, surprised at the rebuke.

Her mistress hadn't organised anything for this evening that Dariah could recall.

'When will my lady return?'

'I don't know,' the guard said. 'She … Lady Greythorpe is dining with Lord Regan.'

For the second time in as many days, she dined with her husband. Lord Regan now knew of his wife's despicable activities, which confused Dariah more than ever. She would have expected him to avoid his wife altogether or throw her into the dungeon – not invite her to dine with him.

It also concerned Dariah that after Lady Greythorpe's previous visit to her husband, she had returned early, on the verge of tears, and locked herself in her bedchambers, not even allowing Gretchen to attend her. She usually appeared in complete control, even when she wasn't, so something significant must have happened for her to be that upset. And she didn't rise until mid-morning, her mood gloomier than usual, and she snapped repeatedly at both Gretchen and Dariah. Something was very wrong.

Dariah located Gretchen and gave orders to alert her at once if anything unusual happened with their mistress again. She fetched a bite to eat and returned to her room. She decided to take the opportunity to visit the Abbey before going to bed. Despite the lateness of the hour, Dariah hoped the Abbot would appreciate knowing about her success with the prince. She hurried through the city, keeping to the main streets where lanterns burned, and Capitol Guards constantly patrolled.

Dariah headed straight for the small door about twenty yards to the left of the main doors and knocked. Even though Lord Owen assured her Prior Fren would no longer be able to bother her, she began to get anxious the longer she waited. She knocked again, and after a short time, the door opened, and a young monk appeared. She recognised him as the novice she had met a few weeks earlier.

'My lady,' Bryan said with concern. 'What brings you here so late in the evening?'

'I was hoping to speak with the Abbot,' she replied.

'He's not here, I'm afraid,' the novice informed her. 'He's out of the city and isn't due back until the day after tomorrow. Are you sure you won't come in out of the cold? You could warm yourself near the fire while I get one of the Priors for you.'

'Thank you, but no. Maybe you could give the Abbot a message for me on his return?' she suggested.

'I most certainly can,' he said eagerly.

'Please tell Abbot Alwen that Winnie has done as he suggested, and everything is going well.'

Dariah hoped the message, though vague, contained enough information for the Abbot to understand without being obvious to anyone else.

'Is that all, my lady?'

She nodded and thanked him for his help. Dariah turned back towards Riverview, confident the young novice would pass on her message.

The following day, Dariah woke early. She bathed, dressed and had her hair done by mid-morning. The afternoon couldn't come quickly enough for her, and she went immediately to report to Lady Greythorpe.

'How was the lady this morning?' Dariah asked Gretchen as she entered her mistress's apartment.

'She didn't return until after dawn.'

'Was she distressed in any way?'

Their mistress would have only stayed the night if Lord Regan wished it.

'She wasn't herself, but nothing like before,' the handmaiden said.

'Did you dress her?'

'Yes, ma'am,' Gretchen said. 'Of course.'

'Any unusual marks on her body?'

'No, ma'am,' Gretchen seemed confused. 'Why do you ask?'

She didn't want to alarm the young girl but thought that her mistress may have been beaten by her husband because of what Dariah had told him.

'You know how men are sometimes,' she said, not wanting to get into a conversation with the young girl.

'Yes, ma'am,' Gretchen said, accepting the glib reply.

Dariah had been appalled at her mistress's plan and remained adamant she had done the right thing by telling Lord Regan. Her faith in Lady Greythorpe had diminished somewhat. She deserved some kind of punishment, but being directly responsible for someone getting hurt made Dariah sick.

'Is our lady in?' she said.

'Yes, and she did ask after you.'

Dariah entered the bedchambers. Her mistress sat at her small desk, writing.

'My lady,' she said.

'Dariah.' she put down the quill. 'You're looking radiant. It went well yesterday evening, I assume?'

She blushed at the comment but nodded.

'Excellent, I knew you could do it.'

Lady Greythorpe went and sat in one of the more comfortable chairs near the open window.

'Now tell me all about it.'

Dariah took a seat opposite.

'I will admit, my lady, I didn't think your plan would work, but His Highness was surprisingly open with me.'

She told her mistress everything that had happened with Prince Leto the day before, except for the conversation about Lord Owen. She also kept the prince's accusation against Lord Regan to herself. To her relief, Lady Greythorpe seemed pleased with her efforts.

'Are you well, my lady?' Dariah said. 'I worry for you.'

Her mistress looked about to brush aside Dariah's concerns, but stopped.

'In truth, my husband has been acting rather oddly of late,' she said. 'It's taken me by surprise. But I won't burden you with my troubles. You have more important things to be worried about.'

They talked some more, mainly court gossip, as Dariah didn't want to push her mistress further about her evenings with Lord Regan. Although she wasn't hungry, nervous worry making her appetite disappear, she still ordered Gretchen to fetch food for the midday meal.

Finally, the time had come to see the prince again. With encouragement from her mistress, Dariah returned to the royal residence. The guards opened the door without a word. Prince Leto sat in front of the fire and didn't seem to notice her at first.

'Your Highness,' she announced after the door closed behind her.

He turned at the sound of her voice, and she curtsied.

'I'm glad you decided to return,' he said, a smile spreading across his face.

'It's not every day a farmer's daughter is invited to walk in the Queen's Gardens with a prince,' she said, feeling more relaxed this time. 'I noticed your grim look when I arrived. No more unwelcome news, I hope, Your Highness?'

His smile disappeared, and Dariah instantly regretted asking.

'You could say that,' he said, beckoning her to sit beside him.

He told her of Lord Regan's visit not two hours prior and of Leto's new marital arrangements.

'She'll be arriving in the capitol soon,' he said.

'He wants you to marry his daughter?' Dariah said, finding it hard to believe. 'But you're already betrothed, are you not?'

'Yes, but Greythorpe doesn't care,' the prince said. 'He thinks that since he rules Avaleen, he can do as he pleases.'

Dariah expected the prince to be angry, but he seemed nonplussed. 'You don't seem very upset?'

'Yesterday, I would've been furious and screamed and cursed the man,' he said, 'but you've given me some hope.'

'Me?'

Dariah never thought she could have such an effect on anyone, let alone a prince of the realm.

'You have allowed me to hope I can escape this place again before he can force me to wed anyone.'

'You're going?' Dariah said. 'How? When?'

'I don't know yet,' he said and looked directly at her. 'Will you help me?'

She opened her mouth, but words would not come. She had only just found someone with whom she could be her true self without having to check her words or concoct lies, and now he was planning to leave. It was a selfish thought, but Dariah would do anything he asked, despite that.

'I'm yours to command.'

'It's not a command,' he said. 'But I will need your help, even if it's just not to speak of my plans to anyone.'

'I … I'd never forsake you,' Dariah said, beginning to panic. 'I'll do whatever you ask of me.'

'Are you sure about that? It may put you in more danger than you are already.'

'I'm quite sure,' she said.

'Thank you.'

They eventually took their walk through the Queen's Gardens as he had promised. He also gave her a tour of the castle, all the time shadowed by at least half a dozen Capitol Guards.

Over the next week, they both played their part in convincing the Greythorpes that the prince had begun to behave himself. Dariah informed her mistress of practically everything she and the prince did together. Begrudgingly, Leto acted with less hostility towards Lord Regan.

A carriage ride down to King Lake was the highlight for Dariah. They left at dawn and didn't return until well after dark. Despite being escorted by a dozen guards, she had a wonderful time, and that night, she returned to her room, exhausted.

The prince had invited her back the following evening but had not said what they'd be doing. She didn't care, delighted just to spend more time in his company. These pleasant thoughts kept her smiling as she undressed and prepared for bed.

29

OWEN

He hated the waiting most of all. It had been over a fortnight since Owen sent the young woman back into the wolf's den. He'd heard nothing for days, but rumours began to fly around the capitol that the prince was in the city.

A few minor allies had visited Owen at Lord Malachy's residence. They'd been a welcome break from the tedium. However, he still urged them to abandon the city as there'd been an escalation in the harassment of Owen and his allies by the Capitol Guard.

He'd also received a visit from the Abbot, just returned from a trip to one of the Brothers' monasteries east of the capitol.

'Young Dariah has come through, it seems,' Abbot Alwen said to Owen. 'At least as far as making contact with His Highness.'

Owen was impressed. 'That was quick.'

'And according to our other contacts, the prince is understandably quite upset. Lady Greythorpe has been charged with trying to placate him,' the Abbot said.

'She's more likely to try and beguile him, the whore ... ' Owen's voice trailed off.

'Err ... yes. But it's given Dariah the access we need.'

'Let's hope he can get a message to us,' Owen said.

'Yes,' Alwen said. 'We'll just have to wait and see.'

Owen sighed.

'Terrific, more waiting. There's nothing to do but eat and drink. I'm getting fatter by the day. Whenever my men or I go into the city, we're badgered by Baltair's dogs.'

'Anything I can do to ease your boredom?' Alwen said.

Owen thought for a moment. There was something he had dearly wanted ever since his unexpected banishment from the castle.

'There is one thing, Father. I want to pay my last respects to Caleb if I can. Do you think it could be arranged?'

It wouldn't alleviate Owen's growing apathy, but he wanted to see if it was possible.

'I'll do my best,' Alwen said. 'However, there's no guarantee Lord Regan will even grant you entry to the castle grounds.'

Owen was doubtful he'd get permission, but two days later, he received an official letter signed by the Steward permitting him to visit the crypt of the King, though it was rife with conditions.

He must arrive at the West Gate just after dusk three days hence with one guard only. He should walk, not ride, into the castle grounds and be accompanied to the royal crypt by a member of the Ruling Council. He would be permitted to stay in the crypt no longer than one-half hour.

Abbot Alwen had been chosen as the council representative to escort him. However, he assumed there'd also be an escort of Capitol Guards. He sat back in his chair and sipped his wine. It would be good to say goodbye to his friend one last time.

Owen's prediction proved correct. It had been just on dusk as he, Captain Archer Janz and four of his soldiers approached the castle gate on horseback. Watchers and members of the Capitol Guard kept an eye on them as they dismounted and waited. Soon after the sun had disappeared, Abbot Alwen approached from inside the castle grounds accompanied by half a dozen of the Capitol Guard, including the Captain of the Capitol Guard, Armen Penna.

Leaving the others to look after the horses, Owen and Archer approached the gate and greeted the Abbot and Captain Penna. They began the walk into the castle, Captain Penna alongside Owen, and the Abbot and Archer a couple of steps behind. Their escort came a few yards further back.

'I must apologise, my Lord,' Armen said, his voice low. 'I don't even begin to understand how it's come to this.'

'It's alright, Armen,' Owen said. 'It is what it is.'

'Sir Baltair tells us nothing and some of the things he's ordered us to do … '

Owen toyed with the idea of telling Armen the truth. Although he was a captain in the Capitol Guard, he was an honourable man, not one of Baltair's puppets. However, revealing the details about the King's murder to the captain would most likely be signing the man's death warrant.

'Continue doing your job and keep your eyes and ears open,' Owen said, 'but do me this one favour if you will.'

'Anything.'

'Look out for the prince. He may need protection from those claiming to have his best interests at heart.'

'I will, my Lord,' Armen nodded his understanding.

They walked on and eventually entered the central courtyard.

'It was wrong,' Armen said, breaking the silence, 'to disband the Noble Guard.'

'It would be in your best interests not to say that out loud around here.'

'I was planning to apply next summer,' Armen said.

'You'd have made an excellent Noble Guard, Armen.'

'Thank you, my lord,' the captain said.

They arrived at the entrance to the crypt. Captain Penna allowed Owen and the Abbot to descend the stairway alone. The foyer of the crypt was about fifty feet round, with half a dozen darkened passages leading off in various directions. It was lit by torches on the walls in between the passages.

Owen knelt in front of the altar and paid his respects to his closest friend. After a while, he stood and glanced around the crypt. Part of him hoped the prince would miraculously appear out of one of the darkened passages, but it was a vain hope.

'Let's go, Father,' Owen said, and he and Alwen ascended the stairs.

The following night, as he lay in bed contemplating his next move, there was a knock at the door. It was after midnight, and he'd had little enough sleep the past few weeks. This had better be damn important.

'Come.'

The door opened, and Archer came in quietly and closed the door. He wasn't wearing armour and looked like he'd just been woken.

'What is it?'

'We have a visitor, my lord,' Archer said. 'He's waiting in the living room.'

Owen got out of bed and headed for the door.

'You may want to get dressed,' Archer said.

'If someone wants to wake me in the middle of the night, they can damn well see me in my nightclothes!'

'My lord,' Archer whispered. 'It would be better to be dressed when meeting one's liege lord.'

Owen gave Archer a quizzical look. His liege lord was dead, and he was about to rebuke his captain when it came to him.

'He's here?' Owen said.

Archer nodded, and Owen began to dress, rushing to pull on his breeches.

'Light the hearth, make him comfortable. Offer him a drink, something to eat.'

Owen grabbed his tunic.

'Already done, my lord.'

Archer opened the door to leave.

'Who else knows he's here?'

'Sergeant Garrat, me, and now you,' the captain said.

Owen pulled on his boots. 'Let's keep it that way – and double the guard.'

'Yes, my lord.'

Archer left, closing the door behind him.

Owen splashed water on his face. His mind raced. Why was the prince here? Was he doing Regan's bidding? Did Regan know he was here at all?

If not, how did he get here unnoticed? Owen prayed the prince had not been followed and that a contingent of Capitol Guards would not soon be banging on the compound gate. He wiped his face dry and went to the living room.

Leto stood near the fire and turned to face Owen as he entered. He glanced around the room and saw only Sergeant Garrat guarding the door. Owen signalled to him to wait outside; the guard quickly complied.

'Your Highness,' Owen approached the prince.

'Lord Owen, it's good to see you.'

'It's a relief to see you alive and well.'

'I'm alive, surprisingly. As to whether I'm well … ' the prince shrugged and stepped towards Owen.

They embraced.

'My condolences for your father.'

Leto acknowledged him with a short nod.

'And Jacob,' Owen added.

Leto closed his eyes tight and lowered his chin. Owen could see the young prince's pain.

'What happened out there?' Owen said.

Leto took a deep breath and looked back up at Owen.

'I don't have much time,' the prince said. 'I have to get back before I'm discovered missing.'

Owen agreed. 'You need to be extra careful. If you're caught, the repercussions could be severe. Greythorpe won't give you a simple reprimand, you know that.'

'All the more reason to escape the city,' Leto said, 'which is why I'm here.'

'Anything you need, you'll have it, but I will not have you trudging the wilds alone again,' Owen said, pleased to finally be doing something useful.

'I'm in your hands,' Leto said.

30

DARIAH

She wore her favourite dress, a green and black ensemble that showed off her slim figure. Dariah and Leto shared a meal in his apartment and talked continuously throughout. She was enjoying their conversation, but he became nervous after they had finished eating.

'What's wrong?' she asked, concerned.

'I want to take you somewhere special,' he said after an awkward silence.

Again, he didn't say where, but she readily agreed.

'Since I've been back in the capitol, I haven't had the courage to visit my father,' he said. 'I just didn't feel ready, but now I ... would you come with me?'

'I'd be honoured.'

They made their way out to the central courtyard and stopped at the entrance to the crypt, then descended the marble stair and entered the royal tomb where the ashes of the King were interred. The air was cool, and she felt goosebumps on her exposed shoulders. In the centre of the tomb, a smooth stone casket rested on a pedestal. Leto approached it and knelt. Dariah remained a few steps behind. She wasn't as uncomfortable as she thought she would be, surrounded by dead kings a hundred feet underground with the entire castle above them.

'Even after all that's happened, I still can't believe he's gone,' Leto's voice cracked.

Dariah could hear him weeping. She stepped forward, placed her hand on his shoulder and gently squeezed. In all their time together, she had never overtly touched the prince, and the only time he had touched her was on the small of her back to guide her somewhere. She hoped she wasn't overstepping her bounds, but it felt right.

'I'm here for you,' Dariah whispered.

He didn't shrug off her hand but turned to face her.

By the gods, what have I done? I shouldn't have touched him. Dariah was about to apologise, but he embraced her and buried his head in her shoulder.

'I miss him so much.'

At first, Dariah didn't know how to react, but she ignored protocols or the fact he was a prince. He was just a young man who had lost his father in the most heinous circumstances; she simply held him and said nothing. Only the sputtering of the torches could be heard above Leto's quiet sobs.

They returned to the prince's apartment in silence. He went out onto the balcony and sat. Even though it was chilly outside, she was about to do the same, but he expressed a desire to be alone and would send for her tomorrow. Dariah was disappointed but didn't object, and bade him a quick goodnight. She went to the door and opened it to leave.

'Dariah, wait,' Leto said, standing at the balcony entrance.

She shut the door and faced him. 'Your Highness?'

'I'd like you to stay,' he said.

'Whatever Your Highness wishes.'

She stayed near the door as he approached the hearth.

'I want you to stay because you wish it, not because I have asked or what your mistress has ordered.'

'I ... I don't want to go.'

'I want to believe you, I do,' the prince said. 'But I am —'

'Your Highness,' Dariah interrupted, surprised at her own boldness. 'At first, I was sent here to get close to you, to be your friend, to ... err ...

308

seduce you. They said it would be better for Avaleen if you would cooperate with them.'

Leto approached her as she spoke.

'I will also admit that initially, I didn't see the harm in trying. I didn't know you and to be honest, I didn't think you'd even notice me.'

She began to tremble.

'But … but I realised I couldn't in all good conscience deceive you in that way. I only began spying on the Greythorpes to help my family, nothing more, and recent events have shown me they are truly evil and …'

Leto stopped an arm's length from her.

' … and I've become very fond of you in the short time we've spent together, Your Highness. You're a good person, and they have –'

She was silenced as he gently put a finger on her lips.

'I'm fond of you, too.'

Leto removed his finger, leaned forward and kissed her.

Dariah stared at the prince in amazement. As much as she wanted this, she had not expected it. He kissed her again.

'But you're betrothed,' she whispered, barely able to catch her breath.

'To a Greythorpe, and against my will,' he said, 'and I only spent a few days with Cordelia. I may not even live to see her.'

Why would he die? Dariah was going to ask, but he continued to talk.

'My father said to me that you should always plan ahead, but live for today, so give the –'

Dariah placed her hands on his cheeks and kissed him back. She felt his arms encircle her and pull her close as she slid her arms around his neck. It seemed to last forever. She eventually broke away and looked up into his beautiful brown eyes.

'Your father was a wise man,' she said, and before her confidence deserted her, grabbed him by the hand and led him to the bed.

They kissed each other again; long, slow and passionate. Dariah had never desired anyone so much, not like this.

'Sit,' she instructed.

Leto gave her a quizzical look but obeyed, and sat on the bed, his legs hanging over the edge with his boots inches above the floor. Dariah knelt, removed one of his boots, and placed it on the floor. She did the same with the other and pulled off his stockings. She stood and reached for his tunic, but he lifted it over his head and threw it behind him in one swift movement. Dariah stared at his slim, muscled torso.

She had seen men's bodies before, watching the Noble Guard in training or seeing men and boys swimming in the waterholes and lakes around the capitol, but this was different – very, very different. He had a few small scars, but they didn't detract from her vision of him. As if in a trance, she reached forward and placed her hand on his chest. It was firm and smooth with a light covering of hair. Dariah was used to the soft curves of Lady Greythorpe, so she was fascinated with how his body compared. She traced her fingers around his right chest muscle and laid her hand on his chest, covering the small, erect nipple. She glanced up at him, removed her hand and turned around.

He slipped off the bed and began to undo the laces of her dress. He had barely loosened half of them before she managed to wriggle out of it, tossing it onto a nearby chair. With her breasts exposed, she removed her underskirt and threw it on top of the dress. She was now completely naked. Her heart beat like thunder in her chest and she would not have been surprised if he could hear it. She took a couple of long slow deep breaths. When the trembling had mostly subsided, she turned to face the prince.

It was strange. When Dariah had her back to him, she felt self-conscious and nearly panicked, but now that she faced him with her nakedness on full display, she found herself relaxing. She didn't even feel uncomfortable when he slowly looked her up and down.

'You are beautiful,' he said, cupping her chin and kissing her again.

He went to remove his breeches, but she stopped him.

'No,' she said with more confidence than she felt.

Dariah had never seen a naked man this close, now more anxious about his nakedness than her own. She knelt in front of him and gripped the tops of the breeches on either side of his waist. Dariah was aware of the bulge and felt a flutter of panic. Taking a few more deep breaths to calm herself, she tugged on his breeches, pulling them down to his ankles. He stepped out of them, and she pushed them aside. Dariah lifted her gaze from the floor and there it was, free of its confines, only inches from her face. He was more than ready, she could see that much. She looked up at the prince and he grabbed her hand and helped her stand.

'Are you sure about this?'

'Yes, Your Highness.'

'I think we're way past formalities,' he grinned. 'Call me Leto.'

'It's just … I've never been with a man before … Leto.'

He kissed her once more, pulling her against his hard body. She responded in kind, holding him tightly and returning his affections. They broke the embrace, and Leto scooped her in his arms and laid her on the bed. He climbed onto the bed and lay on his side facing her.

'Never?' he said, circling one of her breasts with his finger.

Dariah quivered at his touch.

'Never.'

'Only women?' his finger slowly circled closer to the centre.

'Err … yes,' she blushed.

She gasped as Leto brushed the nipple of her other breast with his fingertips. She pulled his head to hers, and their lips locked. She gently stroked the back of his head as he rolled over her, and she wrapped her legs around him as he lowered his body onto hers.

Dariah woke in a daze, but her mind flooded with memories of the previous evening, and she beamed. Her happiness was tinged with disappointment at having been unable to stay the whole night.

'I'd dearly love you to stay, but you can't be discovered here,' Leto said as they lay cuddled up after their lovemaking.

She didn't understand. Perhaps this was his way of saying he didn't want her there anymore. Did she do anything wrong? She thought she had done everything right. It had made her sad and a little angry, and she rolled away from him and propped herself up on her elbow.

'I'm a big girl, Your Highness,' she said. 'If you wish me to leave, you don't need to make up an excuse.'

Earlier that evening, she wouldn't have dared challenge the prince. Maybe it was her familiarity with him or that she was no longer a maiden. Would that make a difference?

'Seriously, if they find you here by yourself without knowing my whereabouts, they'll ask questions of you,' he said, 'and both you and I know what the Greythorpes are capable of.'

'How can you leave here without being noticed? There are dozens of guards outside.'

'I've been sneaking around this castle for most of my life.'

She was about to snap off another retort but instead stared at him and thought about it. It made sense, she supposed. If anyone could get around a place like this without being seen, it would be him.

'I remember that you didn't always go unnoticed,' Dariah smiled, leaned forward, and kissed him.

She liked kissing him. His lips weren't as full as those of her mistress, but she enjoyed it nonetheless, and the hair of his light beard tickled her lips.

'A rare misstep,' he said, smiling.

Dariah now understood why she had to leave, so she pushed aside her disappointment. With her newfound desire and confidence, she got up and sat astride him.

'Not until you make love to me one more time,' she said with a cheeky smile.

She remembered their last bout of lovemaking, more urgent and energetic than their earlier couplings. Reaching down under her slip, she touched herself. She was still tender, and her thighs still ached, but she wouldn't have traded the experience for anything in the world. Eventually, she got out of bed and found Jane, ordering her to draw a bath. She enquired after their mistress.

'She hasn't been in her quarters since last night,' Jane said.

'Is she with Lord Regan again?'

'I don't know, ma'am,' the maid said as she poured hot water into the tub.

'Find Gretchen and tell her to notify me when Lady Greythorpe returns.'

'Yes, ma'am,' Jane said.

As the young handmaiden left, Dariah dipped her fingers into the water. It was a little cooler than she liked, but she removed her slip and stepped into the tub anyway. She lay back in the lukewarm water and began thinking about Lady Greythorpe. Her mistress was most likely with her husband. It was still early, barely past dawn, so it wasn't as if she had been absent from her quarters an unusually long time. A lot of questions began popping into her mind. Would her husband ever punish her, and if so, what would happen to Dariah? If her mistress wasn't punished, why not, and could she go back to sharing her mistress's bed again? The idea had appeal but not on the same level as before.

She could feel her mood darken as she thought more about the Greythorpes, unsure if she could keep up this charade for much longer. The only thing that kept her going now was Leto. She enjoyed how she felt when she was around him. He was a prince of the realm, and Dariah knew she could never be with him, no matter her feelings for him. When he left, she would be sad and disappointed, but she'd treasure the time spent with him.

It was nearly high sun, and with no word of Lady Greythorpe, Dariah's concern began to grow. She waited in her mistress's living room with Gretchen. She considered asking Winston, the Steward of Lord Regan's household, if he knew of their Lady's whereabouts, but a knock at the door interrupted her thoughts.

Gretchen quickly went to the door as Dariah stood. The handmaiden opened it expecting, as Dariah was, news of their mistress. To the surprise of them both, Leto stood in the doorway.

'Your Highness,' Gretchen said and performed an awkward curtsy.

He acknowledged her with a slight nod and looked over to Dariah.

'You're here?' Dariah said, surprised.

He stepped into the room.

'I didn't want to send for you again,' he said. 'You are not a common servant.'

Dariah was at a loss for words but approached the prince. They embraced, and he gave her a tender kiss. Gretchen stared at them, her mouth agape, still holding the door open.

'Are you ready to go?' Leto said.

She nodded and turned to Gretchen. 'When Lady Greythorpe returns, inform her I'm with Prince Leto.'

Gretchen nodded but didn't say anything.

'Good,' Dariah said.

Leto took her by the hand and almost dragged her from the room. After a short walk around the castle grounds, they spent most of the afternoon making love and drinking wine in Leto's apartment.

Dariah stood naked at the balcony entrance with a goblet in her hand, watching the sunset over Kings Falls.

'I think I've had too much wine.'

She had never paraded her nakedness with Lady Greythorpe, usually putting on a slip or a gown if she was getting out of bed for more than a few moments. She wasn't ashamed of her body but was never comfortable exposing herself casually outside the bed. But with Leto, her inhibitions disappeared. It felt natural to walk around naked when they weren't otherwise occupied. Leto came up behind her and slid his arms around her waist. He propped his chin on her shoulder, and she felt his warm body pressed against hers.

'It's not yet dark,' he said. 'I don't want you falling asleep on me just yet. I'll get some food sent up.'

He kissed her neck and let her go, caressing her buttocks as he walked away. Dariah turned to the nearby chair where her dress had been carelessly thrown. She reached for it but stopped at Leto's words.

'No,' he had already slipped on his breeches and was heading for the door. 'Stay as you are.'

'Whatever His Highness wishes,' she said with mock formality and sipped her wine.

Leto left the room, and Dariah turned back towards the balcony. Yes, she had consumed too much wine, she thought, and put down her cup. Knowing it wouldn't last forever, Dariah wanted to spend every moment possible with him. She certainly didn't want to waste it by falling asleep.

It wasn't long before a veritable smorgasbord of food was delivered from the royal kitchen. After the servants had left, Dariah went to fetch a selection for herself and the prince, but again, Leto told her to stay in the sleeping chambers and directed her to the bed.

'Today, I serve you,' he said, disappearing into the living room.

Dariah grinned to herself as she followed his instructions and climbed back up onto the bed. It wasn't every day a girl was served by royalty. Leto returned with a small platter of food. He placed it on the bed and climbed up next to Dariah. She reached for the platter, but he slapped her hand away. He cut off a small piece of cheese and tried to put it in Dariah's mouth, but most of it ended up on the bed. She began laughing at the absurdity of it all; here she was, naked in the bed of a prince, and he was feeding her like a slave would a master.

'You aren't very good at this, are you?' she managed to say after recovering from her fit of giggles. 'I'll starve before you feed me enough.'

'You're probably right, but at least I tried.'

'And a very gallant attempt it was,' she said, reaching for the platter again, this time without interference.

After eating, they lay together on the bed. Dariah rolled onto her stomach and propped herself up on her elbows. Leto lay on his back staring at the ceiling.

'I'll understand if I can't stay the night,' she said, guessing the reason for his dour expression. 'Don't feel bad sending me away.'

'It's true, you cannot spend the night,' he confirmed, 'and this will be our last night together.'

Dariah's heart sank. She knew this was eventually going to happen, but not so soon.

'I'm leaving the capitol tonight,' he continued.

She was silent for a moment and turned away from him, barely able to contain her emotions. 'Where will you go?'

'South, with Lord Owen.'

Dariah's throat tightened, and though she fought back the tears, the first trickled down her cheek Leto was also clearly upset, but it didn't make her feel better.

'I'm sorry,' Leto tried to wipe away her tears. 'I care for you greatly, but I have to go.'

'I … I know you do,' she said. 'But not right now?'

'No, not right now,' he said.

She kissed him and nestled her face into his neck. 'Good.'

For Dariah, the time to leave arrived far too quickly. She thought Leto was asleep and considered slipping out without fuss, but he was up and alert when she climbed off the bed and began to dress.

'Dariah, you'll always occupy a special place in my heart,' he said as she put on her slippers. 'No matter what happens.'

She finished dressing and went up to him. She kissed him one last time, a long, lingering kiss that she never wanted to end.

'Don't die,' she said and hurried out of the bedchamber before he could say anything more.

She fled back to her quarters and threw herself onto her bed. She hadn't realised Leto would be so disarming and so easy to love. She cared for him a great deal but deep down she knew there could never be a future for them. Why did she feel so empty, knowing she would probably never see him again? Dariah didn't know how long she lay there but suddenly didn't want to be alone. She needed a distraction; something or someone else to divert her attention.

She got out of bed and splashed cool water on her face. Patting her face dry with a cloth, she started towards Lady Greythorpe's quarters. Her mistress had been the only other person to whom she had grown close. Despite Dariah's misgivings about her behaviour, she needed someone to hold or be near her, even if it was just sleeping. She hoped it would take the edge off her misery.

The guards paid her no mind as she entered the apartment. She crossed the living room and entered her mistress's sleeping chambers. A single torch burned, but movement on the bed caught her eye. Her mistress must have heard her come in.

'My lady, it's Dariah,' she whispered. 'Are you awake?'

Dariah's eyes adjusted to the darkness, and she stopped dead in her tracks. Her mistress lay naked on the bed, her legs spread wide with the bobbing head of a girl buried between her thighs.

'Hello, Dariah dear,' her mistress purred, turning her head towards her.

'I'm ... sorry to disturb you, my lady,' Dariah said, embarrassed. 'I didn't realise you had company.'

'It's alright,' she said. 'It's only Gretchen.'

At the sound of her name, the girl lifted her head. 'My lady?'

The young girl glanced at Dariah.

'Don't stop, girl!' her mistress commanded.

Gretchen was one of the few familiar with the relationship between Dariah and their mistress, but the young handmaiden shot Dariah a brief look of guilt before she moved her head back between Lady Greythorpe's legs and continued with her task.

Dariah would have understood if it were a man, but it wasn't. Gretchen was in the same position as she had been not six months earlier. She'd been replaced. Now, she felt betrayed and foolish.

'Would you like to join us?' her mistress murmured.

Surely, she couldn't be serious. 'No ... No, thank you,' Dariah said.

'Are you sure? Gretchen's a quick learner.'

Dariah didn't wait to hear anything further. She simply shook her head, left the bedchamber, and returned to her room. She closed the door behind her and leaned against it, her back sliding down the door until she dropped to the floor. Lady Greythorpe had already lost her trust, and now she'd also broken her heart.

Eventually, Dariah dragged herself to her bed, but her mind raced and sleep eluded her. With what she knew about the Greythorpes and her mistress's betrayals, Dariah felt more vulnerable than ever. She had to get out now, away from the Greythorpes and Riverview. Leto had said that he was leaving with Lord Owen. With her patron leaving the capitol, would there be anyone to look out for her? The Abbot was a good man, but she doubted he could protect her.

Dariah was frightened. Lord Regan had killed the King and blackmailed the prince. She herself was spying on his wife and was stuck in the middle of it all without a friend in the world.

The only solace she took was that Lord Owen had promised that if she returned to the Greythorpe household, her family would be looked after no matter what happened. Dariah thought she had done more than enough and deserved to be free of this place. There was only one thing to do.

She sat up and found her boots. She fished a small bag from under the mattress, which held the money she had squirrelled away over the past months. It wasn't much, but it would have to do.

Then she grabbed her cloak, left the room, and ran out of the castle, only slowing to a walk when she reached the main gate. The Watchers on duty recognised her and let her through without comment. She pulled the hood over her head and headed into the city, vowing never to return to this dreadful place again.

31

OWEN

Owen had planned their exit from the capitol down to the last detail, but his heart nearly stopped when he heard this.

'What do you mean you were seen?' Owen exclaimed.

His plans could be all undone before he'd even started.

'It's alright,' Leto reassured him. 'It was Armen Penna.'

Owen breathed a massive sigh of relief. If it were anyone else, they'd have been in real trouble.

'What did he say?'

'That he'll try and steer any investigations away from us.'

'Good, good.'

Owen had a high opinion of the captain of the Capitol Guard, but Owen still had a sick feeling in his stomach. Just nerves, he thought. Stealing the prince from under Greythorpe's nose had immediate dangers and consequences, not just for Owen and the prince, but for his family and allies.

'He was waiting for me,' Leto said with a smile. 'And you had told him to look out for me.'

Owen nodded.

'At the time I had no idea when I'd see you again, if ever.'

'But I'm here now,' Leto said. 'I just hope he doesn't get himself into trouble.'

Armen's life would be forfeit if the Greythorpes discovered his complicity in the prince's escape.

'He's a good man,' Owen said, but he couldn't concern himself with that now. He had to worry about the future. If the plan he had put in place for Greythorpe didn't come to fruition, war would undoubtedly follow. It involved a fair amount of risk and significant expense, but it'd be well worth it if a conflict could be avoided.

Archer helped him don his cloak. With his battle armour packed away, Owen hadn't planned on wearing any armour, but the captain had convinced him to at least wear his light chain mail over his tabard. With his coat, cloak and the darkness, the Watchers wouldn't even notice.

'The prince?' Owen said.

'Everything is as you ordered,' Archer said.

'And the household staff?'

Owen refused to leave anyone behind.

'Everyone's ready, my lord.'

Thankfully, they all fitted into a single, large cart.

'What do you think of our chances?'

The captain finished tying the last piece and grabbed Owen's cloak.

'Does it matter?' his Captain said, lifting the cloak onto Owen's shoulders and fastening it.

No, it didn't. They would be going through with the plan anyway. Owen patted Archer on the shoulder.

'Let's go home.'

Owen followed Archer to the stables, where his soldiers mounted their horses. Owen grabbed the reins of his favourite stallion and pulled himself up into the saddle. Unlike himself, his captain and soldiers were dressed in battle armour, including helmets that covered most of their face. Along with the unarmed servants, the cart contained other precious cargo, and expected two dozen fully armed soldiers to be an effective deterrent against potential bandits.

Owen and Archer led the procession, followed by half a dozen soldiers riding in pairs. The wagon followed with their possessions and household staff, and the rest of his men came behind, riding in threes. They wound their way through the darkened city and arrived at the South Gate.

As expected, the gate had not yet been opened and would remain closed until sunrise. About half a dozen Watchers were stationed above, below and either side of the large stone arch. A huge fat man entered the street as they approached, a torch in one hand, and signalled them to stop.

Archer raised his hand, and the procession stopped as the Watcher waddled towards them.

'Open the gate at once!' Archer demanded.

Owen had expected this, but he let the captain do his duty.

'I will, after I search you and your cart,' the Watcher growled. 'And might I ask why you're leaving the city so early? It's still several hours until dawn.'

He faced two dozen mounted soldiers but didn't seem to care.

'I couldn't sleep,' Owen said, pushing back his hood, 'and who are you to question when I travel?'

The Watcher raised the torch higher and looked at Owen, his smugness vanishing.

'Oh ... Chief Watcher Anders, milord.'

Owen may be banished from the castle, but he still commanded respect.

'Well then, Chief Watcher Anders,' said Owen. 'What do you hope to find in your search?'

'I ... I have my orders, milord.'

Owen glared at the Watcher briefly and nodded his assent.

'Thank you, milord,' the Chief Watcher said and signalled to his men.

One of the Watchers approached Captain Janz's horse and reached for his saddlebags.

'You touch me or my horse, and you'll lose the hand you touched it with,' Archer warned.

The Watcher stepped back and looked at his superior.

'But milord?' the Chief Watcher implored Owen.

'Chief Watcher Anders,' Owen said. 'I'm sure there's nothing you could be looking for that would fit in a saddlebag.'

'I've got the Governor's daughter wrapped in my bedroll,' a voice came from down the line, and the soldiers laughed.

'We'll have to search the cart, milord,' the Chief Watcher said, ignoring the jibe.

Owen wanted to leave with minimal fuss, and he could see the man's frustration building.

'By all means,' Owen said. 'But be quick about it.'

'Thank you, milord,' a relieved Chief Watcher directed his men to the task.

Owen pulled his mount around and stopped short of the wagon, glancing up at the line of soldiers halted behind. They all remained calm, and none seemed nervous. Aside from the comment about the Steward's daughter, none drew any unnecessary attention to themselves.

So far, so good.

The Watchers ordered the servants out of the wagon and began their search. Owen had to admit they knew what they had to do and, before long, had searched all the bags, boxes and sacks. His soldiers carried everything they needed, and Owen travelled with only the essentials. The Watchers even searched under the front seat where Coen the driver sat, much to his steward's annoyance. Owen thought they had finished, but one of the Watchers called the Chief over, and they had a brief discussion.

'Milord, we need to inspect the contents of that large chest,' the Chief Watcher pointed to it.

The chest, nearly as wide as the wagon, had been locked tight, but Owen had expected this request.

'I'd prefer you didn't,' Owen said.

The Chief Watcher licked his lips, nervous.

'I'll have to insist, milord,' Anders said.

Archer had brought his horse around to the other side of the wagon and stopped just short of Anders and the other Watcher.

'Lord Owen has said no.'

The Chief Watcher sighed. 'If you refuse, I'll have to report it to the Guard Captain.'

'Then report it,' Archer said. 'Just open the bloody gate!'

'No, wait,' Owen said. 'I'll allow the chest to be opened, but only you may look inside.'

'That would be suitable, milord,' the Chief Watcher said, relieved.

'Are you sure about this, my lord?' Coen said, now standing next to Owen's horse.

He had to risk it. Normally, he would've lambasted the Chief Watcher and happily stayed here for hours arguing, but he couldn't afford any delays.

'Unlock it, Coen,' Owen said.

His steward clambered onto the wagon. He unlocked the chest and jumped off the back, moving aside to give the Chief Watcher room. The big man looked at the wagon for a few moments. He turned to the nearest Watcher and gave him some orders. The Watcher then looked at the Chief as if he didn't understand.

'Just get it and hurry,' the Chief ordered.

The Watcher hurried off towards the gate and disappeared into an open door. Moments later, the Watcher came out carrying a large wooden box. He lugged it to the rear of the wagon and set it on the ground. With audible effort, the Chief Watcher stepped onto the box and into the wagon.

'Chief Watcher,' Owen moved his horse closer to the wagon so he could look the man in the eye. 'Once you've seen what's in there, you should think very carefully about who you tell what you saw.'

Anders gave Owen a confused look.

'If there's something suspicious, I have to report it.'

'Put it this way,' Owen said. 'If you came through the gate with this chest, it may arouse suspicion, but I am not you. Does that make sense?'

'I think so, milord,' the Chief Watcher said.

'Because if you tell anyone, it could cause me a great deal of trouble,' Owen said. 'I don't like trouble.'

The Chief Watcher now looked worried but reached for the chest anyway. Owen glanced at Archer, who glowered at Anders. The Chief Watcher used two hands to lift the heavy lid and peered inside the chest. He stared at the contents, not moving. He eventually glanced up at Owen, and then back at the chest.

'Do we have an understanding, Chief Watcher Anders?' Owen said as the fat man closed the lid.

'Err … yes, milord. There's nothing here worth troubling anyone about,' Anders said, turning to get off the wagon. 'Help me down.'

A couple of Watchers helped the Chief down from the wagon, and he walked past Owen towards the gate.

Coen and the other household staff climbed back aboard.

'I'll remember this courtesy, Chief Watcher,' Owen said, and with Captain Janz, took his place at the head of the cortege.

323

'Open the gate!' the Chief Watcher shouted. 'Have a safe trip, milord.'

Owen acknowledged him with a nod and looked to Archer. 'Let's go.'

The massive timber and iron gate creaked and rattled as it opened. Archer signalled for the procession to move forward, and Owen finally led his people out of Twin Falls. The first part of his scheme had succeeded. Now they had to make it back to Cliffs End, a trip of nearly two hundred leagues.

They wound their way down the range to the lowlands without incident. The first rays of the dawn touched them as they neared the protection of the Kingswood. One of the soldiers rode up to the front of the column, settling in beside Owen.

'That went well,' the soldier said.

'We aren't out of danger yet,' Owen said, annoyed.

'I don't know how your men wear these things,' the soldier said, removing his helmet and shaking his hair.

'My men do what they have to do, Your Highness,' Owen said. 'Like most good soldiers.'

The soldiers knew Leto rode amongst them, but some of the household staff audibly gasped as they recognised the prince riding next to their lord. He hadn't trusted the servants with that information, except for Coen.

'What's in that chest anyway?' Leto said. 'You seemed quite protective of it.'

'Gold, and the fewer people that know about it, the better. The last thing we need is bandits thinking it would be worth the risk to take on a score of seasoned soldiers.'

Leto ran his hand through his hair and scratched his head.

'Do you think the Chief Watcher will keep his mouth shut?'

'I'm hoping for a few days' head start before he gloats about it in a drunken stupor or gets greedy and sells the information.'

'I'm betting he'll spill his guts within a day,' Archer said. 'But we'll be too far gone by then.'

'How long to Cliffs End?' Leto asked.

'We'll be leaving the wagon and the servants with ten men. They'll cross the river at Southern Brook and travel the western route through the Greenhavens. We're taking the more direct route down the Great South

Road.'

The Lieutenant in charge of the wagon had instructions to make only one other stop along the way, but it shouldn't delay them by more than a day.

'It shouldn't take us more than a week if the weather holds out,' Archer said. 'It might even be snowing when we reach the Shadowlands.'

'It won't take Greythorpe long to discover you're missing, and he'll be incensed,' Lord Owen said. 'So, we'll be riding hard and should easily make it home ahead of whatever force he sends.'

'Will we be safe?'

'For the winter, perhaps,' Owen said.

'Then what … war?'

'If we get home safely, Regan won't have a choice. He'd look weak if he did nothing, especially since you've slipped through his fingers again.'

Owen watched the prince digest the information.

'Do you want to turn back?' Owen added.

'No, no!'

Leto seemed adamant about that, at least.

'Then we'll see what the summer brings.'

The prince looked unsettled as the realisation of his actions hit him. Owen had tried to explain the possible repercussions back in the capitol, but he'd always seemed a bit distant, and Owen didn't know whether the prince had understood anything at all. He'd been through a lot, but it didn't absolve him of his responsibilities.

'Your Highness,' Owen said. 'I find that when it comes to politics and power, you rarely get what you want. Just think what would have happened if you'd stayed.'

Leto sighed. 'Like I said before, I'm in your hands.'

'Then put your helmet back on.'

'Yes, sir,' the prince's smile returned, and he rode back towards the wagon, replacing the helmet on his head.

Owen had stolen the prince from Greythorpe, knowing it could lead to war. Despite this, he found himself smiling.

He was going home.

32

CEDRIC

Cedric leaned back in the chair, took another drink of wine from the goblet, and swirled the liquid around his mouth before swallowing. He'd had better, he thought, much better. He wouldn't have been surprised if the lord of this stinking backwater served him the shittiest wine they had or maybe it was just that they had no taste this far south.

'I still don't believe you.'

Gruffydd Greenwood, Lord of the Greenhavens, was a handsome man of slight build, with short, grey-flecked hair and, usually, an amiable demeanour.

He glared at Cedric. 'I welcome you into my home, invite you to eat at my table, and you call me a liar?'

They were dining in the main hall of Forest Keep, four hundred miles south of Twin Falls. Aside from the Greenhavens guards, four others also occupied the room, seated around the long table at its centre.

At the head of the table sat Gruffydd, not even trying to hide his disdain for Cedric's presence. To his right sat the elderly chief advisor and Chamberlain, Elbert Tanke, and to his left, an equally aged Greenhavens knight, Sir Denis Katerman. Cedric had been seated at the opposite end of the table, as far away as possible from Gruffydd, something that couldn't be construed as anything but a slight. He'd brought Captain Kirby, who sat to his left, thinking it wise to leave Harrow back at the camp, for the moment at least.

'If the boot fits,' Cedric said.

'That's no way to speak to your host, young man,' Sir Denis growled.

'Who are you again?' Cedric countered.

Sir Denis jumped to his feet and glowered at him, resting a hand on the pommel of the sword that hung loose at his side.

'Sir Denis,' Gruffydd said, raising his hand to calm the old knight.

The Greenhavens knight settled back in his chair. Gruffydd glared at Cedric and pointed towards the door.

'I want you out of here. Out of my hall, my castle and off my lands.'

'Not going to happen,' Cedric said, shaking his head, 'until you've given me what the lawful leader of the realm has requested.'

'Hah! Lawful leader, my arse,' Gruffydd stood, and leaning forward, placed both hands on the table. 'I know what really happened to the King and how your father has manipulated the law to fill the council with his cronies.'

Even Cedric didn't know exactly how the King had met his death. Only his father, Sir Baltair and Harrow had been present at the time, and none of them had said anything to him.

'Be careful with your words, my lord,' warned Cedric.

Gruffydd now pointed his finger at Cedric.

'Don't threaten me, boy, and if you think you can scare me with that small army of thugs you've got camped outside my walls, think again!'

Lord Gruffydd's mood had been dark ever since they'd met. Cedric had hoped this would be an opportune time to hone his diplomacy skills, but Gruffydd wasn't cooperating. Cedric's attempts to solicit the whereabouts of Gruffydd's son, Kyle, came to naught. Antagonising the Lord of Forest Keep seemed to be the only thing Cedric had accomplished.

'And whilst on the subject of your men,' Gruffydd continued. 'You've only been here a day, and already they're causing trouble. I don't have a thousand guards to keep the peace like you do in the capitol. Rein them in, or I'll start locking them up, understood?'

Cedric and his small army had camped in the valley a mile from the main gates outside the surrounding town of Hampstead Heath. Cedric had let them come and go as they pleased.

'Get used to it. We could be here a while,' Cedric said. 'However, in the interest of fostering amity between us, I'll instruct my men to exercise some restraint and stay in camp after dark. Would that help?'

Gruffydd grunted his assent and sat back in his chair. He hoped the curfew would mitigate any more incidents and, if possible, make the Lord of Forest Keep more amiable. The man had worn a perpetually sullen expression since Cedric's arrival.

Cedric and Captain Kirby went off to join Harrow at The Twelve Hawks, a small tavern on the outer edge of Hampstead Heath. They took a table in a small alcove at the far corner. Being early afternoon, most of the tables had been filled, but it wasn't so loud that they could not hear themselves.

'I don't think he'll give us anything, do you?' Cedric said.

'No, my lord,' Captain Kirby said. 'Have you heard anything more from him?'

Cedric's attempts at negotiation seemed to have failed, and his patience had been worn thin.

He shook his head. 'Frankly, I'm tired of his delays and belligerent attitude, so we need to get his attention. Show him we're serious.'

'We have more than enough men to raze this place to the ground,' Harrow said in his usual terse manner. 'Let's use them.'

'He's right, my lord,' Captain Kirby said. 'We're here on the authority of the Steward, and Lord Gruffydd hasn't given a sufficient reason not to comply. Refusing this request is like refusing the order of the King, and if someone ignores the King, then –'

'they should hang,' Harrow finished for him.

Gruffydd had refused a direct request from the Steward of the Realm. Cedric held written orders signed by his father, but the Lord of the

Greenhavens had refused to even read them. Cedric had been forced to read it aloud to him, but he didn't want to kill anyone unless necessary.

'Err … I'm not advocating execution or burning,' Tamar said, 'but we do need to show him that we're not to be trifled with, or we may as well break camp and return home now.'

'We all know he's lying through his teeth, but I want some proof before we do anything more drastic,' Cedric said.

'Like what?' Harrow didn't sound impressed.

'Have the men heard anything from their dealings with the townsfolk?' Cedric asked. 'Something that proves he's lying?'

'Nothing, my lord,' the captain said. 'Not even the whores are talking.'

'Then let the men know they'll have to be more persuasive with their enquiries,' Cedric said. 'Start with the innkeepers and the whores. And the Master of Feathers, find him as well.'

'Yes, my lord,' Tamar said.

'I don't want anyone killed, understand?' Cedric said, glaring at Harrow.

Tamar nodded, Harrow grunted. The three rose and returned to the camp.

After a simple meal with Tamar and some of his men, Cedric returned to his tent. They'd departed the capitol in a hurry, which meant Cedric didn't have the usual trappings of a commander's tent, such as chairs, a table, and a real bed. He slept like the other men, a bedroll on the ground. Some rugs for the floor would have been nice, but at least he had a bigger tent.

Yawning, he lay down and pulled the blanket close around his body. He closed his eyes and hoped for a decent night's sleep. As they often had recently, his thoughts wandered back to the Grey Stag and Rosie, and he felt a stirring in his loins. This quickly abated as voices outside suddenly increased in volume. Surely no one could be stupid enough to fight outside the commander's tent? He sighed and stepped out.

'-better let me through, or I'll fucking gut you!'

Harrow stood glaring at the two soldiers tasked with guarding Cedric's tent.

'I have my orders, sir,' the guard said without much confidence.

The grizzled soldier had a sword in one hand, and the other held a body tossed over his shoulder. Harrow intimidated people even when he wasn't angry, and if he had his blade out and threatened to kill you, he could be a tough man to face, but the guards had not wavered. He'd commend them later, but for now, he better intervene before Harrow killed one of them.

'What the hell's going on here?'

The guards stepped aside, visibly relieved when Harrow's attention shifted from them to Cedric. He flinched as Harrow stepped forward and dumped a body at Cedric's feet.

'Who's that?'

'The birdman,' Harrow said. 'I questioned him like you wanted.'

Cedric stifled a yawn. 'It's the middle of the night. Couldn't this have waited until morning?'

The man had taken a beating, his face bruised and bloody. What had Harrow done to him?

'You said you were sick of waiting.'

Cedric commanded Harrow while here in the Greenhavens. However, he still had to be wary when dealing with his father's enforcer, who still never referred to him by name or rank.

'Is he dead?' Cedric wouldn't have been surprised, given Harrow's total lack of regard for human life, whether friend or foe.

'No, but if you want him dead, just say so.'

Cedric rubbed his temple.

'No ... no. So, did you turn up anything useful?'

'Two messages in the past three weeks. One from Redstone and one from the son, two days before we arrived.'

This piqued Cedric's interest. 'What did they say?'

'He claims he didn't know,' Harrow shrugged. 'That he just saw the seals.'

It didn't matter. This was all he needed to decide on his next course of action.

'I knew he'd been hiding something,' Cedric spat. 'Now he'd better give me what I want, or there will be consequences.'

'About fucking time,' Harrow said with a scowl.

Cedric looked down at the unconscious body of Gruffydd's Master of Feathers.

'Get him out of here. We'll discuss our strategy in the morning.'

'What shall I do with him?' Harrow said.

'Dump him somewhere. I don't care. Just take him away so I can get some sleep,' Cedric turned and went back into his tent.

He met with Lord Gruffydd the following evening, again in the main hall. As before, Sir Denis Katerman and Gruffydd's advisor attended. However, this time Cedric had only brought Harrow, who stood near the entrance, making the Greenwood guards uneasy.

The conversation was stilted, but polite. Gruffydd hadn't mentioned anything about his Master of Feathers being beaten senseless, but even if he had made the accusation, it didn't matter. Cedric and his commanders had discussed the new plan of action that morning, and it was going ahead regardless.

They had finished the meal, and the table had been cleared. Cedric was anxious to begin his negotiations again, but this time from a more advantageous position.

'Why are you still here?' Sir Denis said before Cedric could speak. 'My lord's position has not changed. He has nothing for you, and even if he did, I would counsel him not to divulge it.'

Where was Tamar? He should have been here already.

Cedric ignored the old knight and addressed Gruffydd.

'I don't understand your reluctance to give me what I want, what I know you have.'

'I have nothing to say to you,' Gruffydd said, glancing over towards Harrow, 'and I'd appreciate it if you'd take your men and leave.'

Cedric shook his head.

'That's most disappointing.'

Everyone turned at the sound of the door opening. Captain Kirby entered and approached the dining table.

'Excuse my tardiness, my lord,' Tamar addressed Cedric. 'I had to sort out an urgent issue with some of the men.'

'I trust it was resolved to your satisfaction?' Cedric said.

'Yes, sir,' the captain said, stepping to Cedric's right.

Finally, the diplomatic dance could cease.

'It's simple; all I want is the princess,' Cedric said. 'Then I'll leave.'

'I can't give you what I don't have,' Gruffydd said.

'Why so stubborn?' Cedric said. 'I know you've recently received messages from Redstone and your son. No one else needs to get hurt.'

The southern lord seethed. 'Are you threatening me now?'

'We're way past threats.'

Cedric gave his father's enforcer a barely imperceptible nod. Before Gruffydd and his men knew what had happened, Harrow had unsheathed his sword, sliced open the throat of the nearest Greenwood guard, nearly decapitating him, and thrust his blade into the stomach of the other.

Gruffydd and Sir Denis jumped up, knocking back their chairs as Captain Kirby drew his sword.

'This is what happens when you don't cooperate,' Cedric said, staying seated.

The old knight had his blade out and moved between Gruffydd and Captain Kirby. 'Murderous heathens!'

Harrow opened the doors to the hall, and a dozen of Cedric's soldiers rushed in, stepping over the dead guards. Harrow strode towards Gruffydd, leaving a trail of the guard's blood on the floor where it dripped from his blade. The remaining soldiers followed close behind.

Sir Denis turned towards Harrow and raised his sword.

'Stay back, or you'll –'

Harrow batted aside the old man's sword with his own and ran him through. Gruffydd stumbled backwards, tripping over his chair as the blade exited Sir Denis's back. The soldiers stepped past Harrow as he yanked the sword out of the Greenwood knight, who slumped to the ground with a gurgling groan.

Gruffydd's dismay turned back to fury as two of Cedric's soldiers grabbed him by the arms and propelled him towards the doors.

'What the hell?'

'Where … where are you taking him?' the shocked Chamberlain had finally found his voice.

'The Lord of Forest Keep is going to spend a night in his own dungeon,' Cedric said. 'Then we'll see how cooperative he can be.'

'You bastard!' Gruffydd yelled as the soldiers dragged him out of the hall.

Cedric ignored him. 'Captain?'

Tamar sheathed his sword. 'We have complete control of the Keep, my lord.'

'Many deaths?'

Cedric ordered his men to disable or capture the Greenhaven guards, but he knew there would be casualties.

'A few, my lord,' the captain said. 'Couldn't be helped.'

Putting Captain Kirby in charge of that part of the plan instead of Harrow had no doubt kept the number of deaths to a minimum.

'Well done,' Cedric said and turned to the Chamberlain, who had remained seated, too stunned to move. 'Now, Elbert … may I call you Elbert?'

The chamberlain trembled, but nodded.

'Elbert,' Cedric continued, 'this situation isn't permanent. Once I have what I need, I'll be on my way. But until then, I'm the master of Forest Keep, and I expect you to run it as usual.'

'Y … Yes, my lord,' the old man said.

'Good,' Cedric drank the remaining contents of his cup. 'This swill isn't so bad after you've had a few.'

Now that he controlled Forest Keep, he ordered the curfew lifted, and since Gruffydd now occupied a dark cell beneath the keep, Cedric annexed his living quarters. It had a roaring log fire in the hearth and a real bed. He also toyed with the idea of bringing the young wife of Sir Kyle Greenwood to his bed but had second thoughts, as he knew she wouldn't come of her own accord. Bedding an unwilling participant took effort, and the long day had made Cedric weary. Maybe tomorrow night, he thought. Instead, he took one of the kitchen wenches. She wasn't a great beauty, but she had big tits, a nice arse, and her willingness excited him.

He slept soundly that night.

Late the following day, Cedric, Captain Kirby and Harrow descended the steps into the dungeons to see if Gruffydd's attitude had changed, but Sergeant Tolas called them back.

'A rider has arrived with a message from the capitol, my lord,' the sergeant said.

'So where is it?' said Cedric.

'He insisted that he hand it to you personally,' Sergeant Tolas said. 'I've had him taken to Lord Gruffydd's … err … your quarters.'

A personally delivered message usually indicated something of great importance. Cedric nodded, and they all followed the sergeant back up the steps. The Lord of Forest Keep could stew in a cell for a little longer.

The messenger had been taken to the corridor outside Cedric's commandeered quarters and guarded by two soldiers, one of whom opened the door as Cedric approached. The messenger looked young, barely sixteen.

'Come,' Cedric entered the living room ahead of Captain Kirby and Harrow.

Sergeant Tolas ushered in the messenger and closed the door.

Cedric stopped near the hearth and turned. 'Who are you?'

The young man bowed. 'Asmus Thorne, my lord.'

'I know your father,' Cedric said, recognising the name.

Sir Hugo Thorne, the Lord of Stowe and an enthusiastic ally of the Greythorpe family, lived in a town about a hundred miles to the north of Forest Keep.

'Yes,' Asmus said. 'He speaks highly of you and your family.'

As Cedric held out his hand, he remembered that despite his loyalty, his father considered the man a fool. 'The message?'

Asmus reached into a leather satchel and produced a small scroll. 'This is the original. We weren't sure of your exact location, so we made another copy,'

'Where's the other one?' said Captain Kirby.

'My brother is headed towards Cutter Bay and Whitehall,' Asmus said.

Cedric took the proffered scroll and unfurled it.

'Please thank your father for being so thorough,' the captain said. 'The sergeant will arrange some food and refreshments for you, then I suggest you return home.'

Asmus acknowledged Captain Kirby and gave Cedric a bow.

'My lord.'

Cedric ignored him and began reading as the young rider turned and left with Sergeant Tolas, who closed the door behind them.

'Fuck!' Cedric couldn't believe what he had just read.

'Bad news?' Tamar enquired.

'You could say that.' Cedric reread the message, but the meaning didn't change. 'That little prick of a prince has escaped again, and my father has ordered us to find him.'

'Surely he must have had help,' Captain Kirby said.

'Redstone,' Cedric spat.

He thought of sending Harrow. Cedric had already had enough of roughing it, sleeping outdoors in the cold, but his father's message had made it clear he should go and that the importance of recapturing the prince superseded that of finding the princess.

Cedric pondered this for a few moments. He had a hundred and fifty soldiers at his disposal. He could do both.

Within the hour, he and seventy of his soldiers rode hard for the Shadowlands. He'd left the remaining men with an irate Harrow to hold Forest Keep, with orders to try and coax more information out of Lord Gruffydd.

From Hampstead Heath, he headed east towards the Great South Road, hoping to intercept his quarry before they could reach the Shadowlands. Unfortunately, they were more than a day behind. He pushed his men hard, riding throughout the night and the next day, stopping only to gather information and to water and feed the horses.

Deep in enemy territory, they could see the top of the Black Cliffs in the distance. The further south he got, the more Cedric resented the fact that he had to be here at all. His bitterness wasn't directed at his father for sending him on this errand, but at that idiot Baltair for allowing the prince to slip through his fingers a second time. It rankled, and his dark mood wasn't helped by the weather. He had the hooded cloak pulled low over his head and a heavy scarf wrapped around his neck and the lower part of his face, showing only his eyes.

They would stop and sleep tonight. The men would begin dropping from their saddles if they didn't, Cedric concluded. They made camp just outside the village of Abbey's Pool.

'They can't be too far ahead now,' Captain Kirby said.

'I hope so,' Cedric muttered, tired and still in a dark mood.

Early the following day, they stopped in a tiny hamlet of a dozen dilapidated wooden structures. Cedric, Tamar, and a handful of soldiers entered what looked like the tavern and began asking questions. Already irritable from the long ride, Cedric had the innkeeper beaten in the middle of his establishment when he refused to answer. The stubborn man relented after the second beating and informed them that a large group of riders had passed through around dawn but hadn't stopped. He claimed he didn't know the identity of the riders, but Cedric knew otherwise.

Why would someone take a beating for strangers? It didn't matter. They had continued to gain on them, so the hard riding hadn't been wasted.

By high sun, Cedric and his men reached the top of the Burned Range and surveyed the valley below. They now rode through the Shadowlands, territory directly controlled by either Lord Owen or one of his brothers. If he didn't find the prince today, it'd probably be too late.

'My lord!' Captain Kirby pointed towards the valley.

Cedric gazed in that general direction but couldn't see anything, just pockets of trees scattered throughout the plains.

'There, just east of the bend in the river before the woods,' Tamar added.

He had another look and eventually detected movement about ten miles ahead.

'Do you think it's them?' Cedric said, hopeful.

'It has to be,' Tamar said. 'Wes?'

The old tracker dismounted about thirty yards ahead and studied the ground. He walked back and stopped between Cedric and Tamar's horses.

'At least twenty riders, my lord,' Wes directed his findings to Cedric.

'How long ago?' Cedric asked.

'This morning at the earliest,' the old tracker said.

An elated Cedric led his company of mounted soldiers down into the valley. The Last Bridge came into sight, and the group slowed. He considered it ill-named, as another bridge, the Red Pass, had been built only a few miles to the south. The Last Bridge consisted of three separate bridges spanning the river, from the riverbank to a small island, to a second island, and finishing on the opposite bank.

'They didn't cross here, my lord,' Wes said, not even dismounting.

That left only one more choice to them, the Red Pass, named so by the first Redstone lord who had commissioned its construction.

'An hour ahead at the most,' the old tracker added.

Cedric's excitement grew. The idiots thought they had made it to safety and had slowed.

'Lieutenant Frost, take thirty men across the bridge and follow the river south. We'll try and box them in.'

They watered the horses and set out again. Cedric had reservations about riding so deep into Redstone territory, but he did have forty mounted soldiers. No one but a small army would be of any concern, and that this would all be over by the end of the day, buoyed his mood.

He scanned the road ahead for his quarry, around each bend, over each hill, behind every copse of trees they passed. He felt like a hunter and that little orphan prince, his prey.

Cedric's confidence began to slip as the hours crept by and the cliffs loomed ever larger ahead of him. They rode out of another pocket of trees … nothing. It can't be long now, he thought. He thrust aside his concerns as they crested a slight rise.

Not a mile ahead, The Red Pass, a stone structure at the base of the Black Cliffs, spanned the Winding River at its narrowest point this side of the Burned Range. A hundred yards beyond the bridge, the aptly named

Swiftwater Falls cascaded into a dark fissure at the base of the cliffs, known as the Dragon's Throat.

Men and horses milled around the water's edge at the bridge's northern end, and somewhere among them would be his target. Cedric urged his mount forward. Despite being already lathered from hard riding, it accelerated to a full gallop. They had been seen, which was expected. Forty mounted soldiers made a lot of noise, but they closed on the bridge rapidly. Soldiers scrambled for their horses, and the ones already mounted organised themselves into a loose defensive line. This gave Cedric hope. If they didn't just turn and flee over the bridge, the prince must be on this side of the river. Otherwise, why stay and face certain death?

He drew his sword and pointed it forward as his men lined up on either side of him. Redstone's soldiers began their charge, and the gap between the opposing riders closed. At the last moment, Cedric tugged on the reins, and the riders on either side surged ahead, leaving him a full length behind, ensuring the rapidly advancing enemy would attack them ahead of himself.

The lines of mounted soldiers met with a clash of swords and howls of agony. Cedric swung his sword at a passing enemy rider who had just blocked an attack from Captain Kirby, leaving his flank defenceless. The soldier screamed as Cedric opened the side of his neck with a slash of his sword as he rode past.

He kept his mount surging forward, and about fifty yards from the bridge, Cedric saw his prize. The prince had been down near the waterfall but now headed towards the bridge's northern end. Cedric couldn't let him get across the bridge, but the prince probably had a much fresher horse, and his own mount would die under him soon if they kept going for much longer.

He glanced across the river to the southern end of the bridge. Lord Owen sat astride his black stallion, barking orders. Another dozen soldiers galloped across the bridge towards Cedric.

Cedric spurred on his ailing mount, not even checking if his men had followed his lead. The prince had put on a burst of speed and was nearly at the bridge, and Cedric couldn't see any way to stop him. Even if he managed to catch up, getting Leto to stop and engage him would be near impossible. He saw his quarry slipping away, along with his father's approval.

Leto neared the first pillar that denoted the start of the bridge. He could only think of one thing to do. Cedric dug his heels into his mount's sides, and the exhausted creature bounded forward with a last gasp of energy. The prince had begun crossing the bridge when Cedric collided with him, smashing into his side at a full gallop. His mount stumbled to its knees throwing him into the air. With a crushing thump, Cedric hit the ground.

The next thing he knew, he was lying on the muddy embankment, gasping for breath. He tried to sit but fell back to the ground, lightheaded. He closed his eyes for a few moments and reopened them. He had been lucky, landing on the river's edge with one foot submerged in water. Five yards away, a horse struggled to regain its footing as the river splashed around it, but two broken legs had already sealed its fate. The mount wasn't his, so ignoring the thumping pain in his head, he turned and scrambled up the embankment. Realising he didn't have his weapons or helmet, Cedric crouched behind the stone pillar and surveyed the scene.

He expected a battle to be raging about him, but most of his men had assembled about fifty yards north of the bridge. To the south, a couple of riderless horses trotted around a scattering of bodies. At the other end of the deserted bridge, surrounded by a cadre of soldiers, Lord Owen shouted and gesticulated, pointing over the bridge wall towards the waterfall. On the opposite shore, Redstone soldiers had begun to wade into the water.

Cedric's gaze shifted towards the waterfall. He realised the horse in the water belonged to Prince Leto, who had been thrown into the river. The prince was swimming to the other side. Was he mad?

'No, no, no!' Cedric shouted.

But his protestations were in vain as the swift current swept the prince over the falls and out of sight.

'Fuuuuuck!' he roared.

No one ever returned after entering the Dragon's Throat, so the stories went, and now the prince had disappeared, swallowed by the cliffs, and he would be blamed. That Redstone didn't have him either made Cedric feel only marginally better.

'Fuck!' he screamed again.

'My lord!'

Cedric whirled to see Captain Kirby pull up beside him, leading a horse. It wasn't his mount.

'Are you hurt?' Tamar said, concerned.

'Nothing that won't heal.'

His body would register the results of the fall tomorrow, but for the moment, he felt fine, apart from a sore head.

'What's happening? Why aren't we fighting?'

'Reinforcements arrived for Lord Owen just as you fell,' he said. 'They must have been waiting for them when we arrived.'

'How many?' Cedric said and glanced across the bridge again at the Redstone soldiers surrounding the Lord of the Shadowlands.

'At least fifty; too many,' Tamar said. 'And once the prince entered the water, they retreated to the southern shore, so we thought it prudent to withdraw as well.'

Killing Redstone would have been a pleasant bonus. It may have gone part way to making up for the prince's death.

'We're still within bowshot, my lord,' Tamar said. 'We should go.'

Cedric mounted up, and they trotted away from the bridge. 'My sword. I need my sword, my bow … and my helmet,' he said. 'And find my fucking horse.'

'Yes, sir,' Captain Kirby said and barked orders to search the northern embankment.

Bodies of soldiers and horses littered the ground.

'How many did we lose?' Cedric said.

'Fifteen,' Tamar said, his tone solemn, 'including Wes.'

Damn it! Something else his father will not be pleased about.

'What of Lieutenant Frost?'

'No sign of him or his men,' the Captain said.

They were probably dead too. Cedric sighed. He'd be heading back to Hampstead Heath with less than half of the men he'd started out with, though it could have been worse. Capturing the princess now became more important than ever. Hopefully, Harrow had managed to extract information from the stubborn Lord of Greenhavens. He cantered back to what remained of his soldiers.

'Let's go,' he ordered, knowing he couldn't return to the capitol empty-handed.

He pulled on the reins and directed his mount north, back towards the Greenhavens.

What the hell else could go wrong?

ACKNOWLEDGEMENTS

I want to thank all those who encouraged and supported me in the writing of this novel, especially my wife, Linda. Without her, this novel would probably still be sitting in a drawer gathering dust.

Matthew West, for steering me in the right direction every time I veered off course, which was often, you have my sincere gratitude.

And I couldn't finish without acknowledging my family, particularly my stepdaughter, Grace, and the family bookworms, Lauren and Jess, who gave me the confidence to share my work with the world.

ABOUT THE AUTHOR

Paul grew up in country Western Australia, devouring historical fiction, science fiction and fantasy books and movies from an early age. In adulthood, his love of these genres led him to turn his hand to writing his own science fiction/adventure screenplay. Following that, he wrote a short screenplay about a man coping with the onset of Alzheimer's, a topic close to his heart.

A national writing competition inspired Paul to try something slightly different, writing a single scene for a novel. Encouraged, he kept on writing, and *The Blackwater Chronicles* was born.

Paul lives in Perth with his wife, Linda.

The Wooden Crown is his first novel.